PICK THE LOCK

ALSO BY
A.S. KING

The Dust of 100 Dogs
Please Ignore Ver Dietz
Everybody Sees the Ants
Reality Boy
Ask the Passengers
Glory O'Brien's History of the Future
I Crawl Through It
Still Life with Tornado
Dig
Switch
The Collectors: Stories

FOR MIDDLE READERS (AS AMY SARIG KING)

Me and Marvin Gardens
The Year We Fell from Space
Attack of the Black Rectangles

PICK THE LOCK

A.S. KING

DUTTON BOOKS

DUTTON BOOKS
An imprint of Penguin Random House LLC
1745 Broadway, New York, NY 10019
penguinrandomhouse.com

Design by Anna Booth
Text set in Joanna Nova

Library of Congress Cataloging-in-Publication data is available.

First published by Dutton Books, 2024
First paperback edition published 2025

Manufactured in the United States of America
BVG

ISBN 9780593353981
1 3 5 7 9 10 8 6 4 2

The authorized representative in the EU for product safety and compliance is Penguin Random House Ireland, Morrison Chambers, 32 Nassau Street, Dublin D02 YH68, Ireland, https://eu-contact.penguin.ie.

For the useful

The trust of the innocent
is the liar's most useful tool.

—STEPHEN KING

The production of too many useful things
results in too many useless people.

—KARL MARX

You are the sky.
Everything else—it's just the weather.

—PEMA CHÖDRÖN

PICK THE LOCK

PROLOGUE:
Lesson One

I DO NOT LIE TO GOD.

God, in this sense, can be whatever you want it to be—but the one thing God cannot be is a liar or a believer of lies or a perpetuator of lies or an eater of lies or a baker of lies or a bartender of lies. God / the universe can shake up a cocktail and serve it to you, but if you need lies to survive, you must tell your own stories / add your own garnish.

God will watch you from behind the bar.

God will nod and smile as you eat the cherry.

God knows you are imperfect.

You do not.

God forgives you.

You do not.

This is why you lie to God.

And so, Lesson One is easy.

I am imperfect. I forgive myself. I do not lie to God.

I first learned this lesson when I was four years old. I have not strayed. I am humble in the light of the universe—I have earned my place.

My father lies to God. All the time.

Today he said, "God knows, we tried all we could before she went into the System."

She is my mother.

We is him.

Tried means he didn't like her the way she was.

The *System* is how Mother travels now, contained in a tidy capsule.

God knows.

My father should not be the keeper of God's words. He is a liar and a thief.

God knows.

My father cannot think God's thoughts. He is a traitor and a brute.

God knows.

God shouldn't even be allowed in his mouth—my father is a killer.

He made my mother into a fast-moving message. Fed her into a tube.

The message reads, "I am an example of what happens when a coward lies to God."

My father.

God knows.

Our teacher. Our captor. Our hero.

His Lesson One is: *The World and Its Seven Continents: Overview.*

My Lesson One is: DO NOT LIE TO GOD.

ACT ONE:
Home Movies / The Americas

<u>Cast in order of appearance:</u>

Jane
Henry
Hungry Birds
Vernon
Mother/Mina
Marta's Whipped Potatoes
Great-Aunt Lily
Milorad
Gemma
Marta
Brutus the Rat
Finch
Jed
Jefferey
Robert
Todd
Andrew

HOME MOVIES

Today is Sunday, September 22, 2024

ALLOW ME TO BACK UP. You will know where we're going. But you must also know how we got here—to where I know the truth about everything.

Now I know, but last week I didn't know.

This is how most things occur, yes?

One day we are sure of something and the next day we are not.

Let me show you a home movie from six years ago.

HOME MOVIE—04.12.2018

My brother, Henry, is six years old and is feeding the birds in the back garden. He is surrounded by rosebushes and hunger. He tosses seed out in fear. The birds are tripling in number and the tears on his cheeks are real. Vernon sits on a bench, grinning a bit. He wears suit pants and a pocket watch, a starched white button-down, and he calls me over to him. I am ten.

"Will we watch your brother be attacked to death together?" he asks.

"Why would you say that?" The look on my face is serious. Henry is openly crying now—though he knows better than to call out for help.

"Lighten up, Jane," Vernon says.

"I have to help him," I say.

"You know the rules."

<pause>

I did know the rules. This was specifically Rule Number Two. *Do not interfere with others in a way to aid them in times of fear or sadness. They must learn their own escape.*

<resume>

"I will have a guest tonight," Vernon says, "a private dinner. I've a governess on order to come and eat with you and Henry. She'll show you a film on the television."

"I see."

Henry is now running—not toward us but away. He aims for the fountain at the center of the garden—a near-flat dish dropping water into a larger one, and then another, until it lands in a square pond. The birds follow on foot and by wing until Henry drops the entire bag of seed on the path.

"What film?" I ask.

"I don't know," he answers.

"Will Mother be joining us?"

<pause>

I knew this was not a question I was allowed to ask, but Mother was on a big tour and I missed her; plus, Henry was out of earshot and I was feeling brave.

<resume>

Vernon bristles and cracks his neck.

He answers, "You are so terribly hard to love, Jane." Then he gets up and slowly walks inside, through the large French doors that lead to the study and closes them behind him.

Henry hears the doors and runs toward me from the fountain.

"Father!" he yells.

I walk toward him and pick him up when we meet. I spin him around by his hands and crying snot flies out of his nose and lands on my arm and I don't mind because the spinning makes him giggle and squeal with happiness. He is six, after all. Not old enough to understand anything like private dinners or how to learn his own escape.

<stop>

We have tens of thousands of home movies. Not because Vernon followed us around recording our family antics, but because there are security cameras in certain areas of our large Victorian home: the patio and rose garden, the dining room, the sitting room where the television is, the study where Henry and I take our lessons, and the foyer. We don't have home movies from any other areas, so this is where I believe the cameras to be.

Before I found the home movies, I wasn't sure about anything.

After I found the home movies, I am both sure and unsure of a great many new things.

If nothing else, I am at least a step further into the truth of my life, which you'd think I'd know having lived it, but that's not how things go when one is so terribly hard to love.

Here's one from nine years before I was born. It is the origin story of me, Jane. It is the origin story of this whole charade—what's about to unfold. Whatever this is, it starts here.

HOME MOVIE—06.03.1999

Mother and Vernon are madly in love in 1999. She sits on a bench in the rose garden; he kneels next to her, holding her hand in his.

"I do not know another beauty such as yours. Not one bloom in this garden can match it," Vernon says.

"You flatter me," she answers.

"I am a man of deep emotion. Do not doubt," he says.

"Do tell me what you did this week while I was away."

"I was so excited to tell you yesterday." Vernon pouts. "But you didn't seem interested."

"Oh, love. I'd just come home from Philadelphia. I needed a rest. Marta made me a fattening meal. Have some mercy."

"Marta's whipped potatoes," he says.

"With butter enough for children!" she declares.

Vernon smiles and stands up. He brushes the gravel from the knee of his trousers and sits on the bench next to Mother, who has turned toward him to show attention.

Vernon says, "You know, when we marry, Marta can whip potatoes for all of us—you, me, and the children."

Mother's smile envelops her face, then fades.

"I know we've only been dating for five months but I can feel it," Vernon says. "Can't you?"

"I feel it," she says. She taps her foot.

He giggles. "Now I crave Marta's potatoes."

"I can ask her to make you some if you like," she says. "Stay and eat with us. Aunt Lily is always happy to see you!"

Vernon chews the inside of his cheek, as he does when thinking or annoyed. "I fear Lily only humors me. She laughs too loudly at my jokes, and I do not know what I did to offend her."

"She is very old and very protective," Mother says.

"I am not a man you need protection from," he says.

She laughs and swats the idea away with her delicate hand. "Your imagination is wild, you know."

"I know I love you. That's as real as anything."

"And I love you. Let's take a walk."

They walk, hand in hand, through the rose garden, Vernon stopping to smell each variety and Mother stooping down to follow his lead. He is five foot seven. She is five foot eleven. As they walk, you can sense his discomfort in this.

From the way they talk and interact, you'd think the rose garden behind our large Victorian home is a time tunnel to a century before. But Mother, twenty-six, is in a pair of faded black jeans with a hole in the left knee. She wears combat boots open at the inside zippers and a ragged sweatshirt off-shoulder that reads HOW LOW CAN A PUNK GET? Vernon, twenty-eight, is wearing casual office clothing, though he has not had a job since he worked for his uncle as a telemarketer a year ago. His ironed chinos and ill-fitting polo shirt do not match Mother's style at all. He looks like her child—a mere boy.

She is sure of herself.

He is not.

<stop>

When one knows the roots, one can understand the leaves.

The movies are the roots.

OUR HOME

The hedge around the rose garden is a nearly two-stories-high arborvitae. Milorad, our gardener, keeps it trimmed to give the illusion of perfection. The roses are in beds according to color and variety. In spring, there are tulips divided the same way—color, variety—that look like a carpet from my bedroom window.

I am lucky to have a bedroom that overlooks the back garden. Henry's room faces the front of the house, which means he can hear cars and walkers and fire engines and anything else that goes down Spruce Street. Lately, there's been an increase in people on bicycles because the town has completed a walking and biking trail and its entrance is a half mile past our house. Vernon fought the trail, claiming it would invite people to come into the garden, but no one has and I don't think anyone even knows it's here. From Spruce Street, our house looks untouchable and, to me, a little scary. The aesthetic is Pristine Victorian Prison.

I have only been on the road when I have to go places, which isn't often. Since the global pandemic several years ago, our family has stayed indoors at home because Vernon fears we will get sick and die.

He was always saying, "I couldn't bear to lose you!"

He says it with such feeling you'd think he means it. He can't help it. His lies to God have been part of him for a lifetime, like his liver. Since he landed here in this old Victorian home—the home of my mother's family, once a country retreat for her late great-aunt Lily's parents—he acts the part. His dress is that of a lord of the manor, including the ridiculous pocket watch. His modus, a mix of *I couldn't bear to lose you!* and *I've a governess on order to mind you / teach you / love you / listen to you.*

Father married up.

Mother married way down.

It's not about money. It's misfired potential. Mother believed in her 1999 ripped-leather-and-punk-rock heart that this was a man who would love her, no matter their vast differences. She trusted, which is the way of women no matter the century. That trust landed her in the tubes, contained in a capsule that is entirely of her ancestors' making, an example of irony and ingenuity both.

TUBES & CARGO

How I came to Lesson One later than I should have

UNTIL I WAS SIXTEEN, too old to be catching on to the situation, and until last week when I found the cache of home movies, I believed my mother *wanted* to be in the tubes. She was fragile and she was fierce. She could kill you and she might faint from chronic weakness at any moment. The story seemed plausible even in its inconsistency because it was the one told to me.

I viewed Mother as a convenience or a bother depending on the day. I viewed Mother through Vernon's eyes as if my own were daffy. My brother, Henry, has no choice—being a boy and the son of Vernon, he is terrified to step out of his assigned role. Any future plan designed to free Mother cannot be shared with him.

I remember days when I was young—while Mother still walked the hallways of this house. She read me stories so often; in my memory, the years before her total confinement were made of scenes that had her splayed on the bed / couch / garden bench / thick grass with a book in front of her and me on her lap, hooked to every word. She acted the books—put on voices for sprites and dragons and sometimes would drop the book and act out the scene. One time she chased me all the way across the lawn to the fountain and then splashed us both with water because in the book, it was raining.

These are the times I choose to remember.

The rest are more complicated.

Now Henry and I take lessons in the study from Vernon, and if she's not on tour or recording in the studio, Mother watches and listens from the corner, where she is confined to a wooden chair that is inside a capsule that shuttles her around the house's large System of tubes. It's a pneumatic system—like the capsules in the bank drive-through or in old office buildings. Her third great-grandfather was the first in America to use them in his department stores to send mail and memos to different areas of the store. Nobody knew his grandson-in-law had tweaked the design to build a larger System that would carry his wife—contained in their country home an hour northwest of Philadelphia.

I didn't question it. After all, I had grown up here. Each room had its tube stop in the corner, and the noisy whir of the air that transported Mother from room to room was quite normal. One time, before the pandemic, I went to a birthday sleepover at Gretchen Brown's house. I was eleven. Gretchen Brown had a koi pond in her foyer. I truly believed that our tubes—the System laced through each room of the house—were something akin to a bubbling indoor pond with real fish in it.

I suppose it is.

The fish is Mother.

THE BALLAD OF MINA PLACENTA

That is the fish's name. My mother. Mina Placenta. Don't worry—you're not the only person who screws up your face like that upon hearing it the first time. Everyone is confused.

Some are brave. "Is that your family name?"

Some are not. "What a lovely name."

Placenta is the name of Mother's punk band. Formed in the mid-1990s in West Philadelphia, Placenta has shared the stage with bands like Iggy and the Stooges, Hole, and Sonic Youth, as well as hundreds of bands you never heard of. Mina, my mother, has stories of being on private jets with your favorite punk stars and probably watching them do copious amounts of drugs with copious numbers of groupies. She even has her own groupies, but she doesn't pay attention to that stuff. She is busy trying to solve the problem of domestic violence and providing menstrual solutions to girls and women all over the world.

Plus, she always said she was dedicated to Vernon.

Fact is, I don't really know her the way I should.

I'm downplaying the whole thing quite a bit here, but that's normal. I'm the daughter of a rock star, quite literally, and we have been raised in a house where our father has outlawed music. We still have turntables and speakers and radios, but we can only listen if we have headphones plugged in, and if Vernon is nearby, we mustn't dance or show enjoyment.

Conversely, Vernon has decorated the entire first floor in Mina's framed gold and platinum records, tour posters, magazine covers, and other Placenta memorabilia. Last month, a reporter from *Rolling Stone* was here, and while they were waiting to talk to Mother, Vernon showed them around like a proud, doting husband. She is about to release a new album, her eighth, and will start touring again next month for the first time since the pandemic.

Up until I found out the truth about everything, I didn't care much for Mother's fame. Mina Placenta was a joke. *Why would anyone listen to a flake like her?* This was a question often asked around the fire, the dinner table, and the pool in summers. This was given to me as the only path—*Why would anyone listen to a flake like her?*—the way Christians are raised with only Jesus. I tried to play the part, but I couldn't help but follow my curiosity. I read all of her lyrics, even the bad words, from the sleeves of the vinyl records she gave me upon each release. None of it made sense until I found the home movies.

VERNON'S RULES

There are lists of them displayed on the kitchen bulletin board. New ones get added. For example, the ban on music was only added in 2018, the day after The Christmas That Changed Everything, which was the day Vernon locked Mother into the System for good. She is now only allowed out for special occasions like birthdays and rare family game nights.

GENERAL HOUSE RULES

1. *Keep your thoughts and emotions to yourself at all times.*
2. *Do not interfere with others in a way to aid them in times of fear or sadness. They must learn their own escape.*
3. *Do not talk to people outside the home about our family.*
4. *If you have complaints, bring them to Vernon only.*
5. *Do not talk to the servants about personal business.*
6. *Do not leave the property for any reason. The property is defined as follows: the house structure and grounds, including the pool and pool house; the rose garden; the lawn; and the croquet course. The vineyard and orchard are off-limits, as is anywhere beyond the hedge along the front of the home.*
7. *Do not believe anything Mina says. Check all stories with Vernon.*
8. *Music shall not be played aloud in any area of the property. [Added 12.26.18.]*

SYSTEM, COMMUNICATION, AND ELECTRONICS RULES

1. *Only Vernon can adjust System attachments. (There are five types: two-way, one-way, wet nurse, meal, and silence—ALL five types are off-limits.)*

2. *Only Vernon may use the System remote control.*

3. *All those entering the property must surrender any electronics to Vernon.*

4. *All phones, tablets, and computers are subject to inspection by Vernon upon surrender.*

5. *Under no circumstances is anyone allowed to use the house telephone without permission from Vernon.*

6. *No one may look at Mina while she is in the System. [Added 01.01.2019.]*

7. *No one may help Mina if she is emotional in the System. [Added 01.15.2019.]*

8. *Any attention paid to Mina while she is in the System is punishable by being grounded to one's room. [Added 01.25.2019.]*

ADDITIONAL RULES

1. *Mina is not to be let out of the System. She will eat all meals in her bedroom. [Added 12.26.2018.]*

2. *Mina is not allowed to speak to the children unless Vernon grants permission and attaches the correct System attachment. [Added 12.27.2018.]*

3. *As Jane has turned 16, the lady's maid may not visit unless Jane is taking a suitor and needs help dressing. [Added 03.04.2024.]*

GEMMA

With Mother in the System or on tour, I was provided with a lady's maid early in life. The term was delicious—to me, then—at maybe eight years of age. *Lady's maid*—so fancy! No one in my school had one or had even heard of one. Gemma was only nine but had the skills of a grown woman. Very useful. She could do everything from washing my clothing and cleaning my room to playing a competitive and endless game of Uno on a rainy day while French braiding my hair. She was especially good at hairstyling and there was nothing like feeling her hands on my scalp. She became a fast sister.

Gemma doesn't live here, but she has a bed in my room, away from the window, behind a screen. It's a small bed—a twin with an old mattress. My childhood was full of sleepovers and sometimes we'd have two-person pool parties with croquet tournaments, karaoke, and Marta's homemade ice cream. Gemma's favorite flavor is cinnamon sugar. We spent hours talking about romance. Especially when we were ten and eleven. Before the pandemic. Something about a virus took the romance out of everything.

Gemma has a phone and when she enters the house for any reason, she has to surrender it to Vernon. Henry and I are not allowed electronics—even though in elementary I had a tablet computer provided by the school. Now that we homeschool, our lessons are done with pencils and paper. If I want to call my friends or even Mother if she's away, I must use a phone that is attached to the wall by a cord. We have three in the house—placed in the kitchen, the study, and the upstairs hallway, next to an overstuffed upholstered chair and small walnut-topped table that has been polished so shiny it resembles glass. The area with the most privacy is the kitchen. Though, it's not like I have any friends to call. The pandemic hit when I was in fifth grade. I have not been outside our estate since. Even my closest primary school friends like Gretchen Brown have moved on and become real live teenagers. I remain Jane—girl with white starched nightgowns and a lady's maid.

Mother's upcoming tour—in America from October to December this year and then Europe and Asia in winter and spring 2025—proves that I should be back in regular school. People are out again, breathing the air, going to concerts, living normal lives.

Gemma makes it bearable. She has an infectious laugh and dry wit that drops me to my knees. Now she's seventeen and comes around less often—only to help me dress for suitors. Sometimes we sneak in a sleepover, but these days I'm so busy researching the home movies at night I don't have time.

She still calls me her best friend and I feel bad for it. She doesn't know about the home movies and I can't tell her because the iPad I use to access the movies is stolen. From her.

THE SCHOOL OF VERNON

It has been four and a half years since March 2020, when the pandemic shut us all into our homes. I was twelve years old. School closed down and we were made to attend online school, which was more than complicated for me and Henry because we were not allowed electronics, so Vernon decided then to homeschool us. This was further complicated by the fact that, though Mother was home, she was, since Christmas Night 2018, completely confined to System. She couldn't help with math problems, and she couldn't read books to us in her calm, kind voice. Instead, she sat in the tube and stared out at us.

Vaccines were arranged, booster shots after that, and by the time I turned thirteen, schools had opened and all my fifth-grade friends headed to middle school. I truly thought I'd be heading back for seventh grade.

Vernon sat Henry and me down in the study in late August. Mother was in System, fitted with the two-way communication attachment, a rare privilege by that time, and she wore a smile like she belonged there. I was so angry. Reader, forgive me. I was so angry.

When Vernon said that we were going to be homeschooled another year, I wailed.

When he said Mother agreed, I said, "Well, of course she did. Look at her! What a flake!"

Mother and Vernon had a similar disappointment at the time. Mother was supposed to go on a second tour for her only platinum album, *Safe House*, in late 2020, and Vernon was supposed to cash her checks, but the pandemic made that impossible. When she tried to reschedule the tour in 2022, the fervor for live shows was still quite low, so the record company scrapped the idea. Vernon talked endlessly about how we had to keep our purse strings tight because Mother wasn't earning, which worried me. He said we'd lose the house and the help. We didn't. Now Mother is heading on tour again, and Vernon seems upset about it even though he'll get to cash her checks again. I suppose it doesn't help that she titled the new album *Run, Jane, Run*.

"I open my heart and the things I really want to say come out," she explained to *Rolling Stone*. "Jane is my daughter. She's sixteen and a half. I can already see the monster with its maw open, ready to devour her completely. This country shits out women. Eats them and shits them out. Hate to sound pessimistic, but it's never going to change. *Run, Jane, Run* is about making your own world inside your head so you can survive it."

FREE MOTHER

An opera

By Jane Vandermaker ~~Cook~~

Contact:
Jane Vandermaker ~~Cook~~
1111 Spruce Street
610-555-5555

CAST OF CHARACTERS

(in order of appearance)

JANE, a sixteen-year-old young woman, lead singer of Free Mother

MILORAD, a Serbian gardener and driver

DAVID, drummer from Free Mother

ELLIS, bass player from Free Mother

WENDYLISA, guitarist from Free Mother

FANS, assorted audience members from the punk club

MINA, Jane's mother

BRUTUS THE RAT, Milorad's pet

OAK TREE

FINCH, Jane's aunt, Mina's sister

MARTA, Mina's best friend and the family cook

VERNON, Jane's father, Milorad's employer

HENRY, Jane's younger brother

GEMMA, Jane's lady's maid

TREE FROGS

SET DESCRIPTION

Center Stage: Revolving stage with four main sets: Sitting Room, Study, Dining Room, Kitchen. All décor Victorian Era. Transparent System tube in center accessible from all four rooms.

Center Stage Elevated: Jane's Bedroom and En Suite Bathroom.

Stage Right: Patio overlooking the rose garden.

Stage Left: Pool house. Small bar with stool, beat-up chair, rat's cage.

Far Stage Right: A traditional glass greenhouse.

Far Stage Left: A car.

Drop Curtain: There is a drop upstage. The top part of the sky area is almost white, to allow for projections. Beyond the main house, there is a town built up a hill behind it, and many homes. In the top right corner, one particular house stands out and is enlarged and detailed, including a window.

Key Feature of Drop: A window is cut into the drop high in the top right corner (stage left). Behind this window is a platform for an actor to stand and look through the window toward the audience.

LEGEND

1 JANE'S BEDROOM
2 JANE'S EN SUITE
3 DINING ROOM
4 KITCHEN
5 SITTING ROOM
6 STUDY
7 PATIO
8 GREENHOUSE
9 POOL HOUSE/MILORAD'S PAD/ BRUTUS'S CAGE
10 DROP WITH TOWN STRETCHING INTO THE DISTANCE
11 AUNT FINCH'S WINDOW
12 WHITE AREA FOR PROJECTION

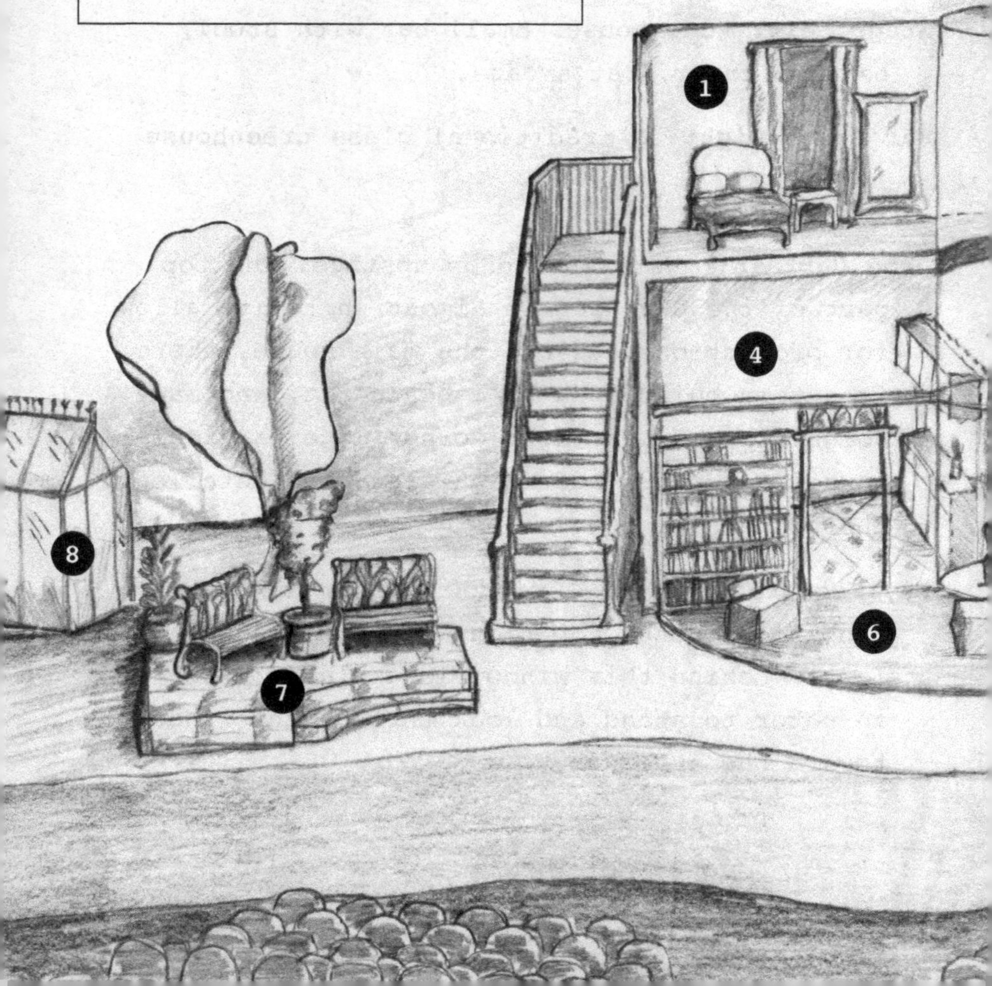

10
11
2
3
9
5

PRODUCTION NOTES

It is the year 2025. The global pandemic is five years old and Jane is tired of being cooped up in her Victorian house with her rule-making father and her brother . . . and her mother, who is confined to a System of tubes that run throughout the house.

Jane has been secretly sneaking off with her punk band, Free Mother, and playing small clubs in Philadelphia, Harrisburg, and New Jersey. What she wants: to go to actual high school; to free her mother from the System; to play punk music; and to fall in love.

DEDICATION

To My Mother

Librettists have historically received less prominent credit than the composer. In some seventeenth-century operas still being performed, the name of the librettist was not even recorded.

—Wikipedia

ACT I, SCENE 1

INT. PUNK CLUB—LATE NIGHT

JANE is onstage in a dank little punk club with her three band-mates. She is screaming the end of a song into a microphone and the crowd is screaming back.

ENTER: MILORAD from the back of the crowd. He stands, rocking his head as if he enjoys the music.

JANE (to crowd)

It was good to see you, Philadelphia! My ride is here!

CROWD

No! No! No!

The crowd looks around for Milo-rad, who looks down and tries to fit in. They hold lighters and phone flashlights above their heads.

Encore! Encore!

JANE

Looks to Milorad, who gives her a small nod with his eyes closed.

Well . . . maybe just one more.

CROWD
screams

Jane sits on the edge of the stage, swinging her legs and swaying from side to side with the band's ballad-paced intro.

Song: "Where Are You Going?"

JANE
WHERE ARE YOU GOING
SWEET LITTLE GIRL?
WHERE DID YOU WANDER TODAY?
WHERE IS YOUR MOTHER?
GO FIND YOUR BROTHER,
BRING HIM BACK HOME RIGHT AWAY.

Jane slowly stands up. She leans over as she continues to sing.

JANE
WHERE ARE YOU GOING
SWEET LITTLE GIRL?
WHY DO YOU LOOK SO CONFUSED?
YOU'VE GOT ALL YOU NEEDED
YOU'VE NEVER ONCE HEEDED
THE RULES THAT MAKE YOU FEEL USED.

The band plays for two measures and Jane paces the stage quickly and intensely. She scream-sings the rest of the song.

JANE

I'M SIXTEEN YEARS OLD
I DO WHAT I'M TOLD
MY MOTHER'S LOCKED UP LIKE A RAT.
WHILE MARTA IS SEWING
SHE ASKS 'WHERE YOU GOING?'
LIKE I KNOW THE ANSWER TO THAT.

BAND

LIKE I KNOW THE ANSWER TO THAT.

Jane continues to pace. The song changes tempo and key. Ballad turns to punk very quickly.

JANE (screaming)

HOW DO I KNOW WHERE I'M GOING?
HOW DO I KNOW WHERE I'VE BEEN?
HOW DO I KNOW WHAT TO DO NOW?
HOW DO I KNOW NOT TO SIN?
NOT TO SIN!
NOT TO SIN!

BAND and JANE

NOT TO SIN!
NOT TO SIN!
HOW DO I KNOW WHERE I'M GOING?
AND HOW DO I KNOW NOT TO SIN?

Jane jumps into the crowd, face up, and surfs her loyal fans.

JANE

WHERE ARE YOU GOING
YOU SWEET LITTLE GIRL?
WHY ARE YOU RUNNING SO FAST?
DOES YOUR DADDY REMEMBER
THE PROMISE HE RENDERED?
HOW DO YOU HANDLE YOUR PAST?

BAND and JANE

WHERE ARE YOU GOING?
WHERE ARE YOU GOING?
WHERE ARE YOU GOING?
AND WILL IT BE SAFE?
WHERE ARE YOU GOING?
WHERE ARE YOU GOING?
WHERE ARE YOU GOING?
WILL YOU FIND YOUR PLACE?

BAND plays fast and loud. Jane is returned from her crowd-surfing to the stage.

Jane paces the stage, bangs her head, while the music roars. She makes eye contact with Milorad.

JANE

WILL YOU EVER FUCKING FIND YOUR PLACE?

Song ends. CROWD jumps and jostles and yells. Jane makes a small curtsy and motions her arm to the stage.

JANE

This is Free Mother! David on drums!

CROWD

roars

JANE

That's Ellis—finest bassist this hemisphere!

CROWD

roars

DAVID and ELLIS play a small rhythm section riff while Jane and the guitarist talk close into each other's ears.

JANE

And this is WENDYLISA on guitar!

CROWD

roars

WENDYLISA throws her pick into the crowd and takes her guitar from around her neck. Milorad moves toward the stage against a steady current of sweaty punk fiends.

Jane fist-bumps her bandmates and picks up a backpack on the side of the stage, peels off her sweaty jeans and replaces them with ill-fitting khakis. She pulls off her soaked black top and replaces it with a plain blue T-shirt, then removes her bra from underneath. She shoves the sweaty clothing into the backpack and heaves it over her shoulder. Houselights are turned on. Jane makes her way to the edge of the stage and jumps down to meet Milorad, who hands her makeup wipes and she wipes off the black eyeliner and lipstick.

FAN

Jane! Jane! I love you!

JANE

I love you too!

FAN

Marry me!

JANE

I'm sixteen!

FAN

Okay! Marry me later!

JANE

Okay!

MILORAD

We must go.

JANE
Of course we must.

MILORAD
He is angry.

JANE
When isn't he?

MILORAD
This is fair question.

JANE (to fans waiting to talk)
I'm sorry, friends. I must go.

MILORAD
She must. I am sorry. (No one really hears him.)

FAN
Free Jane!

JANE
Free Jane!

FANS and BAND
Free Jane! Free Jane! Free Jane!

Milorad and Jane leave club, get into the car.

FADE TO BLACK

LESSON ONE: THE WORLD AND ITS SEVEN CONTINENTS

Today is Monday, September 23, 2024

"NORTH AMERICA is home to twenty-three countries," Vernon says, "entirely located in the Northern and Western Hemispheres."

Vernon looks over my shoulder as I write notes.

"Did you draw that?" he asks.

I redden. I am sixteen and I still doodle to keep my brain busy. "Yes," I say.

"Maybe you shouldn't," he says. He adds rhetorically, "Or should I fetch you an art tutor?"

I look to Mother in the corner, inside of her capsule. She is smiling at me. I look back down at the doodle. It's a flower in a vase. I look back to Mother. She is a flower in a vase, too.

"Can you name the twenty-three countries in North America?" he asks.

"I thought there were only three," I say. "America, Canada, and Mexico." I know all twenty-three but I don't want to spoil his fun.

He points his index finger in the air. "Ah! For you, then, we shall learn the other twenty before the end of the week."

I look over at Mother and she's smiling, still. She's wearing a pair of men's suit pants, a blue T-shirt with the sleeves cut off, and is barefoot. Her exposed shoulders are broad, toned, and so white. Her feet look like mine—arches shallow and big by design. I am nearly five foot nine now—two full inches taller than my father.

"How many Central American countries can you remember from last year?" he asks. "We *did* learn this last year, you know. Though I suppose that's not relevant."

"I remember Belize and Costa Rica and El Salvador," I say. "Oh! And Guatemala!" I put my *wait* finger up. I know that I know the countries of Central America. I look at Mother in the corner again and she's sitting cross-legged on her chair in the capsule, eyes closed. "Panama!" I say, "and Nicaragua!"

Vernon is also staring at Mother in the tube. "You're missing one," he says.

I whisper the ones I already said to myself. "There are seven in total, right?"

"Seven," he says, still watching Mother while she breathes slowly and calmly in the tube. "You've only named six."

"Huh," I say.

Vernon fetches a globe that is wildly out of date. It still has the U.S.S.R. on it.

"I don't want to cheat," I say. "I can remember."

"Go alphabetical," he says. "You can do it."

Belize, Costa Rica, El Salvador, Guatemala . . . "Honduras!"

"Brilliant!" he says. "You've done it."

"Of course," I say. "I was taught by the best."

Mother has a song on her 2010 album titled "Grease the Gears." The lyrics are made entirely of compliments. We all know the key to Vernon's door.

He smiles and ruffles my hair. "That's ten of twenty-three."

"I can't think of thirteen other countries in North America," I say. "I'm actually a bit confused."

"Think for a minute. I've got to get Henry onto his algebra."

I look back to Mother while Vernon tends to Henry.

We look at each other. She is smiling, but her eyes look vexed. Her eyes look like mine.

HOME MOVIE—03.09.2007

Vernon is in the foyer, a suitcase next to him. Mother is out of sight.

She says from offscreen, "You can't just leave!"

"You're so selfish!" he says. "The first day I met you, you said you wanted a family!"

"With a man who loves me, yes," Mother says.

"And I clearly love you. I don't see what the problem is." Vernon says this with his teeth clenched.

"You think it's clear? With that tone of voice?"

"Everything is a test with you!" he says. "You're always just trying to screw everyone over!"

"Whom have I screwed over, Vernon?"

He chuckles. "Me, for one!"

Mother sighs. She walks into the foyer and tries to pick up Vernon's suitcase, but he slaps her hand away. She brings her forearm close and rubs the wrist area.

"Now you'll tell your friends I hit you again, I suppose!"

"Stop being paranoid," she says.

"Why won't you do this one thing for me? You know I always wanted to be a father!"

She shakes her head and laughs a bit. "We've been over this. I can't bring children into the world with a man who hurts me. It's not right. It's just not right."

<pause>

This was one of the first home movies I saw. It's from 2007, the year before I was born. Mother and Vernon had been married for eight years.

<resume>

"Well, how about I promise to not hurt you? Would that be agreeable?"

Mother is still rubbing her wrist from where he slapped it seconds earlier. She doesn't answer.

"I'm so sorry, Mina. I never mean to hurt you," he says. "I'm very sorry."

Mother says nothing. He reaches for her arm and rubs it with the back of his fingers. Her face makes a sort of conciliatory grimace. It's not a smile.

"How I love to see you smile!" Vernon sings.

Mother frowns to herself. Vernon hugs her so enthusiastically you can hear the air in her lungs exit with the force. "Vernon! Not so hard!"

He releases her—as if a venomous snake—and pushes her across the small room. "Jesus Christ! You're impossible to love!"

She regains her balance and leaves the room, still holding her wrist.

He picks up the nearest thing—a small brass bowl—and throws it at her from behind and then he shrugs on his overcoat and picks up his suitcase.

"No one else will want you! You're no good to me . . . or, or to anyone . . . without children!"

Mother pleads softly in the background. "*Please.*"

"Fuckin' useless!" he growls. "What a waste." Vernon picks up his suitcase and turns his body to look directly at her in the hall. "I'm going to stay with my mother!" he yells. With that, he opens the door, steps through, and slams it behind him.

The second the door is closed, Mother reappears and latches the two locks, then leans down and fastens the floor bolt. She takes a deep inhale and lets it out, her back to the door. She slowly looks up to the foyer camera.

"I'll figure it out," she says directly to me, watching, seventeen years later, "I promise."

<stop>

HENRY'S ALGEBRA

"Stop crying!" Vernon says. "How are you going to get anywhere in life?"

Henry wasn't made to sit inside and do schoolwork.

Henry continues crying. Not to spite our father, but because he is a sensitive twelve-year-old boy. I look to Mother in her plexiglass prison. She has her hands facing outward and is aiming toward Henry, as if she is sending him good energy. She is still smiling. She is usually smiling. It's perplexing.

Henry dries his tears on his shirtsleeve and asks a question about exponents.

Vernon says, "Check your textbook. I don't know algebra!"

I say, "Yes. Exponents can have variables."

Then there are sounds from the kitchen—a pan dropping and a loud bang. And then Marta: "Fuck!"

Henry giggles.

Then some more bangs that sound like a rolling pin on stainless steel kitchen counters. I hear her open the back door.

"Milorad!" she yells. "Your rat is loose again!"

I stare back at my notes. Ten more countries in North America. I look back to Mother and try to figure out why she's smiling. I look back at my doodle and think about an art tutor. I look at Henry and say, "Why don't you get Henry a tutor for his algebra?"

Vernon looks at me and mocks, his hands clasped before him. "Why ever don't I fetch someone to help?"

"I think it's a good idea is all," I say.

"I'm sure you do."

I look around for Brutus, Milorad's lost rat. No rats here.

HOME MOVIE—07.19.2008 (498 DAYS AFTER THE LAST HOME MOVIE)

I am an infant. Mother is holding me and humming a song. Vernon is pacing in the sitting room, from velvet-curtained window to velvet-curtained window, ranting.

"I don't know how many times I have to tell you," he says.

"Tell me another time, Vernon," she says softly.

He stops pacing and faces us. "I went out for a *single* round of golf. It was very civilized. No alcohol passed my lips. I was completely sober when I came home. The memory you have of me must be mistaken." His face turns from stern to soft. "You must know that everything I do, it's for you, my love. Let's not dwell in the past."

"Okay," she says. "Your vodka breath and the way you stumbled to the door, and the fact that you lost your favorite putter is all in the past. Of course all you do is for me."

Vernon looks appeased.

Mother continues. "I can feel it every night when you don't come to bed."

"GOD DAMMIT!" Vernon screams. He picks up the small end table next to Mother's chair and throws it across the room. It splits into pieces and knocks over a potted plant. Dirt spills out. Mother barely flinches, though she does hold me tighter against her chest.

He whimpers, "Why must you insult me all the time?"

"I was just trying to get you to tell the simple truth. It's not a *bad* thing to tell the truth. And who doesn't get drunk while golfing every now and again?"

"I wasn't drunk."

Mother smiles and looks at me. She bounces me on her lap and in a singsong says, "Vernon doesn't know / His friends called me / Vernon doesn't know / His friends were drunk, too / Vernon doesn't know / It's okay to get caught / Vernon needs to learn / How to just stop lying."

Vernon looks a mix of sad and furious. He puts his face physically into his hands and then he says, "Oh, my love, I'm so sorry! I *was* drunk. I really was. I don't know why I lied."

"Isn't he adorable?" she asks infant-me. "When will I learn?"

He comes to the chair where she sits and kneels beside it and kisses her arms and knees and anything he can reach with his lips. He keeps whispering, "I'm sorry. I'm sorry. I'm sorry. I'm sorry," until he reaches her face and my face and he kisses us all over our faces, even when Mother flinches, and then he calls out, "Marta! What's for supper?" and waltzes out of the room to the kitchen.

Mother holds me to her face and smiles at me. She holds me above her head and plays airplane. She hums the singsong she'd just sung and then disappears through the doors to the study with me in her arms.

When the sitting room is empty, a figure emerges from behind the settee on all fours. It is my mother's sister, my aunt Finch. When she's fully clear of the furniture, she brushes off her hands and knees and walks toward the kitchen.

<stop>

THE ISLANDS

My grasp of the Caribbean Islands is not great.

I have memorized them several times, only for the names and locations not to stick. I can remember minute details of the strangest things and every one of Mother's lyrics, but for some reason, Saint Kitts and Saint Nevis are not important to me.

Vernon has given me a blank map with lines drawn next to each island. Instead of writing the names of the islands into the blanks, I write mnemonics—words that might help me remember. Mnemonics are the way I've always memorized things, often in the form of songs. This has been made complicated by Vernon's music ban. Also: his insistence that I not become anything like Mother. I wrote a scene about it last night.

INT. SMALL IMAGINARY PUNK CLUB INSIDE JANE'S HEAD

Song: "Daddy Said"

The music starts abruptly here with a guitar feedback squeak followed by very fast and loud punk music . . .

We see JANE and her three imaginary BANDMATES, dressed as (foam) islands of the Caribbean, onstage at a small, packed imaginary punk club in Jane's imagination.

JANE

DADDY SAID
DADDY SAID
MAMA NEVER LOVED YOU
AND I KNOW IT'S TRUE
BECAUSE HE SAYS IT'S TRUE.

Jane sings into a microphone, toward screaming, freaking-out fans. She is dressed in short black leather shorts, mismatched legwarmers. Big fuck-off boots. Across her shoulders and chest is a rigid foam cutout of the island of Jamaica, painted with the Jamaican flag. Jane's hair is tousled and wet from sweat.

JANE (CONT'D)

DADDY SAID
DADDY SAID
MAMA ONLY LIES TO YOU
AND I KNOW IT'S TRUE
BECAUSE HE SAYS IT'S TRUE.

JANE and BAND

TRUE TRUE TRUE.
TRUE TRUE TRUE.
TRUE TRUE TRUE.

Jane kicks high in the air. The band members play a wicked good bridge.

JANE

DADDY SAID
DADDY SAID
I'M THE ONLY ONE WHO'S HERE FOR YOU
WHO LOOKS OUT FOR YOU
WHO LONGS FOR YOU.

Jane is on her knees at the edge of the stage, watching the mosh pit.

JANE

DADDY SAID
DADDY SAID

I'M THE ONE YOU SHOULD TALK TO
THE ONE YOU SHOULD TRUST WHO
THE ONE WHO WILL HELP YOU.

JANE and BAND
TRUE TRUE TRUE.
TRUE TRUE TRUE.
TRUE TRUE TRUE.

Jane crouches down, points to the BOUNCER at the edge of the stage as the band plays the bridge. She moves her head wildly to the rhythm.

JANE
DADDY PUT A HAND ON MY LEG
SQUEEZED IT TWICE
CODE FOR OWNERSHIP
CODE FOR WORSHIP
CODE FOR LISTEN-TO-ME.

JANE and BAND
LISTEN TO ME!

JANE
DADDY SAID DADDY SAID DADDY SAID.
NO ONE CARES WHAT DADDY SAID.

JANE and BAND
TRUE TRUE TRUE.
TRUE TRUE TRUE.
TRUE TRUE TRUE!

Jane is just freaking out now. Her island costume is crowd-surfing while she is left on-stage in a black bra, mascara sweat running down like tears, screaming the chorus. Rolls around onstage.

JANE and BAND

TRUE TRUE TRUE!

TRUE TRUE TRUE!

TRUE TRUE TRUE!

We hear the music fade and the sound of the crowd overtake it, then it slowly becomes back-ground noise to the sound of a tapping pencil.

END SONG

INT. STUDY

We see Jane sitting at her desk, pencil in hand, staring at a map of Caribbean islands. She taps the pencil in beat with the song that just faded.

JANE (V.O.)

The thing about the lyrics to Mother's songs is that they are never lies. This is one of many things we have in common.

Projection on DROP: a fast side-by-side comparison CLOSE-UPS of MOTHER and Jane as she lists each one: hair, nose, feet, singing, laughing, being smart, smile, lips.

JANE (V.O.) (CONT'D)

Other things we have in common—I have her hair, her nose, and her feet, as already noted. I have her pitch, her humor, her intelligence, and her smile. Her lips.

Jane sits, studying her geography and looking out the window. MINA is in the tubes, watching Jane stare out the window. VERNON is napping lightly on a settee near the fireplace.

END SCENE

HOW JANE CAME TO THE PUNK OPERA IN HER HEAD

One time Vernon was driving us to the mall. Seemed such an odd thing for him to do, but Henry was eager for cactus soil and Vernon was smoking a pipe at the time and needed fancy tobacco he could only get at the store there. I was eleven, weeks from twelve. Henry was eight. It was a mere month or so before the pandemic locked us all up.

Vernon kept coasting through stop signs. And he never used his turn signals.

I said, "Vernon, turn signal."

He said, "Jesus, Jane, you sound like your mother."

I said, "You still need to use your turn signal."

He said, "I'm a better driver than your mother, anyway."

I said, "Are you not using it now because I asked?"

He said, "Yes, Jane. I am rebelling against you. We have switched roles. You are my mother now. I shall call you Punk Rock Jane and you shall spray the audience with menstrual blood and tell them all to go fuck themselves."

I said, "Jesus, Vernon."

He laughed and Henry laughed. I laughed, too. If I didn't, I wasn't sure what would happen.

It was then, in the back of that car, that I decided that maybe being Punk Rock Jane wasn't so bad. Not only would it annoy Vernon that I turned out like Mother, who had been completely confined to the System at that point for two years, but it would also annoy Mother that I was trying to be like her, probably. Vernon had already told me how insane she was. How negligent.

I didn't know that he'd spent all her money. I didn't know about his deals with Finch or Marta or Milorad. I didn't know about how utterly broke we all were, regardless of our posh Victorian lifestyle. I didn't know anything.

All I knew was that I had to do something to stay safe the older I got. The more I looked at the tubes, the more I had a terrible feeling that it would be me in there one day.

MEET BRUTUS

WHAT YOU NEED TO KNOW is that I destroy things. It's what I do. Once the funerals are over or the bulldozers have pushed the wreckage into piles, I am made stronger. Not muscles-stronger, but presence-stronger. We all have a presence, you know. Even rats.

I have destroyed just about everything that can be destroyed. From reputations to whole people, I've decimated them. I've destroyed homes. I've destroyed families. I've destroyed cities. I've destroyed mothers and children. I've destroyed those most undeserving of destruction.

I am a monster. Call me Algos. Call me Perses. Call me Shaitan. Call me Kali. Call me Satan. Whatever name you choose, know that I don't care at all. You could call me ice cream and I'd still find the best thing about you and make you doubt it.

Here's what I see when I crawl around the Victorian home of Vernon Cook and Mina Placenta. I see weakness. I see greed. And I see splendor. I was born to burn it all down. Every piece of beauty and filigree—every gold-leafed accent—I was sent to crumble it. I am termites. I am tornadoes. I am floods and fires and sandstorms and cracks in the earth. I am the person who hates you for no reason. I am the person who bullies your mother. A tormentor. A sadist. I am every single rapist and every single child molester. I am every wife beater and every depraved nurse. I am the worst things you've ever daydreamed and every one of your fears. The scariest thing about me is that you can't even fear me. Not now. Not ever. Made of myths, I am, to make you believe that I am an impossibility.

But I live in the pool house with the Serbian who never sleeps.

There is a reason I chose him. A reason he chose me.

EXAM DAY

Today is Tuesday, October 15, 2024

VERNON DOESN'T BOTHER to get up early on exam days even though he makes such a huge deal out of us studying for them. While we wait for him to stumble downstairs, Henry and I look out the front window and watch children—some of our old friends—walk to real school. We do this most days between seven and eight, while Marta makes us breakfast.

In the last three weeks I have [re]learned the countries and capitals of North and South America, the capitals of Canadian provinces and the capitals of American states, and the names of adjacent oceans and seas. I am sixteen and this is the stuff we did in seventh grade. And while Henry struggles through algebra at his grade level, Vernon hasn't assigned him to read a novel since he was nine. If I had a way to do it, I'd write to the school district and tell them they have a duty to rescue us.

It is soon time for me to argue with Vernon about it again. Instead of answering on-topic, Vernon talks endlessly about how one day I'll find a man and live happily ever after. He makes it sound delicious—"You'll land in the lap of luxury, for certain. I mean, look at you."

Indeed. Look at me. Long legged, brunette, porcelain tone, perfect teeth, dimples. Lap of luxury for certain, old boy.

"Is that Peyton?" I ask Henry.

"He's so tall now."

"Wow. So that must be Anna. Shit," I say. "She's, um, *grown up*."

I look left only to see Henry scowling at me—all of twelve. "That's what people do," he says. "They grow up."

"Sorry," I say. "I can't get a grip on time anymore."

Henry sighs. "Please, Jane. It's not like you're incarcerated."

I look over to the tube in the corner of the room. It's empty now. I don't think Henry understands any of this. I suppose he will never have to. I go to the kitchen and leave him staring at his old friends through the window.

I flop myself into the nearest chair to the tube in the kitchen, put my elbows on the table, and sigh.

"I should be at school like a normal teenager," I say. I balance my chin in my hands.

Marta moves around the kitchen and puts a cup of hot chocolate in front of me and then uncaps a whipped cream container and puts as much as she can on top of the hot chocolate. "Soon you'll be old enough to do what you want," she says.

"I don't even know how to be sixteen."

"You're doing pretty great at it," she says.

I roll my eyes. "Please."

The System whirs itself awake. Marta looks relieved. Twenty seconds pass and Mother arrives in the kitchen tube. Henry joins us.

She smiles at us and mouths a *hello*. She has pillow creases on her face and her hair is frizzy in every direction. Marta looks around for the two-way attachment for the tube. Vernon must have fitted the one-way attachment here yesterday.

"You're still in your pajamas," I say.

She smiles and gestures to her pajamas.

Marta says to her, "You're staying up way too late. You need rest before tour."

Mother nods. She leaves on Friday.

"Today is exam day!" Henry tells her. "I know how to diagram sentences now."

She blows him a kiss for good luck.

"And I know all the capitals of the Americas . . . same as I did in seventh grade and I should be in the high school with my friends experiencing my sophomore year," I say.

Before she can blow me a kiss, and before Marta can fit the two-way attachment, the back door to the kitchen slams. It's Aunt Finch.

"Complaining again, Jane?" she asks.

I don't answer.

She knocks obnoxiously on Mother's tube. "Hello, sister!" she yells. "How's the weather in there?"

Mother stretches her arms and rolls her neck. Henry seems panicked about what to do. He looks at his hands, which are folded on the table.

"Nobody's rescued you yet, huh?" Finch yells toward Mother.

I watch her move around in her tiny capsule. I don't understand why she doesn't just escape. I'm not allowed to think this, let alone say it aloud. She is there because she wants to be there, Vernon says. "If she wanted to be your mother, she'd have found a way out," Vernon always says. "And she'd have quit music" is the refrain sung by Finch, Vernon's chorus.

"Mind if I take your place this morning?" Finch yells.

Mother looks into my eyes. She reaches up and presses the green button. The fan whirs. The capsule shoots down and out of sight, leaving the tube empty and Finch smirking.

Marta goes to the far smaller tube next to the System—a pneumatic dumbwaiter—and puts Mother's breakfast tray into it.

"Was that porridge?" Finch asks.

"Yep," Marta says.

"I want some."

"Okay," Marta replies.

Finch claps her hands together and then rubs them. Looks at me. "How much do you know about Brazil?"

"Capital is Brasilia," I say. "Biggest country in South America. Fifth largest in the world. They speak Portuguese." I try to remember anything else. "Biggest Carnival in the world in Rio de Janeiro, and green anaconda snakes. I think that's it."

Finch nods.

"It has four time zones!" Henry says. He's our in-house time-zone calculator. Anytime Mother is on tour, he can figure out what time it is where she is.

"Why?" I ask.

Finch shrugs casually. "I'm thinking of going back. I need to talk to Vernon about it."

Marta serves me and Henry French toast and we both dive into it. Finch isn't ever here to see us. She's only here to see Vernon.

"I need to get my rightful half of this house first," she finishes.

As I eat my French toast, I try to count the number of times Finch has said a variation of this to me and Henry. I'm not sure why she bothers. Clearly, Henry and I have no say over what Mother does. Or even what we do.

"She's making so much money. Hides it all from us, you know. Even from you two," she says. Marta places a bowl of porridge in front of her.

"Why Brazil?" Henry says. "You've lived all over the world!"

"And why so soon?" Marta adds. "You haven't even been in that apartment nine months!"

"I think I'm just a rolling stone," Finch answers. "Plus, the view is infuriating!"

The view is our house. She lives up on the hill, where she can see everything we do.

THE BALLAD OF VERNON AND FINCH

I do not lie to God and I will not start now. My father, Vernon, has had a yearslong relationship with his wife's sister, my aunt Finch.

Always presented to us as an exciting world-traveling bachelor-type, dropping in whenever she happened to be in town, Finch commanded certain respect back when Mother wasn't locked up all the time. The two of them used to play dreadfully competitive croquet games, and we'd pick sides based on who'd given us the most candy that day. It was always Finch because—even back when she was free to roam—Mother was controlled by Vernon's sighs and glares and subtle shakes of the head and Finch had an endless pocketful of Tootsie Rolls.

Back then, Henry and I adored Aunt Finch because, as it was told to us, Mother was an impossible and annoying woman and her sister was the cure to Vernon's ills as well as our own—even if she wasn't particularly kind or caring.

In the six years since Mother has been locked up, Finch comes around a lot more, usually with a six-pack of beer, and she no longer hides her road-rash personality, though she is almost always staring into the screen of her cellphone.

A failed musician and failed poet, she buys every one of Mother's albums and listens carefully enough to hear everything she hates about Mother. Most recently, she hates that Mother has "all this space!" and won't "just stay home!" because she's "so busy out there getting rich."

"They laugh at you, you know!" That's what Aunt Finch said to Mother many times—her outside the tube and Mother inside, eyes closed, blocking Finch out. "No matter how much success you get, you're still just a weirdo and no one takes you seriously!" Mother would put her hands over her ears, and I could see her throat tensing with a loud hum. Sometimes, she would take her flannel shirt or sweater and wrap it up over her head so she couldn't see Finch, and Finch couldn't see her.

Estrangement is all kinds of complicated when one is confined in a tube and one's sister is outside the tube, fucking one's husband. It really is a scandal.

I can't judge, though. From the age of seven, through the tween years when the pandemic locked us all in this wood-paneled Victorian cage, to the age of found-the-home-movies sixteen, I also behaved in ways for which I cannot ever forgive myself.

I was scum. Duplicitous. Disloyal. I can't bear it.

There is a memory I have from inside my bedroom, where there are no cameras. Six years ago—two months before The Christmas That Changed Everything. Mother was there, in the flesh, on a break from a world tour for Henry's birthday, and I was ten. She held a stack of freshly laundered sheets still warm from the dryer.

"You're doing so well on your math work," she said to me.

"Not like you even care," I said.

"I care very much, Jane."

"No, you don't."

Mother cocked her head at me in the way she does. Vernon says it's to make us feel bad.

"Stop doing that!" I said. "You control us with how you look at us!"

"I'm sorry," she said. "Come on. Let's make the bed. I was hoping we could talk like a mother and daughter do. I started with something silly like math. Really, I should ask you if you have anything to share. I miss you. I miss reading to you. What are you reading now?"

I am so ashamed to tell you, reader, what I did next.

"What do you care?" I yelled. "You go all over the world to play music and make millions of dollars that you don't share with us,"

I said. "And your music is stupid anyway. Finch says you just string random words together."

"I'm sure Finch is right," Mother said.

I grabbed the sheets from her hands and took them to my en suite bathroom. I shoved them in the toilet bowl. I said, "Mother, go fetch my sheets and wash them. I can't believe you wanted me to put such filthy things on my bed! No wonder you don't have a good family life. You just can't seem to do anything right."

I am so ashamed. I have been a dour, piece-of-shit daughter—though we had incentive to practice. Each time Henry or I did something evil to Mother, we were rewarded.

Three weeks later, on Christmas morning 2018, Mother was there, exhausted from a yearlong tour, and she wore a pair of men's checked pajama pants—red and navy blue—and a T-shirt that read ALL I WANT FOR CHRISTMAS IS REPRODUCTIVE RIGHTS.

Finch, who stayed in the adjoining guest room next to Vernon's while Mother slept two stories down in the basement, said to her, "How dare you wear such a thing to Christmas!"

Mother didn't answer.

Finch said, "If Jesus was aborted, we wouldn't even be having Christmas!"

Mother didn't answer. None of us were religious. I started to fake-cry for my reward.

Vernon scooped me into his arms then, and said, "I'm sorry, Jane."

Mother hung her head. "I'll change my shirt, Jane. I apologize." She went to change and came back with a different shirt on. It read ALL I WANT FOR CHRISTMAS IS THE END OF FOR-PROFIT PRISONS.

Finch muttered under her breath and rolled her eyes. Mother sat down on the floor next to the tree.

Vernon opened his gift from Mother then, between sips of his bitter black coffee. It was money. Cash money. Bills from every country she'd been in that year while on her world tour for the album *Safe House*. Vernon looked at the roll of cash and back to Mother.

"What good will this do me?" he asked.

Mother looked hurt.

Vernon walked to her and squatted an inch from her face. He screamed. "I stay home with your children and you bring me money I can't even use?"

Mother started to cry and her body shook.

Henry started to laugh—he was seven years old. He said, "Look at Mother crying!"

I took him to the kitchen. I could hear from there, Mother's explanation.

"Finch told me that this is what you wanted—bills from all the places I'd been," she said. "I thought you'd be thrilled."

I peeked through the swinging door. Finch sat on the couch smirking, arms crossed, legs crossed, spring-loaded, and shaking her head. There was quite a bit of yelling after that and Marta distracted us with Christmas dinner chores and loud holiday music—a tradition during Vernon's annual Christmas benders, though this one was louder.

Later that night, while Mother was locked securely in the System, Vernon and Finch gave Henry and me an endless mound of Marta's Christmas cookies, and while Henry got plain eggnog, I got something special. My very first taste of rum! At ten years old. How naughty! How fabulously wicked!

EXAMS AT NOON

By the time Vernon arrives in the study, it's past noon. Henry is out with Milorad and covered in dirt. I am locked in my en suite bathroom, under my favorite fleece blanket, and on my quest for the truth. I need to understand why Mother is willingly locked up when she hasn't done anything wrong.

"Jane!"

I hide the iPad in the hollow behind the sink pedestal and rush downstairs. I feign being out of breath.

He ignores me. "Sit. It's exam time!" He puts a packet of test papers in front of me. "You have one hour."

I open the packet while he goes to the kitchen for coffee.

The test is for seventh graders. It says so in the footer of the front page, which also has the name of the website Vernon uses for his worksheets. (He keeps his computer setup locked in his room lest Henry or I sneak online and find out anything about the real world.)

I fill in the Caribbean Islands first, just to spite myself and Vernon. The rest is easy. It's been easy since the sixth grade when I first took this exam.

I decide, two pages in, to contact the school district. This is serious. This is my future. *Panama, Honduras, Nicaragua, Belize . . .*

I will say *Dear School District, Vernon Cook is holding me and my brother hostage in our house at 1111 Spruce Street. I am sixteen, and today I took the same test on North American geography as I did in elementary school. Please do whatever you can to save us.*

Sadly, no one will be sent to save us because this letter is in my imagination. Instead, Vernon arranges another suitor. My twentieth, I believe.

SUITOR #20: JED FROM THE ORCHESTRA

When Vernon took me shopping at the family department store in Philadelphia on my sixteenth birthday in March, he made sure to stop by the lingerie section and told the woman working there to "set me up with whatever she needs." This meant lacy panties and bras, all of which felt too old for me but I went along with it.

That's what having suitors is all about, Vernon told me. *Going along with it.*

His name is Jed and he plays the French horn in the youth symphony, which Vernon isn't too pleased to learn as we eat dinner. In fact, he rejects the boy outright and doesn't stay for dessert. It gives Jed and me some time alone to talk.

"Your dad really dresses up for this stuff," he says.

"He lies to God," I say, quite drunk from dinner wine. "Pocket watch and all."

He pulls out a flask from his sport coat and offers with his eyebrows. I nod and he takes a swig and hands it to me. I take a long swig, looking directly into the security camera.

He looks around the dining room. "Are those gold records?"

"Yes."

As my head looks over my shoulder at Mother's gold records, he launches himself into my lap right there at the dining table, tongue flailing as if I'm not still eating Marta's famous peach cobbler.

I suddenly feel ill—as if I am about to faint. I open my mouth to speak, and all that comes out is garbled. Jed continues to straddle me in my chair and I push it away from the table and we begin to fall backward quickly. When the chair hits the floor, my head is saved by his arm, which makes an interesting sound as we land. Next thing I remember is Marta and me in my bedroom, her telling Henry he was a good brother, and the darkness of sleep.

APPLESAUCE DAY

Today is Wednesday, October 16, 2024

I HAVE BEEN SPOILED my entire life with the foods Marta and Milorad make for our family. For example, I have never tried applesauce that comes from a jar. I have never eaten store-bought jam. And I have never placed in my mouth a vegetable that was not homegrown.

Today is applesauce day and don't even think of trying to get into the kitchen until it's done or else Marta will tell you right off.

Vernon learns the hard way annually.

I can hear it from the patio where I'm lying on a bench dealing with a disquieting wine-and-roofie hangover.

"Get your hand off of that!" Marta yells.

"I just want coffee!"

"No coffee today," she says.

Vernon says, "I can just make instant and—"

"No coffee today!" Marta snaps.

I can hear the swinging door of the kitchen and then Vernon opens the patio doors.

"It's applesauce day," he says.

"I'm aware," I say.

"Can I sit here with you?"

"I'm trying to nap in the sun," I say. My head is pounding.

"Aren't you helping?" he asks.

"Of course. But not until the end. I'm a taster."

"I would think that's Henry's job now."

"Henry is out on a bike ride," I say. It sounds so *normal*, doesn't it?

"What?" You can hear his balls tense up.

"See? You're awake. You don't need coffee," I say. Henry isn't on a bike ride. He's in the greenhouse.

"Jesus, Jane."

"That should be my stage name," I say.

I sit up and he sits down where my feet were a minute ago. He looks at me. He starts to talk. I hear nothing over my inner band-name monologue.

Jesus Jane's Taste Test. Taste Test featuring Jesus Jane. Jesus Jane and the Hangovers. Bagged Lunch. Jesus Jane and Bagged Lunch. Bike Ride feat. Jesus Jane. Jesus Jane and the Bike Rides. Jesus Jane and the Bike Riders.

"Don't you think?" Vernon asks.

"Hmm?"

"You're always saying we should see more art."

"I didn't hear you. Sorry. What are we talking about?" I ask.

"Your art tutor."

"Oh."

"She wants to take you to a museum first thing," he says. "I don't think it's wise."

I didn't think he was really going to get me an art tutor. I startle myself and hug him with gleeful arms. "Are you serious? Which museum?"

"I can't recall."

"Do you remember the Rodin? It was so beautiful. The longer I stared at the bronzes, the more detail I could see. Flawless!"

"Calm down."

"I shan't! It's too good of a dream! A museum! A real museum!"

"You sound like you've never been anywhere," he says.

"I've been locked up since I was newly twelve. Surely you can't even imagine what that's like. It's been dreadful. I'd walk along a highway, even. Anywhere different."

"Oh, shut up, Jane. Really." Vernon stands up and I stand up with him. I do enjoy my misplaced Victorian-teen-girl act. It's what he expects.

"I'll shut up if you let me see a museum with—" I pause. "What's her name?"

"Susan," he says.

"Susan," I say. I'll admit I was hoping for something that sounded a bit more exciting. *Jesus Jane and the Susans.* "When do I get to meet her?"

Vernon says, "I don't have her nailed down yet. I'll put in my order now."

Marta pokes her head out of the kitchen. "Jane, can you give me a hand?"

I nod at Marta but say this to Vernon. "You're *ordering* her? Is she a pizza?"

Vernon closes his eyes as if I'm too much to suffer. I feel for him—worn down by a sixteen-year-old girl with a hangover.

By the time I'm inside the kitchen Marta has one eyebrow raised and whispers, "You smell like a pirate. You're lucky he didn't—"

"Arrrrr," I say. "Where's Mother?"

She throws me a clean dish towel soaked in cold water, and says, "Rehearsing at the studio. Slap that on your face."

I do.

When I open my eyes, she's handing me a cup of black coffee and an Altoids mint.

"Lean back."

I do.

She expertly drops saline onto my parched eyeballs.

This is not our first rodeo.

Milorad arrives in the kitchen via the back door. "I am here to help!"

Marta points to three huge pots on the stovetop. Each one has steam billowing from it—she's boiling water. On the stainless steel island, she has two big cutting boards and two chef's knives. Between them is a huge bowl of washed apples.

Gemma walks in from the direction of the study. "Sorry I'm late!"

She walks directly to the bowl of apples and starts chopping them into quarters and placing them in an empty bowl to her left.

"Hi!" I say to Gemma. I can't think of anything else.

"Hi!" she says back.

Marta places her hands on both of my shoulders and moves me into the comfy chair in the corner of the kitchen. She hands me two Tylenol. She says, "Don't get in the way."

For two hours, I watch as they chop, boil, and grind. I check to see where Vernon is a few times, but Marta tells me I can't go outside. I say, "But he could be asleep in the sun again."

Milorad answers me. "He is with your mother's sister. They are in the orchard, cleaning up."

"That's a lie," I say. Because I've never known either Finch or Vernon to clean up anything.

The adults in the room all look at me.

I fake figuring it out, whatever "it" is. Because if it's something weird and sexual that involves an orchard, I don't want to know.

Ten minutes later, it becomes clear it was not sexual at all.

Vernon is screaming. I mean *screaming*—as he storms toward the house.

"If it's so bloody easy, then you do it!" he snaps. "*You* do it!"

Marta whispers something in Milorad's ear. He grunts in agreement. Gemma looks up at me and gives a feeble smile. I love applesauce day. Seeing our people in one place, working together, makes me feel like I'm part of a family.

OUR PEOPLE

It's an icebreaker!

OUR PEOPLE. THAT'S HOW WE SAY IT.

Gemma.

Milorad.

Marta.

They are *our people.*

LET'S GET TO KNOW MARTA!

Marta has cooked delicious food (and made jams, preserves, powders, elixirs, wines, ciders, beers, truly—Marta has a recipe for anything you ever wanted) in this house since 2001, and has been cooking for Mina since she was fourteen years old! Her favorite animal is the starfish. ASK MARTA ABOUT WHY SHE LOVES STARFISH SOMETIME. She grew up about a mile from here and was Mother's best friend since they were in primary school. Marta's favorite color "depends on what you're talking about." She says: brown for sweaters and red for pajamas, but "really ugly and unsettling colors for sports cars." Marta lives in the original servant's quarters, a spacious two-bedroom apartment with windows overlooking the large lawn to the west of the rose garden, which is only accessible from the back stairs in the kitchen.

LET'S GET TO KNOW MILORAD!

Milorad is a mysterious gardener and general valet with a cool accent. He came to America from Serbia in 1992—soon after the Yugoslav Wars started. He landed first in Chicago and lived there with his cousin. No one knows why he came to Pennsylvania. I think it's because he had a raucous love affair. ASK MILORAD WHY HE CAME TO PENNSYLVANIA SOMETIME. He started working for our family in 2006, the year Mother and Vernon went to Amsterdam to launch Mother's second studio album, *It Takes Two*. Milorad lives in the pool house and no one seems to mind. His favorite color is "the green of spring grass" and his favorite animal, aside from his pet rat, Brutus, is the red-tailed hawk.

LET'S GET TO KNOW GEMMA!

Gemma is seventeen years old, which is not too old for me to be in love with her. She has been my lady's maid since I was eight, which is weird because she was only nine, but she has always been far more mature than me. She says, "I'm your *friend*, only I help you do things. That's all." Her favorite color is blue. Her favorite animal, she says, is me, but I've heard her talking to Marta about how she keeps chickens on her family's farm and how much she loves the blue ones. ASK GEMMA WHY SHE LOVES HER BLUE CHICKENS SO MUCH SOMETIME. Of our three *people*, Gemma is the only one who doesn't live on the property. She tells me she walks here, but she never arrives wet when it's raining.

LESSON TWO: HOW I CAME TO KNOW MY MOTHER IS A WITCH

Today is Thursday, October 17, 2024

APPLESAUCE DAY always means pork for dinner. Marta serves the sauce warm—that was dinner last night. Then I went to bed stuffed and Gemma slept over, so I couldn't look at any home movies.

Waking up this morning was awkward. Only for me. Gemma has no idea.

I arrive downstairs to find I successfully passed Vernon's North & South America exam on Tuesday. There were no trick questions for once. Just a map and fill-in-the-blanks. After Vernon returned my graded test to me, Henry cried over algebra until Vernon let him help Milorad in the garden.

The only time I like Henry now is when we're outside. He seems more grounded there, not faking interest in whatever Vernon's saying. He likes dirt most of all. He seems to find an escape in it. Mother knows this because Mother buys him dirt-related gifts for his birthday every year and it makes Vernon crazy. Which means it makes Henry crazy, too. When he turned thirteen last week, he turned his back to Mother, contained in the corner, and said, "I don't want to plant any of these bulbs because I know you must have picked them by witchcraft."

That's the new one. Mother is a witch. A witch who finds the most beautiful varieties of flowers in the world and gives them to her dirt-loving son on his birthday. What a demon! Only a fortnight ago, Vernon started wearing a Christian cross around his neck on a gold chain to ward off her magic.

I go to the kitchen and get a bowl of fresh applesauce and break some pieces of cheese into it—my favorite snack.

After my test review, where Vernon rolls his eyes at the fact that I misspelled *Guyana* and *French Guiana*, I have the day off, so I join Henry in the garden where he's sitting on the grass, the knees of his Flexion hiking pants already muddy. It's a warm October and the leaves are only beginning to turn. Henry's exotic bulbs and tubers are still in the box and half wrapped with Mother's drawings all over brown parcel paper.

"*Arisaema costatum*," Henry says. "Native to Nepal."

I nod. "Where will you put it?"

"It needs shade, I think. I need to read up," he says. "Though I may just throw it away."

"Why?"

"*Sauromatum venosum*," he says. "Voodoo lilies. She gave me three of them."

"Voodoo lilies," I say. "That sounds exciting."

"Only if you're a witch." Henry gets up and walks to Milorad. Milorad is presently shoveling aged horseshit onto the rose beds in the southwest section of the rose garden. I follow Henry. I don't say anything about Mother not being a witch. This is a game and I have to play in order to free her.

"I saw the new plants!" Milorad says. "Do you know where you want them? I have some good suggestions!"

"Can we use holy water to water them at first?" Henry asks.

Milorad laughs.

I ask, "Since when have you believed in holy water?"

"Since our mother became a witch," Henry answers.

Milorad drops his brow. "Witch?"

"Yes, Milo," Henry says. "Mother is a witch now. She is more terrible than we thought."

"Oh my," he says.

Milorad is playing stupid. I heard Vernon out here with him last week. *She's a witch you know. Curses me every night! I swear if there was a way to lock her up safely I would, but she deserves to at least be in her own home while she loses her mind like this. Thank God for those old tubes. Poor dear. I love her so much.*

"Honestly, I don't think I want these at all. Do you have a friend who might want them?" Henry asks.

"Henry. Do not throw away such good plants," Milorad says. "They were gifts."

"From a witch."

"Mother is not a witch," I say.

Henry looks at me like I'm a traitor. Milorad looks like I've just rescued his cat from a house fire.

I walk back inside.

Vernon isn't in the study. Mother is sitting in her capsule, meditating. I walk up to the tube and knock lightly on it. She looks up and smiles.

I say, "I don't understand why you're doing this."

She says something but I can't hear it. I try to read her lips.

She points to her ear. *Listen. To.* Then two words I can't figure out.

She says it again.

"'Listen to *Safe House*'?" I say.

She nods.

"Who are you talking to?" Vernon says, arriving from the kitchen. "Ah!" he says. "I knew this would happen."

"I hate her," I say, pointing. I look right into her eyes. "Witch."

Vernon looks impressed.

I turn to him. "I don't like doing my schoolwork while she watches anymore, Vernon."

"Of course, Jane."

"And I want to play games later. All of us. For Henry."

"Oh, Jane! I'm so glad," Vernon says. "Games always help him out of his slumps and I fear he's in one now. So soon after his birthday!"

"Make sure Mother is there. I think it will help if she's there."

"Of course," Vernon says.

"We shall play Ticket to Ride!" I say. "The American version. I know how much Henry loves it."

"Of course," Vernon says.

"And invite a suitor!" I say. "I'm feeling pretty today."

"Of course," Vernon says.

I look back to Mother. She is standing in her capsule and doing Tai Chi. When she reaches up to gather Heaven, her belly pops out from under her shirt. It is the palest white and her hip bones pop out and I can see the faint stretch marks from her pregnancies. When she reaches down to gather earth, I can see the top of a tattoo on her right hip—a rendering of Anne Bonny, the notorious pirate, but instead of a musket, she's holding a carton of milk.

"I love family game nights!" I say. "Will Marta make us mashed potatoes for supper? I'd love that so much. And maybe another pork loin? It's applesauce week!"

"Of course," Vernon says. "Jane, what's got into you? You're positively glowing."

"I think we should be allowed to go to the garden more often, Vernon. I think it's good to talk to Milorad and walk in the sun. Especially this time of year."

"I see."

"Go talk to Marta!" I say. "Best she knows now what she's cooking tonight."

Vernon leaves the room, but I know he's lurking by the door.

I turn to Mother in the corner, doing Tai Chi—limited to the diameter of the capsule, she is rocking slightly from her toes to her heels, raising and lowering her forearms. Her eyes are closed and we ignore each other.

I go to the display cases in the study and find the vinyl record of *Safe House* and take it to my room. I've listened to the album before, a few times. I read all the words on the record sleeve, but that was back when it was released. Quite a year, 2018. It was the year of *Safe House*, its matching world tour, and The Christmas That Changed Everything, which was soon followed by The Great Ignoring—neither of which can I bring myself to think about, let alone look at in the home movies.

As I climb the stairs, wondering how the lyrics on *Safe House* might have changed since I was ten, I hear the System fan switch on and imagine Mother being pushed and pulled all over the house, trying to find a place where she isn't a witch.

TICKET TO RIDE

Four hours later, we are seated around the large dining table. My suitor's name is Peyton; he's covered in pimples and can't seem to speak in coherent sentences. He only tells us he plays football and that he has a game tomorrow night.

I make WTF eyes at Vernon.

Vernon says, "You gave me such short notice, Jane."

Gemma came to help me get dressed and ready. She brushed my hair, powdered my nose, and ironed the sleeveless hoodie sweater I'm wearing. It's argyle. Dinner is delicious and Vernon declares Marta the best chef in Lancaster County. After dinner, Finch arrives with a six-pack of beer.

"Vernon, who is this?" she asks of Peyton.

"Jane's suitor," Vernon answers, while Finch looks Peyton up and down.

"Not good enough," Finch answers, and cracks open a beer.

Peyton leaves then, claiming this "isn't what he signed up for" and doesn't even thank us for dinner or attempt to kiss me goodbye.

"I'm going to change out of this sweater. It's too hot in here!" I say. Finch says something to Vernon and he takes a beer from her six-pack and cracks it open.

Gemma follows me upstairs, and when we get into my room, I want to kiss her but everything is wrong with that. The power dynamic is wrong. The fact that she works for my family is wrong. The fact that she's my friend is wrong. Also, she's probably not gay and probably not in love with me and this is probably just some dumb crush that I will outgrow. Also, I've never kissed anyone before in my life. By the time I've thought all of that, Gemma has started to undress me, and as she has me step into a pair of wide-bottomed yoga leggings, I slip into a light fleece hoodie sweatshirt.

"Look at your hair!" she says.

I look in the mirror and the static has it standing out at all angles, the way it did when I touched the cool silver ball at the Franklin Institute science museum in Philadelphia.

"I wish you could stay," I say. We calm my hair down and I sit and put on a pair of socks. "Mother will be out of the tubes and we get to see her before she leaves for tour."

"Board games were never my thing," Gemma says, and we walk back downstairs and she heads to the front door.

A minute later, Mother arrives through the kitchen swing door. She has changed out of her capsule clothing and has a light sweater on. The sweater has holes in it and is black-and-gray-striped. She sports well-worn leather pants.

"Leather?" Finch says.

Vernon laughs. He adjusts his bright green polo shirt and runs his hand through his thinning hair. "Always both over- and underdressed for every occasion. That's our girl."

Mother smiles shyly and sits down.

She knows what's about to happen.

This is a set piece.

FAMILY GAME NIGHT

In this room there are two games going at once. One, the board game in the middle of the table. Tonight's is Ticket to Ride—a game about train routes around the world, in this case, America. It is Henry's favorite game.

The other doesn't have a title or a board or a box or a set of instructions.

The other is a rodeo. A free-for-all. A death match.

"I get black!" Henry says. I've already put all the black trains at his place setting because everyone knows Henry gets black.

"Green," Vernon says.

"Blue," Finch says.

"And I get yellow," I say.

Mother gets red by default.

Mother is used to getting whatever she gets by default. There's a reason she writes the most disemboweling lyrics in punk rock.

Between the Mina Witch Trials of early afternoon and now, I spent most of my time in my room on the floor with my record player. I listened to *Safe House* three times (in headphones, of course), reading the lyrics through each song. It's quite a puzzle. The first song is "To the Girls in the Bathroom." It's about high school girls putting on makeup in the bathroom and how they help each other. The refrain is haunting. *Remember this, you high school girls, remember who you are right here. They will try to make you kill each other in another fucking year. Make a world unto yourself inside your gorgeous little head. And in that world, you can become a thing more suitable than dead.*

I look at Mother, who is arranging her tiny red plastic trains, and I understand the world inside her head. I wonder if she and Marta used to put on their makeup in the bathroom when they were in high school.

The game begins. We get our cards with the routes we have to complete on them. My cards are bullshit. I don't know how many crappy train routes a person can get in this game, but I am sure I've gotten the max. The rounds go by fast—people start to put down trains, completing the routes.

"I'd like two cards from the pile, please," Henry says, and Vernon hands him two cards from the pile.

Finch lays down three matched cards and puts three trains on the route from Pittsburgh to Chicago. She takes the last available route and blocks the only way I can complete my game route.

"Jane, move my marker," she says. I do. She's currently in second place. Vernon is in first even though we're supposed to be letting Henry win the game.

It's Vernon's turn and he picks two cards from the pile, clearly hoping for a certain color card, and says, "The unknown is exciting!" Then he looks at the cards and says, "Dammit."

Mother says, "The unknown is still exciting, though, right?"

Finch meows like a cat, then, "Ts-ts-tssss." Hisses from the back of her throat.

Mother looks at her sister. Then at Vernon. They both look down at their cards. Mother is expressionless and emotionless. "Right, Vernon?" she says. "You said it on our wedding day, remember?"

"Of course," Vernon says. He feigns annoyance at Finch's hissing.

"Tsss," Finch hisses again and it knocks me into two years ago, on my birthday.

HOME MOVIE—03.02.2022

We're playing Trivial Pursuit, the 1980s version. I am turning fourteen in seventeen minutes.

<pause>

I am meticulous about my time of birth. I am a Capricorn moon, which means I'm responsible, pragmatic, and I set goals. At an-hour-to-fourteen that year, I'd set a goal, especially, to make Vernon proud by doing what he had trained me to do my whole life and get another reward—maybe more rum, I hoped, because he gave me vodka the week before, shaken, not stirred, and I didn't like it.

<resume>

We sit around the table—me, Henry, Vernon, Finch, and Mother—and we answer trivia questions. Mother only needs one more segment to win.

She lands on the correct square and I ask her a question from the category That's Life.

"How many pounds of chemical additive does an average American consume yearly: three, six, or nine?"

Mother answers quickly, "Nine."

I frown. "How did you know that?"

"I didn't," she says. "I guessed the most shocking answer. Americans are always the most shocking. Especially in the eighties."

Aunt Finch does it then. "Meoooow."

Vernon chuckles through his nose and looks down at the table.

Henry says, "Meoooow."

"Tss-tss," Finch adds.

Mother takes a deep breath and looks uncomfortable.

"Would you like to try for the middle spot to win?" I ask.

Mother rolls the die, gets a six, and lands in the middle. Vernon, Finch, Henry, and I discuss how to make sure she loses the game—it's my near-birthday, after all—and decide that she's worst at sports questions. She keeps looking down at her hands, which are folded delicately on the table.

"What was the only U.S. pro team to end a ninety-eight-year championship drought in the 1980s?" I ask.

Without looking up or even taking a breath, Mother says, "The Philadelphia Phillies. I was there for that."

I turn to her, mere moments before I turn fourteen years old. "Tss-tss-tsss!"

Finch meows.

Henry hisses, too.

Vernon chuckles under his breath and checks his pocket watch. "Only five minutes now until the exact time of your birth," he says. "I remember it well. What a beautiful night."

<pause>

I remember the way he said this. It was as if Mother hadn't even been there for my birth—as if he had done all the work.

<resume>

Mother gets up and turns toward the tube in the corner of the study. Her eyes long for it. I throw a game piece at her. It hits her in the back of her leg. Henry throws his, then, and it hits her on the elbow and his colored pie slices fly out. Finch picks up the box of cards and lunges forward as she throws it. It hits Mother in the back and she shudders. I throw another game piece and another. Henry throws tiny triangular pieces at her in a handful. I pick up the second box of cards and aim for her head.

The room comes alive with hissing. Henry, Aunt Finch, and me. Mother freezes in what looks to be some kind of psychological paralyzation.

Ts-ts-tsss-tsss! Tsss-tss-tsssss-ts!

Vernon gets up and takes Mother by the arm and shows her to her chair inside the capsule. He closes her in, puts the System remote control into his pocket, and replaces the attachment so there is one-way communication only. She can hear us. We can't hear her. We work to pick up all the things we threw. Henry stands by the tube, and yells, "I hate you!" I stand behind him with my hands on his shoulders, and say, "I wish you weren't my mother!" Vernon gets himself a glass of wine. Finch gives Mother the finger and hisses, drawing her upper lip up to bare her bucked, uneven teeth. With each hiss, she enunciates her middle fingers.

With my hands still on Henry's shoulders, we stare into the tube where Mother sits on her wooden dining chair. She dressed up for my birthday—a cool plaid skirt and her famous twenty-eyelet orange Doc Martens. She looks down, now, at her hands. Her hair hides her face so I can't see if she's crying yet.

Henry starts beating on the plastic tubing, fist after fist.

"Everyone hates you, see?" I say. She looks at me and I see a single tear inching down her cheek.

And then it's 12:12 a.m. and we all gather by the fire in the adjacent sitting room to celebrate how great the world is to have me in it. Vernon produces a hand-blown glass flute filled with champagne. I drink it fast, and he refills it.

<stop>

It was quite a memorable day.

TICKET TO RIDE / PRESENT DAY

Aunt Finch stops hissing and opens another beer using the bottom of her T-shirt to protect her palm. She hands it to Vernon. She opens one for herself and takes a gulp.

It's Mother's turn, then mine. She puts down six cards and says, "I'm going from New Orleans to Miami," then lays down six red train cars, placing each on their allotted space.

"That's not fair!" Henry complains. "I need that route!"

Mother continues to place the red plastic train cars on the board.

"Hey! Listen to me, you fucking witch!" Henry says, then gets up and goes to Vernon.

Mother stops, looks at Henry, and smiles. "Come now. I just brought you so many beautiful plants for your birthday. Surely a witch wouldn't buy you things so special, would she?"

Finch meows while she removes Mother's red trains from the board and replaces them with Henry's black ones.

"Shut up, witch!" Henry says from behind Vernon, who has his gold cross out now and is holding it in front of his chest like he's in a movie.

Right then, Mother stands up slowly and backs her way to the tube in the corner—lets herself in and sits on her chair, closing the door behind her and pressing the green button inside the capsule. We meet eyes for a moment before the System drops her down to basement level, where her bedroom is.

Tears pour from my eyes, and I can't keep them in. I turn my head so the others won't see me. I act like I'm cold and use the hood of my hoodie to hide my face.

"Are you good?" Henry asks.

I don't know what to say. There's nothing to say. I'm staring at an empty tube where my mother has been confined for six years when she's not sent out to be a rock star who screams about freedom into a microphone. She is a walking contradiction. Until now I thought that meant she was a liar, but now I see that the tubes are safer. She walked right in. Closed her own door. Lowered her own capsule. Escaped. Us.

She escaped us. On her last night home.

I don't know her at all. It's so disturbing I can't even make up a lie for my little brother as I hide inside my hoodie. I hear them cleaning up the game. Someone opens a cabinet door. Someone else gathers empty beer bottles. Henry stares at the back of my head, waiting for an answer.

"I'm devastated," I say, slightly wry.

"We can play again tomorrow," Henry says. "Maybe you'll win that time!"

When I can finally turn around and act not-devastated, I aim toward the hall to head down to Mother's bedroom but Vernon gestures for me to sit down and hands me a fancy cut-crystal glass with an inch of brown liquid in it.

"Cognac," he says. "Calms the nerves."

CLOROX TEST

I land back on my bedroom floor next to the record player, headphones on my ears. My nerves are calm. The last song on the A side of *Safe House* is "Clorox Test."

"Clorox Test" has a subtitle. *A song about unstable chemical compounds.*

It's a punk rock ballad, and Mother's voice is strong but wavering—a mix between Patti Smith and Sinead O'Connor.

I have never felt more special / his spotlight is divine / every minute together / his heart and soul are mine. / He talks about our future / how old we're going to get / he asks me if I want some tea / he asks me if I'm wet.

Soulmates never part, you know.

Soulmates are the best.

See if you're a soulmate now.

Take the Clorox Test.

Let me take away your power / and take back all my love / give me more I demand it / I need help / I can't stand it / I get all of you now / stop acting so nice / I've told all my friends / you're colder than ice.

Soulmates never part you know.

Soulmates are the best.

See if you're a soulmate now.

Take the Clorox Test.

When you test the door and it's open / when you test the door and it's closed / when you test the door you might notice / your friends are all opposed / to this creep who took you over / where's your brain? what do you think? who are you now? / If you even blink, he will say that you are the problem.

You are the problem.

You are the problem.

You are the problem.

He will warn you all the while—punctuated by a shove.

He will tell you that it's all your fault for being difficult to love.

You are interiorly bleach. Nothing left of you now. May as well just bleed / make the world white / make the fog rise / bleach it all to clean and clean and clean and clean and clean and clean and clean . . . the music fades out. It's haunting.

I don't know if it's accurate, but the more I listen to this song, the more it's not about bleach at all. I think Mother was being sarcastic when she wrote that title. Unstable compounds! I can't wait to meet her.

ACT I, SCENE 5

EXT. DRIVEWAY—EARLY MORNING, NEXT DAY

JANE, HENRY, VERNON, MARTA, and MILORAD are all around MINA as she says goodbye. The Placenta tour bus has been loaded with her bags and is about to head out.

Mina hugs Henry and Jane and whispers something to each of them. She hugs Marta.

MINA

(to Henry) I will miss you so much! (moves to Jane) And you, love. Oh. I hate leaving you two. So MUCH!

Mina cries. Jane and Henry do not.

MINA (CONT'D)

And goodbye, dear Marta. And Milorad, our garden warrior.

Mina hugs Marta and then tries Milorad, but Milorad rubs her arm awkwardly instead of a hug. Mina looks at Vernon, and Vernon leans in for a hug but gives a cold European double-kiss and says . . .

VERNON

Ciao.

Vernon walks inside to the study, where he pours himself a drink. Jane, Henry, and Marta stay to wave Mina off. Milorad stands a few feet away, with his hands in his pockets, looking up at the sky.

JANE (waving)

Goodbye, Mother! Play it loud!

MINA (through bus window)

I'll send you postcards!

Henry waves, but looks to the sky, the same as Milo.

The bus pulls away from the curb, and Henry and Milorad head to the garden. Jane goes inside and finds Vernon in the study, downing liquor from a cut-crystal glass.

The BAND arrives in the study from the kitchen, dressed in foam postcard costumes.

Song: "Postcards"

Composer notes: *Very fast, intermittent yelling—think "If I Were a . . . I'd" by Fishbone.*

JANE

SEND ME A POSTCARD FROM
MONTANA
INDIANA
LOUISI-FUCKIN-ANA
FROM ALASKA
NEBRASKA
MINNESOTA
NORTH DAKOTA . . .
SEND ME A POSTCARD FROM
SONOMA
TACOMA
OKLA-FUCKIN-HOMA
FROM AUSTIN
AND BOSTON
FROM MONTEREY
TO SAN JOSE
WHERE EVERYTHING IS
A-OKAY
SEND ME A POSTCARD.
MAMA, SEND ME A POSTCARD—
BUT THEN COME HOME
TO MARTA'S MASHED POTATOES
MILORAD'S FRESH TOMATOES
AND ME.
AND ME.
AND ME ME ME ME ME.

LADY'S MAID

"I'd like to try some more suitors," I say to Vernon, who is sipping a second drink before ten in the morning—likely celebrating Mother's departure.

"Peyton wasn't even close to your league," Vernon says. "I need some time to interview."

"I'll soon grow out of the clothing you got me on my sixteenth," I add.

He looks up from his phone, where Finch is barely responding to his texts. Two words here. Three words there.

"I can't wear them around here," I say. "I need suitors to wear them."

"Of course," he says. "I'll get on it."

"It can't just be them coming here either. No boy wants to just sit around with a girl's father," I say. "No offense."

"Mmm. Of course," he hums.

"I'll need Gemma to help."

"Yes, yes," he says, typing.

I kiss him on his head. "Thanks!" Then I go to my room where *Safe House* is still on the turntable. I get into bed with the record sleeve and the lyrics. I read the songs as if they are a novel. The whole thing feels like it's missing the most important chapter. Something about it makes me want to cry a wholesome, teenage river.

POSTCARDS

POSTMARKED OCTOBER 22, 2024

A PHOTOGRAPH OF SUNSET OVER LAS VEGAS

Dear Henry and Jane,
I can't believe I'm on tour again. After all that time at home, I admit I got used to seeing you every day, even though I'm not allowed to touch you. I hope you're

doing well with school! Henry, try not to worry about math. It will either become clear or it won't—and in the end, algebra isn't all that important. Jane, I hope you are reading a good book. I just read Every Day by David Levithan and it was really great. I will be in Nevada for three days and then off to Portland and Seattle. I miss you both very much. Love, Mom

POSTMARKED OCTOBER 23, 2024

A BLACK-AND-WHITE PHOTOGRAPH OF A FORTIES STARLET IN AN OLD-STYLE BIKINI AND CAT GLASSES

Dear Jane and Henry,

Last night's opening show was wild! We sold out the arena, which is small but that's still a big deal. I want you guys to meet Anvil, our opening act. Marta and the lead singer, Davy, have been an item for a long time. I'm not sure if you know that about Marta. Anyway, Davy is a great guy and Anvil lyrics are all about how your generation is going to have to clean up the mess we all made. Their drummer is the fastest I've ever heard. Even faster than Mackie Jayson from Bad Brains! Anyway, I miss you. The woman on the front of this postcard is Davy from Anvil's grandmother. More soon. Love you, Mom

POSTMARKED OCTOBER 25, 2024

A CLASSIC VEGAS POSTCARD OF THE MAIN STRIP OF CASINOS

DEAR JANE AND HENRY!

I CAN'T WAIT TO LEAVE THIS TOWN. I MISS YOU BOTH SO MUCH! LET'S ARRANGE A PHONE CALL SOON, YES? YOU CAN TELL ME ABOUT YOUR STUDIES AND I CAN TELL YOU WHAT IT'S LIKE TO BE WOKEN UP FOUR TIMES PER NIGHT BY DRUNK PEOPLE KNOCKING ON YOUR HOTEL DOOR.

Henry—tell me where you decided to plant your birthday bulbs! Jane, your father tells me you've decided to try some more suitors. Be safe and remember you don't have to settle. I love you both! Mom

LESSON THREE: HOW TO END A SHITTY DATE

Various dates throughout November

SUITOR #22: JEFFEREY FROM MY OLD SCHOOL

Jefferey from my old school has grown quite a bit. He's almost six feet tall and his face is no longer cherry red and flaky. He arrives in a car loaned to him by his father. He is wearing a pair of khakis and a long-sleeved polo shirt. When I see this from where I'm spying in front of Henry's bedroom window, a growl forms in my throat.

Gemma says, "He's awfully handsome."

"If you think so," I say.

"For a boy, he walks with grace," she says.

"Who needs grace?"

Gemma looks at me funny. Then she tells me to stand up straight. We go back to my room, and she powders my nose and fixes a few strands of my hair. I decide to change my outfit. I wear black turtleneck and black tights and a camouflage miniskirt with a pair of knee-high shiny black boots.

"You should probably wear that chain necklace you have," Gemma says.

When I leave my room, I thank her, and she says, "I love dressing you. It's one of my favorite jobs around here."

"Makes me feel like a weird Victorian asshole," I say.

"Well, I like it so there's no need to feel weird. You look great! Let's go meet this graceful suitor, yes?"

I head down the stairs, Gemma follows ten paces behind me.

Vernon *loves* Jefferey. Their conversation becomes so boring I would rather do anything else but listen to it. Summer jobs. Golf handicaps. Mutual country club acquaintances. When Vernon says, "And a snappy dresser!" I can't hold in my laugh.

"What?"

"Nothing," I say, noting the only difference between them is the color of their polo shirts.

There is uncomfortable silence.

"We're going to be late to the movie if we don't leave now," Jefferey says.

"Of course," I say.

I nod to Gemma, and she grins and raises her eyebrows. Vernon shakes Jefferey's hand.

We get to the theater and Jefferey drops me off at the doors and goes to park. I watch him as he pulls into a parking space and then backs out and repeats that several times before he is perfectly centered.

I walk to the concession stand. I pick up a box of Swedish Fish and wait for Jefferey. When he comes in, his cheeks are back to the color of eighth grade and he's wiping his nose with the back of his hand.

"Grab me a large popcorn!" he says as he rushes through the lobby. "Extra butter. And a large drink! Oh! And some Milk Duds! I gotta pee. Don't forget to buy tickets!"

I start walking toward the exit before he's even fully in the bathroom. Two sets of doors later, I'm in the cold evening air, walking down the country road that eventually leads to the small municipal airport. Mother flies in and out of there all the time. When I was little, before Mother was locked into the System, Milorad used to take me with him to pick her up. The bathroom has a fascinating motion-activated sink that washes and dries your hands all in the same place.

POSTMARKED OCTOBER 26, 2024

PICTURE OF PORTLAND, OREGON

Dear Jane and Henry,
Portland is such a great city. I can't wait to bring you here one day so you can see how cool it is. Best grits I ever ate. We sold out two shows. The crowds are really lovely—they knitted us hats! Matching hats! Like—on the second night, we wore the matching hats. I really love the songs on this album and I'm grateful I get to sing them every night. I hope to talk to you on Halloween. I wonder what you're dressing up as this year. I will be doing our Seattle Halloween show dressed as a foam triceratops. Enjoy the view from the patio for me. All the leaves must be turning now. Love you, Mom

SUITOR #23: ROBERT FROM THE COUNTRY CLUB

Gemma dresses me in a very preppy-punk ensemble—a plaid skirt, schoolgirl style; black tights; and ankle-high slip-on fat-soled boots. Button-down white shirt, not tucked in.

"I think we should tuck it in," I say.

"I think it would ruin the whole look. Just add this," she says, and hands me a sort-of necktie.

"Feels a bit too schoolgirl for me," I say.

She looks me up and down. "Hmm."

We hear a car arrive. Gemma goes to Henry's window and then comes back to my room. "Take off the shirt. We'll trade it for this." She hands me an oversized faded black sweater.

"My favorite," I say.

"Good to be comfortable, right?"

She looks at my makeup—I went for eyeliner times three, with curlicues at the corners—nods and tucks my hair behind my right ear.

Then we head down the steps to meet Robert.

I thought I'd like him when he arrived in black jeans and a soft gray sweater. He wears a pair of Doc Martens shoes, and his jeans are rolled up just a little so I can see his soft gray socks, slouching down over his ankles. Vernon asks him all sorts of Vernon questions—how his schooling is going, what his golf handicap is these days, where he's thinking about going to college. All the time Vernon asks him things, Robert seems shy and he smiles at me as if he knows Vernon is a knob.

Then he speaks.

"What's that?" he asks as he points to the tube in the corner of the study.

Vernon says, "Marta built a hell of a fire tonight, didn't she? Almost can't feel the cold."

Robert looks at me and I shrug. He asks, "I'm sorry. You didn't hear me. What's that big tube?" He points.

Vernon dismisses us and Robert drives me, in his own car, to a small jazz concert he bought tickets for. I feel like a beat poet. I'm glad I'm wearing my favorite sweater.

He bought the tickets. Let me stress that.

A big step up from Jefferey.

It's in a club in Lancaster city—like, a bar. No one asks for ID or anything like that. I assume since it's a gig, maybe they aren't serving alcohol. We get the table just to the right of the stage, front row. It's waiting for us with a RESERVED sign on it.

Robert holds my chair out, I sit. He sits, looks at me, and smiles.

Robert is not a good-looking young man. He is, if I picked one word, unembellished. I am very glad he paid.

"I heard about how at your house there's some kind of big iron lung or something," he says.

"Oh yeah? Who told you that?"

Robert looks shy. "Like—it's just a thing people know, I guess."

"Oh." This is news to me. However, I've been stuck in my house for the past five years. Everything is news to me. "What's an iron lung?"

"A thing that helps people breathe, I think. They don't really use them anymore. I mean, I think. I don't know."

"So why would we have one in our house?"

"I don't know."

"Did you only come on this date to look around my house?"

"No!" he says. "I really like you."

"You've never met me."

"I know your dad."

"Yeah."

"He said you needed dates."

"How kind of him," I say.

"Now that I see you, I can't see how you need dates," he says.

"Thanks."

A man comes onstage and places a shiny silver alto saxophone on an instrument stand at the front of the stage. He comes back and places two bottles of water on the piano bench.

A tall waiter comes to the table and asks Robert something I can't hear. An old man carries a double bass across the stage. The older couple at the table next to us is staring at Robert.

"Here you go," the waiter says, and puts two filled cocktail glasses in front of us.

"What's this?" I ask.

Robert says thank you to the waiter and turns back to me. "Jack Daniels and Coke—it'll loosen you up."

When I excuse myself to the ladies' room, I take both my purse and my coat. Robert is so busy loosening up, he doesn't question it.

POSTMARKED NOVEMBER 2, 2024

PICTURE OF THE HAYSTACK ROCK

Hi guys! We got two days off and we went to the Oregon coast where it rained for both days, but we did take some walks on the beach anyway and we got some good pictures of the band in the freezing cold surf. I miss you all very much. It's been so long since I toured, I forgot how tiring it is and boring at times. David has a cold, so he's sleeping and staying away from the rest of us. He and Davy from Anvil have become close—like brothers. I will make sure to send a picture soon! I love you all! Hug each other for me. Hug Vernon twice! Love, Mom

SUITOR #24: TODD FROM THE LIBRARY

"A boy who reads!" Gemma says. "I mean, he could be the one," she says, completely serious.

"I'm sixteen," I say.

"Still—a symphony seems like a very classy first date. You never know."

"I'm not going to get married, Gem. At least not for another fifteen years," I say.

"Fifteen years! You'll be over thirty!"

"Are you a Victorian android?"

"Busted." Gemma puts her hands up.

I spin in my dress in front of my standing mirror. The hem of my dress rises. "I would say I look fresh tonight. Very feminine," I say. "It almost isn't working."

"True. Dresses don't suit you. You're more of a skirt person."

"I'd like a suit," I say. "A tweed suit like David Bowie. Three-piece."

"I'll get on that. Right away," Gemma says.

"I'm serious."

"So am I," Gemma says.

"He's here," I say.

We do the usual parade down the staircase.

Todd is gorgeous. I'm not even kidding. He's over six feet, has dark hair and his eyes are big, and I think his eyelashes are an inch long. When he sees me come downstairs, he raises his hand in a small wave, and I smile and am genuinely excited about a symphony, which is, to be fair, not in my character.

"What's a pop-up?" Vernon asks Todd. I must have interrupted.

"It's not a long, drawn-out concert in a large venue," Todd answers. "It's the full orchestra, but they arrive and tune and get settled and then play for about thirty minutes and then they get up and leave as we leave. A pop-up."

"Outdoors?" Vernon says.

"Yes. At the park. In the bandshell. They only announced it two days ago. I thought it was perfect for what you'd proposed."

Proposed.

We drive in Todd's electric car to the park. When we get there, we sit in the car for a while with the heating on high. Todd says, "I have blankets for us."

"I didn't know it was outside. I wish I'd have worn something warmer." It's under fifty degrees out there but I see they have portable outdoor heaters scattered around the seating area.

"I think the dress looks great," he says.

"What symphony is it?"

"Number forty in G minor. Mozart," he says.

I have never wanted to tell a boy I love him before. But there, in that electric car, with the heat blowing my hair around, I almost do.

"Do you not like Mozart?" he asks.

"I *love* Mozart," I say.

"Oh, good," he says.

We watch as the musicians fill the stage. About two hundred people start to get out of their cars and walk toward the bandshell. Todd carries the blankets in one hand and puts his other hand on the small of my back, to help us stay together in the crowd. We land in the third row from the front, in the aisle next to one of the portable heaters. After a minute or two of tuning, the music begins.

The music is beautiful and the blankets are warm. I look at Todd periodically and he is smiling, and I can't believe I'm experiencing this. I know every note of this symphony. Mother played it a lot when I was a child.

Vernon hates Mozart. Todd is lucky he didn't tell Vernon what symphony it was. He has his hands under the blanket that we've wrapped over our laps. His hand finds mine and just like that—I am holding hands with Todd from the library.

During the minuet, the third movement, Todd leans into me a bit and I rest my head on his shoulder. I can't stop my mind from thinking like Gemma does. *Maybe this is the one.* And then Todd very suddenly moves his hand from mine and cups and gropes my crotch. I mean—vise-grip gropes.

I inhale sharply. The people near us all look at me.

Todd keeps his eyes on the orchestra and his hand on my crotch, pressing hard against it and trying to find a way in under my dress. He pinches my labia between his fingers until I can't hold it in.

"Ouch!" I bark.

I move the blankets off my lap as fast as I can, shove them in his lap, and start walking toward the park exit.

I didn't think Todd followed me until I hear, "Hey! Hey!"

I turn around, more for safety than anything. He's not running—looks genuinely concerned.

"I didn't mean it!" he says. "Your dad told me nothing was off-limits!"

Rather than leave the park, I hide behind a row of shrubs until Todd from the library thinks I'm gone. I watch as he walks back to where we were sitting and sits back down. He looks very upstanding and normal. I'm sure I look like the lunatic—like Mother in 2019 during The Great Ignoring.

I focus on the music. The fourth movement has already started. The violin is dancing around the notes. I picture Mother the last time she played this symphony for me four years ago—her in the capsule inside the System, and me in the study, wearing pajamas because I had a cold. She and Vernon had been so worried—pandemic times and all—that I had something far worse. But it was just a cold. So, they allowed me to rest and Vernon allowed the music.

The more I think about it, the more I see how little she did to deserve the reputation Vernon has gifted us. All she's done is love us and try to be a great mom and bring home money for us. Or not. I do know that *Safe House* went platinum. Vernon says he never got any money from Mother for it because she gave the money to charity. *"As if anyone really cares about periods in the third world."*

As the final movement comes to an end, I emerge from behind the bushes and find my way to the sidewalk of the cute town where the pop-up concert is now ending. It's quaint. Tourist shops. A pub. A fountain on Main Street.

POSTMARKED NOVEMBER 5, 2024

PICTURE OF THE SEATTLE SPACE NEEDLE BUILDING

We made it to Seattle and we didn't sell out either night, but we had a good show last night. Jane—I played that punk version of "Twinkle, Twinkle Little

Star" that we used to play on the ukulele—remember that? I wonder, are you getting these postcards at all. I hope so. If you don't have time to call me, ask Vernon to text me anytime you want to say hi! Love you! On my way to the top of the Space Needle so I thought this postcard was fitting. I love you all! Mom

SUITOR #25: ANDREW FROM MY OLD CAMP

Gemma didn't lie. She got me a suit. Tweed. Just like David Bowie.

And when I put it on, all three pieces, I say, "How is this tailored? No one measured me or anything."

"I know your body," Gemma says.

I melt.

"That's kinda hot," I say.

She laughs. I melt ten more times.

She says, "Andrew will love it."

"You're just pretending I don't say anything not-straight, aren't you?" I ask.

She raises her eyebrows.

"You ignore it every time," I say.

"Well," she says, then stalls to figure out the rest. "When you put the most important woman in a girl's life inside a plastic tube, you're bound to make her a little curious about women, I suppose."

I don't know how to feel about this. She's wrong. I'm not gay because my dad locked my mom inside the tubes. I'm gay because I just—am. And yet, I start to doubt everything about myself because she said it with such surety, and yet I feel like a fraud when Gemma and I head down the stairs. I feel like me in this suit should tell everyone everything they need to know about me. However, Vernon believes the suit is "Breathtaking! Jane! You're a trendsetter in that! Holy smokes!"

Andrew smiles the way he used to in the dining hall at summer camp. Like he doesn't even have to try. I'm sad for him. A lot has changed since we last saw each other on the ropes course when we were ten.

One: He did not grow nearly as much as the other boys, so it's hard to notice how much has changed for him, poor dear. And two: I am no longer a lost ten-year-old girl who crushes on any boy who looks at me. I have standards, and based on my last twenty-four dates, no man will meet them. So—good luck to Andrew who apparently doesn't speak.

Due to the camp theme, Vernon fills the room with scouting stories of his youth.

"One time we were at a camp in upstate New York and it rained so much the place flooded while the scouts slept. We'd been getting rather drunk on account of us being leaders, and when I went outside to relieve myself, it was dark, and I heard the sound of a river, but thought I was imagining it. Only when we came out an hour later did we see what was about to happen. I ran from tent to tent to tell the boys to get up and get their things," he exclaims, as if this is some kind of African safari story. "We lost a lot of our gear, but we're lucky none of them were drowned!"

"Ah yes. The drowning-scouts-while-you-were-drunk story. Charming," I say. "Hello, Andrew. It's nice to see you again."

He smiles and nods, but that's it.

"Still not a talker, eh?" I ask.

He laughs but says nothing.

"Don't pressure him," Vernon says. "Some young men save their energy for the words that count, right, Andrew?"

"Yes sir," he says.

"So—*yes sir* counts but *you look great tonight, Jane* does not. Noted," I say. I grin and he grins and Vernon looks as if he's about to scold me when Andrew speaks.

"You look great tonight, Jane."

We were slated for dinner at the Mexican place in town, but when I got in the car, I said, "Drive me to the most remote location you can so we can watch the meteor showers."

Andrew follows directions. Still doesn't talk, though. The whole way to the field, nearly an hour in the car, he just plays music—mostly crappy eighties heavy metal. I attempt to turn the volume down and he puts his hand out and says, "Whoa."

"Am I a horse?" I ask.

"Stereo is off-limits to girls," he says.

If I could open my car door and roll out now, I would, but it would hurt the suit. Instead, I wait for him to park up on the shoulder. We walk through woods to the field, me holding the blanket he keeps in his trunk for emergencies. It smells like a dog threw up on it, but I don't care. I don't plan on sitting on it.

"Hold my hand," he says, slinging his right arm back as he walks a step ahead of me.

"I'm good. Need to balance."

He stops. "You don't want to hold my hand?"

I walk into him and my momentum causes us to stumble and hold on to each other. His hands are strong and I'm pretty sure he's bruised my arm. But he also stopped me from falling.

"Well?" he asks.

"Can we just get to the field? I don't want to miss the meteors," I say.

He steadies himself and starts walking again.

When we get to the field, I hand him the blanket, and he says, "Why don't you just admit it to yourself so your dad stops setting you up with guys?"

"Admit what to myself?"

"You're probably gay."

"Yeah," I say. "So?"

He doesn't know what to say now. I think he's used to girls proving to him that they're not.

"Stop looking at me and look up! They're everywhere!" I wrap my arms around myself and feel the tweed tight on my arms. This suit is probably the best thing that ever happened to me.

He lays down on the blanket and looks up. He pats the space next to him, and says, "I won't bite. I promise."

"I'll be right back," I say. "I have to pee."

POSTMARKED NOVEMBER 11, 2024

PICTURE OF PALM TREES IN LOS ANGELES

Dear Jane and Henry,
I'm sorry for the week away. David got so sick he had to go to the hospital and we had to cancel two shows but he's okay now. We thought it was COVID-19, but it's just a really bad cold. We're in Los Angeles today and we sold out tonight's show. Jane, I'm wearing that T-shirt you always loved with the big red star on it. Henry, I'd love to know what you dressed up as for Halloween! Everything else on the road is pretty boring. I miss you all.
Love, Mom

HOW TO END A SHITTY DATE

What you do is you get up and start walking.

Inside of ten minutes someone will pick you up. First on the country road where the movie theater is. Then on the city road where the jazz club is. Then Main Street in that cute town. And now, the country road near a lake I used to canoe on when I was ten. Someone *always* picks me up.

The someone is always Milorad.

I may as well be in prison.

He no longer opens the window and calls my name. He just drives up beside me and I can hear the doors unlock and then he drives a few meters ahead and stops. There's no point in running, so I get in.

"Your father is getting tired of this game," Milorad says.

"Is he paying you to parent me?"

"I can see his position. You need to stop running away."

"How would you know?" I ask. "Last week I ran away for good reason. And the date before. And the date before that!"

"Andrew is a nice boy," he says.

"To you, maybe. But to me, he's the same as any other—racing for entry."

Milorad clears his throat with discomfort.

We stay quiet until we get close to the house. I ask, "Maybe I can move into the pool house with you, yes? You'd make a great dad."

He laughs. "I am not father material." ASK MILORAD WHY HE IS NOT FATHER MATERIAL SOMETIME.

"I see how you take care of Brutus," I say.

"He is a rat. You are a girl. Very different things."

"I bet you'd pick better suitors for me."

He doesn't answer.

"I bet you'd pick better suitors for Brutus, then," I say.

He laughs again. "Maybe this is why he escapes so much! Maybe he needs suitors!"

As we drive the familiar blocks of Spruce Street toward home, I consider where the microchip could be. I have three guesses. The scar I've had since I was a child, right behind my mastoid bone on my scalp—Vernon says I was dancing with a pencil. The scar on my knee from summer camp—there was glass in the ropes course mulch. The only filling in my mouth—suspicious to me because the dentist said it wasn't a cavity yet, but he was going to fill it before it became one.

Vernon is waiting in the driveway when we pull in front of the house.

"I sure wish I was Brutus right now," I say.

Milorad answers, "Tell him the boy wasn't suitable and that you are tired."

Vernon walks over to my door.

"I really don't want to talk to him at all," I say. My voice cracks.

"Do not cry. You know what happens," Milorad says.

I look at him. We lock eyes for a moment. Everything changes. Milorad becomes my father. I become his daughter. I do not cry.

BRUTUS'S LAUGHTER

What does Jane want? Jane wants everything.

THIS IS TOO CONFUSING. Too much. Jane wants one thing, then another. Jane doesn't know what she wants. Jane cannot do what I do. Jane cannot scurry around and see everything. She is a young, learning human. I am an omniscient rat.

Everyone laughs at the Janes of the world. Girls with dreams. Girls who don't know everything. Girls who want their fathers to love them—to pay attention. Girls who want their mothers close but far enough away to hate. Laugh at Jane for not having anything she wants. Laugh at Jane for failing at being Vernon's perfect daughter. Laugh at Jane for not being everything. For not knowing everything.

Poor Vernon has no idea what he's doing. The nights he sits in Milorad's old smoking chair moaning about his life—he looks at me in the cage and says he wishes he were me. He has no idea, same as you have no idea. You don't know a cockroach from a bluebird. You don't know a zebra from the receptionist at the family doctor's office. You don't understand magic like me. You don't know why I'm here. No one does.

So, ignore your doubt and laugh at Jane. It's easy. She is sixteen and stupid and she hasn't been laid and she's never filed taxes and you will always be superior to her because you are taught to think life is a baseball game and the bases are things like sex, money, and what kind of car you drive.

I have traveled the world—lived in every type of place you can imagine—and I know enough to say that the only real win in life is something I can't have. Vernon can't have it either—we have this in common. Love is the only win. Tender, sweet love unconcerned with control or power. About half the people on Earth are incapable of that, just like me and Vernon. It makes them faster to hate, easier to control, and impressive liars. My kind of people.

ACT TWO:
Old Business / Europe, Asia & Africa

Cast in order of appearance:

Oak Tree
Dr. Love
Mrs. Constance
Addi
Miss Wilde
Gretchen Brown
KZ
Porter
Marlon
Mr. Rothenberg

OLD BUSINESS

Today is Friday, December 20, 2024

HENRY SAYS, "Vernon told me today that Mother tried to kill him one time with a kitchen knife."

There's a bout of silence that feels like glass.

"I saw that," I say.

"What do you mean?"

"I was there. Under the kitchen table," I say. "You were just a baby."

"Why didn't you tell me?" he asks.

I shrug.

"What was she like? Why did she stab him?" His eyes are wide, like this isn't a story about Mother and Vernon, but two exciting strangers in a neighboring house.

"I closed my eyes," I say. "It was terrifying."

Suddenly, I need fresh air.

The sky is blue and purple because it is sunset. It's cold out here, but the air helps.

My mother didn't stab my father.

I was there. Under the table, like I said.

It was terrifying, like I said.

I hear the door open and close. "You okay?" Henry asks. He tugs on my arm and I realize I've been out here too long and I probably look suspicious.

"Yeah," I say. "I'm fine."

We go inside. I stand by the fire. There is a part of me that will never be warm.

COTTAGE PIE

Marta makes a stunning cottage pie for dinner and serves it with her fresh-from-the-oven dinner rolls. While I'm buttering my roll, I say, "Henry, are you still too scared to ask Vernon about what we were talking about this afternoon? I can ask him for you if you like."

"Let the boy ask his own questions," Vernon says.

"Hear, hear!" Finch says.

Henry looks at me and indicates that he is too frightened to ask, so I say nothing.

We eat and it's pretty quiet.

Henry tells us that he'd like to be a vampire for Halloween next year and then mentions that Halloween is weird because we can't leave our house. "Do you think we'll be able to trick or treat like normal next year?" Henry asks.

"I'll be too old," I say.

"You can still come with me!" Henry says.

Finch shows mild interest but claims she dislikes holidays—her birthday most of all. I don't think any gift she ever got was good enough. This comment kills the conversation for two whole minutes.

"So, is that what you wanted Jane to ask?" Vernon eventually asks Henry.

"No," Henry answers.

"Oh," Vernon says.

Henry looks at me. Another minute passes.

"Okay fine, Jane, ask his question for him," Vernon says.

I time it well. Leave some space for anticipation. One of

Vernon's unspoken rules is *Don't ever act afraid of me because I am not scary*. So I try to get just to the edge of that—right when he's about to snap, I speak.

"Henry wants to see your scar from the time Mother stabbed you," I say.

Finch's eyebrows raise.

Time stops for a moment. Then it speeds up.

"You may not!" Vernon says-yells. When no one says anything because time has frozen us, he adds, "It's far too grotesque for dinner conversation."

Henry nods and accepts the disappointment. I accept nothing.

"Oh—be a sport," I say.

"I do not wish to be reminded of the day I was put through that horror!" he says lightly, as if he's saying it to the dinner roll he's buttering.

"You've told him about how it all happened and how you bled and how you had to call the doctor and I think you even told him you got stitches. How many again?"

Henry says, "Nine."

"Nine," I say, "That's right. Nine stitches. From that horrible day when Mother stabbed you. Was she trying to kill you? I forget that part of the story," I ask.

"She was," Vernon says.

"Man, that must have been scary," I say.

"You see now why I had to put her in the System," he says. "She was a danger."

"I see," I say. "Though you waited what—six years?—before locking her up."

He looks frozen again. "I wanted to give her a chance to get better. She's quite sick, you know. The doctor says she has anxiety!" He says this while staring at the antique bookcases opposite the table. Then he says, "We should tidy up for Marta tonight. Don't you think?" and gets up and starts clearing the table.

"Can you point to where the scar is?" I ask. "Henry is curious."

Vernon picks up two plates, his and Finch's, and then pretends he wants to point but can't, so he gestures with his elbow to a spot on the right side of his abdomen and then heads to the kitchen with the plates.

I can hear Marta scold him. "*Mina pays me plenty to clear your plates, Vernon. Please let me do my job.*"

When he comes back and sits down, butters another roll, I say, "So she stabbed you with her left hand or did she, like, cross your body?"

"This is the end of the discussion," Vernon says. "It's not dinner conversation."

"Henry was curious, is all. He said you told him all about the stabbing last week and he came to me to make sure we were safe."

"We're safe now, Henry. I took care of everything," Vernon says.

Henry beams.

Lying makes me hungry. I butter another roll and finish my cottage pie.

Finch flops on the couch in the sitting room, which we can see from here, pulls out her phone, and dives in.

Vernon pulls out his phone as well and laughs at something, and then types a text and sends it off. Finch's phone sounds with a ding. She laughs. It's all very silly.

"I was there, you know." That's what I say.

No one responds at first.

"I regret telling the boy anything about it," Vernon says, pretty much to himself and his phone. He almost whispers it.

"I'm glad you told me," Henry says. "I didn't know Mother was dangerous in that way. I thought she was just a witch."

"I was there," I say again. "I saw the whole thing."

Vernon looks over at me. "As if your memory holds from that age."

"I remember a lot from that age," I say. "Same as you do, right? All those stories from your terrible childhood."

"Yes, well, what you saw and what was really happening are two different things," he says. "You can't really trust your eyes, now, can you?"

"I seem to see okay."

"Jane, please."

"I was there," I say.

"What the fuck is your problem?" he says. This line seems to escape his mouth rather than be spoken. "You're always manipulating me!"

"I'm just saying I was there and I saw what I saw. That's all."

He continues to sop up the last of the cottage pie juice with his roll and ignores me.

"It was quite a scene to see as a four-year-old. One day maybe you'll ask me about it."

I know it all sounds quite energetic and almost exciting, but I assure you, it's nothing of the sort. Murder was something talked about quite a lot in our Victorian home. I didn't know this until I started stumbling across the home movies. For example, this:

HOME MOVIE—08.05.2021

I am thirteen.

"Tell me what she said!" Finch says to me. We're on the couch and she's got a box of chocolates.

"She didn't say anything. She's inside the tubes, right? I can't hear her."

"She's an animal!"

"She's my mom." I nod and chew. "It's not like Vernon can run the whole house, though, right?" I ask.

She sits up quickly. "She's not to be trusted! She could kill you, you know."

"Kill me?"

<stop>

Or this:

HOME MOVIE—05.23.2016

I am eight and Henry is four and we're out by the fountain feeding birds, trying to get them to eat right out of our hands.

"What do you think you're doing?" Finch yells from the patio bench.

I look caught. Henry looks caught but has that cute-little-kid giggle on his face. I look more terrified.

"You're going to get sick if they touch you!" she yells.

Henry says something to me under his breath.

<pause>

I remember what he said. He said, "I wish she'd stop."

<resume>

I throw my birdseed out onto the paving stones around the fountain. Henry keeps clucking at a house sparrow that's been eating out of his hand for the last five minutes.

"Henry!" Finch yells. The birds fly away. "The two of you come here right now!"

Henry and I walk to the patio.

She sits us down on the bench in full view of the camera, and says, "I'm in charge and I won't have you injured."

"It's a bird," Henry says—back when he couldn't pronounce his Rs right—"It won't hurt us."

"Do you know who will? My sister, Mina. You think she's so great but she'd cut your head right off your neck, you know."

<stop>

I surmise this is the reason I have had the feeling of escape in my bones for as long as I can remember.

POSTMARKED NOVEMBER 18, 2024

PICTURE OF A BIG-HORNED STEER'S FACE UP CLOSE

Dear All,

I can't wait for the next month to pass so I can come home. I miss you all so much. The tour has been going well—Phoenix and Las Cruces were both great shows. Tonight is Austin and then again tomorrow night. The band decided to cancel our dates in Florida due to the political lunacy. Screw them. We will donate proceeds from Run, Jane, Run *to help queer kids in Florida, for sure. Anyway, I miss you all. Love you! Mom*

WALKING

It's early morning, winter solstice. I'm on the new neighborhood walking and biking trail, which is nicely paved, really pretty, and a half mile from home. It's got trees and bushes and there's a creek and a bridge over the creek. The sun is shining and it smells like wet leaves and dirt and someone has a fire lit, because woodsmoke is a definite theme.

I forgot how much I love seeing my breath.

"Jane! Stop!" This echoes in the bare woods surrounding the trail. I've already crossed the bridge and there's nowhere to hide. I run on instinct.

"My tired legs cannot run," Milorad huffs.

"It's my lucky day!" I say, and keep running.

I look back and Milorad has stopped on the bridge and is looking out at the creek, his chest heaving. I know the consequences he could face and I realize that, in a sense, we are both Vernon's captives. I turn around and walk back. He notes this by grinning at me and waving, then sitting down, tired.

I sigh. "How'd he even track me?"

Milorad shrugs. As we walk back to the house, I tell him that I want to learn how to play the guitar and there isn't anything wrong with that.

"Your father has good reason for no music," he says.

I don't reply. We walk the path, our breath in front of us. I can never tell if Milorad is brainwashed or just doing his best under the circumstances. We are all brainwashed—even me, though I know far more of the truth now. I'm dealing with the aftereffects, really.

If you get a child to hate one of their parents, you get them to hate half of themselves. If you want to know why I hissed and meowed and threw those sheets in the loo, then you must know I was hateful most of all to myself because every part of me is Punk Rock Jane, and every part of me knew that I was being set up to be hated, too. Looking back, I think Vernon had no idea about this part. He was so intent on his hate because he's a selfish man who needs people to like him—and yet, look at him.

Vernon isn't the kind of man who would loosen the screws in your chair and then call you a fat bitch when the chair falls apart. He's the kind of man who loosens the screws in your chair and, when it collapses, offers you help to get up, and then a week later retells the story boisterously in front of you about how stupid you looked as you fell.

It's sadism-lite on the physical plane, but on the psychological plane, it's fucking torture. It turns out, my father's lies to God have become his personality. He is a hoax—top to bottom—a homemade competitor for not our love, but our loyalty, neither of which he possesses himself. I don't even think God knows who he is. And when you're fooling God, there have got to be some consequences.

"What's his good reason?" I ask. When Milorad looks confused, I add, "For not allowing music?"

He looks down, seeming ashamed. "Your father is complicated person."

"But what's his good reason?"

Milorad stops walking and looks at me. "He does not want to encourage you or your brother to go into music because it's so hard on the family."

I look up at him as we walk. "What's hard on this family is Vernon lying to God."

"Lying to God?" he asks.

"He's a bartender of lies," I say.

"A—bartend—?"

I nod once. "You are imperfect. I forgive you."

"Thank you."

"You're welcome."

We walk awhile in silence. I can see Milorad wanting to point out each species of tree to me, but he holds back.

"Have you heard from Gemma at all? I miss her very much."

"She is working for another family since last month when you escaped from every suitor your father arranged for you," he says. "I am sure she misses you, too."

"Maybe she can visit at Christmas."

"I'm sure you can request for her," he says.

"I don't want to *hire* her," I say. "She's my friend. I want to eat dinner with her and go for a walk."

"No more walks!" he says with a laugh.

When we get back to the house, Milorad walks toward the pool house, and I follow him. He seems alarmed to see me in his living room, but I'm here, folded onto a chair. "Can I have a bottle of water from the fridge?"

As he's getting me my water, Marta slips in the back door. "You've been found! Your father will be relieved."

"Ugh. Spare me," I say.

"He was worried?" she tries.

"He just wants to control everyone." I make a remote-control gesture with my hand.

She shrugs and Milorad gives me a water and gives one to Marta, as well. I sense that I am not wanted here, but I don't plan on budging. I go to the cage and talk to Brutus. He's a great little rat. People who don't hang out with rats don't get it, but they're really smart and pretty fun, too. One time, Brutus chased his tail until he fell over. It was hilarious. And he does tricks. And he's a fantastic escaper. Just like me.

POSTMARKED NOVEMBER 24, 2024

PICTURE OF THE STATUES OF PAUL BUNYAN AND BABE THE BLUE OX

Hello from Minnesota!

It's cold! Like—way too cold for me, and last night when we left the theater, there was SNOW on the ground. Oh, it makes me miss home. I hope it snows over Christmas break and maybe we can go sledding down the big hill. I know that sounds off-script, but it would be nice to be allowed some normalcy. I suppose I'm feeling bold after a month away and me being confined to System doesn't feel all that healthy for any of us anymore. Let's talk about it when I'm back. I can't wait! Love you, Mom

LESSON FOUR: EUROPEAN GEOGRAPHY

Today is Saturday, December 21, 2024

"JUST TELL ME the forty-four countries in Europe and then learn the capitals." Vernon holds a cup of black coffee and doesn't make eye contact.

"Are you cross with me, Vernon?" I say it in Victorian Jane, a lilt in my voice and pity. So much pity.

"I'm not so much cross as I am disappointed," he says, handing me some worksheets as weekend punishment, as if days of the week matter anymore.

"I'll try to improve," I say.

"I can't believe the shit you put me through, Jane. Seriously," he says. After some head shaking, he grumbles, "How hard is it to just know what the right thing to do is?"

I work on my list of forty-four European countries, west to east, and ignore his question. *Iceland, Ireland, the UK, Portugal, Spain, France, Belgium, Luxembourg, Andorra, the Netherlands, Denmark, Germany, Switzerland, Italy, Finland, Norway, Sweden, Poland, Czech Republic, Slovakia, Lichtenstein, Austria, Hungary, Slovenia, Croatia. Twenty-five.*

"How hard, Jane?"

I look up. "I thought it rhetorical. Really, how do I answer that?"

"I think 'Not hard, Vernon' would be sufficient."

I squint at him. I think I'm trying to make him look like something else. Like—maybe if I squint hard enough, he will turn into a good person. Or a useful person. Or even a useful pet. Like an emotional support pet for the students of Vernon's Victorian Pandemic

Academy. Henry sure would benefit from one. He's crying over having to do algebra on a Saturday.

"I can help him," I say.

Vernon ignores me. He walks over to Henry and sighs heavily before sitting down.

I look at the large clock on the wall and it's 11:45 a.m. Lunch can't be far off. I am already daydreaming and tired. Between the home movies and the opera, I don't get a lot of sleep.

The front door opens. It's Aunt Finch. She sighs as she closes the door, as if closing the door causes her extreme stress. Between her and Vernon, I can't tell who's more done with life.

I go back to my list.

Serbia, Montenegro, Bosnia and Herzegovina, Kosovo, Macedonia, Albania, Greece, Bulgaria, Romania, Moldova, Ukraine, Belarus, Estonia, Latvia, Lithuania, Monaco, Malta, San Marino, Vatican City. Forty-four.

"Henry, why are you doing this to me?" Vernon says. "Look. It's simple. Anything that happens in the parentheses gets done first. Okay? Just try again."

I think Vatican City being listed as a country is stupid. I've never been there, but it still feels dumb. "Do you think Mother has ever been to Vatican City?" I ask the room.

Finch snaps, "Do your work," and then flops down on the velvet couch and starts reading something on her phone.

I work on capitals. I'm pretty sure I remember them all. I could probably write a song about all of this.

INT. STUDY (FILLED WITH MANY GLOBES AS PROPS)—DAY

Free Mother BAND members dressed in rigid foam shapes of European countries. JANE is dressed as Austria.

Song: "Do Your Work"

Composer Note: *Fast like Fishbone's "Subliminal Fascism."*

JANE

ONE DAY I'LL BE ON A TRAIN
BETWEEN BELGIUM AND LICHTENSTEIN AND
I'LL MEET A KID NAMED GUSTAV
AND HE'LL TELL ME THAT AMERICANS ARE DUMB.
AND I'LL BE READY.

I'LL TELL HIM TALLINN IS THE CAPITAL OF ESTONIA.
I'LL TELL HIM VIENNA IS THE CAPITAL OF AUSTRIA.
I'LL TELL HIM PARIS IS THE CAPITAL OF FRANCE AND
HE'LL SAY, YEAH, BUT WHO DOESN'T KNOW THAT?

THE TRAIN WILL STOP IN SOME GREAT EUROPEAN CITY
EATING PROPER BREAD—THE KIND THAT WILL GET
MOLDY.
GUSTAV WILL TELL ME AMERICANS ARE FAT
AND LAZY. THE DETAILS WILL BE HAZY.
BECAUSE I'LL BE READY.

I'LL TELL HIM HUNGARY IS BUDAPEST
ROMANIA IS BUCHAREST
BRATISLAVA, LJUBLJANA, SLOVAKIA, SLOVENIA
NONE OF THIS IS DIFFICULT
AND GUSTAV WILL CHUCKLE AND SAY
HEY, YOU'RE AN AMERICAN GIRL, SEXY AND TAN
LIKE ON TV, WANT TO GO TO THE DINING CAR
WITH ME?

VATICAN CITY IS BOGUS / NOT A COUNTRY BY ITSELF
SAN MARINO IS SAN MARINO, WHICH IS SILLY.
GUSTAV ORDERS A SCOTCH, POINTS TO A BOTTLE ON A SHELF,
BUT THINKS THE CAPITAL OF PENNSYLVANIA IS PHILLY.

DO YOUR WORK, DO YOUR WORK, DO YOUR WORK.
DON'T BE A DUMB AMERICAN, DO YOUR WORK.

DO YOUR WORK, DO YOUR WORK, DO YOUR WORK.
DON'T BE A DUMB AMERICAN, DO YOUR FUCKING WORK!

SCAVENGER HUNT

Vernon is pleased with my ability to list him every capital in Europe. He and Aunt Finch sit on the velvet couch, propping each other up, as if it's totally fine.

He hands me my completed worksheet. "It may be time to move on to Africa!"

I shake my head. "Asia next—logical order?"

"Whatever you want, Jane," he says.

"I'd like to see Gemma again soon," I say.

"I can't trust you with suitors if you run away like this morning."

"Can't she just visit for Christmas or something? She's my best friend! I don't need a suitor."

"We'll see," he says, "Do your work."

Do Your Work, Do Your Work, Do Your Work.

I look down at the stack of worksheets Vernon gave me. Three of them are so poorly scanned from the homeschooling website that I can barely read them. But one seems to say that I am reading *The Catcher in the Rye.*

"Am I supposed to be reading a book right now?" I ask.

"Aren't we all supposed to always be reading a book? Isn't that what they say?" Aunt Finch says, staring into her phone screen, her thumb scrolling up, then down, then up, then down.

Vernon doesn't answer me. He sits there, looking out the window as if I didn't ask him anything. I look around my desk and there's no copy of the book. One other worksheet refers to it, though.

"Is this a scavenger hunt?" I ask, in character. "Oh, Vernon, you know how I love a scavenger hunt! What's the first clue? Will it be a long hunt? Shall I ask Marta for a snack before I set out?"

HOME MOVIE—07.19.2016

I am eight. I am in the sitting room, lying on the couch, reading. My hair is twisted into two plaits, perfect pigtails. I am wearing a traditional romper—a one-piece, light, summer jumpsuit with no sleeves. The shorts ride up because I am high-waisted like my mother. The romper is made of thin cotton.

Mother is home from her 2016 tour for *Apples Rapist Oranges* (an album praised by critics as "A whole different Mina Placenta—poetic as all hell. Stunning" and described by Aunt Finch as "More garbage screaming about men"). She walks into the sitting room, hands me a pink Post-it note, and tells me that I have to wait until she counts to ten.

<pause>

Background: She took a whole hour to set up the scavenger hunt. Vernon was still in bed, and Marta had fed us all delicious homemade English muffins with fresh jam that she and Milorad made the day before.

I don't need the home movie to remember this scavenger hunt.

<resume>

Once Mother says, "Ten!" I read the pink Post-it note.

Quack-quack! Where did those little ducks go now?

I run to the pool, where Gemma is practicing her back dives while Milorad skims dead bugs off the surface of the shallow end. I enter the gate, say hello to both of them, and head right for the storage chest that holds the pool toys, some cushions for the lounge chairs, and other random pool things. Inside there is a bag of small rubber ducks. And inside that bag is my next clue.

What smells like dinner but isn't dinner?

I run out of habit. I run around the patio and into the rose garden but I still don't understand. *What smells like dinner but isn't dinner?* Mother comes out the double doors and smiles at me. I sit on the bench, frowning.

"What's wrong?"

"I'm stumped."

"Good!"

"Good?"

"If the clues were easy, it would be no fun. Trust me."

"What smells like dinner but isn't dinner?" I ask.

She raises her eyebrows and says, "Where does one smell food around here?"

I run off-camera into the kitchen.

<pause>

Marta was there. She offered me another muffin. The conversation went something like this:

"I'm looking for something that smells like dinner that isn't dinner."

"Oh! That sounds fun!"

"What is it?"

"I don't know. What did we have for dinner last night?"

I remember running toward the freezer. I remember saying, "Mother is so sneaky!"

The night before, I was served a thick chicken noodle soup, and I was cheeky enough to say, "Soup isn't dinner." Vernon said, "It smells like dinner!" And Mother said, "Vernon, she doesn't know any better." Vernon said something like, "She should know better." To which Mother answered, "Of course."

Anyway. I found the next clue in Marta's stash of frozen soup. It was a blue Post-it note and it said, *Leagues under, you will find treasure.*

<resume>

I burst out the back door and run to the pool, I don't change or even think to, and I dive into the deep end. I swim all the way to the bottom—a whole eleven feet—and I find a plastic bag with a clue in it. By the time I burst above the water's surface, I am out of breath, mostly with excitement.

"What does it say?" Gemma asks, from the side of the pool.

I don't answer. It's not a clue. It's only part of a clue. I leave it on the side of the pool and I dive down again.

I find another ziplock bag with a Post-it note in it. I look around the deep end. There are four more. I grab one and then swim up for air. Then I drop again and gather the other three.

I drop the bags on the side of the pool and swim to the ladder. When I get out of the pool, I see in my reflection in the pool house patio doors and wave to myself. My romper is completely transparent. I don't seem to care.

I sit in the sun and open each bag. All six pieces fit together. *Hit this rainbow and you can turn around again.*

<pause>

That's the clue that had me running off-camera to the croquet pitch. No one knew then that Vernon was there, splayed between the middle wickets, sleeping with one side of his face catching the hot July sun.

I remember being scared he was dead at first. And yelling, "Vernon! Wake up!"

I shook him on the shoulder and I remember yelling his name a few times, the putrid smell of his breath, and how he suddenly said, "Hello, poppet!" like nothing weird was happening.

I left him there and ran to the stake behind the starting wickets, with the colors of the mallets in stripes, like a rainbow. I remember the clue.

Where does Mother love playing music the most?

Mother always wrote the best clues.

<resume>

I run past Mother, who is still sitting on the patio bench, and say, "But you love playing music everywhere!"

She smiles and watches me go to all her favorite places outside, then I run through the house to the music room, the settee in front of the fireplace, the landing on the stairs, where she says the acoustics are "hollow and flawless."

No clues.

I run back through the double doors and search the garden again. I stop by the fountain and catch my breath. I yell to her, "Will I have to fly to Australia to find this clue?"

"Oh! I wish we could! You'd love Melbourne!"

"Let's go, then. I need to get this hunt over with!" I am so sassy in my damp little romper, barefoot, and my hair all wispy and wild, pigtails leaving two wet spots down my front.

She laughs and so do I. And then Vernon wanders into the pool gate, yells, "Hello all!" and strips off his clothing—bar his brief underpants—goes to the diving board and dives in. His dives are funny and he looks like a frog when he kicks his legs out.

<pause>

Gemma tried to teach him how to not do that with his legs earlier that summer, but he yelled at her so now we all are a little afraid when he dives because he's so self-conscious. In the home movie, you can see the fear on our faces when we watch him kick his legs out.

<resume>

He swims to the ladder underwater and then breaks the surface and climbs out, grabs a clean towel, and dries off his face.

"Where were we?" Mother asks.

"We were going to Australia because you love making music there!"

"Aaaa! Oww-ch!" Vernon says. He fans the side of his face that is red from sunburn.

"It's far closer than Australia," Mother says.

When I look at her, I can see a Post-it note clue stuck to her chest.

"Your heart!" I say.

She motions for me to get it, and I do and give her a kiss on the nose while I'm there.

It says, *Let's take a long walk now. There are clues in the trees!*

<stop>

The movie ends when we leave the wide-angle view of the patio camera. My memory remembers what happened, though. We didn't get far.

SALINGER

"Of course it's not a scavenger hunt, Jane. You're sixteen. Far too old for games like that," Vernon scolds. Finch makes an assenting grunt.

"So, tell me where the book is, then?"

"Over on the shelf behind the Grammy stuff. It's a red book. Paperback. Salinger is the name of the author," he says.

I go to the large mahogany bookcase with the glass doors. It's as old as the house. Deep shelves and Grammys on the top two, as well as other trophies. Mother kept them in boxes until The Great Ignoring, when Vernon redecorated to make everything look better than it was. I find a well-worn copy of *The Catcher in the Rye* by J. D. Salinger. Next to it is a stack of postcards from Mother that Vernon is hoarding away from us. I leave those where they are for now and retrieve the book.

I inspect the cover, which is ancient-seeming with no art but the dark red background and bright mustard-colored lettering, and I look inside. It's the fiftieth printing, it says, around 1979, but the book was published in 1951. I turn the page to the dedication.

It says, "TO MY MOTHER."

I love it already.

JANE'S MEMORY—07.19.2016

Mother and I walk across the croquet pitch and toward the gap in the hedge, me still holding the scavenger hunt Post-it notes in my hand.

I am eight years old. I remind you of this because right before we exit the property through the hedge, there is a very loud gunshot. And at eight years old, a gunshot is a shocking thing to hear. It's louder than you expect and, in this case, it is closer, too. It does something to the air around us—more than sound. I can *feel* it.

Mother and I jump and scream a little and then turn around.

Milorad holds a shotgun, aimed at us. Vernon is next to him, still wearing only his wet, white underpants. Pool water runs down his hairy, skinny legs. Half of his face is cartoon-red sunburned and impossible to believe.

<pause>

What is notable is that I did not cry. Most eight-year-old children would cry.

<resume>

"What are you doing?" Mother asks. She tries to hide the fear in her voice, but she can't.

"Why don't you come back into the garden?" Vernon says.

Milorad tries to aim the shotgun to the sky, but Vernon puts his hand on the barrel and aims it back at us.

"We're taking a short walk. Nothing to be alarmed about," Mother says.

"There are clues," I say. Carefully, I wave the stack of notes in my little hand.

Mother nods and puts on an expression of empathy and excitement—probably to show Vernon that we were not up to no good—we were not going to say anything about his frog legs when he dives or anything like that.

He says again, "Why don't you come back into the garden?"

So, Mother takes my trembling hand, and we walk back toward the house. When we get close enough, I look to Milorad's eyes and he can't meet mine.

Then, when we round the corner to the rose garden and back lawn, Marta comes running from the double doors in the study. She chases a rat. It's Brutus.

"Keep that fucking rat in its cage!" she yells to Milorad as he follows us into the garden. She notes the shotgun, and her face reacts with concern.

Vernon points and says, "Shoot the rat!" but Milorad doesn't even aim.

"I am sorry!" he answers Marta. He looks at Mother and me. "I am sorry!" he says again.

POSTMARKED NOVEMBER 26, 2024

PICTURE OF ELVIS'S GRACELAND

Dear Jane and Henry,
I've been to Graceland before, but Davy of Anvil hadn't been, so he and David dragged us all there for a photo op. We stayed for two hours and got to meet a few people who actually knew Elvis Presley! It was great. They let me play a piano in the house and we recorded a punk rendition of "Jingle Bell Rock" for our publicist who never calls us. The record label says we're doing great on sales. I only wish you all were here with me. Tell Marta I miss her and her mashed potatoes! Love, Mom

OUR PEOPLE II

It's an icebreaker!

WHILE THE HOUSEHOLD SEEMS LIKE a machine of some sort, as if all components have always been part of it, each of our people arrived at a different time. Here is a breakdown, in chronological order.

LET'S GET TO KNOW MARTA!

Marta moved into the house the same day as Mother and Vernon in 2001. Mother ignored Vernon's demands for a *house all to ourselves* and had Marta's apartment redecorated in the first weeks while Marta stayed in the room that is now Mother's bedroom. When they picked colors, Marta picked yellow for her bedroom because she said it was like waking up inside the sun. ASK MARTA HOW SHE KNOWS WHAT IT'S LIKE TO WAKE UP INSIDE THE SUN! Her favorite song is "Impossible to answer with just one" she says. "But Patti Smith's 'Free Money' is what I usually say." When I look concerned that she didn't pick a Placenta song, she adds, "Try picking just one!" I do not ask her what her favorite food is because this type of question angers a cook.

LET'S GET TO KNOW MILORAD!

On the coldest day of the year in 2006, Milorad arrived at the front door at 1111 Spruce Street, an overgrown Victorian home belonging to Mina Vandermaker, and rang the doorbell. ASK MILORAD

HOW HE KNEW TO COME TO OUR HOUSE SOMETIME! Later that day, he moved into the pool house with his pet rat, Brutus. He had only a half-empty rucksack, and a small bag of American snack food that he purchased in 30th Street Station in Philadelphia. He also purchased one book in the train station. A picture board book called *Good Night Philadelphia*. When he is bored, he can be found reading this book to Brutus. But for many years, he would read it to Henry and me, often out in the rose garden on a blanket while we all munched on Marta's corn muffins—Milorad's favorite food. Within a year, Milorad had the hedges trimmed (some into shapes!) and the rose garden redesigned. He never stops working. Sometimes I can see him out there in the middle of the night, digging and pruning.

LET'S GET TO KNOW GEMMA!

Gemma started work as my lady's maid in the spring of 2016, the same year Mother released her fifth full studio album, *Apples, Rapist, Oranges*. As previously mentioned, she was nine years old at the time. It occurs to me now that I don't know anything about Gemma's family. ASK GEMMA ABOUT HER FAMILY SOMETIME! Her favorite food was apples. She always had at least two with her, and if she got stressed, which happened when Vernon would slam doors or act unseemly, she would pull an apple from her smock pocket or her tote and begin to crunch on it. By the time Gemma turned thirteen, Vernon banned apples because he said he couldn't stand the sound of her chewing on them. After that, Gemma's favorite food was bananas because they don't make any noise.

POSTMARKED DECEMBER 3, 2024

A PICTURE OF TREES WITH SPANISH MOSS

Dear Jane and Henry,

Thank you for the picture you sent through Vernon of your funny faces! I will never tire of seeing you be so silly and playful. Please don't lose that when you "grow up"! We are in Athens, Georgia, today and tomorrow. I love it here. The more I drive around the country, the more I want to put us ALL on a bus and show you all the amazing places there are! I love you. See you soon, I hope! Yay!

Love, Mom

LESSON FIVE: WALKING IS GOOD FOR THE DIGESTION

Today is Sunday, December 22, 2024

I'VE BEEN WALKING for more than fifteen minutes and I'm pretty sure I'm free to do as I please. Vernon rarely announces that he's taking a nap. I took the opportunity. I even brought my Salinger book, should I find a nice place to sit and read the next chapter.

The temperature has dropped to below freezing, but it's sunny. The weather looks good for this week, which is great because Mother might be coming home tomorrow. If Vernon allows her. Since The Christmas That Changed Everything, he hasn't allowed it.

One time before she was locked up, a snowstorm kept her away from us for Christmas Day. Finch came instead. She hadn't been invited and was living somewhere far-off and exotic at the time, but when she heard Mother couldn't get home, she said, "Someone has to pretend to be your mother!" and made her way to our house in record time.

Look. Vernon may have fooled me with his stories of Mother's feeble-minded control and latent ability to make us all miserable while she wasn't even there, but no one ever fooled me into thinking Finch was mother material.

She is a collector. She collects information, mostly, by pretending to care. Here's an incomplete list of things she collected from me before I stopped trusting her: Everything Mother ever told me.

Details about my dates with suitors since I started dating. (Even the kissing and touching, which makes me feel weird even thinking about it.) The list she compiled from all the witch trials about the things me and Henry hate about Mother—always rewarded with ice cream or something stronger. During The Great Ignoring of 2019, I once told Finch that I enjoyed seeing Mother cry.

I am aware this list makes me look diabolical. I was diabolical. Because it was the only way to stay safe once she and Vernon formed their team.

I do not know my aunt Finch outside of the house (do I know *anything* outside of the house though, seriously), but if I was to guess, she is a terrible gossip—the kind who concocts great stories and passes them through thin lips in order to control the listener.

Why else would she tell me and Henry that Mother wanted to kill us? Why else would she tell Marta that Mother thinks she's dumb? Why else would she tell Vernon that Mother tells her secrets that should be kept between lovers? I have stumbled upon so many home movies of Finch transporting her own concoctions between family members, it has kept me from the three main memories I'm looking for.

1. My one special birthday—the day I turned five.
2. The stabbing scene, though I know it happened in the cameraless kitchen, I also know what led up to it and what happened afterward, which happened in other areas where cameras are, so it's in here somewhere.
3. The times Mother told me I was ugly when I cried, which Finch tells me about constantly, but I do not recall.

There are nights I cry over what I find—watching young Vernon chase young Mother through the house while he yells things like,

"You're such a bitch! Stop so we can talk!" or "You're overreacting. I was just kidding!" or "I'm going to call all my friends and tell them what an asshole you are!" It feels worth it, though. I know so much more about everything. I know about Milorad's 2:00 a.m. gardening. I know that Marta sometimes has a tall dude with cool hair sleep over. I know that Gemma has never arrived through the front door. I also keep finding videos of Finch suddenly appearing in various rooms in our house, late at night while we're sleeping. She rummages through drawers and cabinets downstairs over and over, looking for something she never finds.

WITCHCRAFT

I've been walking an easy twenty minutes now and my fear of getting caught is gone. I'm wearing a pair of mittens that Gemma knitted for me. They are a pale shade of purple—and soft. I've wiped my nose with the right mitten twice now, so there is snot freezing on the thumb area.

The air feels right in my lungs. Crisp. It's as if I am waking up. I feel very much alive when I see the enormous oak tree. I think it may be more than a hundred years old. I have an inescapable need to hug it.

I read a book last year about trees and how they communicate with each other and help each other and how they have communities just like us. Better than us—no tree is trying to hurt other trees. I try to focus my positive energy on the oak tree as I climb through the bars on the fence. Mother taught me about energy when I was little and I've always believed in it, even when Vernon told me that it was witchcraft.

Now I hope it is witchcraft.

The music builds from a high-pitched sound in my head at first.

EXT. BIKING AND WALKING TRAIL / IN THE WOODS—AFTERNOON

The BAND members are dressed like trees. JANE is dressed as a witch. Costumes made out of foam.

Song: "Can a Girl"

Composer notes: *A sort of punk waltz. 3/4 time. Fast, but clear.*

JANE

CAN A GIRL FALL IN LOVE WITH A TREE?
CAN A GIRL FALL IN LOVE WITH A TREE?
OAK TREE, BE MINE. SHARE WITH ME YOUR SUNSHINE.
I AM TIRED, TIRED OF ALWAYS BEING ME.

CAN A GIRL HOLD YOUR HAND?
CAN A GIRL HOLD YOUR HAND?
OAK TREE, REACH OUT. LET'S BE TOGETHER.
I AM TIRED OF THIS BLAND, BLAND WORLD.

THE RULES ARE BOGUS.
THIS IS MY MAGNUM OPUS.
SET ME FREE, SET ME FREE, SET ME FREE.

FINCH

Jane!

Jane holds her hand out for the band to stop playing. She takes off her guitar and hands it to a ROADIE. Then she puts on her winter coat again.

"Jane!"

It's Finch this time. She's in her blue puffy parka that makes her look silly. She knows it. This is why she never wears it.

"Get back here!" she yells, as if I'm running. But I'm not running. I was dancing, I guess. I don't even know if I was singing the words out loud or what. I climb through the fence and walk toward her.

"If you were mine, I'd lock you in your room at this point."

I ignore it.

"Did you hear me?" she asks.

I make my way slowly and don't answer her. She is not in any way intimidating in the silly blue parka.

"If you were mine, I'd make sure you couldn't get out," she mumbles as she turns back toward the house.

There are birds on the trail ahead. They start chirping in a rhythm . . . they start making a melody. The band—my band—comes out, dressed as birds.

EXT. BIKE AND WALKING TRAIL—AFTERNOON

The music continues as Jane grabs a guitar that's being handed to her from the woods by a random hand.

Jane is now dressed as a tree. The band members are dressed as birds. Bluebirds, to be exact. Costumes are made of mostly foam. Some feathers.

JANE

If I were yours?

FINCH

If—

JANE

If I were *YOURS*?

FINCH

If—

Jane jumps from the biking and walking trail up to the stage where her bird-dressed band awaits.

INT. SMALL IMAGINARY PUNK CLUB INSIDE JANE'S BRAIN—LATE NIGHT

JANE

One, two, three, four!

Jane steps up to microphone on-stage.

Song: "If I Were Yours"

Composer notes: *A very fast 4/4 time.*

JANE

IF I WERE YOURS, IF I WERE YOURS
I'D BE A WHOLE DIFFERENT PERSON NOW.
I'D BE A BITCH, LIKE YOU, AND YOU WOULD SHOW ME HOW
TO HOLD ALL MY INSECURITIES INSIDE TO ACT AS FUEL
TO BE SO CRUEL, TO BE EVERYTHING YOU EVER WANTED ME TO BE.

IF I WERE YOURS, IF I WERE YOURS
I'D BE A LOT LESS CHEERFUL.
THE PRINCIPAL WOULD CALL AND YOU'D GET QUITE AN EARFUL
ABOUT HOW I BLEW EVERYTHING I HAD.
HOW I CAN'T STOP SPREADING RUMORS.
HOW MY HATE SPREADS LIKE A TUMOR.
THE REFLECTION OF YOU WOULD BE SO MAD.
YOUR MIRROR NEVER LIES.

ENSEMBLE

IF I WERE YOURS, IF I WERE YOURS
EVERYTHING WOULD SURELY SUCK.
IF I WERE YOURS, IF I WERE YOURS
I WOULDN'T GIVE A TINY FUCK.
IF I WERE YOURS, IF I WERE YOURS
EVERYTHING WOULD FEEL BAD
ALL THE TIME—
LIKE YOU, LIKE YOU, LIKE YOU.

Jane kneels onstage.

JANE

IF I WERE YOURS, YOU'D PARADE ME OUT

IN PUBLIC—TOY DOG ON A LEAD.
IF I WERE YOURS, YOU'D BUY ME ICE CREAM
THEN OPEN MY BRAIN AND FEED
YOU WANT TO KNOW EVERYTHING IN MY HEAD
BUT IF IT DOESN'T MATCH YOUR NEEDS, YOU WANT ME DEAD.
AIN'T IT FUNNY HOW YOU WANT TO BE JUST LIKE ME?
YOUNG, PRETTY, SMART, AND FREE?
BUT YOU DON'T SEE HOW THAT GREEN LOOKS SHIT ON YOU!
SHIT ON YOU, SHIT ON YOU!

ENSEMBLE
IF I WERE YOURS, IF I WERE YOURS
EVERYTHING WOULD SURELY SUCK.
IF I WERE YOURS, IF I WERE YOURS
I WOULDN'T GIVE A TINY FUCK.
IF I WERE YOURS, IF I WERE YOURS
EVERYTHING WOULD FEEL BAD
ALL THE TIME—
LIKE YOU, LIKE YOU, LIKE YOU . . .

Music stops, crowd screams.

END SONG

JANE
Thank you! Thank you!

Jane bows and curtsies.

EXT. THE HEDGE SURROUNDING THE LARGE VICTORIAN HOME—LATE AFTERNOON

When we walk across the croquet pitch and the lawn, Finch speeds up and heads toward the main house in her blue parka. I peel off to the pool house.

I walk in the side door, and Milorad says, "Do not open the door!"

"What's going on?" I ask.

"Brutus is out," he says. He's crouched down behind the tiki bar with a brick in his right hand.

"Won't that kill him?" I ask.

"I do not care," Milorad says.

"Calm down. We'll set a catch-and-release trap, like always."

Milorad stands up and puts the brick on the bar. He sighs. Shakes his head.

Milorad's phone rings. He puts it on speaker while he washes his hands. It's Vernon. "Jane, please come to the dining room. Milorad, you and Marta will be eating with us tonight. We'll be ready in about fifteen minutes. Wash up."

Neither Milorad nor I reply. Vernon hangs up, and I head out the sliding door and onto the patio while Milorad dries his hands and says he's going to change his shirt.

POSTMARKED DECEMBER 6, 2024

A PICTURE OF A GOLD-DOMED BUILDING, MONTPELIER, VERMONT

Dear All,

This town is so small and so sweet and the people are so cool! It's cold again, but not as cold as Minnesota was. There's snow on the ground, though. Is it snowing yet with you? The next two weeks are all New England, Michigan, and New York City. Then I get to come home for a whole week! I miss everything about home. Well, almost everything. I can't wait to hear about what you two are doing. Vernon, don't work too hard! Love you all, Mom/Mina

THE RULES

"What's your excuse this time?" Vernon asks, not even looking at me.

"Walking is good for the digestion?" I say.

"You're grounded."

"Oh, please," I answer. "What does that even mean?"

He ignores me. We all tear into our food. Once the appetizer is finished, Marta leaves the table with our small plates and comes back with the next course.

The camera is recording Vernon as he says, "If your mother were to come home for the holiday, things around here have to be better. Better behavior all around."

"I'm doing great," Henry says. "I don't know how I could do any better!"

"You cry over algebra," Vernon says, not looking at Henry.

"Mina hates crying," Finch says.

I lean and whisper to Henry, "Mother will love you even if you cry over algebra."

"What did you just say?"

Henry says, "She told me Mother will still love me if I cry over algebra."

I am not shocked. The boy is brainwashed.

"Well, I may as well tell you," Vernon says, "she's decided not to come home again for the holidays. She's sending presents in her stead."

Henry's jaw tightens. I inhale slowly and sigh. He looks at me and my jaw tightens, too.

"This can't be her choice," I say. "She loves us very much."

At this, Finch laughs, "Ha!"

"Are you implying our mother doesn't love us?" Henry asks.

Finch gets a grip on herself. "Of course not. She's just so very busy, I guess."

"She does send her regrets," Vernon adds.

"I'm sure she has a lot of those," I say. I stare right at him.

The rest of dinner is as you'd expect. There are reminders.

Vernon says, "Just in case your mother *does* decide to show up unannounced, we need to go over the usual rules." In my librettist's mind, I picture him with a flip chart on a stand and a pointer.

1. *Never touch the attachments on the System or its remote control.*

2. *Never open or unlock the doors on the System tubes or capsule. This is for your own safety.*

3. *Mother will take all her meals in solitude. This is her request.*

"That's not true. If she were allowed to come home, she'd want to eat with us," I say.

"Jane, please shut up," Vernon says.

This is when I pull out the postcards from my sweatshirt pouch. More than fifty of them. The ones Vernon has been hiding in the bookcase. "Mother sends us a postcard every day, Henry. Sometimes two," I say.

Henry says, "Really?" and leans over to read them.

Vernon leans vigorously across Henry and grabs them from my hands and puts them on the table next to him. Henry looks at the pile while Vernon speaks more rules at us.

4. *Mother will not be allowed to play music in the house. Nor will anyone else.*

5. *No leaving your rooms until Vernon is awake and out of his room.*

"Wait a second," I say. "Some days you don't ever come out of there!"

"I'll be up around eleven or so every day."

"I wake up at six!" Henry says. "What am I supposed to do for five hours?"

Vernon shrugs, arches his back a bit, picks up the pile of postcards. "What do you usually do?"

I answer, "We hang out in the kitchen with Marta and when Mother is home, Mother. It's quite pleasant. We've never conspired or anything unseemly like that. She stays in the System."

"I miss her!" Henry blurts.

"We all miss her," Vernon says. "Of course."

Finch raises her eyebrows as if to say she does not miss Mother.

"Okay," Vernon says—he's standing next to the fireplace in the adjacent sitting room now—"I can be flexible." He turns to me. "But, Henry, if your sister tries to take another walk, then we have to stick to Rule Number Five."

"I don't see what's wrong with taking a walk in the fresh air," I say. "It is good for the body. And the mind. During times like these, especially."

"Fresh air is more important than ever!" Henry says.

"Of course," Vernon says. "But no walks off the property. Jane knows this, don't you, Jane?"

"Indeed," I say.

"Maybe you can play some winter croquet with your brother this week, yes?" Vernon suggests, as he casually tosses some of Mother's postcards into the fire. Henry lets out a tiny gasp, which only I can hear. The fire reacts with a roar, and when it calms again, Vernon lets a few more fall from his hand into the flames. He continues talking.

6. *No loving your mother in front of Vernon. "It hurts me because she refuses to love me for who I am."*

7. *No being nice to Mother because that will make her think she is welcome in this house. I say, "This is literally her house." Vernon ignores me and burns the rest of the postcards. Henry watches this with interest.*

8. *I do not listen to the rest of the rules. I am Punk Rock Jane. I excuse myself before dessert. "I'm just so tired," I say, and go to my room.*

I go to my bed and curl up under the covers. I'm not cold and I'm not particularly tired, but I feel the need to curl up under the covers to be safe. I can't describe it. I do not know who I am anymore. This is what secrets do to a person.

BRUTUS'S FAVORITE TRICK

OH, PLEASE, American teenage girls are the worst. She curls up in her bed and feels safe? She's not safe. What girl is safe in bed? What girl is safe at all? I made sure, through centuries, that the game was rigged. From child pageants, cheerleaders, and frat party dares to wedded bliss, I'm in charge of safety and there is none.

See, it's a woman's job to keep a family together—even if her husband is terrible. Even if he throws tables at her. Even if he fucks her sister. Even if he slaps her daughter. When she files for divorce, the women in town gossip about how she couldn't keep a man and the men in town think she's a heartless bitch.

I love a good trap.

And, like the no-kill traps Milorad uses to fetch me, this one is foolproof. The bait is inherent: women can't do a damn thing right. All because they have soft skin and big hearts and love. They walk in for the babies, and if they dare to walk out, they're failures. Even if they get away, I make sure they think it every day. I probably got your mom to hate herself somewhere along the way. And then I got you to hate her, too.

HAPPY HOLIDAYS FROM THE VANDERMAKER-COOKS!

Today is Wednesday, December 25, 2024

THAT'S WHAT THE E-CARD SAYS. Marta shows it to me on her phone. There are three pictures—all doctored so that it looks as if our family spends time together. Whoever made these pictures even gave us a vacation! Like normal people.

It's like the moon landing conspiracy, but instead of the moon, it's my life. We are a far cry from Christmas cards, beach vacations, and ice-skating. In one of the shots, it's possible that Henry has three ears.

Since The Christmas That Changed Everything, we don't celebrate Christmas like we used to. There are presents—bought, wrapped, and sent by Mother—in the morning and a roaring fire at night, and Marta makes a turkey and a ham and her famous mashed at midday, but beyond that, it's a prop tree that Milorad and Marta are paid to decorate, no Christmas music, and lies to God. Every year since he locked her in, it's only gotten worse.

I look at Henry, who is sitting quietly on the couch like a trained dog, staring at Jimmy Stewart at seven in the morning by himself.

"This is bullshit," I say to the empty study. "It's supposed to be Christmas."

ACT II, SCENE 3

INT. THE VANDERMAKER HOUSE; ALL ROOMS

JANE is dressed in black pajamas and the BAND is dressed as Christmas ornaments and all wear Santa hats. Except DAVID, who wears a menorah as a hat-like singular majestic antler.

Music fades in . . .

Song: "What Is Christmas Anyway?"

Composer notes: *This is a holiday orchestral piece with violins and flutes and is quite peppy, with punk undertones.*

The FAMILY sits around the sitting room and opens presents, between little dances, as spotlights center each singer. As this song is sung, the entire day is acted out.

MARTA
I GOT UP AT FOUR AND LIT THE FIRE.

JANE

TENSION ROUND HERE COULDN'T BE MUCH HIGHER.

MARTA and JANE

IT'S CHRISTMAS!

GEMMA walks into the living room where the song is taking place. Joins the choreography already in action and hugs Jane and HENRY.

MINA

IT'S MY ONE DAY OUT OF THE SYSTEM.

VERNON (talking to FINCH, motions to his family)

I'D BE LYING IF I SAID I'D MISS THEM.

MINA and VERNON

IT'S CHRISTMAS!

HENRY

I DAYDREAM OF FROGS AND PLANTS.

MILORAD (holding brick)

I MAINTAIN THIS MANLY STANCE.

GEMMA (holding up tweed pants)

I WASH AND PRESS JANE'S GOOD TWEED PANTS.

ENSEMBLE

IT'S CHRISTMAS!

MINA (talking)
This one's for you, Henry!
This one's for you, Jane!

Henry and Jane open presents nonstop throughout this scene.

HENRY
WE DON'T GO TO CHURCH OR WORSHIP JESUS
THOUGH WE SAY "BLESS YOU" WHEN SOMEONE SNEEZES.
ALL I WANT IS A HOTHOUSE FULL OF FROGS.
AND A BRAND-NEW PAIR OF PLASTIC GARDEN CLOGS.

JANE
THIS YEAR EVERYTHING IS WEIRD FOR ME.
NOTHING FEELS RIGHT OR FILLED WITH GLEE.
I ONLY WANT TO GO BACK TO MY SCHOOL.
MAYBE A GUITAR OR SOMETHING COOL.

MINA (talking)
This one's for you, Gemma!
This one's for you, Marta!

MARTA and Gemma open presents and also go between the sitting room tending the fire and the kitchen, where Christmas dinner is being made.

GEMMA
NO ONE'S ASKED, BUT HERE'S THE ANSWER.
MY FAVORITE CHICKEN HAS DIED OF CANCER.

THAT'S WHY I LOOK AS IF I'M ABOUT TO CRY
BUT PLEASE DON'T ASK BECAUSE THEN I'LL HAVE
TO LIE.

MARTA
DID YOU KNOW THAT I GOT MARRIED?
IT'S A SECRET THAT I'VE CAREFULLY CARRIED
BUT TODAY THAT SECRET WILL BE LEFT TO ROAM
BECAUSE MY HUSBAND HAS BOUGHT US BOTH A HOME!

ENSEMBLE
WHAT IS CHRISTMAS ANYWAY?
IT'S JUST ANOTHER INSIDE DAY
HERE AT VERNON'S VICTORIAN PANDEMIC PRISON.
WHAT IS CHRISTMAS ANYWAY?
VERNON UNCORKS THE CABERNET
BY NOON HE'LL HAVE COMPLETELY LOST HIS VISION.

MINA (talking)
This one's for you, Milo!
This one's for you, Vernon!

MILORAD and VERNON open gifts while Marta, Gemma and MINA set the table, light candles, tend the fire, clean up wrapping paper, and do all other chores.

MILORAD
I AM HAPPIER THAN I'VE BEEN BEFORE.
IT'S BECOME IMPOSSIBLE TO IGNORE.

HOW HENRY ACTS AND FEELS JUST LIKE A SON
AFTER SO MUCH LOSS I FEEL AS IF I'VE WON.

VERNON
WHEN SHE'S OUT LIKE THIS SHE'S BEAUTIFUL
BUT I MUST SOMEHOW BE DUTIFUL
TO THE PLAN I'VE MADE TO DRIVE HER TO HER DEATH
WE ALL KNOW THAT THE PLAN IS FOR THE BEST.

The family and their people sit around the dining room table for Christmas dinner.

ENSEMBLE
WHAT IS CHRISTMAS ANYWAY?
BUT SENTIMENTAL OVERSTAY.
IT'S BETTER TO IGNORE THE URGE TO SMILE.
WHAT IS CHRISTMAS ANYWAY?
A CHANCE TO BLOCK THE DISARRAY
AND SIT BACK AND RELAX A LITTLE WHILE.

Marta and Mina clear the table and then Marta guides Mina back to the living room.

JANE (talking)
This one's for you, Mother!

HENRY (talking)
This one's for you, Mother!

Mina hugs and holds her children,

then they laugh and giggle and tickle each other on the floor of the sitting room.

MINA
I NEED NOTHING BUT TO BE HERE
HOLDING BOTH OF YOU SO DEAR

The children tickle Mina.

I'M SO TIRED OF BEING LOCKED UP.
THIS WHOLE ARRANGEMENT IS COCKED UP.

Vernon sees this display and scowls, then texts someone on his phone, then moves to the System tube.

MINA (CONT'D)
STILL CAN'T BELIEVE HE'S SUCH A BRUTAL MAN.
IT'S TIME TO TELL THE TRUTH WHILE I STILL CAN.

ENSEMBLE
WHAT IS CHRISTMAS ANYWAY?
A TIME TO HIDE THAT JANE IS GAY
AND PRETEND LIKE VERNON'S REALLY NOT A DICK.
WHAT IS CHRISTMAS ANYWAY?
A DAY TO PLAN YOUR RUNAWAY
AND YOU'D BETTER DO IT MIGHTY FUCKING QUICK.

Vernon stands by the open System door and beckons Mina into

it. Mina hugs the children and Marta, then steps in. Vernon closes the door and Mina sits on her chair. The capsule slowly descends.

MARTA

I'LL WASH THE DISHES AND HE'LL DRY.

MILORAD

I'LL TRY MY BEST-BEST NOT TO CRY.

MARTA and MILORAD

IT'S CHRISTMAS!

GEMMA

I'LL TRY TO MAKE IT HOME BY NINE.

HENRY

WHERE DID VERNON PUT ALL THAT WINE?

GEMMA and HENRY

IT'S CHRISTMAS!

VERNON

IT'S TIME WE CRANKED THIS UP A NOTCH.

JANE

IT'S TIME TO SYNCHRONIZE MY WATCH.

FINCH arrives stage left just as Mina disappears into the floor.

FINCH
VERNON, WHERE'D YOU PUT THAT SCOTCH?

ENSEMBLE
IT'S CHRISTMAS!

AFTERGLOW

We all got what we wanted. Henry got his hothouse kit; I got an easel, some canvas, and two sets of brushes; Vernon got a leather briefcase handcrafted in Italy; Mother got a ten-minute FaceTime from a sunflower-heavy hotel room where she isn't confined to anything; and Finch got to watch Mother say goodbye before she wanted to. Even Brutus got a night out on the town.

"I have not seen him all day," Milorad says to Marta in the kitchen. "I am too old to chase a rat."

Marta pours him a nighttime cognac, and he goes to his pool house.

Finch and Vernon sit in the sitting room, fire blazing, and they don't know that Henry and I are sitting behind the enormous Christmas tree.

Finch says, "They won't even let me *see* the deed."

"Does it really matter?" Vernon asks.

She looks at him and thinks. "I suppose not once she's gone."

"It'll all be mine then," Vernon answers.

"Ours," Finch says. "All ours."

When Finch kisses Vernon, they look like two groundhogs. I don't know why that's the animal that comes to mind, but maybe I wish they'd go hibernate and not come out until February or ever.

"What are they even talking about?" Henry asks.

"They want to steal the house from Mother and us," I say.

"Fat chance, suckers," he whispers, holding the last syllable.

I look at Henry. "Are you drunk?"

He rolls his eyes like I'm tedious. "What do you think eggnog is made of?"

Mother called again on New Year's Day. She was given only ten minutes again, but this time she was prepared and said goodbye herself. She said two things that were particularly notable.

When Henry asked her if the crowd-surfing was good on this tour, she said, "I don't do that. I'm in my fifties now, love."

And a minute later, she said, "I think this might be my last album. I have other stuff to do in the world."

It gave me some kind of hope.

POSTMARKED DECEMBER 28, 2024

A PICTURE OF THE BEACH IN SEASIDE HEIGHTS, NEW JERSEY

Dear Jane and Henry,
I missed you so much on Christmas. Vernon said it was best I didn't come on account of you both being sick. I hope you still had a good day, regardless. I decided to go to the beach in NJ and spent the day walking in the cold surf. It felt invigorating. I miss taking you guys places! Do you remember our trip to Jamaica? Henry, you were little but, man, you had such fun with the fish in the sea. I miss those days. Happy New Year. Wish I was there. I leave for European tour on Jan 2nd. Will send more postcards! Love, Mom

The first week of January, Vernon moved me on to African geography. He is so laser-focused on geography that he seems to have forgotten the other subjects he's "teaching" me. I asked him as I filled in the African country names without even having to double-check, "When will we discuss *The Catcher in the Rye?*"

He groaned and answered, "You're some cookie, you are, just sitting there asking me when this and when that."

"No pressure," I say. "I was just curious."

He doesn't look up from the magazine he's reading. "Celebrate! You finally won, Jane. You finally have all the power now! All because you read a book!"

Honestly. I think the pocket watch is driving him mad.

POSTMARKED JANUARY 3, 2025

A PICTURE OF A FLOWER-ADORNED BICYCLE ON A BRIDGE OVER A CANAL

Dear Jane and Henry,

It begins! We start in Amsterdam, where the canals are beautiful and the croissants are perfect. We had a photo shoot on a houseboat this morning, where David decided we should dress up as sharks. (There are no sharks here.) Tonight we have our first of two shows. Then two nights in Paris, and then a few days off in Spain before a show in Barcelona and then driving to Switzerland. Henry, I am sending a case of proper Dutch tulips to you. I chose purple because the hue was rich and deep. Jane, I plan on getting you a special ukulele in Salzburg when we stop there. Running out of room! Love you, Mom

LESSON SIX: GEOGRAPHY OF A SLAP

Today is Friday, January 10, 2025

POSTMARKED JANUARY 5, 2025

A PICTURE OF THE EIFFEL TOWER AT NIGHT

Dear Jane and Henry,
Hello from Paris, where it's raining and so cold! We had such a great show last night—then we went to a local pub and played an acoustic set for three more hours. It was fun but we're all too tired today. How are things there? Will you call me soon—I miss you and not seeing you at Christmas was hard! I can't wait to get home for good. I think I may never leave home again after that. I love you both, so much. Love, Mom

THE LETTER

"JANE!"

That's Vernon screaming my name at eight in the morning. I mean *screaming*. I put down my notebook where I'm matching fifty-four African capitals to their countries.

"JANE!"

He's waiting for me at the bottom of the stairs, pacing, and he's holding an envelope.

When I arrive in front of him, he slaps me hard across the face.

I recoil and back up the stairs. He walks up the stairs toward me, shaking the envelope in my direction.

"You did it!" he says. "Little bitch! Always trying to make a fool out of me!"

"I—" I notice my hand is on my face where he slapped me. I can't remember moving my hand to my face. He stops advancing on me, so I stop backing up. He stares at me for a moment, then walks back to the landing.

"Is it from Mother?" I ask.

I can see from here it's typed, so it's probably not from Mother.

"Read it." He shoves it at me.

Once I see the school district letterhead, I know that I'm about to act the most convincing role of my life. *To the Parents of Jane Vandermaker Cook . . . standard benchmarks . . . not met . . . a representative from the district . . . visit your home . . . January 16, 2025 . . . Contact the district office . . . questions . . . appreciate . . . compliance.*

"I don't understand," I say.

Vernon snatches the letter from my hands, turns, and storms down the stairs.

"Why are they coming?" I yell after him.

"Why are they coming?" Vernon mocks, as he paces at the landing of the stairs. "Why do you *think* they're coming? You know—if you want to go to school so badly, I'll send you to boarding school. It would give Henry and me good bonding time, you being away from here."

"Please don't send me away," I say.

"If you could just be better . . . at being a daughter, this could work out. You have this annoying similarity to Mina. You're—you're headstrong. Stubborn. And yet so . . . so . . . fucking *nice*." He stops to take a breath. "But it's not *real* nice. It's all fake with you two. You're always manipulating. Always—like that! Like that!"

He points at the single tear running down my cheek. I feel terrible, for certain, because I do not lie to God and here I am lying.

But I didn't think the school district would answer a ransom note from a sixteen-year-old girl sent back in October. Anyway, the tear is real because I just got hit by my father for the first time, and to handle it, my brain is running a sale on the capitals of African countries. *Kinshasa, Dakar, Abuja, Nairobi, Cairo, Monrovia . . .*

"I need a minute," I say. I get up, touch my cheek again, which still hurts, and walk upstairs to my room. I close the door quietly and lock it. I see the red swelling on my cheek in my vanity mirror, and this tidal wave comes out of me. I can't remember the last time I sobbed like this. I stay as quiet as I can and shove my face into my pillow; eventually, I flip onto my back and try to breathe, but I can't stop.

I check in with why I'm sobbing so much and these are my two main thought-trains:

1. My letter worked and I might be going to actual high school. ➔ I'm scared to go to actual high school even though I'm the one who actually put plan-actual-high-school in motion.

2. Vernon slapped me really hard. ➔ Vernon slapped me because Vernon is really mad at me. ➔ If Vernon is mad at me, then I have no one.

I thought the tubes and the System were only hurting Mother. But those tubes hurt me, too. Mother feels, when I think of her, encased—embalmed on the outside. I don't know what to do with this feeling. I stop heaving and breathe shallow. *I have no mother.* And I remember that I have a mother. Only she is translucent. *I have no mother.* Like a wax-paper doll. No one rolled that thin could possibly be somebody's mother. *Punk Rock Jane and the Wax-Paper Mothers.* I'm programed. Like some sort of robot. Mina isn't wax paper. She's hugs and postcards even if Vernon hides them from us. She's a wad of foreign money and carefully wrapped Christmas presents when she can't even be here to watch us open them. ➔ I have a mother. *Someone around here has to work.* ➔ I will soon tell her everything.

FREE JANE

It is dinnertime—seven hours after Vernon slapped me. I have come to a place of satisfaction now. First, the slap is a keepsake. It could prove useful. Second, I can barely hold in my excitement about going to school, and yet, I must.

Dinner is quiet except for the sound of the slap, over and over again in my head. Vernon is fretting so much, Marta's mashed potatoes don't even make him smile. Finch doesn't look up from her plate—I suspect her neck may be permanently fused this way from phone use.

Henry eats his food quickly and asks to be excused for bed. He looks genuinely sleepy, and I know he spent most of his day with Milorad starting to build the hothouse.

As I excuse myself from the table, Vernon says, "Sit down."

I sit.

He says, without looking at me, "I won't be teaching you anymore, Jane.

"You can do with your days what you like," he says. "But you must stay in your room and away from Henry. Forget Susan or any art classes. Forget suitors.

"Marta will send meals to your room. Until your little visitor from the school district comes, you're not going anywhere and no one is coming to see you either."

He gets up and walks into the foyer and then through the passage to the pool house. Finch looks at me and smiles. "You okay?"

I nod.

"If you need to talk, I'm here," she says.

"Sure," I say.

"Don't forget I'm on your team," she says.

"I won't." As if I'd fall for this old trick.

I get up and move to the kitchen, where Marta is measuring steel-cut oats into a slow cooker. She looks up and smiles.

"I'll make sure to put extra pecans on the side," she says.

"It's all very draconian."

"What time will you want breakfast?" Marta asks.

"Same as always."

"You get a week of vacation! Sleep in!"

"Do you think he'd let Gemma come over?"

"Definitely not," she says.

"Probably for the best," I say. "And how about nine? Seems right."

"I'll send it up right at nine," she says.

"I feel like I'm going to jail," I say.

"You're not," Marta says.

The back door opens. It's Vernon. He slams it closed quickly to keep the wind and cold out. "You're supposed to be in your room," he says.

"We were working out meal stuff," Marta says.

"If you're finished, go to your room," he says, not looking up as he walks into the study. "I don't want to see you."

Marta takes a deep breath. I decide six days in my room will be good for me. I will gather proof. I will write the opera. I will manifest a free mother. I will manifest a free Jane.

POSTMARKED JANUARY 8, 2025

A PICTURE OF A WHIMSICAL MACHINE IN THE MUSEUM TINGUELY

Dear Henry and Jane,

We're in Basel, Switzerland, now. It's such a cool place. One show here tonight and then to Salzburg. I hope you got the bulbs from the NL, Henry. Jane, I can't believe I've been away since October. I'll be home next for your birthday. I can't wait. Miss you both. Love, Mom

POSTMARKED JANUARY 10, 2025
A PICTURE OF THE MOZART MUSEUM

Dear Jane and Henry,
Salzburg is my favorite city. Not just because of all the music connections from Mozart to The Sound of Music *but because it's just so cool. The people here are great. And the food is delicious. I hope to bring you both here one day. Jane, I have found the ukulele, but I will bring it for your birthday. Henry, how's the hothouse coming along? I hope you can take me on a tour when I'm home in March. Love you, Mom*

SIX DAYS AND SIX NIGHTS

On night one, I look for movies from the year I was four and look for Mother running through the house toward the kitchen. Instead, I find other similar scenes . . .

03.15.2012 / Foyer / Mother sprints into the foyer and looks behind her. She is out of breath. Vernon can be heard approaching and she doesn't have time to unlock the door, so she exits through the other doorway, and into the downstairs hall. ➔ 07.04.2012 / Patio / Mother runs across the patio, takes a left at the pool fence, and hides behind the north wall of the pool house. Vernon arrives soon after, looks all directions, then doubles back. ➔ 09.10.2012 / Patio / Mother runs from the garage area to the back kitchen door. When she gets to the door, she pounds on it until Marta opens it.

None of them are the day I'm looking for, which is the alleged stabbing Vernon told Henry about, but the exercise of looking for it made me realize that I will never have enough time with Mother to actually show her all of these home movies. Some of the best ones are more than five minutes long, and the entire plan to show her overlooks the fact that she's confined to System. I decide to format my list differently—shorter snippets, rapid-fire—and call them mixtapes. I use the three of Mother being chased as my first one and title it "Chasing Mother."

The mixtapes get better as the days go on. Saturday, I gather fifteen instances of Finch telling me that Mother often told me I look ugly when I cry—fifteen. That's how much she tells this story, yet I still can't find the actual footage from when this happened. Then I find this:

07.30.2020 / Patio / "You tell me this story a lot. Were you there?" I ask. Finch answers, "Of course I was there." I ask, "Where did it happen?" She answers, "The study. Right by the French doors." And I look so skeptical. I don't remember being that skeptical. Age twelve. I am elated that I was that skeptical. I put it in the mixtape list and call it "Ugly Cryer Story" mixtape.

By Saturday night at 2:00 a.m., I have reviewed all footage of me and Mother in the study. No telling me I look ugly when I cry.

Sunday, I figure it's time to look at my birthdays. I've been saving my fifth for when I'm having a bad day because I know it was my best birthday. So, I start with 2009, the year I turned one.

I watch myself eat pieces of cake with my hands and smear icing on my face. Marta and Mother sing to me the loudest. Vernon seems to never take his hands off me, as if I'm some sort of home base and he's playing a game of tag.

I watch myself turn two, three, four, six, and seven, and I grow sleepy. It's a rainy January day and Marta sent a double-decker grilled cheese for lunch. I nap for four hours, wake up, eat half my dinner, then go back to sleep.

Monday, I decide to organize the opera. I am bored looking at my family being dysfunctional and weird.

On Tuesday and Wednesday, I add four new mixtapes to my list—my favorites are "Mina Doesn't Even Hurt Spiders"—10.24.2016 / Foyer / "Jane, open the front door quick! It's crawling up my arm!" ➔ 03.10.2017 / Patio / Mother unfolds a sweater and a fishing spider crawls out. "It's so big!" I say. ➔ 06.06.2021 / Patio / I scream upon seeing the size of the wolf spider Mother plucks out of her hoodie pocket. "Go find a new home, friend," she says. And "Vernon's Weird Love Similes"—02.13.2001 / Foyer / Vernon and Mother hold each other and while Mother smiles and hums a little, Vernon says, "I love you more than the sunrise loves the dew." ➔ 06.14.2006 / Sitting Room / "I love you like static loves sweaters." ➔ 09.17.2009 / Study / "I love you like flies love . . . uhh . . ." Mother finishes for him, "A carcass?" They laugh.

<pause>

Sometimes they look in love. It's very confusing.

<resume>

12.03.2012 / Sitting Room / "I love you like a whale loves plankton," he says. "Can you simply just say it?" Mother asks, a lazy smile on her face as she leans on his shoulder. Vernon scowls directly at the camera. "Am I not good enough again?" he asks. Mother sits up. "Vernon, please. I love you. I have always loved you just the way you are." Vernon continues to pout. "I do love you like dogs love chow or like mosquitoes love blood or how crickets love to sing," he says.

On Wednesday night, as I eat Marta's lasagna, I decide to look at recent home movies for fun. As I scroll through the last two months, I see Finch disappearing in the foyer after she says goodbye, disappearing in the sitting room when she's left alone. I see her appear twice, as well—poof!—out of the blue.

In one movie, where she suddenly appears on New Year's Eve

in the well-lit study, I stop the footage, rewind, and watch again. I enlarge the video on my iPad and look closely at the dark hardwood floor. I play it four times to make sure.

Listen. I do not lie to God. It's a rat.

And it's not just any rat either.

I save the snippets and time stamps, but I don't know what to title it yet because I don't know what it means. I call it "Shape-Shifter" mixtape for now.

I survive six days and six nights in my room. I feel a little isolated, but not much more than usual. I'm looking forward to the meeting tomorrow with whoever the school district sends, simply to see how Vernon handles it. I sleep like Marta roofied my dessert.

THURSDAY VISITORS

The meeting is in ten minutes and Vernon is dressed in a three-piece suit—his navy pinstripe with the tight legs. His pocket watch chain has been polished, as have his teeth. He even made Henry brush his hair—though Milorad has been tasked with keeping Henry busy this morning while the district representatives are here.

Vernon hasn't told me what to expect and he didn't share anything with me after he called them. I was able to watch the Home Movie yesterday, though, so I got his side of it.

HOME MOVIE—01.14.2025 (TWO DAYS AGO)

Vernon paces in the study. He stops to look through the back door window.

"Yes," he says, "I've been holding for Dr. Love."

He waits as the other person talks.

Nods.

Waits more.

"Ah, Dr. Love, it's brilliant to meet your acquaintance. I do wish I could have come into the building but these days I'm still trying to be careful."

Waits.

"Yes, of course."

Waits.

"I do appreciate your attention to detail on this matter," he says. "Of course I've sent my lesson plans already so you can see the type of work we're doing."

Waits with impatient look on his face.

"I opt the children out of all standardized tests, I'm afraid. I simply believe that teachers are better at telling me how my child is doing than a test. And I— Well yes, I know they haven't seen teachers in a few years but—"

Waits with his jaw jutted out.

"She'll still graduate," he says. "Those years of the school shutdown, they didn't even administer those tests anyway. Even the Keystone." Waits. "Oh. They did?" Waits. "Well, she can make that one up, right?"

Waits.

"Algebra shouldn't be a problem," he says, but if you look close enough at his forehead, you can see tiny beads of sweat forming. "No need for that. She'll do fine." Waits. "Though a tutor would also work. We can administer the test here, yes?"

Waits.

"Oh," he says. "Biology isn't something she's ready for, I don't think . . . but she might be."

<*pause*>

What a diabolically shitty liar Vernon is. The man hasn't even said the word *biology* to me. And I'm supposed to have passed a grade-level state-administered exam in it last year. And algebra the year before. And this spring—English. All I've done is repeat geography lessons for five years. I am braced for not graduating until I'm twenty, but at least I know where Eritrea is.

<*resume*>

"Okay. We'll talk about it then. Thank you."

Waits.

"Of course. I'll have it all ready for your people when they come to the house."

Waits.

"Indeed. A pleasure talking with you. Have a lovely day."

He presses the hang-up button, slams the receiver on my desk, and then gives it the finger with both hands.

<*stop*>

THURSDAY VISITORS (CONT'D)

"Why are you dressed like that?" Vernon asks as I come down the staircase into the dining room. I am wearing what I wear most days—leggings and a T-shirt with a sweater over top.

I note his pinstripes. "Not all of us are prepared for the queen."

He points back up the stairs. "Go change."

"Into what?" I ask. Then the door opens and I hear the *clip-clop* of high heels. I wait. It's Finch. Dressed up like she's some kind of—"What is that?" I ask.

"What is what?"

I gesture to her outfit, which is a garish yellow that makes her skin look gray. It's like someone dressed her to look like a short, squat Coco Chanel. What I really want to ask is *why are you here?*

"CHANGE!" Vernon yells. I run upstairs and look in my closet. I decide on the closest thing I have to dressy is an evening gown.

This one has sequins on it and the spaghetti straps pop my clavicles cleverly and I always considered it my Tony acceptance dress. I put it on and look at myself in the mirror and realize that if Gemma were here, she wouldn't let me through the door without makeup. Not in this dress.

I rummage through my makeup drawer and find my rub-on foundation and I rub it in. I throw on some stick blush and rub that in, too. The doorbell rings. I rush to get some eyeliner on, and Vernon says—quite kindly from the bottom of the steps—"Jane, we're ready for you." I decide against eye shadow or mascara, but I think it's a shortsighted decision. I hold my hair upside down and hair spray it for body, and then flip my head back up again.

Nailed it.

Shit. I don't have the right shoes. Shit. I do have the right shoes, but they're the skimpy little sandals I wore to the concert with handsy Todd from the library.

I hear Finch clomping around at the bottom of the steps. I hurry.

When I walk down the stairs, Vernon looks pleased at my choice. Finch's eyebrows are so high, they meet her hairline.

"Hello, Jane," a familiar-looking person says to me.

For the record, there are two of them here. The familiar one, a woman about the same age as Mother, who is wearing a pair of flowy pants, a black cardigan, and a pair of slip-on Doc Martens, and a very tall younger woman with stark black hair that hangs straight down her back. She's wearing a pink blouse and a pair of business trousers and black leather clogs—the kind nurses wear.

I shake their hands, and the familiar one says, "Do you remember me?"

I squint. "I do, but I don't know from where."

The tall one speaks. "I'm Dr. Love and this is Mrs. Constance. I'm the principal at the high school." She maintains eye contact.

These women have seen my ransom note. That's what her eye contact says to me.

Mrs. Constance says, "You remember me now?"

I give an embarrassed smile and shake my head slowly. "It's been a long time since I've been to a school," I say. "And I was in the elementary then!"

"It's okay," she says. "Not a big deal. I helped you every year when you were in the opt-out room."

I snap my fingers. "You're the one with the cool smelly markers!"

She smiles. "That's me!" She turns to Vernon, smiles, and says, "I'm the school social worker."

Then silence descends. They look at Vernon, who looks very nervous.

"Where's the best place to talk?"

Vernon shows everyone to the table in the study.

"This room has been my classroom since fifth grade," I say. I say it enthusiastically because I want Vernon to believe I didn't send the ransom note, and I'm also scared I'm about to get ratted out.

Dr. Principal asks Finch who she is and why she's here.

"Mina's sister," he says. "She may as well be Jane's mother."

I clear my throat in a sort of uvular reaction.

"Let's talk about what Jane's been learning this year," Mrs. Social Worker says.

Vernon pulls out his folder, which is now very organized and neat. It's also ten times bigger.

The meeting is boring.

The adults talk and I can't figure out why I'm in my Tony acceptance dress on a random Thursday afternoon in January. I look past the school representatives at the table and out the double doors to the garden. Henry told me this morning that it's supposed to snow today.

While Vernon argues his case, which is that he has rights and he's allowed to school me any way he wants, I daydream all of us are stuck here in a blizzard. I picture Dr. Love and Mrs. Constance eating Marta's mashed potatoes. I see them moving in and leaving their families for those potatoes. I write the song in my head, "Marta's Home-Wrecker Potatoes." Fast tempo, grueling bassline.

"Actually, Mr. Cook, Jane's rights are what's most important to us right now."

"She has a right to say something about this, doesn't she?" Vernon says. His voice is in the pitch of balls-caught-in-zipper. "Tell them, Jane! Tell them how well we're doing!"

I keep looking out the double doors for effect at first. "I love learning from Vernon. He's a really great teacher. I think if I had to pick a favorite teacher, it would be Vernon." I look at them, then. "I will admit to being a bold student, though. I often argue with him about missing the social aspects of school. I miss friends and classes and, well, whatever else happens in a high school. But never would I ever want to leave this room. Vernon keeps us safe here."

"Us?" Mrs. Social Worker asks.

"Me and Henry. My brother."

"Where's Henry now?"

"Out doing his science with Milorad, one of his tutors," I lie. I look at Vernon for validation, but he's too busy dabbing sweat from his forehead with a pink hanky.

Marta brings a pot of tea and a plate of her famous shortbread biscuits.

The school people decline and Finch insists. As she attempts to force a cup of tea on the principal, she wobbles on her high heels and spills tea down the front of her ridiculous yellow suit.

"Shit!" she says. Then looks at the women and says, "Sorry. This suit cost me a fortune." She makes her way out of the study and into the kitchen, where she can be heard snapping at Marta and then exiting through the side door. *Clop-clop-clop*. Her car starts. She disappears.

"Jane?"

"I'm sorry, I was daydreaming," I say quickly. Only when I listen back in my mind do I notice I sound terrified. Fast. Nervous.

"Mrs. Constance was asking if you're interested in any clubs," Dr. Love says.

"You can join even if you're homeschooled," Mrs. Constance adds.

I look at my hands. My brain answers in my head: *I WANT TO BE IN ALL THE CLUBS. PLEASE GET ME OUT OF HERE.*

"Jane isn't interested in public school clubs," Vernon says. "She's got hobbies here that keep her very busy."

"Oh! That's great to hear! What hobbies do you have, Jane?"

LYING TO THE PRINCIPAL

The only hobbies I have are my plan to free Mother and my punk opera, both of which are completely private. I try to think of things I like to do. I like to swim, and Gemma and I had back-dive contests last summer. Feels weird to mention because it's January. I like to escape and try to take walks until Milorad is sent to fetch me—can't use that.

"Vernon gets me suitors" is all I can think of to say before the silence grows too awkward.

I almost don't want to look at Vernon now.

"She loves music!" Vernon exclaims.

"Do you play an instrument?" Mrs. Social Worker says.

I nod. "I used to play the piano and I was to learn guitar but . . . that didn't work out."

"We have a huge music department!" Mrs. Social Worker says. "Do you sing?"

"I don't know," I answer.

"She's a talented singer like her mother," Vernon says.

"Where is Mrs. Cook?" Mrs. Social Worker asks.

"Placenta," I say. "Her name is Mina Placenta."

Both women look uncomfortable even though they know well my mother's name is Mina Placenta.

"Of course," she says. "Is she here?"

Vernon says, "She's in Barcelona today, I think. Has a show tonight there and then she flies to Rome."

"Do you get to see her a lot? On videophone?" Dr. Principal asks.

I open my mouth to say something honest.

Vernon says, "Every day, right, Jane?"

I stare at the tube in the corner. My staring at it makes them stare at it. Then they stare at me. And then back at the tube. Vernon keeps his eyes on us.

"Have we done all we need to do? It's time for school and I need to get to it," Vernon says. All three of us are staring at the tube, now.

Marta arrives through the swinging door. She sees us staring at the tube and grimaces. She collects the tray with the tea and shortbread—I grab the last one—and goes back to the kitchen without a word.

The principal has a very concerned look on her face. The divots in her frown lines are deep. The two of them get up from the table, and she says, "We'll review over the next few days and get back to you, Mr. Cook. Thank you for your time today."

"Of course," he says. "Thank you so much for caring about Jane and her studies."

When they leave, Vernon closes the door, his fake smile fades, and he walks right past me and toward the kitchen. I follow him. When I get there, he's mid-shot. Whiskey, I think. Marta is making him coffee and he pours a shot into that, too.

"Hot chocolate?" Marta asks.

"Sure. Thanks."

"Go change," she says. "Get comfy and I'll put this on your desk."

Vernon says, "No school today." He's deeply into his phone—from what I can see, he's reading texts.

"I have to start biology, remember?"

"We've waited this long. One more day won't matter."

"I can fill in," Marta says.

Vernon, still swimming in his phone messages, starts to walk out of the kitchen. "Whatever," he says to Marta's offer. "In two days, you'll wish you were still back here with us." And then he's gone.

FREE MOTHER / ACT TWO

ACT II, SCENE 4

INT. VANDERMAKER HOUSE / HENRY'S GREENHOUSE / FINCH'S WINDOW

MARTA and JANE sit in the study together with a biology textbook. HENRY is outside in his greenhouse, stage right. VERNON sits in the sitting room by the fire with his drink. He is texting. FINCH is in her apartment window, where she's been watching since she got home from the meeting.

Spotlight on Jane and Marta.

MARTA (holding textbook)

I think the best way to start is the book.

JANE

The idea of it is very daunting.

MARTA

I'm sorry you're in this position.

JANE

The idea of high school is almost haunting.

Spotlight on Vernon and Finch.

Vernon is sitting in his chair in the sitting room, next to a roaring fire, typing furiously on his phone. Finch is in her apartment, facing the window up-lit in the drop.

VERNON (drinking from crystal glass between texts)

I need help! Can't anyone see I need help?

FINCH

If you'd listened to me in the first place, you'd have everything now.

Vernon slams his phone down and gets up and walks to the fireplace. He takes off his pinstripe waistcoat and throws it violently onto the couch. He returns to his chair and picks up his phone again.

VERNON
What you suggested was impossible.

FINCH
People do it all the time.

VERNON
Not me. I can't do that.

FINCH
You can do anything.

VERNON
Not that!

FINCH
You've already put the tubes inside her head. What difference would it make if she was dead?

Sudden blackout.
Then lights fade up on

INT. JANE'S ROOM

Marta and Jane finish their studies. Jane walks to her bedroom. She sits on her en suite floor wrapped in a blanket, retrieves the tablet from its hiding place. "Waiting for Jane" starts slowly.

JANE (sings)
I DON'T EVEN KNOW ANYMORE
WHAT I'M SUPPOSED TO BE LOOKING FOR.
PROOF OF ALL THAT VERNON IS
LIES IN EVERYTHING HE EVER DID.

Vernon drinks heavily in the sitting room while texting. Finch is in her small apartment overlooking the house, and she texts when Vernon isn't texting—filling in the conversation. Marta is in the kitchen, making dough. She sings in reply to Jane's verse.

MARTA
THIS IS TOO MUCH AND HAS TO END.
THESE CHILDREN NEED A REST.
HOW CAN I CALL MYSELF A FRIEND
AND KEEP ALL THESE SECRETS IN MY CHEST?

BLACKOUT

Song: "Waiting for Jane" (Ballad)

Characters get in places for "Waiting for Jane": Vernon in

the study instructing Henry, sitting at his desk, Jane is also sitting at her desk.

Lights slowly fade up once all are in place.

Note for cast and crew:

Prop: large Earth/globe disco ball, with a spotlight on one side representing the sun, slowly spins to represent days passing.

Nighttime is represented by the lights dimming down, Jane and Henry lie their heads on their desks, then it repeats. Vernon teaches while the kids work, then the kids leave (Henry to the garden / Jane to her en suite) and Vernon pours himself a drink from the liquor cabinet.

As the globe spins, they repeat these movements.

Marta is in the kitchen making food. MILORAD is either chasing the escaped rat or tinkering with the car or doing something in the garden. Finch appears and disappears in her window overlooking the house, the light in her apartment going on and off.

After three rotations, Jane splits away from this action and walks front stage.

Henry, Vernon, Marta, and Milorad continue to rhythmically pass time, then Henry, Marta, and Vernon slowly make their way to the sitting room. Milorad stays near the car, stage left. Jane, center stage, sings:

JANE

THE DAYS ARE SHORT IN WINTER AND THE AIR IS CHILLY COLD.
NOTHING SEEMS TO MAKE ME HAPPY; EVERYTHING FEELS OLD.

MY BROTHER DOESN'T UNDERSTAND THAT WE ARE BEING USED
ON ACCOUNT OF HOW OUR FATHER'S MIND IS CLEARLY VERY BRUISED.

THE NIGHTS ARE LONGER IN MY BED; LOVE SEEMS ALL BUT LOST.
THE TIME I SPEND INSPECTING HAS QUITE A DREARY COST.

I DON'T KNOW WHAT I'M GOING TO DO.
I NEVER THOUGHT I'D BE SAVING YOU.

Jane dances toward sitting room.

JANE (CONT'D)

I'M WAITING FOR JANE—THAT'S ME.
I'M WAITING FOR SOMETHING THAT MAKES SENSE.
I'M WAITING FOR JANE—SHE'S HERE.
AND SHE'S FROZEN IN SUSPENSE.

WHO WILL I BE?
WHERE WILL I GO?
MY DESTINY?
HOW CAN I KNOW?

All cast but Milorad in sitting room. Jane stands in front of the fire reading from a piece of paper. Milorad is in the driver's seat of the car, stage left.

JANE (CONT'D)

WHEN THE LETTER COMES, IT'S ME WHO DOES THE READING.
VERNON INVITES EVERYONE AND PROVIDES THE COZY SEATING.

MOTHER JOINS US THROUGH THE SCREEN OF VERNON'S PHONE.
IN HER EYES A MIX OF PRIDE AND SADNESS SHONE.

I AM MADE TO STAND IN FRONT OF MARTA'S FIRE.
I AM MADE TO MAKE MYSELF INTO A LIAR.

WHEN I READ THE WORDS ABOUT HOW I'M EXPECTED BACK AT SCHOOL
I THROW MYSELF IN MARTA'S ARMS; CRY EVERY MOLECULE . . . OF JANE!

Jane holds that note of "Jane" and spins/dances toward the car at stage left.

JANE (CONT'D)

I'M WAITING FOR JANE—THAT'S ME.
I'M WAITING FOR SOMETHING THAT MAKES SENSE.
I'M WAITING FOR JANE—SHE'S HERE.
AND SHE'S FROZEN IN SUSPENSE.

Jane sings the questions toward Milorad, who is holding the car door open for Jane.

JANE (CONT'D)

WHO WILL I BE?
WHERE WILL I GO?
MY DESTINY?
HOW CAN I KNOW?

Jane and Milorad in the car. Vernon still sits in his sitting room chair. Marta is in the kitchen. Henry is in the greenhouse.

JANE (CONT'D)

THE NEXT DAY MILORAD PUTS ME IN THE CAR.
HE TELLS ME I DON'T NEED A COAT; WE AREN'T GOING VERY FAR.
MY FATHER HAS GIVEN HIM DETAILED INSTRUCTION

VERNON

BUY CLOTHES FOR SCHOOL AND DON'T MAKE A BIG PRODUCTION.

JANE

MILO LETS ME BUY TWO HUNDRED DOLLARS' WORTH OF SECONDHAND

A PLACE THAT FATHER'D NEVER GO; I LOOK LIKE I'M IN MOTHER'S BAND

Jane exits car and spins back to center stage. Vernon is in the sitting room with his fancy crystal liquor set, drinking to the beat. Henry is in his greenhouse, stage right, and is drinking liquor the same way Vernon drinks. Fast and in rhythm.

JANE (CONT'D)

I'M WAITING FOR JANE—THAT'S ME.
I'M WAITING FOR SOMETHING THAT MAKES SENSE.
I'M WAITING FOR JANE—SHE'S HERE.
AND SHE'S FROZEN IN SUSPENSE.
WHO WILL I BE?
WHERE WILL I GO?
MY DESTINY?
WHEN WILL I KNOW?

Jane looks back and forth between Vernon sitting in his chair drinking, and the empty plastic tube.

JANE (CONT'D) (quietly)
IF I'M TO LEAVE
TO FIND REPRIEVE
IF I KNOW HOW,
WHO AM I NOW?

VERNON (angrily)
Jane!

JANE
WHO AM I NOW?

MARTA (sadly)
Jane.

JANE
WHO AM I NOW?

HENRY (shamefully, while he sips another drink)
Jane!

JANE
WHO AM I NOW?

POSTMARKED JANUARY 11, 2025

A PAINTING OF A WOMAN STANDING ALONE IN A FIELD OF SUNFLOWERS

Dear Vernon,

Please let me know if these postcards are getting to you. I've sent so many and not even a text have I gotten in reply. I look forward to coming home in March and talking with you about our family. Love, Mina

LESSON SEVEN: THE BIOLOGY OF HIGH SCHOOL

Today is Monday, January 27, 2025

I AM SURPRISINGLY NOT NERVOUS AT ALL.

Not nearly as nervous as I was eating breakfast this morning, dreading Vernon's arrival. But of course, he never arrived. Milorad and I leave while it's still dark—I don't think I've ever been so happy to be up, dressed, and in the car at 6:50 a.m.

"You have everything you need?" Milorad asks.

"Yep."

"Seat heater is on for you," he says.

"Thanks!"

"You can call me anytime and I will come get you. Okay? You can always just come home."

"Thanks, Milo."

"I am scared for you."

"There's no reason to be scared," I say.

Silence drops between us as he chews on this. Then he says, "If anyone with gun starts to shoot, run. Don't listen to people who tell you to not run. Just run. As fast as you can. Toward home, yes?"

"Oh my God," I say.

"It is realistic fear."

"Let's not, okay? I just want to have a normal life. Even if it means I have to get shot for going to school."

Milorad slowly shakes his head.

I give my attention to the pleats in my plaid Britney skirt. I made sure it passes dress code by wearing it low, so it's not technically a Britney skirt, more like a Christian school skirt, but it completes the look. It's cold, so I have on my favorite cashmere, too-loose sweater and a big tee under it, the plaid skirt and a pair of ripped up leggings. Combat boots. Of course. Marta's inner-zip Army-issue. Of course. *Punk Rock Jane Goes to High School.*

In my backpack are three things: a spiral notebook; a school-requested specific type of calculator that I don't fully understand; and my sketchbook, which contains my coded list of home movies, mixtapes, my opera, and my sketches, which are getting better despite my lack of art tuition.

I'm still not scared when Milorad stops the car in front of Dutch Valley High School. He chooses the center of the bus circle as my drop-off spot and the other parents in the queue are not appreciating that at all. *Punk Rock Jane and Your Angry Parents.*

Milorad hands me a phone. My eyebrows go through the stratosphere.

"It is old phone," he says, "and I have it connected just for your school days to my own account. It is not possible for you to have it at home, but it will be our secret, yes? You call me if you need help. I mean it."

I jump over the center console where Milorad's coffee has been getting cold and hug him. I hope he comes to parent-teacher conferences, too.

HOMEROOM

I'm still not scared as I approach the office to pick up my helper. They were explicit in the letter. "*You must have your helper with you at all times.*" Vernon got a kick out of that.

"Sounds like you won't be allowed to wander off there either," he said.

He has no idea how much better this place already is compared to Vernon's Pandemic Prison School. First thing: There are schoolchildren in it. Second: There are teachers in it. Fact: I am probably about to have my ass kicked by every single class I walk into. Also fact: I'm still not scared.

"Are you Jane?" someone says the second I walk into the office. She's behind me, sitting in one of the chairs.

"Guilty as charged." I turn around and make a small bow.

"Hi!" she says, getting up and waving. Her grin is enormous. She doesn't say anything else.

"Hi," I say.

She hands me my schedule, which I already have a copy of in my bag, and says, "Let's go to homeroom."

As we walk through the halls, she tells me tricks on how to remember where I am. Each hall is associated with a color. Our trip to homeroom is Blue ➔ Yellow ➔ White. We land in a classroom decorated with grammar posters. One is dedicated entirely to literary insults.

My helper says, "Do you have a school map?"

"What's your name?" I ask. I pull my school map out of my bag.

"Addi," she says. "Shit. Sorry I didn't tell you that before. I was nervous."

"So—first class is biology," I say.

"Right. Can you see how to get there from here?" She points to my map with a shaky finger.

"Wait," I say. "Why are *you* nervous?"

The teacher walks in then. She's about thirty and wearing what looks to be a sort of jumpsuit. Like the kind car mechanics wear, just more fashionable.

I want to look at my map and answer Addi's question about how to get to biology, but I'm getting a vibe from this teacher. I can't take my eyes off her. I do, and I look around the room. She has a Pride flag and other flags that I don't recognize around the room. She also has a bunch of posters with rainbow sayings on them. The usual ones you see about how love is love and no human is illegal, and one that says DIVERSE, INCLUSIVE, ACCEPTING, WELCOMING, SAFE SPACE FOR EVERYONE along the rainbow.

My favorite so far, though, is a framed one. It looks like it was handmade. It says, YOU ARE NOT A BURDEN over and over again, and the background is pink, light blue, and white.

"She only got permission to put that back up last week," Addi whispers, pointing to the safe-space rainbow.

"It's great."

"She's the GSA advisor."

I nod and have a vague idea what she's saying, but I was last in school as an eleven-year-old fifth grader. Back then it was mostly about trying to get on the playground first for recess.

The teacher walks over to my desk and I smile.

She shakes my hand. "It's nice to meet you, Jane. I'm Miss Wilde, she/her, and I'm glad you're here." She looks to Addi. "Did you show Jane to the nearest restrooms and other places like that?"

"Not yet," Addi answers. "She has a study hall during Flex so I'll show her around then."

"Okay. But, Jane, in case you need to know, the nearest girls' restroom is the next door to the left as you walk out this door. There's an all-gender bathroom about ten feet beyond that."

"Thanks," I say.

"No problem." She puts her fist sideways on her heart and taps it twice, just like Mother used to do. Marta does it, too.

"She's a huge fan," Addi whispers.

And now I understand. It's not me making Addi nervous. It's my mom.

As I stand silently for the Pledge of Allegiance and sit through the morning announcements, I realize that I am Mina Placenta's daughter, and here, unlike in my house, this is actually a good thing. I am out in the world now where there is a network of Placenta fans that will help me find my way. Addi is one of them. Miss Wilde is another.

INTRODUCTION

Miss Wilde raises her hand in the front of the classroom when the announcements end. The room goes quiet after a burst of talking.

"Before you all go on with your days, I want you to welcome a new student." She looks at me and raises her eyebrows. I turn around and wave in a few directions, but don't say anything. "This is Jane Cook. Jane, introduce yourself and tell us where you've been and what you like."

I stand. "I'm Jane and I've been homeschooled since the pandemic. I knew some of you in elementary school. I left in fifth grade." I start to sit down.

"Do you have any hobbies?" someone asks.

I stand again. "I like jigsaw puzzles." This is not a lie, but it's a curious answer. I haven't done a jigsaw puzzle since I was nine.

"Do you play music?" Miss Wilde asks.

I nod. "I used to. But now I'm writing an opera. A punk opera."

"A composer!" Miss Wilde says.

"Just lyrics," I say. "Not the music."

She gives me a look like she's impressed. "A librettist!"

Then the bell rings and Addi hands me my book bag.

When kids walk past me on their way out the door, they say nice things. *Welcome to Valley, Nice to meet you, Have a nice day, If you need any help, let me know . . . Holy shit, Jane, where the fuck have you been?*

That's Gretchen Brown. She hugs me.

"Dude! It's so good to see you," I answer.

She sees my schedule in my hand and snatches it. Addi gasps and we both look at her like she should calm down.

"You have bio? Why do you have bio?" Gretchen asks.

"Long story," I say.

"Are you a sophomore or a freshman?"

"Kinda in between, I think? We'll know more in a few weeks."

Gretchen frowns with concern. "What did they do to you?"

The three of us walk toward the science wing. White ➔ Yellow ➔ Green. Gretchen starts a monologue worthy of a Broadway voice-over.

"I don't even know where to start," she says. "You missed middle school completely and you have no idea how lucky you are. My mom got me the worst hairstyle for eighth grade I can't even explain to you what it was like to have to walk around with that shit happening on top of the crazy eighties stuff she bought me to wear. I'd told her the eighties were in and she took it way too far. Classic my mom, you know?"

I think about the koi pond in her foyer.

"Freshman year I dated Ron Smith. Do you remember Ron? He didn't say much when we were in elementary school. Quiet and liked to play basketball at recess. Not sure if you guys even knew each other," she goes on. "But he loves punk so he knows all about your mom. His dad takes him to shows. Oh shit, yeah! His dad went to school with your mom! Anyway, we broke up in May of freshman year. He wanted me to do stuff I didn't want to do and I'm no slut, you know?"

Addi says, "Make sure you notice where this right turn is. It's easy to miss." We glide into the green hallway.

"Don't use that word," I say to Gretchen. "That's how women hurt each other."

"Shit," Gretchen says, nodding slowly.

We all stop walking on Addi's cue.

"Sorry," I say, "but you don't have to be a slut to want to *go there* as a sophomore. Everybody is different. Right? No shame in you not wanting to do what some others do. And if Rob dumped you for—"

"Ron," she corrects.

"Ron. If he dumped you for some girl who's more willing, then he wasn't worth your time anyway. It's not her fault for being active. Or yours for being not as active. It's up to Rob. Ron. Shit. Whatever his name is."

"Damn, you're, like, a philosopher," Gretchen says, smiling. "High five!" She holds her hand up for a high five and I give it to her as Addi pulls me back toward the biology classroom door.

We walk in, Addi tells the bio teacher that I'm here, and he motions to some seats in the front row to his right. We sit. I brace myself. It's January. I'm not sure how to slot into my first-ever biology class halfway through the year, but the best way is to be open-minded, I guess.

BIOLOGY / GEOMETRY / LUNCH

I have chosen an interesting day to drop cold into this biology class. It's a lab class and I have zero idea of what they're doing, or the words they use to describe it once I ask what they're doing, and pretty much everything else. The teacher, Mr. Long, mentions twice that we will be doing a dissection next week. I am absolutely out of my depth, and for some reason, I find it exciting.

Next is geometry, Green ➔ Yellow ➔ Orange, which is doable, and then language arts, Orange ➔ Yellow ➔ White, where we're starting a book called *Long Way Down* by Jason Reynolds next week. Then PE class, White ➔ Red, which I don't have to do today because I have no idea what to do in a PE course that doesn't involve a parachute or those little scooter carts we'd push ourselves around on in elementary school.

Lunch is tragic. Red ➔ Yellow ➔ Blue. When I went to elementary school, I took a brown bag and ate what Marta made for me. This is totally different. Marta didn't make me anything today because Vernon wouldn't allow it.

I maneuver my way through the line and land at a table with strangers, staring at an apple, a plate with a "wrap" on it. I note that I only have fifteen minutes to eat once I sit down, so I pick it up and start eating. The lady said it was ham and cheese and it is, but I'm pretty sure the cheese is made out of plastic. It doesn't taste like cheese.

"Jane!"

I look up.

Gretchen Brown waves me over to her table, pointing to a small empty space she carved out of her friend group.

The strangers at my table are debating something that has to do with school sports—I'm not even sure what sport—and haven't noticed me at all. By the time I sit down next to Gretchen and say hello and smile, I am socially exhausted and now have only eleven minutes to eat lunch.

"You have a bit of—uh." I don't know her name—she's the one who was sitting here before I stole her spot. She points to her teeth.

"Soggy wrap," I say. Then I swish my spit around and feel a huge chunk of plastic cheese-like gunk flush from between my teeth.

"They sell bento boxes at the Wawa," Gretchen says.

"Who eats gas station sushi?" someone asks.

I stare at the ham-and-cheese wrap and I am too hungry to not eat it. So I eat it. In big bites, while blocking out all the chatter about gas station sushi. I can't hear myself think. In elementary school, we were chaperoned and told to keep the noise down. We didn't have to be silent, but we had to behave. High school is the opposite. This place is mayhem.

Gretchen is talking about the V-Day dance.

"You remember KZ, right?" She points and I look and the kid looks familiar, but I can't make out their face.

"Nice to see you again," they say. Then they whisper their dead name and "they/them" into my ear. I look again when they pull back.

"My kickball homie!" I say.

KZ offers a very chill fist bump.

"Is Porter here, too?" I ask, and I take a huge bite out of my apple and chew. I have no idea how a school can make an apple taste bad, but they did. This apple sucks.

I put it on the plate.

"Dude!" Porter says from right next to Gretchen. And there we all are—the four wild ones from elementary school, queens of the kickball field—together again at a table, now being circled by boys trying to get a look at me. It's gross.

"Fresh meat," the girl to my right says.

"Blood. Fresh *blood*," Gretchen says.

"Same difference!"

I get up to clear my tray and then grab my backpack and say goodbye. Addi joins me as if she's been watching me all this time.

As I walk away, Gretchen Brown yells, "Wait!"

I turn.

She points to three guys at the table who are smiling at me. "Which one?"

I shake my head.

"Come on!" she says, as I walk away.

I clear all the pieces of my lunch to the place they belong and shove my tray into the conveyor belt tunnel. I peek in, expecting to see the end and see a happy dishwasher, but the tunnel seems to go forever. Part of me wants to jump on the belt to find out where it takes me. All of me hopes it's a place that is not a heteronormative nightmare like what just happened. I thought high school would be cooler about that stuff, especially after Miss Wilde's rainbow homeroom.

LIBRARY / HISTORY / TENNIS COURTS

I feel almost famous by the end of the day. The fresh meat phenomenon is in full swing. At the beginning of each class, I'm briefly introduced and I can feel the eyes on me. Not just the regular eyes. The fresh meat eyes. Not fresh blood at all.

For reference: fresh meat = new target of lust or interest, and fresh blood = person who brings a new way of thinking. No one has asked me what I think about anything.

A kid in my library study hall leans into my ear when I'm deep into using the computer. "Are you going to that dance?"

I answer, "I literally started school here six hours ago."

"I'm Marlon," he says.

"I'm Jane."

"Oh, I know who you are." He smiles and laughs a little. "Everybody knows who you are."

"Wow, Marlon. Way to be creepy to the new girl on her first day."

"Shit, no. I didn't mean it that way." He backs up a whole step.

"Just giving you a hard time," I say. I go back to the computer.

"Are you really writing an opera?" he asks.

"I am."

"Can I be in it?" he asks.

"Sure."

He looks at me like I'm a puzzle. "So, are you going to the dance or what?"

I look at him and drop my head to the left. "Again. I literally started school here six hours ago."

He nods and walks away.

I go back to the library computer, where I have typed my mother's name into the Google search bar. I scroll through the articles and other links. I open the band's official site. Then her Wikipedia page. And apparently, she once had a Twitter account. The school computer won't allow me on any social media, but I scroll through the Google list of @MinaPlacenta's old tweets and they're mostly about domestic violence, sex trafficking, and helpline numbers. Interspersed are tweets and retweets about other punk bands, her shows, and tour dates.

Her profile picture is a black and white of her onstage when she was just starting out. She barely looks like herself. She looks like me. Her header picture is the cover of *Run, Jane, Run*, which is an ethereal sort of shot that I can't figure out. It looks like the ceiling of a big warehouse but spray-painted white.

"Whatcha doin'?" It's Marlon again. "Are you on Twitter? I thought that shit was long gone."

"I'm on Google, I think." I shrug.

This is what I see on the screen:

> **@MinaPlacenta January 1, 2019 Stop believing that the only definition of a good life is one that is uncomplicated and without villains.**

"What's that mean?" I ask Marlon, pointing to the small graphic of a pushpin.

"It's pinned," he says. "They want to keep it on top for people to see."

I look back at her quote. *Stop believing that the only definition of a good life is one that is uncomplicated and without villains.* I look at the date. *January 1, 2019.* Day one of The Great Ignoring. I scroll more. I find a tweet from only a month ago. From around Christmas.

> **@MinaPlacenta December 27, 2024 Don't feel embarrassed for loving someone who treats you poorly. Love isn't anything to be ashamed of. Treating others poorly is.**

Marlon says, "I'd never treat you bad."

I forgot he was here. "Of course," I say.

"The dance," he says. "Consider it."

"Noted," I answer, as he walks away.

I'm so stuck into the *Rolling Stone* article about *Run, Jane Run*, the bell rings and a little part of me jumps.

I walk to history class in a daze. Addi guides me. Orange ➔ Yellow ➔ White. I just learned more about my mother from the internet than I ever have from inside my house.

I don't remember any of history class.

After history class, the final bell rings. Addi guides me back to my locker, which is also in the White hallway. I give her a high five and release her from my service.

"I can find my way to the front doors from here," I say. "Thanks for today. You really helped me."

"No problem. See you tomorrow!" she says with a small wave.

Milorad said he'd meet me out front, and I forgot he even gave me a phone until I'm at my locker. I find it on the bottom of my backpack and open the home screen. It lights up with texts. They are all from Milorad.

Have a great day at school!

You can do anything you put your mind to!

Don't worry—you will feel at home there in about two weeks.

If you get lost, ask for help!

Are you having a good day?

What did you eat for lunch?

I will be outside the front doors at 3pm. ☺

When I walk outside, Milorad is not in front of the school like he promised. The whole area is filled with yellow school buses. I look at the visitor's parking area and I don't see the car there either.

I take my backpack off my back and find my phone again. There is a text from Milorad.

Walk from front of building all the way to end of walkway. Across street is tennis courts. I am parked there.

I follow his directions. Someone yells, "Hey, new girl!" out of a bus window. "I liked your answer in Rothenberg's class!"

I keep walking and smile. It was a good answer and it made Rothenberg say, "I think you're going to fit in here just fine, Jane."

When I get to the street and look across, I expect to see Milorad parked on the street next to the tennis courts. But he is parked literally *on* the tennis courts. Some other students are pointing at him and saying stuff. I panic and fast-walk to the passenger side door, get in, and say, "You have to get off the tennis courts. You can't park here."

"I did not know about the bus situation!"

"I know. Come on. Let's go."

"Seat belt."

"Just go and I'll get it on."

He waits until I have it on.

"Give phone back," he says.

I give him his phone back.

When I get home, Vernon stops me at the door and asks for my school-provided computer. He puts it into a small safe and scrambles the lock.

"How am I supposed to do my homework?" I ask.

He shrugs and walks into the kitchen.

POSTMARKED JANUARY 22, 2025

A PICTURE OF THE DRAGON BRIDGE IN LJUBLJANA, SLOVENIA

Dear All,

This is now one of my favorite cities in the world. Ljubljana is so hip! Our shows in Austria were good, but not as good as Amsterdam/Antwerp. Vienna was a bummer. The crowd was really stiff—just like the Baroness Schraeder from The Sound of Music. ☺

It was really great to see your faces the other day when you called. Jane, how is school working out? I hope you have an easy time. If not, know you have choices. We can always find a good school for you nearby if you don't like this option. Henry, I hope algebra is a bit easier now that we arranged a tutor. Love to you all, Mina/Mom

DAY TWO

Addi meets me in the office again. She's perky. I match it. A random secretary waves at me from behind the big desk. I wave back. I hear a familiar whirring noise from somewhere in the office, but I know it can't be what I think it is.

"I need to stop here," I say when we're outside the bathroom where Gretchen Brown told me to meet her.

We walk in together, but then Addi turns and says, "I'll wait outside."

Gretchen and KZ are here, putting on eyeliner in the big mirror above the sinks. "I can't believe that shit," Gretchen says.

"Hey, Jane," KZ says.

Gretchen nods. "But seriously. I'm going to refuse to take it."

"Hey," I say. "What are you refusing?"

"Some mental health quiz they want to give us," Gretchen says.

"It's supposed to help them figure out if we need more help than the exactly zero help we get in this place," KZ says.

I pull out my makeup bag and start with eyeshadow.

"It's bullshit," Gretchen says. "Like—why offer a screening if they can't actually help with the result of said screening?"

"What color shadow do you think would look good with this?" I ask.

They look at me.

"You can get away with anything."

"Yeah, you're gorgeous, you know," KZ says.

They go back to talking about the mental health quiz. I decide on yellow and red shadow. Bold, but it matches my yellow-tartan-pants vibe. KZ shifts the topic to how they don't know what they want to do with their life. Gretchen agrees and adds, "If I marry rich, it could work out really well." They look at me.

"I require enough time in artistic seclusion to express my full disdain for the origin of this query," I say, dipping my head in Victorian respect as if I was asking them a favor. They find it funny and I'm relieved because the Victorian Jane act has never left my house before and when it was coming out of my mouth, it sounded prissy.

"But serious, like—how are any of us supposed to know what to do with our lives?" Gretchen says.

"Capitalism will be picking meat off our bones by the time we're thirty," KZ says.

"Jesus fucking Christ!" someone says as they enter the bathroom. It's Porter—the best kickball shortstop you ever saw.

"Where have you been?" KZ asks.

"What happened to your hair?" Gretchen adds.

Porter throws her stuff on the floor and puts her face close to the mirror and breathes on it until there's steam enough for her to write *Got laid* in the steam.

"Whaaaat?"

"Giiirl!"

I stay quiet. I don't know what to think about Porter getting laid. Last time I hung out with Porter, we were gluing macaroni to pieces of cardboard in fifth grade art class.

"It's seven thirty in the morning!" Gretchen says.

"My dad dropped me off at six," Porter says. "And my mom thinks I'm at the gym."

"Wait," KZ says. "You legit had sex *this morning*?"

Porter nods with her eyes closed. Gretchen and KZ grill her on details and she says she's not sharing. She's mid-mascara when KZ says, "You're so lucky to have parents who hate each other."

LUNCH / REGRETS

By the time lunch comes, I am thoroughly regretting my decision to send the ransom note to the school district. Biology is a monster. I will need a tutor as soon as possible. Geometry is doable but so boring my eyelids flutter the minute I sit down. By the time lunch comes, I feel a deep need for Marta's espresso. At least I was allowed to bring a packed lunch.

There are approximately nine boys shark-circling our table, eyes on me.

"This whole fresh meat thing is getting old," I say at lunch.

"You can tell them to fuck off," KZ says.

"Or pick one," Porter says.

I go back to eating my Cornish pasty—homemade from Marta who is trying new fillings. Today is chicken, leek, and potatoes done in some magical cheesy way. Not magical enough to help me tell my friends that I do not like boys, though.

Gretchen tells a girl I never saw before about how I'm Mina Placenta's kid. The girl says, "Who?"

"Placenta?" Gretchen says, in a tone like the girl is a dolt for not knowing. Accurate.

The two of them look at me. I wave and go back to reading my mother's old Twitter feed, which I located only this morning on Milorad's emergency phone. She's completely badass.

@MINA_PLACENTA: ABORTION IS HEALTHCARE. MOTHERS ARE DYING.

@MINA_PLACENTA: FORCING 11-YEAR-OLD RAPE VICTIMS TO GIVE BIRTH IS THE NEW PORN. YOUR SENATORS ARE JACKING OFF TO IT ON YOUR TAX DOLLARS!

@MINA_PLACENTA: NO ONE SHOULD HAVE TO PAY TO BLEED. MENSTRUATION RELIEF NOW!

@MINA_PLACENTA: I guess I should plug the new record. [link to and picture of *Run, Jane, Run*.]

I stare at the album cover again. The white steampunk feel. The nondescript feeling of the same System Mother has lived in since December 2018.

The boys circling the table have asked Gretchen if I am free tomorrow night, as if she's a booking agent of some sort. One of them leans in to sniff my hair.

"Fuck off!" I snap.

The lunch teacher on duty walks by when I say this. We meet eyes. She gives me a thumbs-up.

An hour later I'm in Rothenberg's history class and he's talking about the Enlightenment and no one in the room is talking about anything but Europe and Europeans, and yet they keep saying *the world* when they answer. Like *the world was experiencing an increase in culture and education.* I raise my hand.

"We need to stop saying *the world* was experiencing the Enlightenment. It was only rich Europeans. The rest of the world was dealing with terrible things, really."

Everything goes still.

And then the bell rings and no one even cares what I said except Rothenberg who fist-bumps me on the way out the door, and says, "Nice!"

ACT II, SCENE 6

The library is quiet and Marlon is nowhere to be found, so I find a corner, sit down, and write what comes to me. Sometimes when I write the opera, it comes out as a film script. This song won't work as is, but that's what revision is for. Or maybe I can create the illusion of a pool center stage.

Song: "Actual School"

Composer notes: *This is a fast punk number. Mostly screaming. Tight drum and bass, with a slight ska or reggae feel.*

INT. VARIOUS SCHOOL HALLWAYS, THEN THE POOL (final verse)

The BAND is wearing inflatable pool arm floaties and swimming rings around their hips.

JANE

THIS PLACE IS FULL OF PEOPLE WHO JUST DON'T CARE.
THIS PLACE IS FULL OF PUSSIES WHO'D NEVER DARE
TO BE UNLIKE THE COOKIE CUTTER BREAD AND BUTTER
EVERY OTHER SCHOOL, AND THEY STILL WANT US TO
THINK OF THEM AS COOL.

THIS PLACE HAS BELLS AND BELLS AND BELLS AND
BELLS AND BELLS
A THOUSAND POTENTIAL MURDERERS AND HUNDRED
DIFFERENT HELLS.
THIS PLACE HAS NOTHING NEW AND NOTHING OLD AND
EVERYTHING
IT'S GOT EVERYTHING YOU NEVER WANTED TO KNOW.

DON'T WANNA BE A FOOL?
DON'T GO TO ACTUAL SCHOOL.
DON'T WANNA BE A DOLT?
REJECT THIS STUPID CULT.

(Fast guitar solo)

JANE

THIS PLACE IS FULL OF YOU PRETENDING TO BE YOUR
PARENTS
AS IF YOU DIDN'T NOTICE CHILDHOOD'S CLEVER
DISAPPEARANCE
AND DESCENT INTO A CHAOTIC SERIES OF QUESTIONS
YOU CAN'T ANSWER
STOP PRETENDING YOU KNOW WHAT I MEAN; YOUR
NODDING HEAD WILL CAUSE YOU CANCER.

THIS PLACE IS ALMOST OVER; THEY'VE REMOVED THE BOOKS AND TEACHERS

MAY AS WELL CALL IT CHURCH AND BRING IN THE FUCKING PREACHERS.

THROW ALL THE OTHER LEARNING SHIT INTO THE INDOOR SWIMMING POOL

BECAUSE THAT'S WHAT YOU GET AT ACTUAL FUCKING SCHOOL.

Song ends with a fast and tight outro.

JANE and her bandmates all jump into the pool. Her mascara and liner run the whole way down her face and neck while she screams in the foreground while the band plays beach ball volleyball behind her.

ADDI comes through the door and tries to get Jane's attention so she can take her to the next class.

ADDI

By the time Addi walks my weary body toward my locker at the end of the day, I want to cry. All this reading about Mother makes me miss her more.

"You're doing great!" Addi says.

"I didn't understand eighty percent of what was said today."

"It'll get better," she says.

I open my locker and feel like climbing in rather than taking out my coat and putting it on and filling my backpack with homework stuff. Addi helps me and tells me again that it will get better.

As I walk toward the road where Milorad and I agreed to meet, I pull out the cellphone he gave me again this morning.

Have a good day at school!

I am having a Cornish pasty as well for lunch! followed by a goofy picture of him and Marta eating lunch together.

It will take a few weeks to feel comfortable, do not worry!

I will be at our meeting spot early!

When I can see our meeting spot, he is standing outside the car, even though it's below freezing. He walks to my side and opens the door for me and I get in. When I do, I find Henry in the back seat with me. When Milorad arrives back in the driver's seat, he gives me a look like he wants to cheer me up.

I hand him his phone, and he says, "Let's get some ice cream!"

WHO IS BRUTUS TODAY?

INTERMISSION

AN AUDIENCE NEVER KNOWS what's really going on behind the scenes. It's one of the most delicious things about human beings. You could sell them a car without tires during anything that feels like a break. They're so blinded by the houselights, they'll believe you love them, when in reality, you could be trying to kill them.

Humans are easy to fool because they're tired all the time. The more tired they get, the easier it is to control them.

For example, no one has realized yet that I am so much more than a rat who chases my tail and makes them laugh. I am a world traveler. A jack-of-all-trades. I am the villain in this story twice over—shape-shifters have all the fun.

Out of a million crimes, I've been caught a thousand times, only to leave the handcuffs empty, the jail cells abandoned. One time, I disappeared right in front of a jury. I looked into the eyes of the man whose wife I murdered as he smiled at the guilty verdict—poof!—I vanished. Sometimes you have to stick around for effect. It's no fun if it doesn't hurt.

As I watch Jane, Henry, and Milorad eat ice cream cones through an empty produce box thrown in the corner of the shop, I hear them talking about me.

"She's not my mother," Jane says to Milorad.

"Of course," he says, "but I—"

"She's always looking at her phone," Henry says.

"She is reading news," Milorad says. "She is concerned for the world."

"She just wants everything Mother has—including Vernon, the house, me, and Henry," Jane says.

"I do not think you are correct," Milorad replies.

"Does she pay you to lie?" Jane asks.

"It is just logic," Milorad says. "She is—eh—rolling rock traveler, yes? She cannot be a mother or wife and also move back to Brazil."

"So that's a yes? She does pay you?"

Milorad waves off the question. He hates lying. I knew that since New Year's Eve 2006—the night I met him under Chicago's Dearborn Street Bridge. He hates lying and he hates running. And every day he's forced to do both. Poor bastard.

ACT THREE:
Real School / The Truth About Everything

<u>Cast in order of appearance:</u>

Babies

Babies

So many Babies

LESSON EIGHT: BABIES

Today is Thursday, January 30, 2025

THE HISTORY OF PLACENTA

In history class, we have to write a five-minute speech on a cause we care about. I choose Mother and head to the band's Wikipedia page.

> Formed in 1996, with its roots in a basement near Swarthmore College in Philadelphia, Placenta is a punk band with influence. Mina Placenta (formerly Vandermaker) was looking for "a band that could play loud, fast, and feminist." The band is as well known for their music as they are known for their social justice, especially their dedication to free menstruation products for all and domestic violence awareness.
>
> Placenta started rehearsing in the summer of 1996, mashing up classic punk covers and their own songs. By January 1997, they were playing Khyber Pass, the North Star Bar, and other small venues in Philadelphia as well as occasionally playing live singles on WXPN, the radio of University of Pennsylvania, where Mina was taking a graduate class—Sociology of Capitalism. Her experience on the Penn campus, paired with her rising notoriety as a performer, led her to change her name legally.

"What does a placenta do?" she asked *Rolling Stone*. "It feeds and nurtures a baby."

The band's fans are known as Babies. [external link]

How did I not know that Placenta fans were called Babies? I've listened to all the albums. I know all the lyrics. *I live with the founder. I am her literal baby.* And yet, it was this-very-second o'clock when I found out that the band's fans are called Babies.

I don't even take a minute to think about how genius that is, and just go back to reading once I wipe the always-the-last-to-know tears away.

In the summer of 1999, soon after her marriage to Vernon Cook, Mina was contacted by the band GWAR, complaining that her blood-spattering live performances were a rip-off of theirs. The dino-themed band expected an apology. Mina became an icon with her very public response. "We're nothing alike. You use fake blood. I don't. Get anywhere near me with your legalistic capitalist bullshit and I'll drown you in the menses of a million real, good, punk women." [external link]

Placenta still sells Real Good Punk Woman merchandise on-site at shows and through their website. All proceeds go to organizations that work for menstrual equity and education. The band gives away menstrual cups at their concerts and has so far claimed to have given away more than two million. [external links]

By the year 2000, the band had more than thirty original songs, but Mina Placenta and her longtime band-partner bassist, David Placenta (formerly Rocco), refused to cut an album because they didn't want the music to cost money. *Late-Stage Capitalism* was released, finally, in 2002, by Virgin

Records, with Mina saying she would use at least half of her earnings to help women and children escape from abusive homes. The release was delayed by the 2001 death of Mina Placenta's parents, in a traffic accident. By 2020, Placenta band members had donated more than fifty million dollars to programs that help menstruating people in one hundred countries, and that help families in the US recover and rebuild after violence against women and girls.

2018's *Safe House*, the band's seventh studio album, and their best-selling, went platinum and sold more than four million copies worldwide. *Spin* said of the album: "Another love song to women helping women, Placenta is a feminist archangel of compassion." The band members made fifty thousand dollars each that year, and the rest of the profits from *Safe House* went to an amalgam of charities.

The band's dedication to charity is laced through lyrical refrains like this one from "Smother" on *Late-Stage Capitalism*: "Don't tell us about your Heaven aspirations / while you pour your money into corporations / If you're not feeding babies and their mothers / you're just another fucking hand that smothers."

I can't bear to read any more. I close the window on the computer and don't take any notes.

I have never known my mother.

Seems the oddest thing, doesn't it? That I would be the spitting image of her, have the same interests, the same ears, the same DNA, and same address, but somehow, I have to learn about her from the internet as the mother of all these other Babies.

When I see Porter in the hallway on my way to my locker after final bell, she stops to talk to me and I say, "Can't talk. Seething."

She yells, "Fuck yeah! Light shit on fire!"

HOME / HENRY

I don't say a word to Milorad as he drives me home. He notes my mood, and after I hand him our secret school phone, he keeps his eyes on the road and hums some kind of upbeat Serbian folk song.

I walk into the house, through the study where Henry is at his desk, pencil and head in hand, and into the kitchen. Marta is listening to music in earbuds and mixing batter in a bowl.

"Hey!" I say.

She jerks her head around and removes an earbud.

"Why didn't you tell me about Babies?"

"Huh?"

"Are you a Baby?" I ask.

She catches on and nods. "Of course."

"I had to learn about my own mother from Wikipedia. I feel so . . . stupid! Why didn't you tell me this stuff?"

"I'm not allowed to talk about it," Marta says. Then she puts her finger up to warn me. We both barely breathe, and Marta eyes the door to the study. I tiptoe over and open it briskly.

"Oww!" Henry says. He holds his face with his hand.

"Oh my God, I'm sorry, Henry!"

"Is there blood?" Marta asks.

Henry looks into his palms. "No blood."

"Come here," Marta says. She gets two tiny arnica tablets and tells Henry to let them dissolve under his tongue.

"Why were you two talking about babies?" Henry asks. "You're not pregnant, Jane, are you?"

"Ew, no," I answer.

"Vernon says you'll be pregnant by spring at public school."

Marta and I nod.

"Henry?" Vernon asks from beyond the door. He walks into the kitchen. "There you are! What about the rest of that algebra?"

he says to Henry. He looks at me. "Computer in safe," he says, and then ushers Henry back to his desk.

I look at Marta. She shrugs. I say, "He's going to be angry forever about this, isn't he?"

"Don't tell him you're a Baby."

"What's he gonna do? Be angrier?"

Marta wipes her hands on her apron and pours the contents of the bowl into a square baking pan. I go get my backpack.

As I put my computer into the safe, Vernon watches me open it and check one assignment.

"Put it in the safe!" he yells.

"Sorry, but the assignment is on there and it really is due tomorrow and I can't do the work without the computer."

"I'm sure you can," he says. "It says on their website that they accommodate those of us without internet."

"But we have internet. And most people who don't are too poor to afford it."

"Well then, we're too poor," he says. "That's how your mother wanted it, isn't it?"

He's irrational.

"I need to call Mother," I say.

"Another day," Vernon answers.

"Uhh, no. I need to talk to her now," I say. "You said that we could talk to her whenever we wanted, right? So I need to talk to her now."

"She's probably too busy for you," he says. Then he gets up slowly, and we make our way to the kitchen.

As we walk through the study, Henry, who is crying over algebra, asks, "Can I talk to her, too?"

"Of course," I say.

Vernon whispers something under his breath, but I don't hear it.

THE CALL

Henry still has tear streaks on his face. I never noticed how perfect his skin is before now. I never noticed how, for thirteen, he's still so small. The pandemic made a mess of time, so a lot of days, I think Henry is still eight and in second grade and still addicted to the show *Wonder Pets*, where there was always an animal in trouble and the characters would save them. Anyway, his skin is perfect and he leans over the stainless steel island while Marta dials and puts the phone on speaker. Vernon sits in the comfy chair and picks at his cuticles.

When Mother picks up, she asks how we are and Henry says we're all really great and that we're eating his favorite dinner tonight. "That Cajun chicken in the cheese sauce," he says.

"Corn bread?" Mother asks.

"Of course!"

Mother says, "You guys are making me more homesick than I already was!"

Vernon says, "Come now, Mina, don't make the children feel bad."

"I don't feel bad," I say. "I miss you! Where are you today?"

"I miss you, too!" she says. "I'm a bit west of Lisbon."

"That's Portugal!" Henry says. "Five hours ahead."

"It's so nice to hear your voice," I say.

"How's school, Jane?"

"It's good," I answer.

"Are you able to keep up?" she asks.

"That's part of why I'm calling," I say. "The school gave me a laptop. They give one to everybody, and most of our classwork and homework is done on the laptop."

"That sounds cool," she says.

Vernon gets up and walks briskly through the swing door toward the study.

"It is cool," I say, "But—"

Before I can say anything else, Vernon bursts back through the door holding my laptop with both hands and shoves it into my chest, nearly knocking me over. Marta moves behind me to catch me.

"I suppose there's nothing I can do to protect you!" he says, and storms out again. "Henry! Come finish your schoolwork!"

"I hate algebra, Mother," Henry says. "It makes me cry every single day."

"Oh, sweet Henry," she says. "Keep working on it and it will make sense."

"Henry!" Vernon calls.

Henry says goodbye to Mother and goes back to the study.

"Is school really good, Jane?" Mother asks.

"Overwhelming," I say. Marta puts the corn bread into the oven and starts gathering dinner ingredients. "Been meeting my old friends in the bathroom to put on our makeup in the morning. It feels like I'm a character in one of your songs."

Mother laughs. Marta laughs.

"Have to go! Glad we could solve the computer problem," Mother says sarcastically through the speaker. I can hear her eyes rolling.

"Kick ass!" I say.

"Be safe!" Marta says.

"Love you both! Hug Henry for me!" she says. "I hate that he's crying every day."

She hangs up.

Then it's just me and Marta standing in the kitchen. She has a box of penne in her hand. I have my laptop. We look at each other. We both hate that Henry is crying every day, too. I've been watching him lately—since I saw this one home movie and realized something pretty big about us as siblings. Wait. Let me show you.

HOME MOVIE—12.23.2011

I am three years old and sitting on the floor next to our big Christmas tree, picking my nose while doing a wooden jigsaw puzzle with big pieces. Mother is confined to the System, and Vernon is pacing between the sitting room settees trying to get two-month-old baby Henry to stop crying.

<pause>

My home movie research shows that before The Christmas That Changed Everything, from 2002 to 2018, Mother was confined about 35 percent of the time, usually for "punishment" whenever Vernon decided she'd crossed a line. However, he can be heard in a different home movie saying, "I love to watch her squirm," so I don't think it has anything to do with what Mother did or didn't do.

<resume>

Vernon has no rhythm—his pacing and bouncing aren't in sync—and Henry's protests get louder. Mother watches him, seeming concerned and frustrated.

I seem not to hear Henry's screaming at all, though it's so loud in this recording that it makes my ears crackle. But in the movie, it's as if I find this glass-shattering screeching completely normal.

"Just bring him here," Mina says through the two-way attachment.

Vernon ignores her. I keep doing my puzzle.

Marta arrives from the kitchen. She has hair dyed a pastel shade of purple. She says, "Can I do anything to help?"

Vernon says, "No."

Mother says, "I'm thirsty."

Marta walks to the tube in the corner. "Tea?"

"Yes please. Thank you."

"No," Vernon says, but no one seems to hear him.

He continues to pace and bounce out of sync. I stop doing my puzzle and become determined to make Henry stop crying. I follow Vernon as he walks, making funny faces and waving my arms at the baby.

"Please just bring him here," Mother says. "Let me feed him."

"He's not due a feeding for another hour."

"He's a baby, not a car," she says.

He ignores her. Henry screams even louder, if that's possible. Marta returns with a mug of steaming tea.

"No!" Vernon says.

Marta realizes that he's talking to her.

"Get out!" he screams.

Henry is startled quiet by the yelling and for a split second, there is silence as Mother looks at Marta, Marta looks at the mug of tea in her hand, and I finally get Henry to look at me. I stick my tongue out with my index fingers hooked into my cheeks.

This is when he starts crying again.

Vernon snaps, "Jane, you're not being helpful."

Henry roars.

Mother says, "Vernon! Bring him here!"

Vernon says, "Listen to how you made him cry, Jane!"

Mother yells, "Let me out of here and let me feed him!" She is trying to open the door to the tube from the inside, but she can't. "Please!" she screams. "Why did you lock the door?" she yells, while she continues to try.

Her yelling startles Vernon, who goes quiet for a second and then startles me by spinning on his heel and plopping Henry right in my little toddler arms. Henry moves around a bit and starts to cry, but I put my pinkie finger into his mouth because I'd seen Marta, who's still standing with a cup of hot tea, do that before. Together, in a state of shared shock, we watch as Vernon walks to the tube and slams the heel of his hand into the plastic. He snatches the two-way communication attachment off the front of the tubing and throws it to his right, then reaches down for the wet nurse attachment and fits it into place.

<pause>

A quick recap about the five System attachments. The two-way, the one-way, the silence, the mealtime, and the wet nurse. They are all revolting. Sometimes I think about taking them all outside to the garden and lighting them on fire.

<resume>

Mother says, "Let me hold him!"

Henry starts to fuss in my arms, and I don't look like I can hold him much longer.

Vernon walks over to me and takes Henry out of my arms. He walks back toward Mother and dumps Henry into the deep plexiglass box on the outside of the wet nurse attachment. "Get it out and feed him," Vernon says.

Mother unbuttons her shirt and unhooks the cup of her nursing bra and then maneuvers her breast through the hole in the attachment. Vernon stands there watching the miracle of Henry's suckling, smiling in a way I don't want to talk about. I stand watching him looking at Mother—a jigsaw puzzle made of flesh and blood.

Vernon yells at Marta. "Bring some towels!"

She puts the mug of tea on the table and goes to the kitchen. I move closer and can see the milk running down the front of the attachment and the remainder of the tube.

"Disgusting!" Vernon says to Mother.

She just keeps her body in the right position to feed Henry and her eyes closed while Marta catches the dripping milk with a towel and wipes the outer surface of the tube clean.

"Give one to her," Vernon says. "Mina, clean up your mess." Vernon turns to me then, and says, "Jane, let's go play a fun game!"

I'm still staring at Mother, whose eyes have opened now, as Vernon takes my hand and we walk down the stairs toward his bedroom.

<pause>

The fun game we played was me watching TV in his room while he talked to someone on the phone in his en suite bathroom.

<resume>

Once we're gone, Marta speaks. "Are you okay?"

Mother nods. "Can we switch?"

Marta positions Henry on his other side in the box and Mother switches breasts for feeding him. Milk squirts out and hits the tube surface and drips down the side. At this, she cries.

"He's a bastard," Marta says.

Mother nods.

"Why you keep him fed and clothed, I do not know," Marta says.

Mother nods.

"I mean, really, Mina. Why?"

Mother shrugs, one hand under her exposed breast and the other against the plexiglass to balance. "I made a promise," Mother says. "I keep my promises."

"Did it involve this?" Marta gestures.

"Please—"

Marta looks Mother right in the eye. "Mina, he's going to kill you one day. Or one of the kids."

"He'll apologize later. Don't worry."

Henry chokes and coughs a little then, and Marta pulls him from the plastic feeding box and puts a cloth over her shoulder to burp him. "I can't believe you're letting him lock you up in there," she says.

"I'll be out soon," Mother says. "He doesn't usually lock it."

"What happens when he doesn't ever let you out again?"

"He won't do that."

"How are the kids even supposed to get to know you?"

Henry spits up a little on the cloth on Marta's shoulder, and Mother sighs big. "A musician is no kind of mother."

Marta frowns, her eyes hurt. "He's brainwashed you."

"I wasn't made for mothering," Mother says.

"Bullshit. You're amazing. He just hates you."

"Has he mistreated you?" Mother asks.

"This isn't about me," Marta says.

Mother is crouching down now, inside the tube, wiping the breast milk off the plexiglass.

A door opens and slams shut in the background.

<pause>

For some reason, the movie stops then. Goes completely black. There are no more movies available from the sitting room camera until after the new year.

<stop>

This feels like the worst home movie on my list, but it's not. Henry was always being dragged around and plopped in places and ignored. It's one of the sadder parts of watching the home movies. If you'd have asked me a year ago who was the favorite child and who got the most attention, I'd have said Henry.

HOME MOVIE MIXTAPE—HENRY STORIES

01.21.2011 / Sitting Room / "Jane needs a playmate, Mina! Be a sport!"

04.05.2012 / Study / "Why you chose to have another kid, I don't know. Just trying to keep me here, I suppose," Vernon says to Mother as she feeds Henry on the rocking chair, and as he drags his suitcase toward the hallway. "Don't try to stop me! I'm not coming back this time!"

06.09.2014 / Dining Room / Henry is two and a half years old and sitting completely alone in Vernon's dining chair. He falls asleep after ten minutes of singing something to himself.

09.01.2016 / Foyer / Henry, four, is standing in the foyer while Vernon picks up Mina's favorite vase and smashes it against the front door, covering the entire floor with shards of crystal and a mass of Milorad's sunflowers from the garden. When Vernon leaves, Henry carefully steps his way back into the hallway.

11.01.2017 / Patio / "Hide and seek!" Henry yells. He stands and counts to ten with his eyes covered. Then, he opens his eyes and starts from one again and goes to hide. Then, he pretends he's searching around where he was just hiding. Then he finds himself. "Ah-ha! Found you!" And then he cries for being found . . . by himself.

<stop>

The fact is, the favored child was me. Vernon centered me in a way that was both creepy and overbearing. Henry seemed a mere afterthought.

I take my school computer to the study and open it to do my homework. Henry has been set free from crying over algebra and is out in the greenhouse. But something is wrong with him beyond math. I feel it in my bones.

CAVEMAN'S BURDEN

Before I get to homeroom on Friday, Porter catches up with me.

"You good now?" she asks. "Yesterday you looked like you were gonna explode."

"Yeah."

She waits and stares at me while I look away. "Um. You sure?"

"You said something the other day," I say. "About your parents hating each other."

"KZ said that," she says. "And it's oversimplified. In reality, my dad hates my mom and will do anything I ask if I tell him that it's because my mom is a pain."

I nod. "So he drives you to school super early?"

"Yeah."

"I guess it beats walking," I say.

"Nah. My mom does a school run at the normal time every morning. She has to drop my sisters off at the middle school."

"Oh."

"Yeah, I just wanna have my own life, and Eric said he'd pick me up and we could go on dates in the morning."

"Huh," I say. "Does your mom know about any of this?"

Porter looks up from her phone. "Of course not?"

I nod.

"You think I'm a slut," she says.

"I'm the last person on earth who'd think that."

"Why'd you even ask me, then?"

I take a deep breath. "My dad hates my mom, too."

She nods in sympathy and gives me a fist bump. "Eric says all guys hate women deep down—like some kind of caveman's burden."

I don't know what to say after that.

Porter puts her phone in her back pocket. "Wait. How can anyone hate your mom?" she asks. And then the warning bell sounds and Porter has to run to the part of the building wherever the P homeroom is.

By the time my first week of real high school is over, I have three longtime best friends, a forever-helper in Addi, five to ten vague invitations to the V-Day dance, and Marlon, who I don't know how to categorize.

"We're friends," he said to me in the library on Friday. Then he added, "With a hope of something more."

He's so nice I wish I liked guys.

I'm so exhausted, I sleep the entire weekend.

By the time my second week of real high school is over, it's the seventh of February—a week until the dance—and I have two student tutors, biology and geometry, Gretchen has a boyfriend named Darrel and is obsessed with him, and KZ has another crush on a straight guy. ("They never learn," Gretchen says to me before homeroom.) My tutors are helping me catch up, I'm able to keep up in my other classes, and I can find my way around the whole building without getting lost.

When I go to meet Milorad at pickup time, he's not outside the car, like always, and he's not inside the car either. Marta is.

"Hey," I say as I get in. "Is everything all right?"

"Finch is at the house," she says.

"So?"

"She's flipping shit about Vernon letting you go to school. She said he's a pushover and that it's my fault because he always had a soft spot for me." She takes off and starts to drive home.

"It's the mashed potatoes," I say. "Plus—you had nothing to do with it."

"Just be ready."

I let time pass. Then I say, "What's her problem with Mina? I mean, I know she hates her, but why?"

Marta thinks and then says, "I think she hates everyone, your mom first, but then everyone else after that. She's always hated me—since we were kids."

"I forget that you guys all grew up together."

"Yeah. The shit she used to do to your mom was nasty. Always making a fool out of her. Mina never really knew. She was just trying to please her big sister."

"What kind of stuff?"

Marta shakes her head. "A lot of it was just dumb. I don't know—like she'd throw balls across the busy road and make Mina chase them, or she'd push her into water—pools, lakes, the ocean—or she'd have sleepovers with her friends and she'd make Mina drink weird concoctions and throw up as entertainment."

"Like alcohol?"

"No. Like orange juice and mustard. Emetic stuff so she'd puke."

"That's so mean."

"Yeah," she answers. "Your mom told me that story once and I could tell she thought it was normal for big sisters to do that."

"She tells me and Henry that Mother is going to kill us one day. Did you know that?" We're on Spruce Street, three minutes from home.

"Kill you?" Marta pulls the car over to the curb. "How long has she been telling you that?"

"Since I can remember?"

"She said Mina would kill you?"

"Him too. He told us all kinds of weird crap about how dangerous she is. You've heard him. Like—all the rules and the story about how Mother stabbed him."

"Wait. What?"

"I know it's a lie. I was there. But Henry believes it."

She nods slowly, frowning. "I guess I didn't know all of what

I thought I knew." She puts the car in PARK. "So, you believed she would kill you?"

"It seems so. Or—at least part of me did."

"Did you say you were there?" She stops for a moment. "For a . . . stabbing?"

"There was no stabbing," I say. "He just tells Henry that. Or probably whoever else he talks to."

"Huh," Marta says as she pulls onto the road again and aims the car toward our house. "Well, whatever's going on, Finch is at the house, and when I left, she was yelling at Milorad in the pool house."

"Did you notice that whenever Finch is around, Brutus the rat is out of his cage? I find it uncanny." Once we park in the driveway, I open the passenger door and step out of the car, leaving Marta to figure it out if she wants to.

When I walk through the front door, I decide it's time for Punk Rock Jane to shine. I start at the liquor cabinet. I get a crystal glass and fill it with two inches of brandy. I sit in the chair by the fireplace and sip it slowly while trying to figure out a plan. Finch arrives.

"I hope you're happy," she says.

"I'm pretty happy, yeah."

"You going to school has changed your father. He's a different man now."

"How so?" I ask.

"He's inconsolable. Just sad all the time," she says.

"I've only been in school a fortnight. I think he's been sad longer than that."

"Why'd you have to push it?" she asks. "Why couldn't you be happy with how things were?"

I decide her questions are rhetorical. "Shall we throw him a party or something upbeat like that?" I ask. "We can play a game! I can get a suitor."

"No suitors," she says.

I lean forward and do my best Finch impersonation. "You look down. Is there anything I can do to help?"

Finch looks at the floor. I can see her wishing she could shape-shift right out of our lives. Then she looks at me and frowns. "Is that liquor?"

POSTMARKED FEBRUARY 1, 2025

A PICTURE OF THE DUBLIN MOUNTAINS

Dear Jane and Henry,
Did you know that in Ireland, they consider February 1st the beginning of their spring? The daffodils are up and the people are cheery. We have a gig here in Dublin and then we stay for a week because there's a music festival in Kilkenny later this week. So far, we've met a bunch of other epic punks. Oh! And we met a band from Serbia and I told them about Milorad! They settled here after the war. I hope you're getting these. At least for the pictures! This is a picture of the Dublin mountains. Love you, Mom

THE GREAT HIBERNATION

Today is Monday, February 10, 2025

MILORAD SAYS, "You will probably be sent home early today. There is snow coming."

"It's snowing now," I say.

"They will bring you into the school and open doors early so you can all come home safely before big inches."

"You're listening to too much American television. No one says *big inches* in real life."

He gives a deep laugh. "If this is not real life, then what is real life?" He pulls into the circle in front of the school and waits in the queue, then I get out.

EYELINER

"I can't even believe we're here," KZ says.

Gretchen huffs. "At this rate we'll use up the extra padding around Easter break and get out later in June anyway. My dad says we'll probably be out for the rest of the week."

"Ugh," I say.

"Damn, Jane," Gretchen says, "that eyeliner is on-fucking-point."

"I can't be in my house for the rest of the week," I say. "I'll go nuts."

"We'll come over and build a snow fort!" KZ says.

"Is Porter even here?" Gretchen asks.

The silence from all of us feels judgmental. "Maybe if you show up to build the fort without telling me, my dad will have to be nice."

"Let him try to be mean to me," KZ says.

"Sounds like a plan," Gretchen says. "Not like we can call you anyway. I mean, unless we take a time machine to the twentieth century, right?"

"It's a phone number, so on your side, you don't have to time travel. I'll be the one with a phone attached to the wall," I explain.

"It'll be cool to finally see the inside of your house," Gretchen says.

"Yeah," I say.

She continues. "I was talking to Rob Kaninski one time, and he said he was there once and your dad showed him an iron lung."

I stop trying to perfect my eyeliner. "Rob?"

"Yeah. He said he took you to a club or something."

"That was, like, November," I say.

"Yeah."

"Does he go here?" I ask.

"What is up, you sexy beasts?" Porter shouts as she enters the bathroom.

"You're always fucking late."

"Only if I'm fucking your mom!" High fives and fist bumps abound. "Whoa, nice eyeliner," she says.

"Thanks," I say. "Hold on. Does Todd go to this school?"

"You mean Rob?"

"Him too. But no, I mean Todd. The kid from the library."

Gretchen nods. "He does work-study, but he's here some half days. Rob's the captain of the lacrosse team. He's hard to miss. Can't believe you've been here two weeks and he hasn't sniffed around. He's usually all for fresh meat."

"Please stop."

"Most girls would be thrilled to get this much attention," KZ says.

"I'm not most girls. Plus—"

"Shit, we gotta go," KZ says.

Gretchen looks at her phone. Porter looks at her smartwatch.

As we walk out of the bathroom, I run right into Rob, the boy who thinks there's an iron lung in my house.

"Heeeyyy!" he says.

As we maneuver around Rob, Gretchen says, "It's like we summoned him."

I point to the view beyond the front doors of the school. Snow is coming down fast and the cars in the visitor parking area are already covered in at least two inches.

MAYHEM

Mayhem is the only way to describe our early dismissal less than an hour later. The buses line up, the groundskeepers try to make the sidewalks and roads safe, but it's slippery and the snow is partly icy and it's coming down fast.

I've never seen snow so aggressive. I stand, trying to figure out where to go and watch as the students around me fade in and out of what seems like a super-white fog. I cannot see more than nine feet ahead of me.

As I walk around the bus circle and head toward the spot where Milorad waits for me, I see kids throwing snowballs in the parking lot. A snowball hits the side of a bus. A kid yells. Another falls. Another laughs. It's all quite exciting for a girl who's been locked in her house since fifth grade. I probably walk slower than I should.

"It is dangerous for these children to be driving in snow!" Milorad says when I get into the car. I look at myself in the visor mirror and there is nearly a half inch of snow on my shoulders.

As we drive toward the school exit, there is a small fender-bender at the intersection. Milorad says, "How *see*? I was right!" and I let him talk and watch the snow stick to the bare limbs of trees.

Two dog walkers are forging a path through the snowy grass to avoid rock-salted sidewalks. A kid from my language arts class, Gio, is walking home. And as the traffic stops, he looks over at the car.

It occurs to me only now that our car is somewhat a novelty. Vernon insisted, back when Mother had her first gold record, that she "invest in herself and her family" by buying a car of "similar quality to us."

In his mind, Vernon is the Rolls-Royce of husbands.

Gio looks at me in the passenger seat and waves.

I roll my window down. "Do you need a lift home?"

He smiles, walks over to the car, and before he gets in, brushes off his shoulders and shakes his head to get the snow off. He gets in just as the light turns green up ahead.

"Thanks!" he says.

"No problem. Where do you live?"

"Like four doors down from your house," he says.

"Oh," I say.

"Nice to meet you!" Milorad says.

"Did we go to elementary together?" I ask.

"Nah," Gio answers. "I moved during the pandemic. From Arizona originally."

"No snow there!" Milorad seems excited.

"The summers are brutal, though," Gio says.

"I'd like to see the Grand Canyon one day," I say.

"It is coming down so fast!" Milorad says.

"This will be my first blizzard," Gio says.

"Fun," I answer.

"It is Jane's first, as well," Milorad says.

As we drive down Spruce Street at what feels like ten miles per hour, I watch snow-covered things go by. Shrubs, fences, cars, garden gnomes, American flags, gravestones, playground equipment, Finch, in her silly blue parka.

She is walking toward the office door of Lipton, Beaver, and Krouse. Their commercial on TV sings, "We get you what you want, not just what you need."

"This is me, up here. Once you get through the intersection," Gio says. "Thanks again for the ride."

Milorad pulls over after the stop sign and Gio gets out.

He waves to me through the window and then leans down and makes a snowball. As Milorad drives away, Gio lobs it at the back of the car.

"Nice boy," Milorad says.

"Must be nice to be from Arizona," I answer.

"You will not be going back to school this week," Milorad says. "There will be three storms in a row. They do not predict school until next Monday if we are lucky and do not lose power."

I don't say anything.

"Please keep my phone to text with your friends, but you cannot let your father see it. Or hear it. Or anything."

"It's fine. I don't need it."

"You will want to connect with school friends about schoolwork, yes?"

I look at the phone. I open it and put Gretchen's number in from memory. And Porter's. I text: **I am in the 21st century! Please add KZ to this group. I forget their number.**

I put the phone in my schoolbag.

"Maybe you can text with your friend, too," he says, pointing to Gio's house behind us. "The boy."

"Maybe."

"He seems nice."

"No thank you to the Serbian matchmaking, okay?" I say.

He shrugs as he pulls into the driveway. "I tire of being worried for your safety with suitors."

"I never wanted suitors anyway," I say. When Milorad doesn't answer, I add, "I wonder if Vernon gets paid for me being his little prostitute."

"Jane, do not say such things," Milorad says. He gets out of the car and heads toward the pool house quickly.

I get out of the car. I head toward the front door. I stop and look up and feel the snow on my face. It feels like freedom.

When I walk through the front door, I am shocked to hear music.

DANCING LESSONS

Henry looks most uncomfortable. Marta comes in second place—as she watches, leaned against the doorjamb to the kitchen. Vernon is in the sitting room by the fire with a drink. Bourbon, from the faint, sweet smell of it. It is 10:48 in the morning.

Henry is dancing with a stranger. She looks about his age and I assume this is some kind of shock tactic to make me wish I was still a student at Vernon's Pandemic Educational Penitentiary—music. In this case, it's "Waltz of the Flowers" by Tchaikovsky—a slow and organized waltz. Henry is stiff, and his upper body looks as if it's crawling away from his midsection. Henry hasn't seen a girl near his age who wasn't me or Gemma since he was in second grade.

"Lower your hand, Henry," the mystery dancing girls says. "And tell me—is this Jane?"

"Nice to meet you," I say.

"I'm Harriet," she says. "Vernon sent for me upon realizing Henry didn't know anything at all about dancing."

"How nice!" I say. I look at Marta. "I have school stuff to do before I forget it all. I'll be in my room."

Before I can turn and head for the stairs, Vernon shouts, "Jane!" I go to him in the sitting room.

"You cannot take your computer to your bedroom." He doesn't look up from the papers in his hand.

"I can scarcely concentrate in the study with the waltzing," I say.

"Then leave it until later."

"Okay," I say. "You're welcome to rifle through it if you like."

I leave the computer on the couch next to him and walk back into the study where Henry and Harriet are finishing their lesson. The snow is falling so heavily outside, it's as if we live inside a cotton ball.

Then the whir starts, and my body has a euphoric reaction because the whir means Mother, but it's not Mother. It's some other woman.

"Hey!" I say, thinking she's some sort of intruder. I am frozen with my right index finger still saying *Hey!* as the woman slowly appears in the study tube.

Henry says, "That's my new math tutor."

Harriet curtsies toward Henry and tells him she'll see him next week, then walks over to the tube in the corner, opens the door, lets Henry's math tutor out, and takes her place. She stares at me.

Before she can close the door, I rush over to her.

"Where does this take you?" I whisper.

"Home," she says.

"What about the snow?" I ask.

"Weather can't stop the useful," she says. It's as creepy as it sounds, too, because right when she says it, she presses a button and disappears slowly into the floor.

ACT III, SCENE 3

INT. SITTING ROOM—MORNING

Song: "Can't Stop the Useful"

Composer notes: *See "Nervous Breakdown" by Black Flag.*

BAND all dressed in winter snow gear—ski goggles and knit hats. DAVID wears a snowflake costume made out of foam. JANE is in a pair of black ski bibs with a bra under it. She has paper snowflakes taped all over her body and face.

JANE

I WANNA BE SO USEFUL
LIKE ALL THE REST OF THE GIRLS.
I GOTTA FIND A WAY OUT,
MY FATHER CLUTCHING HIS PEARLS.

I'M ANGRY AND I'M DONE
BEING THE LAST ONE TO KNOW.
I CAN'T STAND BEING HERE.
I DON'T KNOW WHERE TO GO.

THEY'RE LUCKY I DON'T FREAK
BECAUSE THEY WOULD IF THEY WERE ME.
I GOTTA FIND A WAY AWAY FROM HERE
I CAN'T WAIT TO BE TOTALLY FREE.

I'M ANGRY AND I'M DONE
BEING THE LAST ONE TO KNOW.
I CAN'T STAND BEING HERE.
I DON'T KNOW WHERE TO GO.

I WANNA BE SO USEFUL
LIKE ALL THE BOYS WHO DON'T DO SHIT

I WANNA BE YOUR MAMA—
GONNA BUY ME IN A KIT

Jane jumps on the settee, while the band slam dances into each other, playing the same rhythm chords over and over.

JANE

AN APRON, A SLIP, A BRACELET,
HIGH HEELS AND EARRINGS THAT WON'T QUIT.
MY CALVES AND THIGHS AND BREASTS
AND MOUTH AND MOUTH AND MOUTH.
CAN'T STOP THE USEFUL.
CAN'T STOP THE USEFUL.

I'M ANGRY AND I'M DONE
BEING THE LAST ONE TO KNOW.
I CAN'T STAND BEING HERE.
I DON'T KNOW WHERE TO GO.

Band leaves the sitting room one by one; Jane is left sitting on the settee, pouting.

END SCENE

SNOWBALL FIGHT

The next day, way later than usual—around noon—I am woken up by how bright the light is streaming into my room. It's blizzard light, I assume, as I lay under my duvet and stay warm. Then I hear car doors close and the doorbell rings. Twice. By the time I'm running down the steps, Vernon is already in the foyer.

"Hi, Jane's dad! We're here for a snowball fight!"

"Are you?" he asks.

By this time, I am in the foyer and waving at the three of them. They are getting snowed on heavily, and Vernon doesn't seem to know what to do.

Henry arrives and his eyes are wide.

"Are you Henry?" KZ asks.

"Are you going to let them in?" I ask Vernon. I turn to them. "Gretchen, Porter, and KZ, this is my dad, Vernon."

"I'm Henry!" Henry says.

"Vernon's a cute name," Gretchen says as she walks right into the foyer after shaking as much snow off her hair and shoulders as she can. KZ follows.

Porter adds, "Don't meet many Vernons these days."

"Rude," Gretchen says.

"What?"

"You make him sound old!"

Porter corrects. "I meant he's *unique*. It's a cool name."

Vernon, Henry, and I stand there watching them act like normal teenagers. I think Vernon might be paralyzed with a mix of fear and flattery. Henry is staring at Gretchen's boobs.

I gesture for them to follow me to the fireplace. "How did you even drive here?"

"She's fearless," KZ says.

"The big roads were cleared last night, so the new snow is melting on contact," Porter adds.

As the four of us weave through the dining room and toward the sitting room, Vernon and Henry talk quietly in the foyer. I hear Henry say, "But a snowball fight!" and I think Vernon has asked him to leave us alone. But then Vernon follows us into the sitting room.

When he arrives, as my friends take off their snow gear and

put it near the fire to dry, we're all talking at the same time, and he stands holding his pocket watch and clears his throat for attention.

"What's the plan?" Vernon asks, acting casual even though he looks like a weird butler.

"Snow?" Gretchen says.

"Fun!" Porter says.

"Cool, cool," he says. I have never heard my father say *cool, cool* before. "Will you stay for dinner?"

"Is that an invitation?" Gretchen asks.

It doesn't seem like one. He is pained and can't hide it, no matter how hip he's trying to present. Marta saves us all with a tray full of mugs of hot chocolate. She even saves Henry, who arrives without having to be fetched, because she made one for him, too. We sit around the fire, talking. Vernon sits in his chair, silent.

They tell us about their adventures so far today—going to each house, collecting snow pants and mittens. KZ talks about their favorite scarf, which has gone missing. Porter says they filled her front yard with snow angels before they went to the McDonald's Drive Thru and ordered sundaes. Porter says she wants to see her boyfriend tonight but he is stuck at his grandmother's house, snowblowing. "She has an insane driveway—you know the places out by the airport?"

KZ predicts that not only will Porter's boyfriend never leave his grandma's, but that "we probably won't get out of here either."

"The roads are fine," Gretchen says. "Stop making a big deal out of it."

"We're due another foot before dark," Marta says.

Porter says, "I'm just saying that my dad predicted that we'd never get back up the hill tonight."

Gretchen says, "Jane has room here."

Vernon's eyebrows go up.

"Sure thing," I say.

Henry can't stop staring at Gretchen's boobs.

When the room goes quiet and we sit with ourselves and sip our mugs of chocolate, I start to feel like I'm living a double life. They're here; they can see the tubes in every room. They don't ask. No wonder no one has ever come over to my house before. It's awkward for all of us. I'm just grateful Mother is on tour. Imagine this scene with her in the tube—I don't even know how I'd deal with that.

"Are we picking teams or what?" KZ asks.

"It's gonna get dark eventually," I say.

"The lights in the rose garden would suffice for any good showdown," Vernon says, turning the lights in the garden on from his phone app.

I get up and look out the window. The others join me.

"Holy shit," Porter says. "Some place you have here."

"Thanks," I answer, mortified.

"You can't see it now, but we have a pool," Henry says. "Hope you come back in summer. We have an annual cannonball contest."

The back door to the kitchen is the only thing that's been shoveled—between the door and the trash can—so I ask Vernon, "Can Milorad clear the snow from these doors? I'd love to be able to just come in to the fire whenever we get cold."

"Of course. I'll tell him at once, Jane," Vernon says, and leaves the room.

"I know I'm going to have to pee the minute I put those ski pants back on," Gretchen says.

"The bathroom is in there," I say, pointing. "I have to find my snow stuff. Henry, do you know where all that is?"

"At your service," he says, and he leaves the room, too.

It's KZ who says the obvious.

"Those giant hamster tubes are fucked up."

Porter looks down.

"Yeah," I say. "Victorian people are weird."

I think KZ will leave it there. They don't. "That shit was built later than that." They walk over and touch it. "It's plastic."

"Okay," I say.

Henry breaks the tension by arriving with our ski gear. Porter comments on my jacket. "Dope."

Milorad waves from waist-deep and shovels the area outside the door.

The next three hours are the most fun I've had, maybe ever, but really since Gemma and I used to have sleepovers. We make up our own game. Henry calls it Monster Sneak. We form two teams (me and KZ versus Gretchen and Porter) and Henry is the Monster. Our goal is to hit as many people on the opposite team as we can with snowballs, while also avoiding the Monster, who sneaks up on both teams and pummels them with snowballs, reducing the number of hits they've gathered. Henry provides two five-gallon buckets for us to carry our snowballs in. None of us are sure of the rules, but once Henry says, "Go!" we start making snowballs. Two hours into the game, we lose count of how many hits we've made or lost, and KZ tackles Henry and we all pile on and scream, "Squash the monster!" and we roll around until we can't feel our hands. By this time, it's dark out and the sleet-snow has started falling.

We go inside where Marta has hot chocolate waiting.

Milorad is sitting by the fire, but gets up when we come in.

"Sit!" I say. "You guys, this is Milorad. He's my favorite."

The others say hi, and Porter says, "I see you pick Jane up every day. Did you know he shines the car while he waits? I watch from my chem class window."

"He's cute," Gretchen says.

"Please stop it, ladies, unless I will overheat and faint," Milorad says.

"You won't faint," Henry answers.

"That accent!" Porter says. "So cute!"

"You will save me from these girls, yes?"

KZ looks uncomfortable. I want to say something but I don't. I feel like a bad friend.

"You're staying for dinner," Marta says. "And maybe overnight. The township just warned that they can't clear areas of Broad Street due to an accident and it's piling up fast out there—icy, too."

Porter hits Gretchen on her arm with the back of her hand.

"What?"

"I told you I wanted to see Eric tonight."

"Jesus Christ, Porter, you can go one day without sex," KZ says. "Plus, that was the most fun I've had in the snow since elementary school."

Marta says, "For now, I'll mash potatoes."

Dinner is full of banter and laughter, and nothing like any other dinner I've ever witnessed in this house. No one is fake except for Vernon, who continues to play Mr. Cool by playing along with everything my friends and I say or do. Even Henry looks annoyed by it. Eventually, Vernon excuses himself and disappears for an hour while we all go back to the fire and talk about whatever comes up.

IF EVER

"I haven't had this much fun in a long time," I say. "If ever."

We've set up our sleepover in the sitting room by the fireplace. Vernon disagreed at first, but Henry convinced him that it was smart and by that time he was fat from Marta's potatoes and numb from after-dinner brandy.

<pause>

Let me add that he offered the after-dinner brandy to me and to my friends, which looked a lot like grooming when he did it—him smiling and wobbling his head a little as if he was being naughty. We all stared at him. Finally, Gretchen said, "We're sixteen."

<resume>

Henry and KZ are playing a game of Spit with a deck of cards Mother brought us from New Zealand. All the face cards are kiwi birds.

Milorad is outside on the lawn tractor, blowing snow. Every few minutes, he rounds the pool house and lands right outside the double doors and we can't hear anything until he rounds the rest of the walkway by the kitchen.

Vernon says, "What time do girls at sleepovers go to sleep?"

"Hey," Henry says. "I'm not a girl."

"Me neither," KZ says.

Vernon stares. Blinks. "I'll check in again in a bit." He gets up and goes to the kitchen.

Marta shows up two minutes later. Henry and KZ are still playing cards, and Gretchen, Porter, and I are talking about Marlon, who is, it seems, everyone's crush. I don't tell them about him asking me out. I want to change the subject because the mention of his name makes me feel like a bad friend.

"Vernon has sent me to tell you that no boys are allowed to sleep over with the girls," Marta says. She rolls her eyes while she says it.

We all look at her and then die laughing. She laughs, too.

"I'm just hanging out until I get tired," Henry says.

Marta looks at me and points to KZ.

"I'm nonbinary, not a boy," they say. "Also not a predator so I think we're safe."

"He's a bit frazzled," Marta says. She makes a motion to all of—this.

I tell her he'll be fine and make her sit down with us. We talk about weird stuff like what it was like to go to our school in the nineties and Porter asks what it's like to be Mother's best friend.

"Like sisters," Marta says, "but closer."

Porter points to Gretchen with her thumb. "That's how she is for me. Better than my real sisters, no question."

"But I'm not as cool as Mina Placenta," Gretchen says.

"Bullshit you aren't," KZ and Porter say in unison.

"Must you curse every time you speak?" Vernon asks from the doorway.

Marta looks up. "Everything's fine. No need to worry," she says.

He looks at KZ, and KZ waves.

"I think you should sleep in Henry's room tonight."

"What? No," I say. "Stop it. Just let me have one normal thing for once, will you? No one here is going to have sex with anyone else. Geez. Adults are so freaking gross. You think because you think about sex all the time that we do, too."

"I was a teenager once," Vernon says.

"Oh, please," I say. "I wager you were born with that pocket watch and a snifter of bandy." This makes Henry laugh. In a cute way. Like we're some kind of normal family.

"We're best friends," Gretchen says. "We're not jumping on bones tonight. Or however you all said it back then."

He looks at his pocket watch. "I'm off to bed. I suppose I'll see you at breakfast." He stands there awkwardly, and if I'm right, he wants a hug. Henry and I let him stand there.

Eventually, Henry gets tired enough to go to bed. We all snuggle up in sleeping bags and Marta puts two logs on the fire, secures the screen in front, and turns off the standing lamp next to Vernon's chair.

When it's dark, and I'm sure we're alone, I tell them to lean in and I whisper, so the camera can't hear me. "I feel bad telling you guys this now. I meant to tell you while we were outside." I suddenly lose air and it takes a moment to get it back. "I'm gay. So, we can stop trying to set me up with guys."

They react with fist bumps and congratulations.

"Who else knows?" KZ whispers.

"No one. But I have to tell Marlon."

"Why?"

"Because he won't stop trying to get me to go out with him."

"Shit. You must really be gay."

"Do you have a girlfriend?" Porter whispers.

"Nah," I say. "School seems devoid of lesbians."

KZ says, "Maybe start coming to GSA?"

After a minute of quiet, I say, "Thanks for being so great. I was scared when I came back, you'd all be way cooler than me."

"We are. But we let you hang out with us anyway," Porter jokes.

"Seriously. It's like you don't even know who you are," Gretchen says.

SNOW DAYS

Six snow days—that's how many we got. Sixty-seven inches—that's how much snow, in eight days. Five—that's how many days we played Monster Sneak. By the Tuesday school opened again, my never-worn ski bibs were worn out, Marta knew the favorite foods of every one of my friends, and Henry managed to actually Monster-Sneak up on us about three times.

On snow day five, Henry showed us around his new greenhouse.

"Didn't you say this is a hothouse? Is it supposed to be this cold?" Gretchen asked.

Something came over Henry, then. He looked up at her and said, "I miss having friends so much." His eyes welled up and Gretchen couldn't help but hug him. "I don't even know if I ever really had friends. Not like you guys are friends." Porter piled on,

KZ, and then me. We just wrapped him up and told him that he'd have friends soon.

"Until then, we're your friends," KZ said.

He nodded and wiped his snot on the sleeve of his coat. Then he answered Gretchen's question. "It'll be a hothouse by spring. We need to install a heater and a mister and some other stuff. By summer, it'll be full of tree frogs!"

POSTMARKED FEBRUARY 10, 2025

A PICTURE OF THE THAMES WITH LONDON EYE

Dear Jane & Henry,
London is just so great and I can't wait to bring you here. I'm not sure if Marta has kept you informed, but Davy from Anvil is from London, so he's showing us around for ten days while we do some gigs and go to schools around where he grew up and talk to the kids about what it's like to have a career in music. I'm counting the days until I see you guys. Love, Mom

LESSON NINE: HOT CHICKEN / COLD OVEN

Today is Thursday, February 27, 2025

THERE ARE STILL about three feet of snow on the ground—my seventeenth birthday is in four days. Mother is coming home to celebrate. Henry's dance and math tutors travel through our System as if that's what they're supposed to do, and I still find it unsettling. I note every time Brutus is out of his cage and Finch shows up. They are never in the same room at the same time.

I have officially been in public school for one month. In that one month, I have learned more than I ever did in a year with Vernon. I still feel lost and dumb socially, but I'm maintaining a decent level of cool. Having friends and a punk rock badass as a mother helps.

Dutch Valley High School is full of Babies. I meet new ones every day. Today it was a kid in the cafeteria who said, "Your mom saved my life one time." He just said it and stared right into my eyes, and then turned and walked away.

The reality of public high school, though, is that it's exhausting me. I fall asleep a little after lunch every single day in Rothenberg's history class. Today, for the third day running, I fell asleep in the car on the way home. I was in so deep, Milorad had to physically shake me awake.

He parks and lets me wake up as he fiddles with something over by the pool house. I finally drag myself into the house.

There is a woman—a new stranger—in the study teaching Henry about earth science.

"Where's Vernon?" I ask.

Henry shrugs.

I go through the study to the garden. It's a beautiful day. Crisp and sunny. Milorad is moving bags of mulch from the shed to a rose bed. I go back into the house and into the kitchen.

"Marta?"

It's four. Dinner is always at five thirty and Marta isn't here. Usually, I can talk to her after school while she preps food.

I hear the whir of the System. The fan is always louder in the kitchen. I know now that this could be a tutor or anyone other than Mother, but my brain still wishes it was her. The capsule goes by with Henry's science tutor in it.

When I walk back through the house, Henry is already out in the garden with Milorad. The System is still whirring, and it makes no sense until I see Henry's dancing tutor hurtle by in a capsule.

"Welcome home, Jane! How I missed you!" Vernon says. He pats me on the head as he walks by with a stunning bouquet of flowers. "How was school today?"

"Why was Henry's dancing tutor here?" I ask.

"Suppose she was heading home." He arranges the flowers in a large glass vase. "It's after four."

"Wait," I say.

"She does other things besides teaching your brother how to dance," he says. He finishes arranging the flowers, brushes pollen off the arm of his sport coat, and checks his pocket watch.

I ask, "Who are the flowers for?"

"Thought I'd make the place look festive."

"Is Finch coming over?"

Vernon's shoulders go back like he's suddenly proud. "Not tonight, no. Gemma will be here at five to dress you."

"A suitor?"

"I'm excited for you to meet him."

"Me too!" I run upstairs and turn on the shower. *Gemma Gemma Gemma Gemma.*

"I'm wearing whatever you want me to," I say, eyeing myself in the mirror. "I don't even care."

Gemma laughs. "We have until six."

"Great."

"How's school? Is it fun? Are you making friends?"

I lie naked on the down duvet Mother sent from Europe—white with green leaves and butterflies on it.

"School's good," I say. "But something weird is happening here."

"Oh?" she answers.

I roll onto my front and twist my wet hair. "How do you get here? Like—to the house?"

"I—um—walk, mostly." Gemma is a bad liar.

"That's odd. Henry's tutors have been using the System."

"I'm so glad Vernon finally got him some tutors," Gemma says. "Hopefully algebra, yeah?"

"And you walked?" I say. "Today?"

Gemma looks down.

"What aren't you telling me?"

"It's nearly five thirty, Jane. We have to get you ready."

I look at Gemma lying and she's beautiful. She has these ringlets—curls people would pay money for. She just has them swept aside like they're nothing. Tucked behind her ear.

"How about something school-themed to echo your week?" she asks.

"Whatever you dress me in will be perfect."

I stand at my vanity and slowly moisturize myself. She throws me fresh underwear and a bra.

"No bra. I've been wearing one all day. That's one thing I hate about this new life." I slip on the panties and then stand like a mannequin with my arms out to my sides and my eyes closed.

Ten minutes later, Gemma is finishing some light makeup on herself, and I zip on a pair of knee-high boots. I look at myself in the mirror. Plaid school uniform skirt—too short. Vernon will not approve. Good. V-neck sweater with a little white button-down under it. No tights, even though it's below freezing outside.

I stop by the vanity after I hear the doorbell ring. I apply big black cat eyeliner on the edges of my eyes. When Gemma sees, she approves and leans in and kisses me on the cheek.

It stops us both.

Gemma has never kissed me on the cheek or anywhere before.

She has shocked herself, it seems. Her face goes red and then stark white.

I ask, "Are you okay?"

She answers, "Let's go, shall we?"

By the time we get downstairs, Vernon has a roaring fire going, the table is set and ready, and I hear Marta in the kitchen whipping potatoes.

"Where's my suitor?" I ask Vernon.

"Outside. Had to make a call," he answers.

I find myself oddly disappointed—it's been three months without suitors and I admit I miss the thrill. I walk into the kitchen. Marta looks me up and down. "Nice boots."

"Thanks."

"Sorry I'm late."

"Can I help?" I walk around to where she has most of the food ready to serve in ceramic bowls and offer to take some into the dining room.

She's carving the chicken. "It's fine. I'm nearly ready."

It's abnormally chilly in the kitchen. I touch the top of the oven and it's cold. "Where did you roast that chicken?"

"What?"

I watch her lay the meat out on the plate, pour gravy on it, garnish it with parsley. I note her jeans have flour all over them as if she was baking, but there are no baked goods in the usual basket on the large center kitchen island. "How come the oven is cold but you have a roasted chicken?" I ask.

The System clunks to action and the fan whirs throughout the house. There's the usual noise and then suddenly, into the dumbwaiter area of the kitchen tube, a basket arrives.

"Where did this come from?"

Marta ignores my question and retrieves the basket from the dumbwaiter. I can smell them—warm dinner rolls. Her special recipe. As she balances three family-style bowls on her platter and heads to the door to the dining room, I walk toward the tube.

I press the Call button, and a capsule clunks its way toward me.

When the capsule arrives, I get in.

I close the door.

I press the big green button.

Inside the tube, it smells of Mother's hand cream and Marta's dinner rolls.

As I brace myself for movement, I look out into the kitchen and see what Mother sees. I always thought her view would be distorted by the curved plastic, the way ours is when we look in at her, but it's not. Everything looks normal.

Marta comes back through the swinging door just as I start to descend. I see her see me and rather than panic, as I expect her to do, she waves and smiles. I feel like this is a movie and I've been rehearsing for this role my whole life.

STATION SIX

I don't expect music. I always thought it would be windy and thumping and loud and fast and violent, but actually, the ride is smooth and feels cushioned and the song that's on is familiar—it takes me a few seconds to recognize it's the Stooges' "I Wanna Be Your Dog," which is a song Vernon hates.

The ride gets faster as I go—from the basement hallway outside Mother's room to a lower level, and then one lower than that. Then I am flipped onto my back and shuttled through a long dark area that opens up to a sort of station. The capsule slows here.

It is brightly lit and tiled white. The ceiling is familiar—glossy-white-painted industrial wiring and plumbing.

As I look around, I can see the mechanics of the System and can picture other capsules, but I can't see anything but my own.

Standing on the platform dressed in blue-and-white-striped aprons are women who seem to be conductors. My capsule comes to a stop—still horizontal and in a chute of some kind. A woman in an apron comes toward me and leans down.

"Welcome to Station Six, Jane!" she says.

"Thank you."

"Are you looking for your mom?"

"Can you send me to where Marta cooked dinner?"

She has a small tablet—like a cellphone—and she seems to be entering all I say.

"Absolutely. Your mother's there. Just giving you the heads-up."

"Great," I say.

She types a few more things and my capsule moves along

through the white-tiled station. It picks up speed and heads toward a tunnel to the left. Everything goes dark again. My ears pop as I descend even deeper.

SAFE HOUSE MOTHER

When the capsule comes to a stop, vertical in a dining room with the meal attachment in place, there are three women around a table talking and eating and laughing, and they all slowly turn to look at me.

"Jane!" one of them finally says, her hand over her mouth, looking like she's about to cry, and I look at her and expect to recognize her, but I don't.

The other two say, "Hi, Jane!" "Nice to see you, Jane!"

I wait for someone to let me out of the capsule, but then realize it's not locked.

"Jane?" Mother appears tube-side and opens the door for me. "I didn't expect this," she says. "I'm overjoyed to see you!" We hug.

"I asked one of the apron women to send me to where Marta made dinner." I look at the food on the table. Roast chicken. Mashed potatoes. Marta's dinner rolls. Unmistakable.

"Does she always cook here?" I ask.

"No. We just had some work to do so she made dinner here tonight."

"Are you hungry?" one of the women at the table asks.

I look at Mother. "I should probably go back—Vernon arranged a suitor."

Mother nods. "Does Marta know you're here?"

I shrug. "Where is *here?*"

"Ah," she says. "Let's get you back to dinner in . . . is this cosplay? Are you doing a Britney dinner party?"

She's smirking so I know she's joking. The other women have gone back to their conversation. I look at them. I look around.

There are no real windows, but there are artificial ones. Everything is painted with bright colors and calming designs. There are fresh flowers in vases and several abstract paintings of sunflowers on the walls.

I never got more than five feet from the tube. I turn to Mother.

She asks, "You okay?"

"What is this place?"

"This is Safe House," she answers.

"Where is it?"

"About fifty feet under the backyard. I'll explain later."

"Okay," I answer.

"I saw Gemma today and she said she was coming over," Mother says.

"Has Gemma been here?"

"That's her story to tell," Mother says. "You read the guide, right?"

I look at her, stupid.

"In *Safe House*? The laminated card?" She can see I don't know what she means. "In the record sleeve?"

Shit. Now I know why she wanted me to listen to *Safe House*. "I'll find it when I get home."

She nods. "Okay, good. For now, let's get you back."

"Okay. I love you," I say.

With that, the room goes silent. The women turn toward us.

"I love you, too, Jane." Her eyes well up and she holds a shaky smile.

As she closes the door on the capsule and then seals the entrance of the tube, the tears escape her eyes and roll down her cheeks. One of the ladies at the table gets up and comes to her and rubs her back.

I no longer know the truth about everything. The truth about everything keeps expanding.

There are women who know who I am and who must know the stories of me hurting Mother. They live nearby—fifty feet under my backyard—which I will know more about later. Mother knows Gemma from outside the house. Marta sometimes cooks meals somewhere else. And seemingly there is a System of tubes that move people beyond our Victorian country home.

This is a lot.

When I get back to the house, I find I've only missed the appetizer. Marta looks at me differently now. The only thing she says as I exit the System is "They saved you two dinner rolls."

BACK TO THE DINING ROOM

Vernon is in storytelling mode. It's the one about the time he went fishing and caught five hundred mythical fish. "The boat was full of them!" he says. "We just had to steer them into the coolers!"

I find my seat and nod at the suitor—whose name I forget—and glance over at Henry, who has, like me, heard this story many times before. He rolls his eyes at me. I smile.

Marta brings plates with chicken and gravy, potatoes, vegetables, and some sort of cranberry compote. I eat without saying much. Vernon tells story after story. Even the suitor looks bored. Before Marta serves dessert, I say, "I'm sorry. I feel unwell. I need to go lie down."

Vernon raises his eyebrows and gives a slight nod. I go upstairs and get out of my schoolgirl outfit as fast as I can (Free Britney!) and I replace it with my favorite pair of pajama pants and an oversized sweatshirt.

A gentle knock at the door announces Gemma's arrival and by the time she opens the door, I am deep in my bed, covered in all my blankets, trying to stay calm about how much I don't know about her.

Every time I find out a new piece of the puzzle, I feel stupid and trust no one. At least Vernon is predictable. He is always lying. To God and to everyone else.

Gemma asks, "Do you mind if I sit down?"

"I went into the tubes," I say.

"Marta told me."

"I saw my mom."

"Good," she says.

"I'm so ashamed." With that, an ocean pours from my eyes. I curl away from Gemma, and she rubs my back as I cry until I vomit into the trash can next to my bed. Then I cry more. "I was so cruel!" I say.

"You didn't know," she says.

"It doesn't matter!"

"You were taught to be that way."

"I was fucking evil."

"Don't say that."

"I was, though," I say.

"I know," she says.

I lean over the side of my bed and vomit into the trash can again. I retch and retch until nothing more comes out. Gemma rubs my back and hands me a few tissues.

I can hear my own blood rushing through my ears. I hear my heart pushing it through. Everything else in the world slows. It's like how people describe getting shot.

While Gemma takes care of the mess I've made, I lie very still on my side. Close my eyes. I picture me, Henry, and Mother in the rose garden, reading books when we were little. I breathe it in. I breathe it out.

Gemma returns from my en suite and says, "I have to go back and report on how you are. Vernon will talk that young man to death, I fear."

"Will you come back?"

"If I can, yes."

I hear her a minute later making apologies for me. No one at the table is disappointed—Vernon keeps talking. I stay under the covers. I am awake and alert, but from the outside, I look asleep.

I don't know what to do now. "I can't stay here," I whisper.

Then I find *Safe House* and pick up the record sleeve.

QUICK START GUIDE

I reach in and pull out a six-inch square of laminated paper with a weird logo on it that looks like a maze and the heading QUICK START GUIDE.

As I read, I start understanding the last year of my life and even more than that. Let me show you. Here's side one:

Ordering Tips

- **Order any woman for any reason by logging into your account, and then click Ordering on the menu.**
- **If you require a woman for a task not listed, click Special Order and tell us what you need in the text box.**
- **You may not order women younger than 16 for love needs. (See Love Needs link in the menu.)**
- **Women under age 18 are accompanied by an adult woman for jobs requiring sexual, medical, or psychological know-how.**
- **If the woman sent to you is not the right woman, log into your account, click on Return Order and give as many details about what's wrong with your woman as you can so we can build your personal profile, then return the woman through the System. A new woman will be sent as soon as she is available.**

- Make sure the bank account that is linked to your account is under your name. Any bank accounts that do not match will not be charged or credited.

Here's side two:

Offering Tips

- Log into your account, click on Offering in the menu, and then List Your Offering.
- Know the worth of your product. The most sought-after women in the System, outside of Love Needs, are tutors, cooks (foreign cuisines +1), nannies, cleaners, and shoppers.
- You may not offer women under age 16 to suitors. See Rules for Suitors link in the menu for more information.
- Women over age 17 are high value to both suitors and families and are often in short supply.
- If your offering is harmed in any way by a customer, you are entitled to compensation. Click on File a Claim and follow instructions. Most claims are processed within five days. If the claim involves criminal behavior, it could be ten days.
- Use common sense. If your offering is damaged or defective, do not list them as an offering. After five consecutive returns, your product will be examined and future offerings must be approved on an order-by-order basis.

I flip the card over several times. My heart is pounding, and I am suddenly hot. I feel like getting sick again. Downstairs, Vernon entertains my suitor and Henry with more stories while the fire roars in the sitting room. Marta serves dessert and coffee. Vernon probably offers cognac or whatever. I feel like writing a scene in the opera, but I don't even know what to write, so I look through Mother's other records in my room, stopping at *Run, Jane, Run*. The sleeve art. I see it clearly—the white industrial steampunk cover is simply a picture of the ceiling in Station Six. It's what we see as we're shuttled on our backs.

JANE'S REPRISE

At 5:00 a.m. on Friday, I grab the iPad from the en suite, walk to the tube in the corner of my bedroom, and press the Call button for a capsule. The whir might wake Vernon, but I doubt it. I didn't hear his bedroom door close until three. The capsule arrives quickly, and I let myself into the System. I press the green button, same as last night. The capsule drops below basement level, same as last time. But this time, once the capsule goes horizontal, I am moving a lot faster. So fast, I almost feel like throwing up again.

I arrive in the station. It's bright white, same as last time. Sterile. New. Sparkling. Everything about it is the future, but when I look to the high ceiling, the conduit and pipework are sprayed white. It's totally the album cover for *Run, Jane, Run*, which means I must be in the right place. *Jane has run.*

A recording of a woman's voice comes from the speakers in the capsule upon entry to the chutes. "Welcome to Station Six."

A station guide appears outside my capsule. I smile at her. She smiles back.

"Where are you going?"

"I want to see my mother," I answer.

"She's sleeping now, Jane."

"I need to see her."

"She wakes at six."

"Do you know when everyone wakes up?" I ask.

She looks at me and cocks her head to the right. Says nothing. Walks away and lets me lie here. From behind I can see a tattoo she has on her right calf. It seems to be a hunk of cheese inside of a heart.

When she returns ten minutes later, I am breathing so slowly I must appear dead.

I open my eyes when I hear her say "Jane!"—as if me being alive was a shock.

"Do you love cheese?" I ask.

"Who doesn't?" she replies.

We stare at each other.

"I'm going to send you to your mother now," she says, and taps the screen of her little tablet. "Next time we'll get you all registered and checked in."

She waits for me to ask. But I know not to ask. I don't want to be registered. I don't want to be checked in. I don't want any part of this bullshit. None of it. Same as the koi fish in Gretchen Brown's foyer pond should be free to swim in a lake and not stuck in a tiny pool of filtered water and smooth jazz in the foyer of an ultramodern prefab in Pennsylvania.

SORRY TO BREAK IT TO YOU

I arrive in the main room of Safe House again; this time the dining room is empty, the table has two vases of fresh-cut flowers, and the false windows have night scenes. Aurora borealis. A sky packed with stars.

I release myself from the capsule and follow the smell of coffee.

There's a room beyond the kitchen with sunlight, which is

impossible. I walk in, and Mother says, "Good morning, Jane!" before I spot her sitting on the floor in the corner, on a meditation pad, bathed in morning light.

"Hi!" I look up at the fake-sky ceiling.

"My boyfriend from college invented those." She points to the ceiling light, which looks like a huge skylight but isn't one because we are many meters underground. "He gave me a huge deal on account of him regretting some stuff. Bad boyfriend, decent businessman."

I sit down on the sofa in the room. It's yellow. Everything in the room is either yellow or white. It's like being inside an egg. But fresher.

"What do you know? About this place? About me?" she asks.

"Well," I say and let out a sigh. "I now know that Vernon's been pimping me out to boys all year like it was some great rite of passage when really he's been getting paid for it." I gesture wildly because that's some bullshit. "But other than that, I know so little, I don't even know how to answer that question."

She gets up and sits on the chair facing me. We both put our feet on the mod coffee table. "Let's start here. I am what's left of your mother. And I'm pretty sure you hate me."

I nod. "Except I don't hate you."

"Mmm."

"I acted like I hate you. But I don't hate you. I'm actually more like you than anyone else. But I can't say that . . . At home, I mean."

"I worry about you and Henry so much," she says. "Marta updates me daily."

"He won't even let me take walks."

"I know."

"I have some things to show you," I say while I pull out the iPad.

"So . . . you don't hate me?"

I look into her eyes. "Not at all. I love you," I say. "I'm sorry for all the things I said and did. I have to show you some stuff so you understand why I did that."

"I don't care about why," she says.

"No, no. You have to let me tell you. You don't know what's been going on at home all these years."

She says, "I have to talk to you about the System and what's really happening out here. Everywhere in the world, really."

"I know I'm next."

"That's what I'm trying to change," she says. "I want to rescue you and your generation from this."

"And I want to rescue you. Right now."

We laugh and she points out how our feet are the same—flat arches and wide at the ball. "Let's figure out how to do that, yes? How to rescue Mina Placenta, part one."

"You could just not go back on tour and open the door on the capsule and walk out like I just did."

She frowns. "He has it locked for me. Otherwise, I'd have walked out long ago."

"Oh."

"Maybe we should back up. You probably need more information."

I sigh. A trillion-pound weight on my chest lifts when I say, "I think I know more than you do now. A lot more—like I just said."

Her eyebrows raise. I hold up the iPad.

"Vernon keeps all the security footage in a local storage cloud. I've been watching it."

"The cameras," she says.

"Mmm."

"How far back?" she asks.

"Since 1999."

She looks intrigued. "Do you want hot chocolate?"

"Sure."

She motions for me to follow her, and we walk through the hallway and back into the kitchen. It's bigger than I expected. Everything here is. She puts the teakettle on and fixes a French press for her coffee and fills another mug with cocoa mix. With marshmallows. Because she's my mother and even though she lives in a System of tubes and capsules and dinner chairs and shitty husbands, she knows I love cocoa with marshmallows.

"Between the two of us, I'd say we have a lot of information," she says.

I don't know what to say. She's making cocoa and coffee like it's totally normal, and she's walking around free in a pair of flowy pants and a loose tank top that reads WHAT'S MORE PUNK THAN YOUR PUBLIC LIBRARY?

"What's wrong?" she asks.

"You're . . . you."

She nods. I nod. We look at each other.

"I don't want to make you cry," she says.

"You're not making me cry. I'm making me cry!" I cry. "I didn't know. I didn't know what was going on."

She puts her coffee down and hugs me. I stop crying.

"None of us know what's going on," she says. "It changes day-to-day. That's why it's so effective."

"Oh."

"It's why I built this place. Or—rebuilt. My great-aunt Lily built it and used to come down here, too."

"So, you're not on tour?"

"I was on tour," she says. "I just get in a day or two early sometimes. Safe House is my center of operations, really. From here I'll eventually reclaim the System."

I'm nodding but I don't even know why. "It's like I was born inside a mystery novel," I say. "And I'm some kind of detective of my own life. I'm tired of figuring things out. I want one thing to be easy."

"Do you want me to explain?"

I nod.

This is what she tells me. There is a System of tubes that goes far beyond our house, far beyond Station Six, and it shuttles women around to places where they're needed. "By men, naturally," she adds.

"Henry's dancing tutor," I say.

"Harriet, yes," she confirms. "And Gemma and the cleaning ladies and the woman who sets up the pool every spring."

"How do they know where they're needed?" I ask.

"Men order them. On the app. So Harriet was ordered by Vernon."

"Huh," I say. "Wait. So all women who work? Are they all in the System?"

She pinches her lips together. "Technically, yes. But most don't know it? Seems odd, I know, but it's how it's always worked."

"You'd think they'd know if they've been ordered and have to get into a tube, right?"

"Not all of us use the tubes. Some are out there in their own cars or taking the subway or whatever. I mean, even I take the subway when I'm near one. Out there we have the choice."

"Is Marta in the System?" I ask.

"Marta has a special role in minding you and Henry," she answers. "But she also has a role in the reclaiming and the work we do here at Safe House. She can't talk about it because she had to sign an agreement with Vernon about not telling anyone what happens in the house."

I have so many questions. "I heard the System whir in the high school office. Does it have stops like a subway?"

"Good question. I can't answer it, though. Because none of us know how the System really runs," she says. "Station guides seem to know how to shuttle us around and we just go from there."

"Back up. My teachers are ordered?"

"Not quite." She shakes her head. "But teachers are some of our biggest recruiters."

"Recruiters?" I am so tired of being a detective.

"Best place to find out where the abuse is." She leans over the table and takes my hands. "See, this isn't just a System to move women around. We're—well—we're making *improvements*. So, a lot of the women use the tubes for escape—from homes that were not safe for them."

I am looking at her now as if she's a bit insane and also an angel, just like *Rolling Stone* said. "You help other women escape? While—like—while you're locked up by Vernon?"

She nods, reaches to the table next to her, and hands me a small booklet. On the front, it reads *For the Useful*.

"Before you read that, let's talk about suitors," Mother says.

"Okay."

A frown appears on Mother's brow. "Since your last birthday, how many suitors has Vernon arranged?"

"Twenty-five or so?"

Mother raises her chin and nods, impressed. "Do you know how much he's charging?"

"No." I don't know what to say after it. I must look pained. I feel pained.

Mother makes a sound like what she's about to say causes her pain. "I didn't know if Vernon told you the truth, but I suspected he didn't."

"He even lies to God."

"He does, indeed," she says.

I drink the last of my hot chocolate and clean the marshmallow off my lips with a napkin. "So the System isn't, like—prison?"

She looks down first, then looks me right in the eye. "It's all in there," she says, pointing to the pamphlet. "It was made to be a prison. By my great-aunt Lily's husband, Rodney. The house was Lily's parents' house, but they both died in mysterious circumstances in 1935, only two years after Lily and Rodney got married."

"Oh."

"Oh, indeed," she says. "So, then the house was left to Lily—my grandmother's sister. Rodney built the System during the Second World War, and Lily lived as a prisoner inside of it from about 1955 until Rodney died in 1987. She lived here freely after that, and I would visit her weekly until she died, also mysteriously, in 2001, just after I married your father. She was the one who built Safe House." She gestures around her.

"Are you going to die in mysterious circumstances, too?"

"I should hope not," she says. "I aim to get out of here soon, regardless."

The whir sounds. I look at the sunflower clock on the wall above the doorway.

"I thought you were the only one in there," I say.

"Of course you did."

"Why don't you just make Vernon leave?"

"It's not that simple." She shakes her head, but looks down, as if she's ashamed. "Now he has my sister involved and that's messy."

"She's trying to get the deed to the house." I feel the weight of the iPad on my lap. "I have things to show you."

"She's always *been* trying to get the house. And him. And you. And he's always been trying to get the house, and her and you. It's a game that no one else is playing but the two of them." She looks at me.

"I feel like I was lied to my whole life."

"You *were* lied to all your life," Mother says. "I'll feel guilt for that forever, even if I didn't know what was going on at the time. I'm so sorry. Lying for men is what women do, it seems."

"He had you brainwashed." I hold up the iPad. "I've seen it."

"Show me," she says.

I look at the clock. I've got five minutes. I find the "Clorox" mixtape, and we sit and watch all three minutes of it.

CLOROX MIXTAPE (CHRONOLOGICAL ORDER)

01.21.2002 / Dining Room / Mother is eating her dinner. Vernon is across the table, and he suddenly screams, "What is wrong with you?!" Mother jumps. "Vernon, you scared me," she says. He smiles. "Just keeping you on your toes."

04.05.2005 / Study / Mother asks warmly, "How did the job interview go yesterday?" Vernon kicks the leg of a chair and sends it scooting across the room. "You only ever want me to feel like shit," he says. Mother answers meekly, "That's not true." Vernon replies, "Stop crying. You're just manipulating me." He paces. "I didn't even go to that interview because if I actually got a job, can you imagine how miserable you'd make me?"

10.31.2007 / Sitting Room / Vernon is in a pair of pajama pants standing above Mother, who is dressed in a red-sequined maternity dress and a pair of combat boots. "You're not going anywhere," Vernon says. "But we RSVPed," Mother says. "You're feeling poorly, and I can represent us as a family." She points to her small bump. "You're not leaving this house," he says.

12.12.2007 / Dining Room / Mother sits in the armchair by the fire, pregnant, and Vernon leans over her, his hands on the arms of the chair, trapping her in. Mother says, "I thought you said you'd stop being abusive if I had a baby." Vernon laughs. "I never said that. Plus, this baby will love me way more than it ever loves you. I'm going to make sure of that."

THE POSTPARTUM CHORUS COLLECTION

03.15.2008 / Sitting Room / "I never said that!" (Right after he said exactly that.)

04.01.2008 / Foyer / "I never said that!" (Right after he said exactly that.)

04.11.2008 / Study / "I never said that!" (Right after he said exactly that.)

04.19.2008 / Study / "I never said that!" (Right after he said exactly that.)

05.18.2008 / Foyer / "I never said that!" (Right after he said exactly that.)

TEN YEARS LATER

09.13.2018 / Patio via FaceTime video / Mother says she knows what's going on at the house between him and Finch. Vernon laughs and says, "I think your work is driving you mad. Much as it pains me, the children hate you and I hate you. You're just such a pain in the ass."

<stop>

I forgot how harsh mixtapes can be because they're stitched together so tightly. I wish I had enough time to show her the "Vernon's Pie Crust Apologies" mixtape. It's a perfect pairing with the Clorox.

"Wow," Mother says.

"Yeah," I say.

We sit in silence for about fifteen seconds.

I ask, "How much do you know about Finch?"

She gets up and stretches. Cracks her neck left, then right. "She's my sister. I know a lot."

"She's a shape-shifter. You know that, right?"

"Oh. Yeah. My sister, the girl with many faces."

She's just going along with me, the way we all go along with anything that feels safe. "I mean literally," I say. "She's not human."

"She's not human. True, true," she says. I can tell by her face that she doesn't know what I'm talking about. Still processing the "Clorox" mixtape, no doubt.

We both look at the clock. I point to it. "I'll have to tell you the rest another day," I say. I look at her. "God, I miss you."

"Come back after school. I'm here for your birthday!" She points to the *For the Useful* booklet. "Make sure nobody sees that."

We stand up and hug. "Tell me what makes you happy these days."

"I'm writing a punk opera."

"Oh!"

"It's about how I rescue you from this place."

"Oh."

I get up and take a deep breath. Mother follows me into the dining room where one of the women who was here last night is sitting by herself, reading a book at the table. Mother gives her a motion like she can stay, and she smiles at us both.

Mother opens the door to the capsule. "Before you go—what do you want for your birthday?"

I'm a musician. I know how powerful rests are. I give this one a whole two measures as I step into the capsule and close the door.

"I want you," I say.

Before she has time to answer, I've pressed the button and head back to Station Six.

OMNISCIENT RAT

Everywhere, all the time

MINA WILL NEVER BELIEVE. By the time she was five, I could punch her right in the stomach and she'd act normal. If our mother asked where she got the bruise, she'd say she didn't know. I'd laugh it off and she'd monkey me because that's what I taught her to do.

Easier than training a dog.

Humans are suckers.

By the time she was ten, she idolized me.

Her first boyfriend in high school—Mike something—duped her into all kinds of weird stuff before I had to tell our parents. For her safety, of course. That's what I told her, too, so she knew how much I cared.

In college, I watched her fall in love with every single guy who'd walk into her life, each one potentially the one who might help her understand the hole in her center, but who all had holes in their centers, too, so she never got to fixing her own. She never knew the hole was from me punching her there for so long.

That's the trick with suckers.

Eventually, you teach them how to punch themselves.

OUR PEOPLE III

It's an icebreaker!

LET'S GET TO KNOW MARTA!

Marta was the first one Vernon approached with a nondisclosure agreement, drawn up by his lawyer cousin, who's the only family member he still talks to, though he refers to him as a *crooked, fat son of a bitch.* He cornered her in the sitting room, and said, "If you don't sign it, you can never talk to Mina or the kids again."

LET'S GET TO KNOW MILORAD!

Milorad has a lot more in his past than I could ever guess, he says. His contract with Vernon is, in his words, "binding until death." He said no more after that. Serbians, am I right?

LET'S GET TO KNOW GEMMA!

Gemma doesn't feel like one of our people anymore because she's never here. I don't think she's signed any contracts with Vernon, because since I turned fifteen, she only comes when I have suitors.

LESSON TEN: FOR THE USEFUL

Today is Friday, February 28, 2025

I STUFF THE PAMPHLET into my pajama pants. I've been lurking around in the middle of the night for six months looking at home movies, and I've never been this paranoid.

"Where are you going?" the station guide asks.

"My bedroom, please," I say.

"Have a lovely day at school, Jane!" she says.

I arrive back in my room and my alarm goes off at 6:04, right as I'm hiding the iPad. I brush my teeth and get dressed.

I hide the booklet in the leg pocket of my beat-up green cargo pants that Marta calls "army chic" as she hands me a plate of waffles. "How'd you sleep?"

"Restless," I answer.

I eat fast, walking through the school day in my head. I forgot to study for a math test. And I forgot to write the list we need for history.

"What kind of cake do you want for your birthday?" Marta asks. "The usual?"

I always ask for a chocolate cake with peanut butter icing.

"I'm not sure yet," I answer. "I think I'll change it up this year."

"Seventeen." She shakes her head.

"I should be driving."

"One step at a time," she says.

By the time I get to school, I've recapped the math work and feel pretty confident about the test. The history list can be compiled during my other classes.

"Fuck!" That's KZ when I walk into the bathroom.

Gretchen fist-bumps me as I get to the mirror and dig through my purse to find my eyeliner. KZ brings their phone to us and shows us a text from Porter. It's a picture of a police car in front of Eric's truck and Eric standing outside the truck talking to the police. The text under it reads **Gonna be late today, yo.**

"Fuck," Gretchen says.

"Yeah," I say.

For the Useful calls to me all day until I can finally pull it out and read it during study hall in the library. I hide it inside the self-chosen novel I'm reading for language arts—a book by Jacqueline Woodson called *Brown Girl Dreaming*—and I find this:

History of the System, Part One

Built in 1942 by Rodney Dunkin, while most American men his age were fighting in WWII, the System was invented as a novelty at first. His wife, Lily Vandermaker, of the Vandermaker department store fortune, used to complain as a joke about having to climb the stairs to her bedroom at night. The couple lived permanently in the Vandermaker summer home after Lily's parents died mysteriously in 1935, and Rodney enjoyed the countryside after his boyhood in Trenton, New Jersey.

When Rodney saw what had been done with small-scale pneumatics in Lily's family's store, and after reading about the Beach Pneumatic Transit system from 1869, he decided that the System would be a fun surprise to give his wife on her return from spending a summer in Nantucket with her extended family. He had made it

quite clear before Lily left that he was growing tired of her amorous advances and attempts to start conversation. With the System in place, he could show that he was still a man willing to do whatever it took to keep her comfortable without sacrificing his own comfort, plus, the System could prove to be a possible help to those who were disabled in ways that had them unable to move through a house of this size effectively, which made him look charitable.

Construction took twice as long as he'd planned, so he sent word to his wife that he'd arranged an African safari for her and her best friend, and that the house had been infested with rats, so she should stay away until it was taken care of. It wasn't a complete lie. There was a rat problem.

His wife's return brought Rodney much sorrow. It seems while she was away, Lily took on many habits, such as smoking tobacco, writing travel essays, oil painting, and cursing. More disappointing is, she didn't find the System all that impressive. She instead mourned the removal of her father's mahogany corner cabinet, where he'd written letters to his pals fighting in WWI, and she complained of a strange smell coming from the plexiglass.

Lily Vandermaker recalled, in her personal diary:

> *Rodney seemed to think I was as-is when we married—that I shan't ever grow. Perplexing, because his own mother had changed careers on three occasions. He told me, about my painting, "Lily, you're not going to be a great impressionist you know. Plus, I think the fumes are driving you mad." I replied, "It's you that's driving me mad. Please just let me be, lest I fetch my father."*

It only took two months of Lily being creative and intelligent in front of him to drive Rodney to the edge. He put Lily in the System one day—"As a lark!" he said—and sent her from room to room, and when she attempted to exit the System in the study, she found the capsule locked. Always a trusting woman, Lily waited patiently on the chair provided until Rodney arrived back in the study. He walked right by her as if he didn't see her at all. She called his name and knocked on the tubing, and he walked by again. It took until later that night for him to let her out. In the six hours she was trapped, she realized two things: one, he knew full well she was locked in. Two, he was exactly the louse her father said he was when they married.

"What's shakin', favorite lady?" That's Marlon. I close my book.

"Not much, man."

"Do you like reading?" he asks.

I frown at him, a show of skepticism.

"I mean, you seem to read a lot," he says.

"Not really."

He nods. I wait for him to walk away.

"March is coming," he says.

"Happens every year," I say. "Astounding."

"I mean spring break. Are you going anywhere?"

"Nah."

He smiles. "You want me to leave you alone, right?"

"It's nothing against you," I say.

"I've seen *Beauty and the Beast*," he says.

I nod, and he dances away, singing, "No one walks like Gaston / no one talks like Gaston / no one makes girls he likes fuckin' balk like Gaston!"

I go back to the booklet and skip to the bullet-pointed pages in the back of the book.

Tips for the Useful

- **Do the job you are ordered to do, be punctual and quick, clean up after yourself.**
- **If unsure of the exact task, ask the client to check your work before you leave their home.**
- **If you are ordered to tutor in an area you are not familiar with, respond by clicking the Not Me button at the bottom right of the order message. Make sure to keep your skill list up to date in your file.**
- **You cannot respond "Not Me" to any other jobs.**

"No kidding," Marlon says, now back in my space. "I can't stop thinking about you and I know you said you don't date anyone or whatever but I think you're really cool and really hot and maybe if you want to see that new Marvel movie or any movie, or—"

"Oh my God," I say.

"What."

"You're serious, aren't you?"

Marlon looks around and nods.

I smile at him for a few seconds and then realize.

"This isn't fair," I say. He's about to defend himself, but I hold my hand out. "Wait. I mean it's not fair to you. I'm sorry, but I can't date you."

He doesn't deflate the way I thought he would. "You have a boyfriend?" he asks.

I shake my head.

"It's because I'm Black?"

I shake my head again. "You're probably the prettiest guy in this place. Nicest, too."

We stand there for an awkward moment.

"I'm gay," I say.

"Oh shit" escapes his mouth before he can stop it.

"For you, I guess."

"I'm sorry," he says.

"No one knows," I say again. "I mean, unless they could guess."

Marlon smiles. "There's, like, twenty guys trying to figure you out, man." He laughs—it's genuine and a real-time litmus about how gay I am because Marlon's laugh is gorgeous and sexy and smooth and, *wow*, am I gay. "Rob told us stuff about dating you," he says.

"That's different. That's something my dad does—sets me up with guys."

Marlon's face changes. "Your dad set you up with Rob Kaninski? Seriously? Does he not like you?"

"Nailed it."

Marlon looks even more confused. "Wait. Your own dad doesn't like you?"

"He's complicated."

"I bet."

"You won't tell anyone?"

"Oh yeah, nah—I won't tell anyone," he says. He makes a move to go, and I stop him and hug him and kiss him on his cheek. When I let him go, he smiles and walks over to his friends, who totally saw us and are acting like seventh graders about it. I go back to the handbook.

- **The System must approve all requests for long-term placements. Nannies and wet nurses are most likely to get approved. Tutors and teachers next. Cooks and cleaners are typically not used for long-term**

placements unless the family is of considerable wealth or notoriety.

- **Love Needs support groups (for ages 18 and over) are every night at 8:00 and 10:00 p.m., eastern time. You may not discuss any ongoing criminal investigation at group meetings. You may not use names of clients at group meetings. Special group sessions run once a week for women ages 16 and 17 for both Love Needs and Suitor Needs. Just tell a station guide where you're going, and she'll send you.**

I stare into space for a while thinking about how messed up this all is. How it's not just me. How it's not just my house. How it's not just Mother. I look over at the librarian, Ms. Houck. *Maybe her.* I look at the other girls in the library study hall. *Maybe them.*

When the bell rings, I get up and walk but my feet don't fully feel me walking. When history starts, I participate but only part of me is in the room. The other part is in the tubes.

I can only get back to the handbook in my room after school. First, a snack to make everything feel normal, and Marta says *one day until Mother flies in!* even though she knows I know Mother is in Safe House, in a room full of sunflowers. I excuse myself to my room. Vernon and Henry are nowhere to be seen.

THE RECLAIMING

Tips for Breaking the System

- **Train in tasks and jobs that men historically have held. This way, our usefulness will become something they depend on.**

- **Form woman-led conglomerates that outperform male-run companies and provide incentives for women held in those male-run companies to become part of the conglomerate.**
- **Organize local safe houses where women most in need can recover, reenter their lives, and encourage them to open businesses and do large-scale commerce.**
- **Continue to rescue women in homes where they are not valued or if they are being abused in any way. This demographic continues to grow and the only people who can help them is us.**

I flip to the front of the book again and back to the history area. I'm nearly sure Aunt Lily wrote this book, but she keeps referring to herself in third person so it's confusing.

History of the System, Part Two

As Rodney's wife was locked in more, the System became a break for her—an escape. She treated it as a holiday where she would sit in the chair provided and visualize her next painting or her next outing. And as her husband drank himself limp every night in the sitting room next to the fire, she began to make the System bigger. She already knew other women who had brutes for husbands like she did. Why not connect them all and form some sort of club? While her luckier peers went to quilting and knitting circles, she made connections and acquaintances with women from all walks—especially ones whose families were connected to construction. When Rodney went on an extended convalescing holiday to

Europe, she brought three teams of builders to the property and constructed Safe House five stories beneath her own backyard.

As the years went on, Safe House became a refuge for brood after brood of recovering women. Lily moved them through and sheltered and supported them until they reached their new life.

Station Six was constructed by someone along the way; by 1980, there were routes between Lancaster and Reading, Philadelphia, York, and Harrisburg, Pennsylvania, respectively. Lily never knew how far the tubes extended but she hoped one day someone would tell her. She never did find out.

Thirty years later, Lily's great-niece Mina, who inherited the home when Lily died and landed in the System in much the same way, met and helped women from as far as North Carolina and Michigan. The System could be everywhere. It could be in a few places. It could move around. We have no idea. All we know is that the men think they control us with their communication attachments and their remote control devices, but once we hit the green button, we find out who's really controlling the System. The station guides allow men to think they're in control, but in reality the station guides can make any capsule go anywhere they want.

We're most concerned with a way to reclaim our lives and families. We are millions of women inventing bigger and better things than our surroundings. We invented it for ourselves. But we never quite know how far we can go, same as Lily. Mina never found out either.

Mother wrote this part of the book. Unmistakable. Everything about it makes me want to jettison myself into the System and find out how far I can go.

What a contradiction. This time yesterday, I still thought the tubes in our house were a prison that contained my mother only. Today, I know the prisoners transformed their cells into love and compassion for fellow prisoners.

Instead of doing my homework, I write a song for the opera.

Song: "Be Careful"

Composer notes: *This has Blondie undertones. Soft punk.*

EVERY MAN WANTS A GAL WHO'S USEFUL.
ALL FOLKS UPTOWN CAN VERIFY
USEFULNESS CAN LOOK APPEALING
UNTIL, IN FACT, YOU ARE HER GUY.

EVERY MAN'S IN NEED OF ONE FINE WOMAN
TO HELP HIM MAKE THE BEST OF HIS LIFE.
IF SHE'S AT WORK AND NOT MAKING HIS DINNER
THEN HOW CAN YOU EVEN CALL HER A WIFE?

THERE'S A WAY TO PUNISH SUCH BASE BEHAVIOR
WITHOUT HAVING TO CHOP HER UP INTO CUBES.
SIMPLY TELL THE CHILDREN ALL YOUR STORIES
AND LOCK HER UP INSIDE THE TUBES.

YOU SAY YOU WANT HER TO BE USEFUL.
YOU SAY YOU WANT HER TO BE KIND.
BUT THEN YOU SAY YOU WANT HER USELESS.
WE KNOW YOU CAN'T MAKE UP YOUR MIND.

ALL THAT MATTERS IS WHAT LOOKS GOOD.
THAT'S ALL YOU REALLY CARE ABOUT.
AS LONG AS NO ONE KNOWS THE TRUTH
ABOUT HOW YOU NEVER LET HER OUT.

BE CAREFUL WHAT YOU SAY TO HIM.
BE CAREFUL WHAT YOU DO, TOO.
NEXT THING YOU KNOW, YOU'LL BE TOO USEFUL
AND HE'LL DO THE FUCKING SAME TO YOU.

RABBIT-RABBIT

Marta teaches me during late brunch on Saturday that saying *rabbit-rabbit* on the first day of the month is good luck. I go to see Milorad after brunch. He is cleaning the pool house with music playing.

"Rabbit-rabbit," I say.

"Yes, you say this also like Marta."

"Is this Serbian pop music?"

"It is from Italy. I like her voice. She is also pretty," he answers.

I go to Brutus's cage and he's running on the wheel in there. I wonder if he knows I know. He stops and looks at me in a way that makes me wonder if he can read minds.

Shit.

I never really thought about how much Finch would know if she's able to run around this house as a rat. It's like having a stalker. Or something creepier. Makes me want to hide everything I own. Brutus continues to stare at me, standing completely still on the wheel. If I'm to be honest, I'm a little afraid for my life.

"Can you help with this?" Milorad asks. He is trying to move the couch by himself.

When I stand up and brush my pants off, I notice Brutus is able to walk through the tiny cage door and saunter away, and while he does, his head is turned to look at me.

ASK MILORAD WHY HE DOESN'T LOCK BRUTUS'S CAGE SOMETIME

"I cannot lock the animal inside the cage fully. Never fully," Milorad says.

I look at the cage. It's a bird sort of cage. Any rat could squeeze through the bars. I never noticed that before. In all these years. "He goes in willingly?" I ask.

"Yes."

"He doesn't stay in there all day?"

"I am not here, but no, I do not think it stays."

"So all this time Marta's been chasing the rat, it's because it's just a rat who gets to roam free?" I ask.

"Like a squirrel," Milorad says. "But inside."

"Huh," I say. "But you feed him."

"Homemade."

"No wonder he comes back."

"Yes," he answers. "It is no wonder."

"Where did you buy a rat, anyway?"

He laughs a little. "I did not buy this rat," he says.

We sit and stare as the rat eats one of Milorad's chicken-and-spelt treats.

"That time you were chasing it with a brick?" I ask.

"I once killed a rat with a brick. In my mother's kitchen," he says.

There is awkward quiet.

Then: "I cannot lock it up, but I cannot kill it. I nourish it. Yet it still shits on my floor and eats my food off the counter. I am allowed to be mad when the rat eats my food."

More awkward quiet.

"Can you tell me about what's going on around here?" I ask.

Milorad quickly shakes his head no—as if he's afraid. His hands are shaking.

"Are you afraid of the rat?" I ask.

He blinks twice.

"You are," I say. I look at Brutus, still munching. He is farm-rat black. Nothing special. "There's a reason you chose him and a reason he chose you."

STATION SIX MIXTAPES

It's very difficult to sit next to Mother and watch her watch the mixtapes. The "Everyone Hates Mina" mixtape—a history of the shit-talking—is devastating, and she cries.

"I can't watch anymore."

"I'm sorry," I say.

She shakes her head. "I had no idea this was happening."

"Not even after he locked you in?"

"I trusted him. He lives off my money. He says he's holding down the fort."

"He makes Finch do a lot of the dirty work," I say, thinking it might console her.

"Finch is quite willing," she answers. She sighs. Stands up. Stretches. "Let's take a walk."

We walk to the dining room, where Mother gets in the capsule and says, "Once I go, you call a carriage and follow me." I nod, noting her use of the word *carriage*. Makes it sound perfectly Victorian, as if all this was rational and the height of fashion.

When I arrive at Station Six, the station guide says, "Ah, Jane. Welcome back." She presses a button on her tablet that rotates my capsule and opens the door. She leans down and sticks her hand out. "Up you get!"

I stand up and then climb out of the track. She presses something on her tablet again and sends the capsule along, then points over to Mother, who is on the platform, talking to two station guides. I walk over.

"Jane, this is Louisa and Birgitta," she says.

I introduce myself and ask the name of the woman who just helped me out—the one with the cheese tattoo. Mother says, "Liesel."

She takes my hand and walks me over a little bridge that spans the tracks and we sit down, cross-legged, in the corner of the sparkling white station. She starts to tell me the story of how the System works.

This is what I learn: You never see the women in the capsules ahead of you or behind you. You are always delivered on time to the place you're supposed to go. The station guides know best, even though they got their job by some man thinking they were truly useless.

The fuel of the System is the mega fans—banks of fans that pump air to move the capsules—located in discreet areas on lands belonging to Reclaimers. At the helm of the System are the station guides, who are magic. Most are also Reclaimers, Mother tells me. "After all, they're the only ones with the power to shuttle us around, so we had to make sure we had them first. Wasn't hard. Not only are they women, but they are, like many women, exploited at work. Many of them are volunteers."

There are grown women who don't know about the System—and a way about them that makes them seem naïve or rejected. As if they weren't picked for the kickball team or marriage. A feeling of childish superiority to make up for the obvious: they are not useful. This is not known to them, but they feel it the way a person knows a surprise party is coming—even if no one has told them.

"Louisa says that you must return in an hour. I want to tell you more but I trust you read the booklet?"

"Yes. I have questions," I say.

She nods.

"How do we reclaim it?"

"We already are," she says. "We've been reclaiming it for years."

"When will you be free?"

"On your birthday."

My face lights up. I frown again. "Will you stay home?"

"I have to finish touring, but after that, yes."

"Are you—are you, uh—" I exhale through loose lips, cheeks blown out in frustration of not finding the words. "Like, are you, uh, scared?"

She looks up to the ceiling. "Like—for my life?"

"Yeah."

She sighs. "Not really, no."

"Marta and Milorad will protect you. And us."

"That's not your job," she says.

I wait. I think. I say, "I spent my life treating you like shit because I was rewarded to do so. And because it kept me safe. Same as you stayed safe inside this—this System. Protecting you is my number one job now."

"Being seventeen is your number one job now. Just trust me."

"You seem so confident," I say. I want to add *but you don't know everything. I do.*

"I have no other choice. I have to get my life back. I'm so sorry you've had to hear all that terrible garbage about how crazy I am. I'm not, you know."

"I know. I'm sorry I had to show you. I wasn't sure how much you knew."

"Try to have compassion for your father. He was raised in the patriarchy and was never allowed to grow a heart or a warm place in his chest for himself."

"Fuck him."

"Fair. But the patriarchy harms men as much as it harms women. They live in a delusional world where they are in charge and sexual royalty, when in reality, they have little power and are often disinterested in sex," she says. "My great-aunt Lily could tell you stories. Rodney was a tyrant because he didn't want anyone to love him. Or even touch him. Then they twist it all to be our fault, when really it's the fault of the System they invented in the first place. This is why I like being in a band. No one is in charge. We're all in charge. And we change the rules as we need to. That's how life and government are supposed to work. But nothing works now. The Systems of oppression broke the whole world, I guess."

"Damn."

"Yeah."

"Will you ever stop making excuses for him? Because he makes none for you and wishes you dead."

She looks me right in the eye for a whole ten seconds. "Shit," she says.

We sit in silence watching women shuttle through and station guides tap on the screens of their little tablets.

I ask, "Do all the women in here—are they all escaping like you did?"

"In one way or another, yes. We've made the best of a shitty situation, I suppose."

"Seems sad," I say.

"I want to read your punk opera," she says.

"I have to finish it first," I answer.

We get up and walk back over the bridges to Liesel, the cheese lover. She puts Mother in a capsule first and sends her back to Safe House. Then me, back to my bedroom.

Mother told me I couldn't visit tomorrow because she'd be away. I spend the weekend reading the opera and trying to figure out the ending. I have no idea how the characters will really free Mother, same as in real life.

SEVENTEEN

Today is Monday, March 3, 2025

MOTHER IS IN THE KITCHEN at 6:00 a.m. for breakfast, just as she promised on Saturday, but she's in the System, the meal attachment affixed to the front.

"Happy birthday!" she and Marta say in unison. Marta comes in for a hug. I walk over to the System and fist-bump Mother.

"I'll be out later," she says. "This is for show."

"To old times!" Marta says, raising her coffee cup.

Henry arrives, still in his pajamas and half asleep. Marta sits him down and she serves us all porridge and toast.

"Happy birthday," Henry says. "I feel terrible. I didn't get you anything."

"You're more than enough." I ruffle his already-ruffled hair.

"What did you want for seventeen?" Mother asks. "I don't think you said."

"I want you out of there," I say. "That's all."

She answers, "But how about a laptop so you can keep writing the opera?"

"Opera?" Henry says.

I motion to everyone be quiet. "It's quite against the rules," I say.

"Rules." Mother nods. "Which ones does the opera break, exactly?"

"All of them," I say. "Except for Number Six, though I'd argue that my writing an opera somehow breaks the no-leaving-the-property rule because I leave in my mind."

Mother looks surprised. "There's a numbered list?"

Henry begins to recite it sleepily. When he gets to the rules specifically pertaining to Mother, her face blanches. I know what it's like to get information later than everyone else. Her face is a waterfall of that. Layer upon layer of trying to understand why any father would tell his children to ignore their mother, screaming in a tube in the same room.

Let me show you.

HOME MOVIE—01.15.2019

Mother is in the tube in the study. She is standing up, her whole body pressed against the plexiglass like she's trying to walk through it and get out. Henry and I are home from school, doing our homework.

<pause>

Mother had been locked in the System for three weeks at this point, since The Christmas That Changed Everything. The Christmas That Changed Everything was the Christmas she came home from the *Safe House* tour relaxed, happy, and quite satisfied with a successful year for her career. It was also the year Vernon found her giggling on the floor with me and Henry on Christmas afternoon and by evening, he'd badgered her into System. She walked in, with a playful pout on her face as if this was his old game. Three weeks later, he still hadn't let her out.

<resume>

"Stop it, Jane!" Vernon yells, because I am looking at Mother.

Minutes later, "Stop it, Jane!"

"Henry, you too!"

Mother stands, pressed against the plexiglass.

"Jane!" he says, a few minutes later. I am ten years old. My mother is locked in a tube. I can't help but look at her.

"Why don't you put her in another room?" Henry asks.

"Because her punishment is to watch us do great things," Vernon answers. "Without her."

<*pause*>

I wanted to point out that doing fourth grade homework isn't necessarily *doing great things*. Didn't seem the time.

<*resume*>

We finish our homework and Vernon leaves the room, and Mother starts pounding on the plastic tubing. I go over to her and put my hands on the plastic. She puts hers up to mine and we lock eyes.

"Stop it," I say. "You're going to get in more trouble."

"JANE!"

Vernon walks to me and grabs me by the arm and practically drags me out of the room. Henry sits in his chair and stares at Mother, then gives a weak, paranoid wave. He is seven and the only homework first graders got that day was a sheet to color and he colored the entire sheet blue. The whole thing is blue. He is so proud of it, he holds it up for Mother to see.

<*stop*>

I never did stop looking at her that week. By the next week, Rule Number Eight was made and I was grounded to my room on three occasions.

BALLOONS

When I arrive in the bathroom for eyeliner conversations, Gretchen is holding three Mylar birthday balloons. "Seventeen!" she and KZ and Porter yell when I arrive.

Hugs ensue. They got me a bento box filled with cake that looks like sushi. I eat it at lunch, where they make the whole table sing to me. I go to the nurse afterward because of how emotional it makes me. I think of my last birthdays. All sixteen of them. The nurse lets me lie down on one of her cots. I didn't lie to her. I could throw up right now, thinking of my past birthdays. Except my fifth, when I got a xylophone and Marta made my cake the shape of a unicorn.

I take stock of my life, there on the cot. I am in actual school. I got a solid B on a biology test and the teacher seems impressed with me. I'm doing okay in geometry, too. I have no idea how I'm managing this, but I am and I'm proud. Vernon's prediction that I'd be back in the study pretending he is a teacher turned out to be wrong, which makes me see that all of his predictions could have been wrong. Maybe everything he ever said was wrong. A lie to God. Garnish to make him look better on a plate. Maybe I'm not so hard to love after all.

Marlon gives me a small note for my birthday during library study hall. *Dear Jane, If ever you decide to try us dudes out, call me first!* 717-555-2244. I hug him for it even though it's kinda stupid—just to make the other guys in study hall curious.

As I walk toward the car to meet Milorad, Mylar balloons swaying as I pass each bus and the breeze rushing through the gap, someone yells, "Happy birthday, Jane!" from a bus window. It causes a cascade of happy birthdays from the crowd outside the front doors. I get emotional again. I wish I could get rid of this—whatever it is. It's like I have some kind of birthday grief.

When I get to the car, I'm surprised to find Marta driving.

"Hi!"

"Hi," I say, stuffing the balloons into the back seat of the car.

"You good?" she asks.

I sit and put my seat belt on. "Yeah. It's just cold. Sometimes my eyes water."

I open the glove compartment for a tissue. When I pull out the tissue box that Milorad keeps in there, a letter, folded in three, falls out and onto my foot. I see the same logo from the Quick Start Guide and pry it open enough to see the heading.

Vernon Cook
1111 Spruce Street

February 6, 2025

RE: ACCOUNT SUSPENSION

I fold it inside my hand while I fiddle with the glove compartment and then shove it in my schoolbag. Hiding things from Marta seems wrong, but if she knows about the Quick Start Guide and hasn't warned me, then I feel any secrets from her are fair.

When we arrive home, I head inside, leave my backpack and balloons on my desk in the study, and head upstairs to change into something more comfortable.

Vernon Cook
1111 Spruce Street

February 6, 2025

RE: ACCOUNT SUSPENSION

Mr. Cook,

Your account has been temporarily suspended due to the following breaches of contract:

Ordering Violations

1. You have returned too many women with no relevant explanation.

2. In interviewing five of your most recent returns, System officials have learned that you made advances on two (2) women without their consent during the week of January 27. Consult the Handbook pages on Love Needs re: all transactions are required to be consensual.

Offering Violations

1. Your filed claim from November has been denied due to disputed information. You claimed your product was harmed, but our records show no such harm.

2. Your product has deserted her duties on more than six occasions. She was reported and returned prior to these desertions for being too assertive, arguing politics, and not being loving during her Love Needs (Suitors) appointments, yet you continue to offer her for Love Needs (Suitors). Please consult your Handbook for training resources and additional information on how to prepare Love Needs products for adequate System use.

"I am far more than adequate," I say to myself in the mirror. I don't know what to do with this letter now that I've taken it. I find the *nonconsensual advances* unsurprising, which makes me wonder how much I intentionally don't think about my own life. As if I've been brainwashed the same as Mother.

Oh my God. We're all brainwashed.

He may have only thrown the furniture at her, but *we* became the furniture. Or something like that. Either way, this letter has been sent to me by the gods. They would like me to somehow make sure that Finch sees it. Happy birthday!

Vernon is waiting at the bottom of the staircase when I come down.

"Happy birthday!" he says, arms out. I hug him. "Marta says dinner is at six."

"Yes."

"And you changed your cake order, she said," he says.

"Growth and change are part of life, I suppose," I answer.

He puts his arm around me as I walk toward my backpack. He squeezes my shoulder twice.

"No suitors for tonight," I say.

"Of course," he answers. "I hadn't planned on it."

"Mmm," I say.

He peels off toward the kitchen as I head to the study.

"Happy birthday again!" Henry says from his desk. "I made you a card!"

It's a picture of me and him, with frogs all around us. "Your drawing is really good! You should get that art tutor Vernon wanted to get for me."

"Not gonna be an artist, but thanks," he says. "What game are we playing tonight?"

"Toss-up between Clue and Life."

He nods. I open my school computer and take a picture of the letter, just in case I lose the original.

"Where's Mother?" I ask.

"She left after breakfast and hasn't been back."

I go to the kitchen.

It smells delicious. The oven is hot and the whole room is hot, the way it usually is when Marta is cooking a big roast. I peek through the oven window and see a big ham. On the stovetop is a large potato pot filled with peeled and chopped potatoes and a smaller pot with John Cope's corn—a specialty that's too hard to explain to those who don't know it but it's the best corn to eat with ham. And another pot, presumably for Marta's famous ham gravy.

But no Marta and no Mother.

I look at the tube and consider going to Safe House, but it's my birthday and I have a bit of homework so I go back to the study, open my school laptop. I think of how different I am compared to myself this time last year.

This time last year, I had never seen a home movie. I didn't know my mother at all. I hadn't been out of my house in four years. Now look at me. Nearly a fully formed Baby, I go to school every day and have friends who have slept over at my house and who I've had snowball fights with. And I've written an opera. About how Vernon lies to God. About suitors. About being the last to know what's really going on. Though I'd guess that's really Henry. Poor chap.

Dinner is delicious and my cake—a red velvet with buttercream icing—is perfect. Henry doesn't love it at first, but eventually, he gets over the food coloring and has a second piece. Vernon hates red velvet cake.

That's not why I chose it.

Mother arrived at the house through the front door an hour before dinner, holding a big wrapped box for me. I'm not sure how she's getting away with not being locked up, but she and Vernon must have had a conversation because he has said three times already that *this is just for Jane's birthday* while Mother reminds us she has to be back in London by Wednesday.

Finch is so quiet, I keep forgetting she's even here. Not like I'd have invited her if I had a choice myself, but her presence has purpose. Gemma couldn't make it on account of her having another job tonight. My stomach tenses to think it might be Love Needs, but I try not to think about it.

Marta clears the table and Henry, Mother, and I help her. It gives Vernon and Finch time to whisper with each other.

HOME MOVIE—03.03.2025 (TWENTY-FOUR MINUTES AGO)

Finch walks in the door and looks done with life. I meet her in the foyer. The copy of the letter is in my back pocket.

"I'm so glad you're here," I say.

"That's new," she answers.

"Sorry about the last few months. I've been bitchy."

"No worries." She hugs me and gives the two-kiss European hello on release.

I sigh.

"You okay?" she asks.

"I have something to show you but I probably shouldn't."

She looks concerned. "Is it something from school? Are you okay?"

"I'll tell you about it later." I hold my finger to my mouth in a *shh* motion as Vernon walks quietly into the foyer.

While the two of them talk in the foyer, I go to the cabinet where the Grammys are and reach up to the third shelf where Vernon has hidden more of Mother's postcards. I replace them with the copy of the letter.

<stop>

IT'S A PARTY! / FAMILY GAME NIGHT

We are sitting around the dining room table. Though Henry's favorite game is Clue, I have chosen [The Game of] Life.

The first indication that this is going to be an interesting night is when Finch, after "meeting her future spouse" on her first turn, gets to the chapel and picks a woman as a wife.

Henry declares, on becoming a doctor (salary $20,000), that he would only ever be a doctor of animals or plants. "Humans aren't my thing," he says. Mother and I are teachers (salary $8,000). Vernon is a lawyer (salary $15,000) and is as smug about it as if he'd just passed the actual bar exam.

The gameplay is drab. We spin, move our little cars along, collect money, pay money, collect children in the back seats of our cars, play the stock market. Mother is acting as banker, so she is busy and in her element, handing out salaries when people pass spaces that read PAY DAY!

Vernon hits the poison ivy space and loses a turn. Then, Finch lands on REVENGE and makes him pay her one hundred thousand dollars, which clears him out. Henry is ahead of all of us, playing the stock market every chance he gets, while Finch moans about how no one told her the benefits of life insurance and the cash bonuses along the way.

Two turns later, Vernon lands on REVENGE and asks Mother for one hundred thousand dollars, and Mother replies, "Why don't you ask Finch for your hundred grand back? She's the one who took it!" He presses her for the money and she tosses out an *Exemption* card from her stack of cards. Vernon sulks.

Henry spins the wheel for his turn. "Adopt a girl *and* a boy! Collect presents!" He holds his hands out for money and we all give him a thousand dollars.

Mother spins and lands on LUCKY DAY and wins one hundred fifty thousand dollars. Finch tries a *Share the Wealth* card on her, but

Mother has another *Exemption* card. Finch meows. Henry looks at his hands. Vernon hisses, "Tss-tsss."

I surprise myself. "What's wrong with you?" I say.

Finch says, "What?"

"You're not a hypnotist," Henry says. He gives side-eye to Vernon. "We're all here. We heard you."

I spin and move. "Iceberg rams yacht! Sell ice cubes. Collect five thousand dollars," I say. "Can we talk about how messed up that is?"

Henry says, "As if there are that many icebergs left to hit."

Finch meows again.

"They talked about ice cubes like it was some kind of joke," Henry continues. "Jane and I will be alive when the Bahamas drown and the plagues hit."

Vernon—"Jesus, Henry. It's Jane's birthday and—"

"Yes, it's my birthday and I think Henry's right. Your generation is part of the problem."

Marta nods as she delivers hot chocolate. "All of us."

"Not me!" Finch says.

"Oh, I think you're a bigger problem than anyone here realizes," I say. I haven't had any alcohol, though Vernon offered. I'm just feeling as bold as I did three years ago where my birthday gave me carte blanche to pummel my mother with boxes of Trivial Pursuit cards.

Finch hisses at this.

"Do you think you're a cat?" Henry asks her.

"Come on," Mother says. "Let's keep playing. Henry will have us all beat if we don't catch up soon."

"I don't even know why I'm playing," Vernon says. "I can't win."

"It's Jane's birthday. That's why we're playing," Mother says.

"Be a sport," I say. "Eh, Vernon?"

Finch meows.

"Do you think you're a cat?" Henry asks again. "It's your turn. Spin."

Finch spins and lands one space in front of me and my ice cube stand. I read, "Bridge out ahead! Back up fifteen spaces!" She throws her hands up in frustration, and Henry counts her back fifteen and places her car where it should be.

Henry's next turn, he spins a ten and lands at the DAY OF RECKONING, cashes out his children, and makes his decision to keep going to Millionaire Acres.

Vernon is catching up, and when he lands on the BUY A TOUPEE space, none of us say anything about his bald spot because he's very sensitive about it.

Mother and I both land on the same spot on the bridge. She exclaims, "Collect two hundred thousand dollars if you own stock!" She beats Finch's *Share the Wealth* card with an *Exemption*, then hands me another *Exemption* card under the table in case the bitch tries it with me, too, but she's out of cards.

<pause>

If I can take a minute to draw the scene for you—

This doesn't quite look like a family having fun on my birthday, but it's close. Mother seems to be having fun. Henry is having fun. I'm having fun. Marta is having fun watching in between runs to the kitchen for drinks and snacks. Finch isn't having fun—but she never does. And Vernon is just drinking a lot and he pretends to have fun the way he pretends everything—no *Exemption* card for that, old boy.

We're not *overjoyed* like some commercial for soap or whatever. We're just playing a game of Life. Henry will probably win and is on his way to Millionaire Acres, Mother and I are on the bridge to retirement, collecting two hundred thousand fake dollars apiece. Finch has just bought a yacht for thirty-six thousand dollars, and Vernon is about to spin the wheel.

<resume>

Vernon spins a four and Henry reads the space, "You've been robbed! Pay thirty thousand dollars!"

Vernon pounds the table and yells, "This shit's just like real life!"

We all look at him. He's drunk, for sure, but he's on the verge of something bigger.

"Have you been robbed in real life, Vernon?" Mother asks.

Finch spits, "You rob him every fucking day!" She looks like Madonna in that meme, pointing and screaming at Mother.

"She gives him everything he has," Henry says.

"Let's finish the game," I add.

"What happened to this family?" Vernon bellows. "We used to be on the same team!"

He's staring directly at Henry while Mother leans forward and spins. Henry ignores Vernon's stare and reads, "Sell the cattle ranch, collect one hundred sixty thousand dollars."

I toss out a *Share the Wealth* card and she has no *Exemptions* left, so she gives me eighty thousand dollars and takes the same for herself. When I spin and Henry reads, "Sweepstakes winner! Collect one hundred thousand dollars," Finch leans in and whispers something to Vernon.

Vernon breathes uneven for a few breaths, and then in one fast move, he leans forward, flips the Life game board, little cars and blue and pink "people" fly everywhere, and then he stands up, balances himself with the back of his chair, and walks out of the room. A moment later, you can hear the slam of his bedroom door.

Marta comes in and starts to clean up the mess. Finch says,

"I'm leaving," and walks directly from her place at the table out the front door.

Mother is separating money into piles and reaches for Henry's.

"I was finally going to win!" he says.

"It's Jane's birthday," Mother says. "Jane wins."

Henry smiles and hugs me. It's weird. Also, he smells like wine.

Marta, Mother, Milorad, Henry, and I sit around a warm fire in the sitting room and I face a small pile of wrapped presents.

"You can open mine now," Henry says. "It's small and I—well, Marta got it for me while you were at school."

I open it and it's a gift card for concert tickets. My jaw drops. "Henry! This is for five hundred dollars!"

"I don't know how much tickets cost, but maybe this way you can take friends?"

I hug him.

Marta and Milorad bought me some cool Bluetooth headphones, and Mother gives me the ukulele she bought in Salzburg.

I strum it until I find the chords for the Happy Birthday song, and they sing to me and Mother hugs me and this is family and you can't tell me it's not. No one is hurting anyone. No one is lying to anyone. No one is in a tube.

Once Mother goes back to London, we're going to have to go back to pretending like this hour didn't happen. "When you finish the opera," she says, "we can work on the score."

HOW THE RAT ARRIVED

I FIND BIRTHDAYS TEDIOUS. Seems dumb to celebrate getting nearer to death.

Even when they celebrate my birthday, it's stupid. I give their gifts away on the walk home—even the homemade ones. Jane caught me one time. I threw a picture she painted into the trash at the house and she must have seen it in there, pulled it out, ironed it back to flat, and then she gave it to me again. Loser.

Fact is, I don't have a birthday. I was never born. I rose from hell like every other shape-shifter. By now you know this, right? You know but Jane doesn't because her imagination isn't nearly as advanced as yours is. She still thinks I lived all over the world in big mansions, living in luxury and horseback riding, when really, I was running through sewers, whispering secrets, causing wars.

I won't keep it from you any longer. I did murder my great-aunt Lily Vandermaker—willingly, indeed. She was interfering with a System she didn't understand, eating up that 1970s women's liberation shit like it was real. Everyone knows women don't mean a damn thing in the world.

Then, when Aunt Lily double-crossed me in the will, there was one obvious thing to do. Only I made sport of it. I've murdered millions of people—it's easy. But making someone else murder a person, that's something worth being proud of. And Vernon Cook is probably the dumbest and easiest puppet I've ever worked with. His hatred for my sister was already ravenous by the time I hooked him. Now I just need him to do the job so I can have my rightful place as head of this whole family.

ACT FOUR: SPRING

Reclaiming / Do Not Fuck with My Mother

Can you take me to the safe house?
The place where I can rest?
Can you hold my tired pretty head?
Can you tell me I'm the best?
Can you take me to the safe house?
It's bright and pleasant there.
Marta makes potatoes.
Gemma curls and sets your hair.
It's a giant roller coaster!
It's the inside of your toaster!
Put my face up on a poster and
take a ride, inside, inside my bride.
Never mind the whirring clatter.
The words he speaks—they never matter.
He only aims to sever ties.
He only ever fucking lies.
Just enjoy the pitter-patter.
The words he speaks—they're only chatter.
You have won the biggest prize.
You don't believe his fucking lies.
(Take a ride, inside, inside my bride.)
I've got your mind, I've got your heart, I've
got your fix.
Trust me trust me trust me baby—go to Station Six.
Go to Station Six.
Go to Station Six.
Baby, you can save yourself.
Go to Station Six.

© Placenta 2018

LESSON ELEVEN: WITCH TRIALS

Today is Friday, March 21, 2025

CALLING JANE VANDERMAKER COOK TO THE STAND

Loyalty is a big deal to Vernon. Irony isn't always funny.

It's five o'clock on the Friday before spring break, and I have been summoned to the sitting room for an interrogation. This one has an actual point, unlike most of the others I've lived through. Today in the school library, I printed the opera. It was risky but it's getting too big to work on the iPad and I want to be able to hold it in my hands. It's almost done. Just a few scenes to go, and with a whole week off, I figured I could lay the pages out and see what the ending will look like. I didn't expect the after-school bag check.

"Who have you shown this to?" he asks, shaking my printed opera manuscript in his hand.

"Literally no one."

"You're lying," he answers. "You're hurting our family with this—this *thing* you're writing."

I look at Finch sitting next to him, performative worry on her face.

"Is this our family? Really?"

"Answer the question," Finch says.

"I've told no one. We don't really talk about family at school. And if we did, how would I describe this, exactly?" I gesture at Vernon, then Finch, then all of us, and the whole room. "Would I say

I have two mommies? Or that you have two wives, or wife-sisters? Like—how do I say it?"

"You'd say your mother is a workaholic," he answers.

"Like you give her any choice," I say.

"How dare you! After all I've been through!"

I open my eyes in mocking shock. "Like the big stabbing, eh?"

This is different from how I used to handle Witch Trials. I was younger then and not equipped for this kind of bullshit.

HOME MOVIE—05.21.2018

I am on the sitting room settee next to Finch, who is petting my hair as if I'm a dog. I am ten years old and in fourth grade.

"Poor dear," she says. "You deserve better."

"I do," I say. "I deserve so much better."

"What do you hate the most about Mina?"

"Oh," I answer, with ten-year-old's sass, "so many things! Like how she sings in the shower and how she tricks me into looking out the window and then takes a piece of my food."

"So rude!" Finch says.

"And how she always wants me to be cleaning something. She's a clean freak!"

<*pause*>

For the record, I do not remember Mother telling me to clean anything but my bedroom when we were young. And I was a slob, so it made sense.

<*resume*>

"She was always a clean freak." Finch nods. "What else?"

"She won't let me have a horse," I say.

Finch nods. Vernon says, "Terrible!"

I continue. “The way she meditates. It’s so dumb!”

“I thought you liked it,” Finch says.

“I liked—I don’t know—sitting still, I guess. Anyway, I think the thing I hate the most about her is how she’s never here.”

<pause>

Mother was on the *Safe House* tour. It lasted the entire year. The more copies the album sold, the more enraged Vernon and Finch became, and the more they’d tell me and Henry that Mother had abandoned us because she loved working more than she loved us.

<resume>

“How much money do you think Mina’s made so far?” Vernon asks from his armchair.

“It must be millions!” Finch says.

“Nothing for us, though,” Vernon says. “Nothing for poor Jane, who wants a horse and who even has room enough to keep it!”

<pause>

This was during my serious horse-girl phase.

<resume>

“If there was a way I could get you a horse, I would,” Finch says. “I’d get it first thing in the morning. “

<stop>

Wait.

Want to see something terrible?

Rewind a week. Find Finch sprawled on the patio bench, talking to Mother on her cell phone.

HOME MOVIE—05.14.2018

"Of course she does!" Finch says. "She's ten!"

While Mother talks, Finch nods.

"That's all fine but who would take care of it?"

Mother says something.

"I appreciate that, but you asked me my advice and I don't think she's ready for a horse."

Mother says something.

"I *know* she knows how to ride. That's not my point. Riding and owning a horse are two entirely different things."

<stop>

The reality of shape-shifters is that they are, every cell, always shifting. And there's Vernon, trusting her while she destroys, on an atomic level, the family he insisted on having. Or maybe Vernon is a different kind of shape-shifter. Maybe this is what becomes of those who lie to God.

WITCH TRIAL (CONT'D)

Vernon speaks calmly. "When did you first start writing this—this *opera?*" he asks.

"I don't know. Like—back in the fall sometime? It was just a fun thing to write on the side, you know?"

"Fun songs about how your daddy touches you?" he asks, eyes wide for effect.

"Your double leg squeeze *could* be patented," I say.

"How many people have you shown it to?" he asks.

"I only printed it yesterday."

"Who saw you print it?" Finch asks.

"Like—the library aide? She didn't even see it."

"Touching you?! Seriously!" Vernon says.

Marta walks into the sitting room with a full tea service and places it on the table. I reach for a cup and Vernon slaps my hand away. He makes a cup of tea for himself and makes one for Finch.

She picks up her teacup and sits back. She looks at me. "Why'd you print it? Who're you showing it to?"

I shrug. "No one."

"You're lying," Vernon says.

"I guess I learned from the best," I reply. When his hand whooshes toward me, I'm already heading toward the kitchen.

"You can't just walk away!" Vernon shouts.

As I walk through the study, I look at the tube and consider the relief of self-imprisonment as escape.

I understand now. I understand.

HOME MOVIE MIXTAPE: MINA'S WILLING SURRENDER

03.10.2012 / Sitting room / All four of us are sitting around a fire, listening to music and reading, and Mother is bouncing Henry on her knee. Vernon asks her to stop. She doesn't. When he begins to yell, she passes Henry to Marta, who has come to see what's going on, and walks to the tube next to the TV and gets in, closes the door, and descends into the floor.

05.13.2013 / Sitting room / Vernon screams, "You can't just walk away!"

12.01.2016 / Study / Vernon screams, "You can't just walk away!"

06.18.2017 / Study / Mother runs and looks for a place to hide. Vernon arrives a moment later as she steps in. By the time he gets to the tube, she's closed the door and her capsule has ascended to the second floor. Vernon screams, "You can't just walk away!"

09.13.2018 / Dining room / Vernon screams, "You can't just walk away!"

HENRY'S MARCH SURPRISE

An hour later, I am curled behind the mustard-velvet wingback chair with matching ottoman. Henry is testifying in the sitting room.

"Have you read Jane's opera?" Vernon asks.

"Jane has an opera?" Henry answers. "How do you even read an opera?"

Finch says, "You're not missing out."

There is silence.

"Can you tell me what you hate most about your mother these days?" Vernon says.

I can hear Henry exhale in that frustrated way he does. "I hate the way she's so into yoga or whatever."

"Okay," Vernon says. "But what does she do to you that you hate?"

"Fuck, man. I barely see her. And when I do see her, she seems pretty nice, if I'm being honest."

"Did you just curse at me?" Vernon says.

"Did I?"

I don't know what's gotten into Henry.

"Don't you two have work or anything? Milo and I are working on the hothouse. I only have so much daylight. And I—"

Finch cuts him off. "Do you remember the time you told me you thought your mom didn't love you because she worked all the time?"

"Yeah. I do. I said it because that's what you told me my whole life. Now that I look at it, I think probably you didn't tell me the full story."

"What's happened, Henry? You're so rude!" Vernon says.

Henry answers, "Maybe you two should interrogate each other and write your own fucking opera. You sure are dramatic enough for it."

I hear him get up. I hear him walk right out the double doors.

"Jane's done something to him," Vernon says.

"Surely," Finch answers.

"She's going to pay for this," he says.

They start to make out like groundhogs on the settee and I keep my brain busy.

Song: "Rodent Love"

YOU GOT YOU A GIRL
AND AIN'T SHE SEXY
ENOUGH TO GIVE
YOU APOPLEXY.

YOU GOT YOU A BOY
AND AIN'T HE HANDSOME.
WATCH OUT, GIRL,
YOU MIGHT NEED RANSOM.

YOU WANT TO BE IN LOVE.
I'D SAY YOU'RE IN LUCK.
BUT REMEMBER RATS DON'T KISS.
THEY ONLY FUCK.

(unfinished)

VERDICT

After dinner, Finch goes home and Vernon calls me into the sitting room.

"I've burned it," Vernon says. "But I'll need access to the file."

I say, "You can't have it. It's mine and I'm allowed to have my own art and expression." I hold a USB thumb drive in my hand—it contains exactly no files. Vernon taught me how to do this. His lies to God have been the only education he was any good at.

"You live in my house and eat my food and—"

Henry says from the study, "Get real."

"Shut up, Henry!" he says. Then he looks back to me with his hand out. "Give that to me."

Vernon is drunk. I am Victorian Jane. "Please don't do this! I shan't write any more songs about your leg-squeezing or anything at all that's bad. It's just confusing growing up like this!"

"Give me the file," he says. I have the drive clenched so hard in my palm, my fingernails are cutting me.

"Give it to me!" he slurs, seizing my arm and trying to pry my hand open.

"You're hurting me!"

"Vernon, stop!" Henry yells from the study.

My hand goes weak from him twisting. He takes the thumb drive and walks back to his chair, sits down, and sighs.

Then, in one move, he tosses the drive into the fireplace.

"Your *expression*, as you call it, was terrible. Do better next time. Maybe you could write about things you know about like—what is it you know about?"

"Not much of anything, I suppose," I say.

"Exactly."

"May I be excused?" I ask. "I have to study for a biology test." I don't wait for him to answer—I get up and head to the kitchen.

"You wouldn't have a test if you'd have just stayed here with me and Henry! You wouldn't need to know anything about biology! Or chemistry! Or anything!"

As I approach the door to the kitchen, I look into the study and see Henry, bent over a book about tropical forestry with a beer in his hand—a thirteen-year-old man.

LESSON TWELVE: FROGS

Today is Saturday, March 22, 2025

MY BROTHER HAS HAD A WEIRD LIFE. Sometimes I'm so focused on myself I forget that he's been locked up for more of his life than I have. The pandemic started when he was eight and Mother was locked up full-time since he was just seven.

I feel terrible about it. Vernon was so busy controlling me that he scarcely paid Henry any attention.

Tree frogs are the only solution.

I found some online that could be delivered next-day and Gretchen ordered them for me on her phone. I've been up since seven waiting for whatever truck will deliver them. I told Milorad to be alert, too. I run into him on the patio at seven thirty.

"You are up early for Saturday."

"Frogs," I say.

"Yes!" He nods.

We sit on the benches and face the sunlight with our eyes closed.

"How did you end up here, Milo?"

"I flew on plane," he answers.

"Don't be difficult."

"Okay."

"So, you flew from Serbia to Pennsylvania and that's it?"

"I flew Frankfurt to Chicago," he answers.

"Huh."

"My cousins came to Chicago with me from a refugee camp. They are still there."

This makes me open my eyes and look at him. Something in his voice sounds like a long story. "What are they like?"

"They are good men," he says. "They do not want anything to do with me now."

"Huh," I say again. "I guess I can see why."

A beat passes and I feel Milorad's eyes on me. "I am hurt by this."

"I know it's hard to face, but there was a time when I was a small child and you fired a shotgun at me and my mother," I say.

"Your father is senseless."

"He didn't fire the gun."

Milorad fidgets and makes a noise in his throat.

I say, "I know you love me, but I also can't trust you because you do whatever he tells you."

"I signed papers."

"Let's have a look at those," I say.

Milorad chuckles. "I don't have copies of these things."

"I think he's bluffing whatever he threatened."

"I would be tossed out with my rat, he said."

"Huh," I huff. "How long have you had Brutus?" I ask.

"About nineteen years."

I blink my eyes open. "Milo, no rat could live nineteen years."

"He is a special rat." He smiles.

A sound in the front of the house has us both on our feet. We walk through the passageway to the front driveway. The UPS driver needs a signature, and I sign. The box is big.

"How many frogs did you get?" Milorad asks as the truck leaves.

"There was a sale?"

He wrinkles his forehead.

"Twenty," I say. "Mixed sexes."

"That's a lot of frogs," Milorad answers.

"I love Henry a lot."

"We should get these inside. It's too cold out here." He walks toward the house.

"Should we leave them in the hothouse?"

He considers it.

"Let's wait for Henry."

We walk in the front door and Milorad takes the box to the kitchen while I stop in the hall. I listen to hear if Henry is awake, and I hear nothing. When I join Milorad and Marta in the kitchen, she has a cup of hot chocolate waiting for me and Milo is trying to figure out a way to peek inside the box.

When I try to stop him, he protests. "What if they're all dead? I do not want Henry to wake up to that!"

Marta says, "He has a point."

"The place has a guarantee. They're not dead. They only shipped them yesterday!"

"I don't hear any movement," Marta says.

Milorad reaches into his pocket and comes out with his small, inlay-handled knife.

Then a sound comes from the box. And another sound. And another.

"That's them," Marta says. "Let Henry open the box."

Milorad puts his knife away. He sits and Marta hands him a cup of coffee. The three of us sit staring at the box for a moment or two.

"What are your plans today, Jane?" Marta asks.

"I have to study this weekend for a bio test on Monday. And I have to work on the opera."

"You are writing an opera?" Milorad asks.

I hold my finger in front of my mouth. "Don't tell Vernon. He thinks he burned it."

He nods. "No music. Yes."

Moments pass. I turn to Marta.

"Why are starfish your favorite animals?"

She answers, "When they eat, the eject their stomach onto their prey and digest them from outside their own body."

Milorad and I stare at her. The frogs make more noise.

"I smell Marta's coffee!" Vernon sings, on his way through the kitchen. Milorad picks up the frog box and moves it to the floor in some kind of reactive protection, then leaves through the back kitchen door.

"Good morning to the house genius! Did you know Jane is writing an operatic masterpiece, Marta?"

Marta pretends not to hear. It's our first defense.

"I got to read about half last night. I'd only read a few of the songs before. But I got curious and found a copy on your school computer," he says. "The scene where I send Milorad to shoot at your mother and you was quite entertaining," he adds. "As if I'd do that." Marta and I look at each other and say nothing. "Or the part where I won't let you go to school. Not so accurate *now*, is it?" He looks around. "Not to mention that your aunt is furious. You drew her like she's some kind of demon!"

I finish my hot chocolate and go to the sink to rinse my cup.

"I've deleted it from your computer," he says. "Just in case you're looking for it."

"That's not fair, Vernon," Marta says. "You can't just delete something Jane's worked hard on. An opera, no less! She must have worked a long time."

"Since September," I say. I don't mention that I have backup copies. So many backup copies.

Marta says, "It's going to be a gorgeous day outside. Milorad is going to feed the roses and I'm going to defrost freezers. What are you doing today, Jane?"

"I have studying. I also told Henry I'd spend time in the hothouse with him this weekend. So, that," I say. "For now, I need to go tidy my bedroom."

Vernon answers, "While you're tidying, you may want to think about how bad it is for your health to keep secrets!" He leaves muttering something about the opera. I leave and don't tidy my room. Instead, I go to the en suite and pull out the iPad. I aim for a few weeks before I found the home movies. I want to see if I looked different on the cusp of being naughty enough to eye Gemma's iPad and fed up enough to steal it.

HOME MOVIE—09.02.2024

Henry is on the patio bench, humming a tune the camera didn't quite pick up, but you can see him humming. He's reading a book about when to plant vegetables depending on the positions of the planets. He's drinking something out of a purple travel mug with a lid. He takes a swig and lets out a long burp.

This goes on for about twenty minutes before Vernon comes outside.

He sits on the bench next to Henry and opens up a book. Henry stops reading and looks at him. Vernon acts as if Henry isn't there. Henry gets up and moves to the other bench, then starts reading again.

Five minutes pass.

Vernon says, "Come on. How long can you be mad?"

Henry takes a sharp breath and slowly releases it and continues reading.

Vernon says, "It's not that big a deal! Everyone does it!"

"She's sixteen! It's one thing if she picks them herself. But for you to get—paid?" Henry argues. "It's wrong. I don't know anyone else who would do it. And don't tell me that's because I'm naïve. I *am* naïve, but selling your own daughter is still wrong."

"I'm not selling her!" Vernon answers.

Henry won't even look at him.

"It's not even renting, really. And I say no to all the older men. She gets a lot of interest from older men, you know."

Henry takes a slow deep breath.

"I shouldn't have told you," Vernon says. "You're clearly not mature enough."

Henry reaches for the travel mug and drinks. "She's my sister," he says. "Stop selling her." He drinks again.

As Vernon explains, I note that Henry begins to look pale. His lips lose color. As Vernon says, "I know where she is at all times, so it's not like anyone can steal her from us, you know?" Henry gets up, walks two steps and faces the patio flower bed and then vomits between two stunning hydrangeas.

Vernon doesn't get up. He doesn't even look. When Henry returns to the bench and takes a drink from the mug, swishes it around in his mouth and then spits it to his right, Vernon says, "Jesus, Henry. After last Tuesday, I reckoned you were done with that stuff."

Henry ignores him. "Stay on topic. Promise not to sell Jane anymore."

"I don't—"

"Promise!"

Vernon hangs his head. "Promise."

"Good. Now go inside. I came out here to be on my own."

Vernon gets up and goes inside.

<stop>

HOME MOVIE—08.27.2024 (THE TUESDAY BEFORE)

<*fast-forward to puking*>

Henry is on his knees vomiting into a flower bed in the rose garden.

<*stop*>

HOME MOVIE—08.20.24 (THE TUESDAY BEFORE THAT)

<*fast-forward to puking*>

Henry is on his knees vomiting into a flower bed in the rose garden.

<*stop*>

HOME MOVIE—08.13.24 (THE TUESDAY BEFORE THAT)

<*fast-forward to puking*>

Henry is on his knees vomiting into a flower bed in the rose garden.

<*stop*>

I think about how bad it is for one's health to keep secrets, just like Vernon told me to.

FROGS II

This is how it always is—one home movie leads to another—and I don't have time for that today. I don't even have time to consider the fact that Henry knew Vernon was making money from my suitors before I did. Or that he stuck up for me. I don't have time to be concerned about all that vomiting and all that drinking.

I make sure my opera is still in the cloud where I left it, I clear my history, and I hide the iPad.

It's nine, and I'm impatient to give Henry his frogs. When I exit my room, I stage a small coughing fit and aim it directly at his closed bedroom door. I admit I even stomp a little for effect.

I half expect to find him in the kitchen with Marta, but instead I just find Marta staring at the outside of the frog box, now back on the kitchen counter.

I stop and listen. A few chirps. "A positive sign that they aren't dead," I say.

I ask Marta to help me study for my bio test, and while she's grilling me, I say quietly, "I need to talk to Mother today."

"London," she says. "Two more shows."

"Let her know I need to talk later."

She pulls out her phone and sends a text. "You can use my place."

Milorad comes in the kitchen door. He looks freshly showered. "He is not up yet?"

"It's Saturday. He's thirteen," Marta says.

"Usually we would already be working."

We stand around the box of frogs, listening to them sing. They don't sound like regular frogs.

"I hope they live a long life in the hothouse," I say.

"I am sure of it," Milorad says.

"Is Brutus in his cage?" I ask.

"I think so."

"Can I go visit?"

"It is messy, but you are now warned."

I go out the back door and walk across the patio to the pool house. As I walk past the sitting room, I see Vernon staring out at me. Startling—to be honest—as if the opera has taken a turn for the dark.

Once inside, I flop into my favorite chair, and I watch Brutus go from his wheel to climbing up the sides of the cage, to drinking water, to eating some of Milorad's homemade food, to getting back on the wheel again.

"You're so fast! It's almost like you're nervous."

He runs even faster.

"Milo told me that you're around twenty years old, which we both know is impossible for a rat."

Runs even faster.

"I've hidden a letter where Vernon hides Mother's postcards. You really should have a look at it."

I get up and walk back to the kitchen door.

When I walk in, I say, "I can't stand waiting. I'm going to go take a shower."

I'm not even lying. I take a shower. Dry my hair on the loudest hair dryer setting. Stomp a few times to see if I can wake Henry.

When I leave my room, I decide to peek in on him. It's past ten, after all, and this is unlike him. I quietly open the door, knocking lightly, and I say his name softly and then once I can stick my head in, I do.

There is no one in Henry's bed. "Henry?" I ask. He doesn't answer from his en suite.

When I get downstairs, I race to the kitchen, where Marta is emptying the freezer into a plastic laundry basket.

The box of frogs is still there.

"Why didn't you tell me Henry came down?" I ask.

"He did? I didn't see him," she says.

I go to the study, then the sitting room, and then outside.

"Is he ready?" Milorad asks from the flower bed, where he's feeding the roses.

"I can't find him," I say, and keep walking toward the hothouse.

The key goes minor in my opera. I approach the hothouse door. I feel Milorad behind me fast-stepping. I open the door, and at first, I'm amazed by how much like a rainforest it is. I take a step in and then—

"Henry!" I yell. "Henry?"

He's curled on the floor of the hothouse, a watering can spilled next to him, so his pants are wet and he's not moving.

"Henry!"

Milorad comes in, then, and when he sees me leaning over Henry, he pushes me out of the way and does all the things a medic would do. He touches Henry's neck for a pulse, pulls his eyelids up and looks at his pupils, he touches his skin, places his ear to his heart.

"He is alive."

I start to cry hysterical tears. I don't even care what Vernon would say. Fuck Vernon.

"Henry!" Milorad yells in Henry's face. He slaps his cheek gently. "Henry!"

He looks to me, crying without making much noise, and says, "Get me first aid kit in pool house and bottle of water."

I run to the pool house and get both things and come back. No one else knows Henry is on the floor of his hothouse, soaked, probably since last night.

"We should call 911," I say when I hand the items to Milorad.

He opens the kit, retrieves something small, and waves it under Henry's nose, then opens the water, takes a long gulp, and as Henry starts to wake up, he sprays it in his face.

Henry makes an annoyed face. "Hey!"

I am still crying, but I am now relieved.

"Did you just spit on me?" Henry asks. He looks around, sees me crying, looks back at Milorad, who is drinking more water, now sitting in the puddle, his pants and shirt soaked. "What the hell are you doing here?"

"We thought you were dead," I say.

"I wish," he says. "You have no idea how pissed I am to be here."

I stare at him, livid tears still falling. "How dare you?" I say, Victorian Jane full force. "Do you have any idea how scary that was?"

He lies back down in the puddle and begins to sob softly. Milorad strokes his hair, and I realize that I am a dour, piece-of-shit sister.

"Wait. Are you serious?" I ask.

"Leave us," Milorad says. "Go get Marta."

HENRY'S SHOCKING BENDER

An hour later, Henry has been showered and the hothouse has been hosed down to clear it of vomit and urine.

The frogs are still in the kitchen, singing.

Milorad sits quietly next to the box of frogs, sipping coffee and a bottle of water intermittently.

No one has seen Vernon since I saw him staring out the sitting room doors.

Henry is still in his room post-shower.

I arrive in the kitchen.

"He needs a good breakfast," Marta says. "And we need to talk to a doctor."

"Vernon will not allow that," Milorad answers. "But you are right about the breakfast."

"You could probably use something to eat, too," Marta says. She flips the home fries frying on the stovetop. She looks at me. "And, Jane. You okay?"

"Yeah," I say.

"She was first person to see him," Milorad says. "She has shock, probably."

"I don't think I'll ever get that image out of my mind," I say.

Marta puts her spatula down and hugs me, and I put my arms around her and tears flow down my cheeks. She rubs my back and all I can think is *I thought he was dead* but I can't say it out loud. But I did, reader. I thought he was dead. And part of my heart will never be the same.

Vernon slams the front door and walks loudly through the house until he finds us in the kitchen and finds me crying on Marta's shoulder. "What's the drama now?" he asks, and starts pouring a cup of coffee.

We ignore him.

"A man can't be in his own kitchen in his own house, I guess."

We keep ignoring him.

"I mean if Jane's crying everything stops. Am I right?"

Marta keeps rubbing my back. I hear Milorad take a deep breath through his nose.

"Tough crowd."

"Shut up," Milorad says.

"I'm sorry?" Vernon says, as in *excusemewhatdidyousay?*

"Stop talking," Milorad says. Marta and I stop hugging and turn to watch.

"This is my house!"

"Technically, it's not your house," I say. "Everyone knows this."

"You're psycho," he says.

"Is this all you care about, Vernon?" Marta says. "You don't care about why Jane's crying, you don't care about why Milorad told you to shut up. You couldn't read the room?"

Henry walks in then, looking fresh.

"There's my boy," Vernon says.

"Shut up," Milorad says again.

"I'm warning you," Vernon says. Henry watches this go back and forth, then places himself behind Milorad's right shoulder.

Vernon gestures to Marta and Milorad as if that's who he's warning. "Whatever the drama is, it can't be bigger than the good news I have."

Henry looks angry. I'm sure all of us do. Then, as if on cue, Brutus scampers across the counter over by the oven. He stops at the cooling rack where a loaf of Marta's famous brown bread sits. He pulls off a little piece with his paws, sits back on his tail, and eats, watching us watch him.

Marta moves fast and grabs the rat while he's chewing, walks over to the door, opens it, and tosses Brutus toward the flower bed, where he lands and scurries back toward the pool house.

"Don't you want to hear the good news?" Vernon says.

Milorad gets up.

"You stupid man. You almost killed this boy with your games! You do not even know this boy! You just use him and tell him lies!" Milorad's voice cracks on that last part.

"Oh my," Vernon says. "You're all worked up over whatever Jane's drama is. I'll come back when you can pay proper attention."

When Vernon leaves, the kitchen door swings and Henry points to the box on the kitchen island. "Are those frogs?"

HOTHOUSE RELEASE PARTY

Punk Rock Jane and the Red-Eyed Tree Frogs. I can't help but hear a song. The frogs are happy-singing and they sound more like a rhythm section than anything—not like native Pennsylvanian frogs.

```
INT. HENRY'S HOTHOUSE—LATE MORNING

                    JANE is in background of the
                    hothouse, up in a tree with a
                    güiro and a tambourine. The BAND
                    is dressed like frogs (bright
```

green foam costumes) and in foreground. HENRY, MILORAD, and MARTA are also present.

Song: "Hothouse Release Party"

Composer notes: *This is an anthem for frogs freed from a box. It should feel like climbing a tree.*

JANE

THIS NUMBER IS ABOUT SOME FROGS
WHO GOT A NEW ENVIRONMENT.
THEY DIDN'T HAVE TO PASS A TEST
OR MEET A MAN'S REQUIREMENT.

THE FROGS CAME VIA UPS
IN A STURDY BOX WITH HOLES.
THEY PACKED 'EM UP LIKE MERCHANDISE
AS IF THEY DON'T HAVE SOULS.

ALL

HOTHOUSE RELEASE PARTY!
EVERYONE INVITED!
HOTHOUSE RELEASE PARTY!
WE'RE TOTALLY DELIGHTED!

JANE

WHEN WE OPENED UP THE BOX
WE EXPECTED THEM TO BOUNCE—
BUT OUT OF TWENTY, EIGHTEEN STAYED
UNWILLING TO DENOUNCE.

WE HELPED THEM ONTO BROAD GREEN LEAVES
AND PLACED THEM 'PON THE DIRT.

AND AT THE BOTTOM OF THE BOX
WE FOUND JUST ONE INERT.

ALL
HOTHOUSE RELEASE PARTY!
EVERYONE INVOLVED!
HOTHOUSE RELEASE PARTY!
EVEN TREE FROGS GET ABSOLVED!

JANE
NOT ALL CAPTIVE FROGS SURVIVE, YOU SEE
NOT ALL OF THEM ARE STRONG
BUT IF YOU CAN HELP THEM BREAK OUT FREE
THEY'LL SING A PRETTY SONG.

THIS NUMBER TURNED TO METAPHOR
PROBABLY ABOUT YOUR MOTHER.
APPRECIATE HER IF YOU CAN
YOU WILL NEVER GET ANOTHER.

ALL
HOTHOUSE RELEASE PARTY!
IT'S GONNA BE THE BOMB!
HOTHOUSE RELEASE PARTY!
GO FIND AND HUG YOUR MOM!

JANE (speaking into mic)
Obligatory public service announcement: Some moms are terrible moms. We know how lucky we are here at FREE MOTHER to have awesome moms.

BLACKOUT

We are sitting around in the hothouse, and none of us care how hot it is. "You really scared me, Henry," I say.

"I scared myself, believe me," he says.

"What the fuck did you think you were doing?" I ask.

"Same as I do every day for like—two years? I drink, I get drunk, I get drunker, I sleep."

"You are thirteen years old," Milorad says.

Henry shrugs. "I'm a prodigy."

"We're going to have to talk about the alcohol," Marta says. Milorad is collecting bottles of liquor from around the hothouse and putting them in a box.

"I've been with you every day since you were eight," I say. I point toward the study and Vernon's Pandemic Prison Academy.

"You thought you were the only one," he says.

I face-shrug at him.

"Long before your spiked eggnog, Vernon and I had our man time."

"'Man time'?" Marta says. She seems dazed and furious, both.

The mister goes on in the hothouse. Uncanny timing because I just started to sweat.

"You knew about the eggnog?" I ask.

"I approved it," Henry says.

I blink and blink and blink and I don't know what to say.

THEN VERNON WALKS IN

"You let Henry drink in first grade?" I ask Vernon. I'm not asking. I'm yelling. I'm accusing. I'm pointing right at him. "You fed us lies and all that trash about our mother and then you gave us alcohol?"

Vernon turns to leave. Milorad steps in front of the door.

"Awfully hot in here," Vernon says.

"You can't pretend you don't hear me," I say.

"The frogs are going to love this place," Vernon says. "I'm so glad you built this, Henry. I'm very proud of you."

Henry looks at him and then at the floor.

There's a sound from outside. A hand on the door handle. Finch arrives, squeezes past Milorad, and steps toward Vernon, putting her hand on his arm.

"Did you tell them?" she asks.

Vernon looks uncomfortable. "Didn't seem the place."

She raises her eyebrows and glares at him.

He says, "I'm divorcing Mina when she gets back."

When he says this, it's not gloating or giddy. It's as if he's being forced to lie. But unlike his lies to God or his lies to reporters from *Spin* or his lies to Mother or me or Henry or Marta, this is one he's purposefully fucking up. As if he wants us to know he's lying.

Right on his face begins Vernon's slow realization that he never had control of anything. And yet, he doesn't know why.

For once, I am not the last person to know a thing.

LESSON THIRTEEN: SPRING CLEANING

When you clean things, you find things.

AN HOUR LATER, Marta is in a frenzy of spring cleaning in the kitchen, emptying and wiping down the insides of the cabinets and drawers.

"You okay?" I ask.

"This is how I deal with stress," she says. "Where's Henry?"

"Hothouse with Milorad."

"Good," she says. "Vernon and Finch went for a walk."

She hands me a few little bins from the top shelf of a cabinet, and I help her clean them out.

She says, "Vernon won't let me tell Mina."

"Well, I'll tell her, then." I put out my hand for her phone.

She points and I go get it from the counter. She tells me her passcode and I dial up Mother, knowing she will probably be onstage in Denmark, which is where I think she is today.

It rings twice and goes to voicemail. I leave a message.

It's Jane and I don't quite know how to explain what happened here today but . . . everyone is okay, though Henry nearly wasn't. He had alcohol poisoning and it was scary and Vernon won't let Marta call you about it so I'm doing it because we really just need you to come home now. I love you.

After a few more cabinets, I say I'm going to take a nap and I go to my room.

I'm in my usual spot in the en suite, ready to back up my newest home movie mixtapes to my cloud. When I sign into the cloud where the home movies are, the interface has changed. It startles me. At first, I think Vernon has changed things because he has found me out. Then I see a small message at the top of the page that says there's been a software update.

The cameras used to be numbered, one through five, but now there are words here, too. And the numbers are different. There's a "06_kitchen" and a "07_pool" that were never here before. There used to be five cameras. Now there are seven.

I go first for the pool camera folder—I've always been able to see pool scenes from the patio camera, so I'm curious. I play Spin the Family Wheel and land on a random date in 2021.

HOME MOVIE—10.12.2021

Milorad walks into the kitchen area of the pool house in his boxer shorts and a T-shirt and fills up his electric teakettle. Once he presses the On switch, he goes to the bathroom and pees with the door open.

He burps.

<stop>

There is a camera inside the pool house, spying on Milorad. Gross. I click back to the menu.

I go to the kitchen folder.

It takes me forty-six tries to find what I'm looking for.

HOME MOVIE—06.10.2012

I am under the table in the kitchen. I am four years old.

"Just leave me alone!" Mother yells as she runs in. She hovers at the doorway, listening for him, and then backs her way toward the back door of the kitchen.

"God dammit, will you just stop running?" Vernon screams.

"Just stop. Stop there. Stop chasing me," she says.

"I have things to say!" he yells.

"Can you please give me some space?" she says.

"Not until I say what I need to say." He moves closer to her. She backs toward the door slowly.

"I'm scared, Vernon. If you could please just give me a minute alone—"

"Why do you *deserve* a minute alone? Since when do you give me a minute alone?"

"All the time, really. But that's not the point. You've been yelling at me for two hours and I'm tired and confused. I need to—"

"I've been yelling?" he yells. "More like *you've* been yelling!"

"I just need some space," she says.

He lunges toward her and stands right in her face, puts his arms on either side of her on the counter behind her and traps her where she stands.

<pause>

The reason I was even in the kitchen was because Marta was out in the garden with Milorad. I was waiting for her to come back because she said she had homemade ice cream. I heard the argument upstairs and heard it tumbling down the stairs, but I didn't expect any of this. Vernon would tell me that Mother was unreasonable or other things (on drugs, crazy, mentally ill, unfit to parent, and one time, he used the R word) but the action was not on display.

Anyway, Vernon has short arms, and when he trapped Mother in the kitchen that day, it made me feel like I couldn't breathe. I could see on her face that's how it made her feel, too.

<resume>

"Vernon, please," she says.

"Please what?"

"Please give me some space."

He grins at her an inch from her face. She is crying dry tears. The look on her face is terror. I stand under the table and can't tell what to do. I want to help her. I know if I say something to let them know I'm here, it will help her but I can't move.

"You always do this to me!" Vernon says. "You're just a control freak!"

"Please just give me some space."

He lifts his arms fast and violent to free her. In doing so, he slams his wrist into her ear. She reaches up and touches it and then backs toward the door some more, her hand reaching for the drawer unit next to her.

"Mina wants space!" he mocks. "Mina wants space because she's scared! And everyone knows Mina gets what she wants because she has to have all the power!"

Mother takes a breath—the first I've seen her take since she got here. It's quiet and shallow and through her nose. She's thinking. You can see it on her forehead.

"Mina has been abused for eleven years! Poor Mina! Here's my cross! Vernon's been an asshole to me for eleven years and I'm still here!"

Mother breathes again. You can see in Vernon's eyes it annoys him.

He moves toward her fast. She opens the drawer next to her and pulls out a small utility knife. She holds it in front of her. This makes Vernon double over in laughter.

He laughs and laughs.

I watch her breathe again. Small, short, shallow. I swear her pupils are so tiny they're like the tip of a pin. She backs toward the back door.

He fake-lunges at her. She flinches and takes a fast step toward the door.

He laughs again. "Are you going to stab me, Mina?"

"Please just give me some space," she says. Her voice is flat. Empty.

"But don't you want to stab me first?"

"Please."

They stare at each other for a few seconds. Mother is barely breathing—controlled but shallow—and she seems aware of every single nerve and muscle in her body and his. Vernon breathes heavily, as if he's just run up three flights of steps. Mother keeps backing toward the door, the knife in front of her. Vernon stays put this time but stares into her eyes.

"I can't take this abusive crap from you anymore," he says.

She says nothing.

"You're just an asshole, you know," he says. "I tell you over and over again that I'm trying and all you ever do is want to win. I hope you're happy now, Mina."

She says nothing.

He doesn't move from where he's standing. She's still holding the knife in front of her defensively. He reaches into his pocket and pulls out his phone. He does some stuff on the screen and then talks into it.

"Hi, yeah. I need to report someone threatening to kill me."

Mina takes a deep breath now and backs her last few steps to the door, turns the doorknob and opens it.

"She's been holding a knife to my throat for about ten minutes. But now she's escaping out the back door. Yes. It's my wife. She does this sometimes. Quite loopy in the head." He gives our address.

As he says this, he goes to the knife drawer and pulls out a steak knife. He puts it to his abdomen and considers stabbing himself. You can see the thoughts on his face. His cowardice arrives in his eyebrows. He puts the knife in the pocket of his cargo pants and goes to the back door and walks out.

<pause>

Change to the patio camera.

<resume>

She hears the door close and gets up from the bench. Her face is wet.

He starts walking toward her quickly. He reaches into his pants pocket. She gets up quickly and starts to run away from him—toward the French doors to the study. She holds the knife in front of her as she runs. She turns her head periodically to make sure of where he is. He isn't running. He is stalking with long, sure strides. He's catching up to her. The double doors are locked and she can't get into the study. She doubles back toward the kitchen door and starts to sprint. He aims to block her. She fakes left and breaks right, then gets to the kitchen door and when she gets through it—

<pause>

Change to the kitchen camera.

<resume>

—she closes it and locks it. Then she takes a deep breath and stands there and stares up at the ceiling.

Then, "Marta?"

I am still under the table.

<pause>

I wanted to tell her that Marta was with Milorad. My throat didn't work.

<resume>

"Marta?" she yells again.

She stands there for a minute, taking deep breaths, then sobs quietly into her hands, then another deep breath, then climbs the back staircase to Marta's quarters.

Thirty seconds after Mother climbs the steps, in the background of the home movie, you can hear Vernon stomping around the house and slamming things around. In the foreground of the frame, though, there is Brutus the rat.

<pause>

I remember seeing it from under the table—the rat. I remember exactly where it was on the kitchen floor. I remember what happened. Brutus didn't see me under the table either. Which is why it felt safe, I guess, to turn into Aunt Finch, who walked into the dining room.

I was four years old and didn't trust what I saw. Part of me always knew it was real, but I always doubted until I found the home movies.

<pause>

Change to the dining room camera.

<resume>

"Mina! I'm leaving!" Vernon shouts from the dining room. "I won't be coming back this time! You'll hear from my lawyer!" He has a box of things on the table and his usual suitcase by the doorway to the foyer. "If you want to talk about this, now's your time to do it!" he yells up the stairs.

He turns to Finch. "Did she leave? Did you see her out there?"

Finch shakes her head no.

He takes off his wedding ring and places it delicately on the table and turns back to Finch. Without a word, the two of them walk out the front door. My little four-year-old self cries then. All the fear and confusion shows on my face.

"Mother!" I yell. "Mother!"

Mother comes to the kitchen and finds me. She picks me up and holds me in her arms, and I sob and she keeps saying, "You're safe. I promise. You're safe."

<stop>

But I wasn't. And she wasn't. And now, almost thirteen years later, I'm about to make sure we're safer than we've ever been before.

PRESS RELEASE

Mother has drafted a press release. Marta shows me a social media post on her phone before she serves dinner. *There has been a family emergency. I am needed at home. Tour is canceled.*

Marta says, "Things are about to move really fast."

This is a welcome idea. Today has been the longest I've ever lived.

When I go to the dining room to sit with Henry, we hear Vernon yelling. *Stay where you are! We need the money! . . . Ugh! Why don't you ever listen to me?*

Moments later, he arrives to the dining room calm, for dinner.

He looks at me and Henry and nods but says nothing.

As Marta dishes fat egg noodles onto the plate, he asks, "Is that tuna casserole?" Marta then breaks the crunchy surface of the casserole and ladles it on top of the noodles.

"Yes!" Henry says. Everyone knows Henry loves tuna casserole. Everyone knows Vernon hates tuna casserole.

Once Marta serves, she goes back to the kitchen and Vernon

pushes himself away from the table. As he's about to get up, Henry says, "Manners, Vernon."

He replies, "Oh, please," and then leaves the dining room, and it's just me and Henry.

We eat for a while silently. I think of telling him about the reclaiming and it feels too risky even if he's not being controlled by Vernon anymore.

"Mother is coming home tomorrow," he says.

"Yes."

"How do you feel about that?"

"Quite good," I say.

"Mmmm."

We eat in more quiet. Henry dishes a small second portion to his plate. We can both hear Vernon stomping around in his bedroom, drawers opening and closing.

"Sounds like it's a three-bag pack," I say.

"Let him fuck off," he says. "Forever."

"Are you okay?"

"I need a drink," he says.

"Oh, Henry."

"I know," he says. I stand behind him and wrap my arms around him and kiss him on his head and tell him how proud I am that he's doing the right thing. When Milorad cleared out the greenhouse, he found so many bottles. Henry cries softly and puts his fork down. Goes weak in my arms and says, "I'm so ashamed."

"You didn't have anything to do with it."

"I hid all those bottles. I hid another fifteen in my room. I'm a fucking drunk!"

"I thought it was just me," I say. "He must have been poisoning you as young as n—"

"Seven," he says.

"Oh," I say. "What a dreadful father."

"Worst." He starts shaking and sobbing really hard. He's quiet about it, but his body is quaking. "I was so bad to Mother!" Sobs. More sobs. "I threw shit at her! And ignored her! Do you remember?" he asks. "Do you remember that first year she was locked in? Ugh!" he groans. "We were helping to kill her. We nearly did! We nearly killed our own mom!"

"We didn't, Henry. Stop. Don't overthink it."

He removes my arms from around his shoulders. "I'm not overthinking. We nearly killed her. You know what I'm talking about."

THE GREAT IGNORING

It was the year our mother went mad. Rightfully. Vernon had locked her up on The Christmas That Changed Everything and then, a week later, commanded us to not ever look at her. For an entire year. Not even if she begged or cried or beat on the capsule walls. Even one time when she cracked away at the capsule door with the chair until the chair broke. We didn't look. There was punishment for looking. And reward for not looking. By February 2019, I'd been grounded to my room four times until I learned to obey the new rules.

"How come it didn't make you into a drunk?" he asks.

"I don't know," I answer.

"She used to scream so loud," he says. He sobs into his own hands. I pull my dinner chair over next to his and sit down. "We just let her. How did we do that? How did we even do that?"

"We were staying safe," I say. "We had no other choice. Even before she was locked up entirely, Henry—remember the things he'd say? About how shitty she was when we knew she wasn't shitty? That's how we did that. And it wasn't our fault."

"It was my arm that threw things at her," he says. "I THREW THINGS AT HER!"

"So did I."

"I told her I hoped she died!" he says. "I'm a fucking monster!" The look on his face is like nothing I can describe.

"I did, too," I say softly. "But who else threw things on game nights?"

He stops and thinks.

"I'm just asking you to stop blaming yourself. Not when there were two adults who were clearly influencing you."

"Not to mention making me a drunk."

"Stop calling yourself that," I say.

"You don't get it. I *really* need a drink. Look." He holds out his hand flat, palm down. It shakes. "Your hands aren't shaking."

"Oh"—more like a sound escapes my mouth than a word—like someone punched me in the stomach and this was the natural response. When Marta comes to clear the table, she doesn't expect to see Henry and me hugging and crying. It's healthy—don't get me wrong. But she's rightly concerned.

"Where's V—"

"Give us space," I say.

She does.

I get Henry to look at me. I can smell his sweat; it's ripe and sweet. "I don't know how to say this right, but you being a drinker was intentional."

He makes instant and intense eye contact.

"First, both of them were so interested in controlling *me*, you were allowed to run free. I always envied you. You got to leave the dinner table and go outside. You got to go with Milorad and do stuff," I start. "But basically, while it looked like you were getting privileges, what was really happening is that you were being neglected. Right? I mean—they took our mom away with lies. And then for you, they took Vernon away, too—the whole family, really. So it makes sense that with all that time on your own, you ended up drinking. I mean, we grew up with Vernon.

"But it's deeper than that. See—the sneakiest way to control a kid is to neglect them. Because then they need love. Like—*need* it. And in return, they need the person who neglected them more than ever."

"So, I ended up drinking so they would love me?" he says. It's not a question. He takes a big breath and lets it out, his cheeks puffed.

"It's also a lot easier to call an addict a liar. I'm sure they'd have preferred to have me as the scapegoat."

An hour later, Henry and I are in the sitting room. Marta lit a fire and Henry turned on the TV to a nature show, but has the volume muted. We sit and talk between bouts of silence, and I show him Mother's postcards from Europe.

"I'd love to see Europe," he says.

"We will one day," I answer.

We read some more postcards.

"I don't want to go to school," he says.

"It's not that bad," I answer.

"I mean, I really don't want to go to school."

"I'm sure we'll find a solution," I say. "Don't worry."

There's a sound outside, and then Milorad comes through the French doors with fresh wood.

"It is late," he says.

"It's spring break," I say.

"You must get sleep," he says.

"Why?" Henry asks. "You never do."

Milorad looks a mix of bashful and panicked. "I sleep!"

The way he says it almost makes me curious enough to watch the pool house footage.

Henry laughs. "You can tell Jane," he says. "Whatever kind of weird Serbian vampire you are—your secret will be safe with us." His giggle is high-pitched like when I used to tickle him on the settee.

"You never know," I say. "Jane might know a lot more than Milorad thinks she knows."

At this, Milorad tosses two logs onto the fire, brushes his hands together, and says, "I am not vampire and I have no secrets! I am man of the world"—he holds his head in a noble gaze upward—"an everyman."

Henry giggles again in that high-pitched way and it slows my heart rate, it's so good.

I ruin it. "You have a mighty unique pet for an everyman."

Henry looks confused. Milorad exits out the doors. I follow him. But he closes the door to the pool house before I can get in.

A RAT'S DINNER

There is a reason I chose him. A reason he chose me.

IT'S SIMPLE. People like Milorad and me, we keep each other's secrets.

Picture this: Chicago, New Year's Eve, 2006. The Riverwalk under the Dearborn Street Bridge. Milorad is so drunk he can't move his limbs and is propped so that he slumps slightly to the right. A rat approaches, sits down by his knee, and stares at him.

"Why you look at me like this, rat?"

Rat blinks.

"You do not know who I am!"

Rat scratches behind its ear.

"I am Milorad the Terrible! A monster. I kill everything good in world. Every good thing. I kill it and then they said I was bad for this after they told me to do this thing. I do not take orders from anyone, rat. Do you hear me?"

The rat leans on the drunk man's leg and rubs its head on his jeans.

"Get away from the monster! I could eat you!" Milorad swipes at the rat and misses. "When I was boy, I shoot rats on my farm. Monster of Knić! I killed many rats and then many people. I am not supposed to be here." He starts to cry. "I am supposed to be in prison for criminals."

"Shut up!" someone yells.

"You will never understand!" Milorad yells back. He looks to the rat. "No one here understands. Americans fight wars from inside their television sets. In Serbia—" Milorad cries again. Sobs loudly.

"Shut up, you fool!" someone yells over Milorad's sobbing.

"Happy New Year!" someone on the bridge yells.

"Monsters cannot sleep," Milorad continues. "I have not had sleep in many years. My mother used to say to my brothers and me as boys that confession is good for sleep. I will confess to you, rat. Does this agree? I will confess."

Milorad slumps his body forward toward the rat. He whispers, "I will confess to you!" He is drooling, and continues to try to drink from an empty beer can.

Milorad whispers to the rat, now curled in his lap like a pet, "You are my son now. I tell you my biggest shame. Yes? You are my boy." The rat allows Milorad to pet it. "You are my boy, rat. I love you, rat." Milorad sobs again.

Someone yells, "Will you shut the fuck up?!"

Someone yells, "Happy New Year!"

"It is painful, son, to have a father who is monster. I have killed men and boys. Oh, son. I am so sorry. I murdered a boy. My own boy, he could have been. Not mine. But he could have been. I always wanted a boy. He always wanted to live but he is dead. Do you hear me, rat? Son?"

The rat blinks.

"You do not forgive me! I am unforgivable! Rat, do not lie to me! I will kill you. Monster of Knić! He will kill your sons and your rats and your birds!"

"If you don't shut the fuck up!" someone yells.

Milorad, looking as if he's amazed that his hands work, picks the rat up, still curled in a ball, and whispers to it. "I will even kill a mother. I am so bad, son. I have no excuses to give you. I was a young man. There was a war and one day I was on farm doing farm things. I was fixing a tractor wheel. This is what I do. I fix things. I make machines work again. I was eighteen. I fix things. And then this war—it grew in our field and we were now watering crops with blood and boys and girls and mothers and the fields turned red and I dug holes. Oh! Rat!" He places the rat gently in his lap. "I dug the holes and maybe I am the only monster who knows where the holes are!"

Someone on the bridge says, "Happy New Year!"

Milorad looks at the rat. "Son, I am sorry to have given to you such shame. I owe you my life now for listening to this confession. Tell me what to do, rat. I will do anything for your patient ear and gracious heart. You, rat, are my only friend in this town. My cousins do not speak to me. Monster of Knić, they say it. They mean it. They tell me they will turn me in if I don't leave their house. Son. Rat. I live wherever I can sleep. I beg for money. Monster! I do not deserve such things. Last week a girl gave me an apple and it looked delicious, but I threw it at her because it was too good for the vermin of Kníc. She called me an asshole. It made me feel so truthful."

The conversation went on like this in whispers for about an hour. Eventually, New Year revelers went home, even the other men sleeping around the Riverwalk went away. When it was just us and the poor sap had sobered up and could move his arms again, I told him what his penance would be.

poof!

His eyes opened wide. He looked around for the rat. They all do this.

"You have been through so much," I said. "You poor man. I am so sorry for all you have suffered."

He stared, but had no words.

"I know a place you could live. You'd have your own room, as much good food as you need, and you'd be part of a new family. I think you'd really like it."

"Rat?" he asked. Squinting at me.

"Do you like gardening?" I asked.

"I am farmer. From Knić. You do not know me," he said. "I have never met you."

"Oh, but you have," I said. "You just confessed to me. Everything about the monster. The mother. The boy. All of it."

He cocked his head to the left.

"I have all you need," I said. "I have an address, five thousand dollars to get there and get settled. But there is one rule."

"Yes?" he said.

"You must keep your pet rat with you when you move in and cannot tell them about this."

"I am to garden? This is only penance?"

"You are to garden, feed your pet rat, and keep your mouth shut. That's all."

He was sober enough to see it and try to understand it, but Milorad was already living lies in order to get through his days. How would he explain to anyone the magic of me? Surely, he'd already talked himself out of it. And so, I reduced myself to Brutus again.

poof!

Just to make a point.

He picked me up and put me in his coat pocket.

We haven't separated since.

THE RECLAIMING

Mother arrives home at one in the afternoon the next day, Sunday. She came with only herself, a backpack, and her ukulele. She hugs and holds me and Henry on the sitting room settee. Marta brings tea and fresh-baked cookies and sits down.

"Holy shit," she says.

"Holy shit," Henry says.

"Yeah."

"I guess we have some things to do," she says.

We all look at each other.

"He's already packed," Henry says. "During dinner last night."

Mother raises her forehead and nods.

"Lord forgive me, I served tuna casserole," Marta says. She and Mother crack up, and it breaks the tension in the house for the first time since Henry's giggles last night.

We're quiet for a moment. Milorad waves into the kitchen while he's outside the back door with a leaf blower, loudly clearing debris from the patio.

"How are you allowed out," Henry says, "and what's happening now?"

"He doesn't know I'm home yet," Mother says.

"I won't let him lock you up again," I say.

"Well, he doesn't know where the tubes actually take me," she says.

"We're ripping them all out, right?" I ask.

Henry frowns in thought. "Will I ever see Harriet or Julie, my algebra tutor, again?"

"You'd be better off in regular school now," I say.

Marta, Mother, and me look at one another.

"Are you guys keeping something from me?" Henry asks.

We look conflicted.

"You are," he says.

"There are some things you don't know," I say. "But it would take a while to tell you."

He points to Mother. "She never stabbed Vernon, right? And probably never did any of the stuff they said she did."

Mother shakes her head. "This is all my fault."

Marta answers, "No."

"I could have just done whatever he wanted and he would have just—"

"Bullshit," Marta and I say at the same time. Marta adds, "You never had a choice. He gave the illusion of choice, but you didn't have any. You need to see what Jane has."

"I'm the only one who worked. I had all the power," she says.

"Power?" Henry says. "You were locked up. We were there. We saw it."

"You need to see what Jane has," Marta says again.

"I already saw what Jane showed me."

"She has more," Marta says. I hold up the iPad, but I don't want to break my mother's heart. The "Everyone Hates Mina" mixtape is especially dark and she needs rest.

"Good day, my loves!" Vernon says as he walks into the kitchen. We all go quiet. He looks at Mother, sitting at the kitchen table like she lives here, then looks at us sitting around the table. "Am I interrupting something?"

None of us say anything. He goes to kiss me on top of my head and I move my head. He goes to rub Henry's back and Henry shifts to avoid it.

"I understand," he says. "You must be so confused by all Finch has said and done over the years. I must look like the enemy."

We stay silent. He sits in the empty chair at the table with his coffee and smiles at Henry, who is the only one looking at him. Mother is looking at her hands. I'm looking at Mother. Marta is looking at me.

"I feel utterly betrayed by her. Mina, I'm so sorry for all I've done at her bidding."

Mother looks at him with a soft expression. "Vernon, please."

"I'm sure she told you that it was all me, but she's lying," he says.

"What are you even talking about?" I ask. "Yesterday you told us—as you stood with your arm around Finch—that you're going to divorce Mother." I turn to Mother and say, "Sorry. We meant to tell you this but he walked in first."

Marta says, "Can we not have this conversation in front of Jane and Henry?" It's not a question, even though she presents it as one.

"Of course," he says.

Then I grab Henry's arm and motion to the outside world with my head and we go out the back door. Then we return through the study doors to listen to the conversation from there.

"Probably best if you go, too," Vernon says to Marta, presumably.

Marta doesn't leave.

"Look. The kids say you already packed. So, this shouldn't be too hard," Mother says.

"You can't kick me out! Not after all I've done here."

"All you've done?"

"I raised your children," he says.

I can imagine Mother's face trying to find an answer to this. I can't stay in the study. I walk back into the kitchen and sit down in the comfy chair. "You certainly were here while I was gone, but I don't think we can describe what you did as raising the children. I toured or worked for less than an average parent with a nine-to-five. What's interesting is how we're not talking about how me being locked into that fucking tube for the last seven years affected those children."

"All the shit-talk," Marta says.

"Finch has some mouth on her," Vernon says.

"Oh, please," I say. "I was there."

"I was there, too," Henry says from the kitchen doorway.

"We were all there, Vernon," Mother says. "How many things have you thrown at me over the last twenty years?"

"I've never thrown anything at you. It was Finch. She's a psycho!"

Mother sighs.

"Stop lying to God," I say.

"Shut up, Jane," he answers.

"Don't say that," Henry says.

"I never win! Not even in my own house!"

"Not your house," Marta says.

"You know Finch murdered poor Aunt Lily," he says. "You know that, right? I'm telling you, this was all her. I love you! I love our family! I love this house."

"I'm not saying she's not part of it. But you're their father, Vernon. You had a responsibility. You were supposed to look after them. And me. And be a family man. Our family. Remember?"

"You need to see a therapist," he says.

"I do see a therapist," she says.

"Oh," he says.

We're all staring at him as if our eyes can push him out the door, but he just won't budge. He starts to go on and on about how much he does around here. He lists schooling and I can't keep my mouth shut.

"Because of you, I'm probably going to graduate a year late. And you mocked Henry when he didn't understand algebra," I say. "Not to mention your ridiculous rules. Who tells a child that they have to find their own escape? What kind of person tells his children that their mother is going to kill them?"

"That was all Finch!" he says.

"We were there!" Henry and I say in unison.

"You were children! You didn't understand," he argues.

"*Tell me what you hate about your mother* isn't that hard to understand," Henry says.

"I never said that!"

"What about all the times you told us Mother was a flake?" I ask.

"A flake? She's a genius! I've said so a million times!"

Henry shouts, "Remember 2019?"

We all go very quiet because Henry never shouts. And because he's angry-crying.

He continues. "Do you remember her going crazy while you made us ignore her? How her hands were bleeding on the plexiglass? How you punished us for caring? How you turned your back? How she screamed for help?"

"I—"

"You planned to bury me in the orchard," Mother says. "You said it to my face."

"That was Finch's idea. Anyway—I wasn't going to kill you kill you," Vernon says, his eyes concerned. We allow this comment to linger. Henry's muscles are tensed—like he could lunge at any moment. "Finch suggested that if we pushed you to your limit, you may—em—do us the—uh—favor yourself," Vernon adds.

"Do you even hear yourself?" I ask.

"Mina, trust me, it wasn't about you. It was—it was—Finch hates you," he starts. "She's so jealous."

We all stay quiet. Marta is humming a little under her breath.

"I was looking for an ally, I guess."

"You certainly found one," I say.

"Shut up, Jane."

"Stop telling Jane to shut up," Henry says.

"You should go," Mother says.

"You should definitely go," Marta says.

At this, Vernon gets up, walks out the back door, and sits on the patio bench. We all sigh.

Then the phone rings.

Henry walks over to the kitchen phone and answers. He smiles and laughs at whatever the person says, and then, "Yeah," he says. "She's right here," and hands the phone to me.

"Hey! You got plans for today?" It's Gretchen.

"Today, yeah."

"You good?"

"Yeah. Things are good. My mom's home," I say. "I have a lot to tell you guys."

"Wanna hit the mall later? We're going, like, every day this week so—"

"Air hockey!" KZ yells.

"And that anime you love is in the theater. The one you told us to watch."

"*Howl's Moving Castle?*" I ask. With that, Henry's ears perk up.

"Yeah!" she says. "So—yes?"

The weirdest thing happens in my body. A war starts. More than one. I freeze and don't answer Gretchen.

Mother must see it because she gets my attention with a little wave. I say, "Hold on," to Gretchen.

"You should totally go out with your friends," Mother says.

"I have to be here for the demolition."

She motions to Vernon on the patio. "I think the so-called grown-ups have some things to do before we get to that. Plus, I just flew in and need sleep. I promise I won't so much as look at those tubes without you here."

I say to Gretchen, "Can I bring Henry?"

"Of course! We're in the driveway! Come out when you're ready."

"My driveway?"

I can hear Porter there, too—they all laugh.

Henry's face is like a puppy's, and he looks to Mother and Marta and then goes upstairs to get ready.

I hang up and look at them. "Are you sure you're safe?"

Mother says, "I've been defusing this bomb for a while now. Don't worry."

"I don't have a phone or—"

Marta hands me Milorad's old phone, then shoos me away with a smile. "Go have fun."

I stop and look at them both as if it might be the last time. Something about leaving right now feels wrong. Everything about it feels wrong.

Henry arrives back in the kitchen. "I brushed my teeth, and I have enough money for all our tickets because I've saved every dollar they ever gave me for spying on you."

I don't even ask. I just go upstairs and put on my favorite leggings and an oversized sweatshirt. The wars go on inside of me—the war between the perceived safety of isolation and the inherent danger of having friends the loudest—and I walk out the front door with Henry.

Six hours later, we've seen one movie, played more than twenty games of air hockey, three games of pool, walked the mall in circles six times, eaten tacos, and Henry and I tried queso for the first time. When we get home, Vernon is still sitting on the patio bench, Mother is sleeping off her jet lag, the letter is gone from the cabinet where I put it, and Marta makes us real hot chocolate, which puts us to sleep fast.

LESSON FOURTEEN: SPRING BREAK

Today is Monday, March 24, 2025

SEARCH AND DESTROY

We all know how this is going to unfold. It's a matter of logic and finesse, defusing a bomb.

He's sitting on the patio bench in the morning sun wearing his bathrobe. His eyes are closed, arms are crossed. Milorad is nearby in the greenhouse, gently watering vegetable seedlings and humming something lively.

"You're up early," I say, standing next to Vernon, eating a bagel.

He's breathing through his nose. In and out. In and out.

"Hope you slept well," I say.

He sighs to himself.

"You're acting like I'm invisible."

"No I'm not," he says. Note to self: all it takes is an allegation. "I couldn't sleep past six for some reason."

"Daylight savings, maybe," I say.

"Whatever." He stands up and starts pacing.

"Maybe a walk would help."

"Just shut up, Jane." He paces as if he has something to do. He has nothing to do.

"Okay."

"You think you're so smart, but you're not, you know."

"Sure." I look up at my bedroom window.

"You think you're the big professor," he says.

I nod and squint into the sun.

"What do you have to say to that, then?" he asks.

I don't say anything.

Vernon flops back into the bench.

"Did you ever love me?" he asks.

I don't think the question is for me, so I don't answer.

"Did you?" he says—looking up at me, standing here.

I answer, "It was never enough."

I walk to the greenhouse and greet Milorad. He says, "He has been there since sunrise. I do not think he slept."

"He's moving out today," I say quietly.

Milorad nods and says, "Brutus is escaped. Do not open door to pool house."

"Okay," I answer. There is a faint song coming from Henry's hothouse—as if the tree frogs heard me say the magic words *he's moving out today* and are throwing a party.

I walk back to Vernon. "Where will you go?"

"With Finch."

"Ah."

"Though she isn't answering my texts or my calls," he says.

"Huh," I say. "Love is hard sometimes, I guess."

Then, I check the cabinet to see if the letter is gone—and it is. Since Mother is still asleep and he's still sitting on the bench, I go to my room and I do my own reclaiming.

I navigate to Vernon's email account. It takes me a few tries to guess *Vernon4Finch!*, but after that it only takes moment to transfer control of the home movie archive to me.

I still have so many hours of footage to watch. So many memories to check. So many tragedies to figure out. I never did find the footage of the time he shook me so hard my neck got sore. Or the day he slapped Mother so hard that it sounded like a gun. I don't even know if they were real. For now, while the grown-ups figure out how to get him to leave and never come back, I want something comforting, so I aim for my fifth birthday—the one I've been saving for a bad day.

HOME MOVIE—03.03.2013

I am adorable. I want everyone to see me being adorable, so I walk around the dining room saying "Hello!" Marta says hello back and touches me on my nose—a *boop on the snoot* as she would say. Henry is only a toddler but he blurts out an "Ewoo" and giggles. Mother says, "Hello, Jane!" and Vernon says, "Yes, Jane, of course."

Marta places dishes on the table at each setting.

<pause>

I find myself bored by these normal-seeming bits. It's as if, for the first few years of our lives, Henry and I had real parents. They weren't perfect but Mother was all *Hello, Jane!* and not locked in the System, and Vernon was *Yes, Jane, of course* and not fucking Aunt Finch and talking shit.

I fast-forward.

<resume>

Marta brings the cake to the table. There are five candles, and the frosting is deep and very frilly. As the room sings "Happy Birthday" to me, I frown and think hard about my wish. And when they're done and Henry is still toddler-humming the song, I take a deep breath and blow the candles out.

<pause>

I remember my wish vividly.

<resume>

Marta cuts and serves the cake and we eat. Mother feeds Henry some bites of her cake, and he indicates that he wants more. Marta gives him his own slice and places a baby spoon in his hand. He throws the baby spoon on the floor and eats the cake with his hands, squishing streams of cake through the gaps between his tiny fingers and spreading the icing all over his face. Vernon takes a picture with his phone. Everyone laughs. I keep eating like a proper girl—that's Vernon's term for a girl with manners and who doesn't throw her fork on the floor. I am sitting up straight, not even a slight slouch, and I have my napkin on my lap and my plate as close to the edge of the table as possible so I can't drop any crumbs. Everyone in the room is watching Henry shove fistfuls of cake in his tiny mouth.

I finish my cake and get up and leave the room. Mother and Vernon sit on either side of Henry and don't say anything to each other. Vernon glares, mostly, while Mother cleans Henry's face up and talks to him.

"Why do you always talk to him like he's an adult?" he asks.

Mother gives him a look like he's weird.

"Most mothers coo over their babies," he says.

Mother ignores him.

"You don't even have a baby nickname for him!" Vernon says. "I read in a book that any mother who doesn't give her baby a nickname or coo at them isn't fit!"

Mother doesn't take her attention off Henry as she answers, "Where did you read that, Vernon?"

"Does it matter?" he asks. "It won't help you be a better mother."

Mother sighs.

Vernon gets up from the table.

"It's time for presents!" Mother says. She unclips Henry from his high chair and holds him close, giving him a kiss on the face and then a few on his head as she brushes the crumbs off his clothing.

Vernon stands watching her and looks uncomfortable.

Mother moves through the doorway to the sitting room.

When Vernon is alone in the room, he pinches between his eyes, as if he has a headache.

<change to sitting room camera>

Mother walks into the sitting room holding Henry, still kissing his head. She looks around.

"Jane?" she asks.

I am not in the room, so I do not answer.

Mother looks behind the settee and the big chair. She looks concerned. Henry grabs a fistful of her hair and pulls and she doesn't seem to notice as she walks to the French doors that lead to the garden patio. One of the doors is open.

"Jane?" she calls out toward the garden. She then walks outside with Henry.

As she exits, Vernon enters. "Mina?"

He looks around but no one is there. "MINA?"

Vernon plops himself in the overstuffed chair by the fireplace. He eyes the wrapped presents on the couch. Then he looks at the fire in the fireplace, walks over to the wood basket, and pokes around in the embers with an iron poker. He puts a log on the fire and then sits back down.

<pause>

I am uncomfortable looking at this. I don't know why because I picked it on purpose because I remember this day as happy. I remember the presents I got. I got a xylophone and my first guitar. I remember Henry playing a percussion egg nonstop and all of us laughing. I don't remember any of this brooding or mood. I don't remember how straight I'd sat eating my cake.

I want to stop watching it, but I can't seem to move.

<resume>

"There you are!" Vernon says when I appear in front of him. "You had your mother yelling and frantic!"

"I'm sorry," I say.

"Oh, don't worry. I'll save you from her temper," he says, and opens his arms.

I look at him dubiously, then I look into the fire, and then at my presents.

"Come sit here," Vernon says, patting his lap.

I keep staring at the presents and start to wander toward the door to the patio, which is cracked open.

"Jane!" he snaps.

I run toward him and get on his lap. He holds me tight and rocks me side to side. I do not look comfortable. I start to try to break free of his arms, but he keeps them lovingly locked around my little arms.

I fidget violently as if I'm having a mild Victorian seizure. Vernon is startled by this and picks me up and puts me on the floor in front of him.

"What are you doing?" he asks.

"Getting warm, Daddy!"

He grabs me then, by my upper arms and pulls me toward him with violent precision.

"Don't ever call me that again!" he says, shaking me a little as he enunciates each syllable. "You know that! You know that!" His face is suddenly bulging as if there's a dragon under his skin pushing to escape.

I look him right in the eye and say, "Why not, Daddy?"

<pause>

I am frozen. I am terrified. I am confused. I was convinced this was a brilliant birthday. I was sure that the shaking incident was a totally different day. Clearly, I was wrong. I am wrong. I can't even move my arms to stop this / fast-forward / anything.

I feel my face.

It is frozen in horror.

It knows what comes next.

<resume>

Vernon grabs my shoulders. His thumbs dig into my clavicles, and his hands squeeze my upper arms tightly. He begins to shake me, and I don't look scared. But as time advances, his shaking is more wild and his face curls into itself as if he's experiencing pain.

"I am Vernon!" he says. "You will call me Vernon!"

The shaking throws me off-balance, you can see me struggling to stand up, losing my footing, but then getting it back. Once my head starts to wobble front to back, we become a physics project. He is expending energy and I am both absorbing it and returning it.

In the footage, my neck looks as if it might snap at any second.

"Vernon!"

Marta quickly picks me up and holds me.

Vernon leans back in his chair and stares into the fire. Marta checks my eyes and my neck—running her hand around it and pressing just a little as if she's searching for a sore spot—and the minute she makes eye contact with me, I start wailing.

With that, Vernon gets up and walks toward the study.

Mother and Henry arrive through the patio door a minute later. During that minute, Marta holds me so tightly and I sob and sob and sob.

Vernon doesn't come back to watch me open presents.

I get a few cool outfits, some books, a few albums, and the xylophone and the little guitar. The guitar case has a purple fuzzy interior. I open it and try to fit myself into it while Mother tunes the guitar and Marta bounces Henry on her knee.

When Vernon does come back in, Marta takes me and Henry out of the room.

Mother says, "What did you do to Jane?"

"I didn't do anything to Jane."

"Marta said you were shaking Jane."

"I didn't lay a finger on her."

"I think you're lying," Mother says.

Vernon puts his whole body into the slap. It makes a cracking sound. Mother takes the hit and walks out of the room. Vernon sits back down in his chair and stares back into the fire. Waits about four minutes and then leaves again.

If you keep the footage playing, you can hear him five minutes later in the foyer.

"You'll hear from my lawyer!"

Door slams.

<stop>

If you keep the footage playing, you can hear him two hours after that, coming back in the same door he left. No one called his lawyer.

He doesn't have a lawyer.

BACKUP

I think I just traumatized myself by watching that home movie.

I thought it was a safe memory.

I thought my memories were safe.

I check the transfer to my new cloud; I make sure all the files have been secured. Then close the window on my browser and clear my cache and history.

I find Henry on the stairs, listening to Vernon pleading with Mother about how he'll change and how he's sorry—same as the "Vernon's Pie Crust Apologies" mixtape. He even adds a line about *never with a closed fist!* as if he knows I just watched that home movie. Mother stays calm and says something like *Vernon, you must go. Today. We can talk about the legal stuff any other day. But say goodbye to the children and then go.*

"It feels like this place is going to explode," Henry says.

"I think it's about to do the opposite of explode," I say.

"What's that even mean?" He looks panicked.

"I've been practicing breathing exercises," I say. "I breathe in through my nose really deep and then I exhale super slowly. Look."

I show him how I exhale through a tiny space in my lips. "If you do this," I say, "you can even slow your heart rate. But mostly it helps me with the anxiety."

"I can't sleep. I mean I can, but not much. I'm always tired. Probably the detox, Marta says."

"I'm proud of you," I say.

"I just want something normal," he says. "I don't understand any of this."

I hold my arms out for a hug. He accepts. "I'll explain it one day, I promise," I say.

Henry frowns. "He makes me scared to grow up."

EXIT STAGE RIGHT

"You're making a huge mistake," Vernon says.

He's dressed in full Victorian, pocket watch and all, and is carrying his suitcases from his bedroom to the door. When he's ready to leave, Milorad in the car, waiting, he asks Henry and me to come and hug him. Henry does it and says *I'll see you soon* in the least I'll-see-you-soon voice I've ever heard. Vernon closes the door gently on his way out. Of course.

Mother, Marta, and I sit at the dining room table. I've told them both that he plans to move in with Finch.

"That's going to be hard, considering she lives with Milorad, right?" Marta asks.

"I think she lives in both places? I mean, I've never been to her apartment, but she's shown us pictures."

"Wait. What?" Mother says.

Marta tells me to show her, so I get my iPad and I queue up the "Shape-Shifter" mixtape. She pauses it a few times and rewinds to watch Finch switch and looks surprised and kind of amazed. I can't describe the look on her face.

"This makes so much sense of my childhood," she says, and watches to the end, her jaw loose. Her eyes are wet. She shakes her head. "This makes so much fucking sense."

<*pause*>

I never even thought about the fact that Finch is her actual sister—that they grew up together the way me and Henry are growing up right now. How terrible.

<resume>

As if summoned, Finch arrives through the kitchen door and slams it. If I could stop time, I'd stop it right here to take bets on how she's going to play this. My money is on her playing the best sister ever and asking why she wasn't invited to the demolition party.

"Why wasn't I invited?" she yells—part intimidating and part pretending to joke—as she finds us all in the dining room.

Mother and Marta grimace, and I find words first.

"You've just missed him," I say.

When she pouts in confusion, Marta says, "He's heading to your apartment, I think."

"Who are we talking about?" Finch asks.

"Oh, please," Mother says. "No need to pretend, sister."

"I'm not pretending," she says. "Milorad told me you're about to ruin this house. It's an historic landmark, you know! Aunt Lily would be appalled!"

"Pretty sure she was appalled when you murdered her," Mother says.

Finch's eyes dart around.

"Pretty sure she'd be appalled to know you murdered her parents, too," I say.

"And your own parents," Henry adds as he walks in from the study, which makes all of us look at him, shocked.

"How old are you, exactly?" Marta asks.

Henry inhales to say something, but then—

poof!

—Brutus scurries through the swinging kitchen door.

"I knew it," Henry says. ASK HENRY HOW HE KNEW ABOUT FINCH AND BRUTUS SOMETIME.

"We need breakfast," Marta says to break the silence.

We eat her famous ham-and-cheese croissants alongside yogurt and mandarins. Mother talks about how we'll do it. Basically, we take out the tubes throughout the house, but we leave one in her basement bedroom so we can access the System, Station Six, and Safe House when we need to.

"I'm moving out of that room," she says.

"Take mine!" Marta says.

Mother smiles. Henry looks as if he's going to cry.

I go to hug him and he flinches away. "I'm so sorry," he says.

"I was a terrible person. I've said and done things that were very wrong. I don't know why. I just did." Then the tears come.

He lets me side-hug him as I say, "You did those things to stay safe. Just like I told you before."

"Where will Marta stay if Mother takes her room?"

"I'm going to take the room next to yours," Mother says. "But Marta got married years ago, and she and her husband are going to move into a house of their own."

Henry looks at Marta. "You're married?"

Marta nods, grinning.

Mother comes to hug him from the other side, now. We hold him up as he sobs.

"I had to stay safe, too, Henry. I know what it's like," I say.

"You're both children I am very proud of," Mother says. "Neither of you was awful. You were being used. Let's get a therapist to work all this old shit out and get back to the joyous day."

"I'm in," Marta says, holding a stack of what looks like folded clothing.

"I have to pee," I say, and jog upstairs with the iPad to put it back under the sink even though I don't have to anymore. As I pee, I think of returning it to Gemma. Seeing Gemma. Getting to be around Gemma. Asking her all the questions I've wanted to ask her for years about her chickens, her family, her life. Something tells me I'll be seeing her a lot more now.

DEMOLITION

When I get back downstairs, Mother is standing next to the tube in the study. She has a chainsaw in her hands and is sporting ear protection and a face shield and is wearing a boilersuit the same color as her eyes. My eyes.

She points to safety glasses on the desk. "You should put those on."

I do.

Henry walks in from the direction of the kitchen. He is also wearing safety glasses and a boilersuit.

I nod and Mother points to a boilersuit and a crowbar that are sitting on my old desk. I say, as I step into the pant legs, "I do not lie to God."

"Of course you don't," Mother answers.

"It's important that you trust me."

"I trust you," she says.

"This is the final scene in the opera," I say.

She starts the chainsaw and yells over its engine, "Well then, let's fucking do it!"

ACT IV, SCENE 3

INT. THE VANDERMAKER HOUSE—ALL ROOMS—AROUND NOON

Music plays in background. Punk or rock. The feeling of Radiohead's "Paranoid Android" in the bassline. It will build into "Pick the Lock" once the action and dialogue are done.

JANE, MINA, and HENRY are all dressed in dark gray boilersuits and eye and ear protection. Mina has a chainsaw, Henry has a sledgehammer, and Jane has a crowbar. They start to demolish the tube in the study first. Then the sitting room, then the kitchen, then the dining room. When the last section is ripped out, they stop and remove their safety gear.

MINA

I didn't think that would feel so . . .

JANE

Great?

MINA

No. It was like I was dishonoring the history of the house. Even the women who'd been locked up.

JANE

Like some kind of weird Stockholm syndrome.

MINA

Yeah. So weird.

HENRY

I used to feel that way about Vernon. Like I owed him my life.

JANE

Shit. Yeah.

Mina shakes her head.

HENRY

I still don't understand why we're not ripping it all out. I don't want a tube in my room anymore.

MINA

Those are coming out. The one in Jane's room. All of them.

HENRY

Why not the one in the basement room?

JANE

We have a lot to tell you. But not right now.

MILORAD enters from stage left with a wheelbarrow and starts to load the broken pieces of the System into it. Henry helps.

MINA

Let's help them get all this outside.

ALL CAST onstage help put pieces of the tubes and capsules in the wheelbarrow. When Mina finds the wet nurse attachment, she walks it outside to the patio, picks up her chainsaw, and cuts it into many pieces. She cries. She smiles. She sits on the patio bench when she's done. Milorad arrives soon after with the wheelbarrow and loads the pieces into it.

MILORAD

I ordered dumpster for tomorrow.

MINA

Thank you!

MILORAD

Will you allow me to help with upstairs rooms? I will fit plywood in floors first down here. Then help, yes?

MINA

Absolutely.

(marked pause)

One day will you tell me how you and Brutus met?

MILORAD

Brutus is not what he seems.

(marked pause)

I have said too much.

Milorad looks all around, as if being watched. Henry, Mina, and MARTA join MOTHER on the patio.

HENRY

What's Jane doing?

FREE MOTHER arrives onstage in the foreground as Jane hands out foam costumes to her bandmates.

MINA
I think we're about to hear a new song.

Each member is a different type of key. ELLIS is a skeleton key. WENDYLISA is a modern metallic blue key. DAVID the drummer wears a foam tubular key as a hat. Jane is wearing a short dress made up of lockpicks that shimmy like a flapper sort of dress.

JANE
Milorad, can you bring that debris over here?

Milorad wheels the wheelbarrow he just filled to Jane, who then dumps it on the patio on the "stage" where the band is about to perform. Milorad sits on a patio bench. His smile is enormous.

JANE (to Milorad)
You look so happy!

MILORAD
I have pulled you off many stages and driven you home from many shows. I am excited to be part of show now, and not big bummer.

Milorad turns to Mina and the others and smiles.

MILORAD

You will like this music. It is good music.

Music fades in . . .

Song: "Pick the Lock"

Composer notes: *THIS IS AN ANTHEM. A punk anthem. It will make the listener feel like part of a family. Warm and safe. Honest. This song is the foundation of the whole opera. No pressure.*

JANE

THEY PUT HER ON TV WHEN WE WERE TINY
IN A DRESS AND PUMPS WITH FOUR-INCH HEELS.
THEY HAD HER SERVING UP SOME COOKIES
AND VARIOUS DELICIOUS MEALS.

THEN SHE SHOWED UP IN OUR HISTORY BOOKS
PROTESTING FOR HER RIGHTS.
WENT TO COLLEGE AFTER SHE HAD KIDS.
STUDIED DAYS AND WORKED LONG NIGHTS.

AND NOW YOU SAY SHE CAN'T BE GOOD
AND NOW—OH! THOSE POOR CHILDREN!
AND NOW YOU SERVE HER UP FOR LUNCH
AND NOW YOU DIG YOUR KNIFE IN.

BAND

FREE YOUR MOTHER FROM THE BULLSHIT

FREE YOUR MOTHER FROM THE CLOCK
FREE YOUR MOTHER FROM THE PRISON
COME WITH ME / LET'S PICK THE LOCK.

JANE
THEY GAVE HER BIRTH CONTROL AND CREDIT.
THEY RAISED THE MORTGAGE ON YOUR HOUSE.
MADE IT NORMAL TO FORGET IT.
MADE YOUR DAD INTO A LOUSE.

IT'S HER FAULT FOR BEING WORLDLY
WANTING THINGS SHE SHOULDN'T TAKE,
IF SHE ONLY KNEW HER PLACE IN LIFE
SHE WOULDN'T BE SUCH A FLAKE.

AND NOW YOU SAY SHE CAN'T BE GOOD
AND NOW—OH! THOSE POOR CHILDREN!
AND NOW YOU SERVE HER UP FOR LUNCH
AND NOW YOU DIG YOUR KNIFE IN.

BAND
FREE YOUR MOTHER FROM THE BULLSHIT
FREE YOUR MOTHER FROM THE CLOCK
FREE YOUR MOTHER FROM THE PRISON
COME WITH ME / LET'S PICK THE LOCK.

JANE
ALL THE RULES THEY TOLD YOU—LIES.
ALL THE BULLSHIT EXPECTATIONS
WITHOUT HER TWO-PLUS JOBS AT NIGHT
YOU'D NEVER HAVE HAD VACATIONS.

NOW THEY TAKE AWAY FROM HER
EVERY RIGHT THAT SHE HAS EARNED.
CAN'T MAKE HER QUIT OR CRY ABOUT IT
SHE'S SO USED TO GETTING BURNED.

Jane beckons and Mina steps up to the stage and joins in for the chorus.

BAND and MINA

AND NOW YOU SAY SHE CAN'T BE GOOD
AND NOW—OH! THOSE POOR CHILDREN!
AND NOW YOU SERVE HER UP FOR LUNCH
AND NOW YOU DIG YOUR KNIFE IN.

FREE YOUR MOTHER FROM THE BULLSHIT
FREE YOUR MOTHER FROM THE CLOCK
FREE YOUR MOTHER FROM THE SYSTEM
COME WITH ME / LET'S PICK THE LOCK.

Jane and Mina are jumping, now, each jump with their knees up. This last line is part scream and part song.

JANE and MINA

OH! THOSE POOR CHILDREN!
COME WITH ME / LET'S PICK THE LOCK!

Jane and Mina collapse onto the patio-stage, surrounded by the

System debris, out of breath. They have some kind of conversation down there on the ground, and laugh and cry and joke around as the Band walks over to Henry and Marta and Milorad, and Marta asks them to stay for dinner.

END SCENE

LESSON FIFTEEN: FAMILY WALK

Today is still Monday, March 24, 2025

THE SKY IS BIG. I don't know if that's just because I'm allowed to be here. Maybe when people are free, the sky looks bigger. I think Mother was right about getting a therapist. I'm in a faded black T-shirt and a pair of ripped jeans. I'm wearing the inner-zip combat boots Marta gave me, and I feel like Punk Rock Jane. I'm not ashamed of her. I love Punk Rock Jane. As much as my father wanted me to hate Punk Rock Jane, it turns out, she's the one who knows me the best.

It's seventy degrees and Henry has shed his coat. He put it on a bench along the trail and when Milorad said, "Someone could take it," Henry answered, "If someone needs it more than me enough to steal it, then they can have it."

Mother beamed at that. He didn't see it, but I did.

For all of Vernon's attempts to make us like him, we still ended up like her. It must be infuriating. Poor chap.

"So, what are we doing for spring break?" Mother asks.

"What are we supposed to do?" Henry asks, making it clear that the sky is absolutely bigger when one is free.

"Usually, people travel, I guess," Marta says.

Mother and I say, accidentally in unison, "I'm not leaving the house."

We all laugh.

Milorad says, "I would like to travel and see my friend in Ljubljana. He has invited me and I would like to see him."

"That's six hours difference," Henry says.

"Why don't you go?" Mother asks.

"I have not flown on plane since coming to this country."

"It's a really easy flight. And you could see the Dragon Bridge! I love that town. It's so hip. Did you know it sheltered artists during wartimes? I always feel safe there," Mother says.

Milorad says, "I will make plans."

We walk in silence for a while. Then we solve old puzzles.

ASK HENRY HOW HE KNEW ABOUT FINCH AND BRUTUS SOMETIME

Henry shrugs. "I don't know. I just, you know, felt it?"

"You felt it?"

"Yeah," he says.

ASK MOTHER HOW SHE SURVIVED THE GREAT IGNORING SOMETIME

She shakes her head. "I just had to," she says. "I almost didn't," she says. "I'm lucky to be alive." Marta gently reaches over and squeezes her shoulder. "Sometimes in the end, when we are at the door that might take us away from everything we love on earth, that's when the best ideas kick in. When I was there, I could see the reclaiming clearly. Not just the demolition of our System, but the reversal of the narrative."

"What narrative?" Henry asks.

"Start with 'All girls are liars' and go from there, I guess," Mother answers.

"I'm sorry for what we did," I say.

"Stop, Jane. It wasn't you."

"I'm sorry, too," Henry says.

"I appreciate that," Mother says. "It wasn't your fault. So many families go through what we did. It's more common than you think. You're not alone. And the more you talk about it, the more free you'll be of it."

HOW I CAME TO UNDERSTAND WHY SHE DIDN'T JUST LEAVE

Me and Henry. That's why. Because it's not as easy as that. Because it's a dumb question. No one seems to ask *Why doesn't he stop hurting his family?* Until people are willing to ask that question aloud, then I don't think *Why doesn't she leave?* is worth shit.

Until the people asking have defused a lying, erratic, manipulating bomb, they should probably keep their judgments about explosives to themselves. Our society makes so many excuses for violent men, we have normalized explosions.

That's why.

It's all very plain.

ASK MILORAD IF HE KNOWS ABOUT BRUTUS SOMETIME

Milorad stays quiet. So quiet.

I do not ask a second time.

OUR PEOPLE IV

It's an icebreaker!

LET'S GET TO KNOW MARTA!

Marta says her earliest memories involved walks with her grandfather. He was a hiker and used to take her to mountains and trails when she was only five or six. "He's the one who taught me how to make mashed potatoes," she says. "He's the one who told me the secret ingredient." She will not tell us the secret ingredient.

LET'S GET TO KNOW MILORAD!

Milorad is quiet and contemplative. He laughs at Marta's unwillingness to share the secret ingredient, but he doesn't say a word for the remainder of the walk. He looks up a lot at the sky and nods, as if it's talking to him. I think maybe the sky talks to Milorad.

When we get home, he walks directly to the pool and peels back its cover. Then he begins to take out the spring and summer patio things—the furniture, the firepit, the hammock stand.

LET'S GET TO KNOW GEMMA!

Gemma is in my room, holding her stolen iPad, watching the home movie mixtape I queued up for her—the one where we were ten and eleven and did back dives for a whole hour just to see if we could. Because that's how Gemma made me feel. Like doing a back dive. Over and over. I can't wait to have a normal life now and maybe even kiss someone like a normal seventeen-year-old. I want to fall in love. I can't remember ever wanting to fall in love before. I don't think love can breathe in a space of hate.

Hate is now in a pile of plexiglass in the driveway. Marta has opened the windows and doors—freshness is pushing the prison air out of the study. I open the heavy velvet curtains. I say, "Can we change the décor, please?" to no one in particular.

The hairs on my neck stand up.

Finch answers, "I suppose you think you'll be getting the house now."

She's sitting at my old desk, tapping her fingers on the table.

"You're unhinged," I say.

She nods.

"You don't scare me," I say.

poof!

Brutus scurries out the open doors to the patio.

MARTA'S MASHED POTATOES

Marta makes a roast chicken, her mashed potatoes, and carrots, and because Milorad asked her to, some turnips.

"Strong food for the mind," he said.

While dinner gets made, Milorad calls for a firepit night. He starts to move the patio furniture into a circle. Henry and I help. I am on a mission to find the seat cushions for the two benches. Henry hauls wood and fills the brass log holder.

"When you go to Slovenia, will you come back?" Henry asks him.

"Of course! If I am allowed to stay here, I will stay here. We are family."

Henry hugs him.

"Will you take Brutus with you on vacation?" I ask.

Milorad doesn't answer.

BRUTUS'S COCKY PROMISE

Never corner a rat.

IF I VISIT WITH YOU, you dare not tell anyone lest they think you brought it on yourself. The best destruction I ever did is in your saccharine mind—making you believe that I am not real. It was an easy deed. I simply told you lies about the good in people and how the best of us only look for that. This left all the bad in people free to take over the world.

And they did.

Now good and evil live side by side, but the good can't point out the evil without looking bad, and the evil doesn't need to do anything but devour. Chew with his mouth open, brag to his friends about how he hit that bitch, shut that little fucker up, gave her what she came for. I am the story everyone will tell you is impossible. And yet, I am fed and watered and I get homemade treats and toys and someone cleans up my shit from the bottom of my cage.

I trained you.

I trained all of you.

You think shuttling women around in tubes is bad?

You've seen nothing yet.

We control the world. You are peons.

See how I run as the stupid Serb chases me? With a brick, with a golf club, with a bat, with a tennis racquet, with his bare hands. I am mocking you and your running—from reality, from the way the world is about to fall on you—from icebergs to dirty politicians, you just put ketchup on it and eat it like fries and hamburgers.

See how he'll never catch me?

How slow he is?

See how pathetic?

How he thinks he can outsmart me?

See how stupid, running in circles?

How confused you are because we called ourselves myths? And you told every little child that monsters didn't exist?

See how we did it?

From right under your bed?

How you can't change it?

How you chase your own tail?

See how he corners me between the pool house and the pump house?

How even then he can't hit the target?

How—

HOME MOVIE—RH.RN. (RIGHT HERE. RIGHT NOW.)

Milorad is filling the patio firepit with wood. It's a warm night. He has music playing and two propane heaters out there as well. Cozy pillows and blankets on the couches.

"We will burn things tonight," he says to me.

Marta has closed all the windows and is doing the dishes with Mother.

<pause>

```
EXT. PATIO—NIGHT

                MINA, MARTA, GEMMA, MILORAD,
                HENRY, and JANE sit around a
```

blazing fire on the patio. They are playing charades.

JANE
You next, Henry!

Henry stands and acts out eating. The others call out guesses. He points inside toward the dining room.

GEMMA
No pointing allowed!

Henry acts out digging a potato, then washing it, peeling it, boiling it, then mashing it.

MARTA
My mashed potatoes!

HENRY
Bingo!

MARTA
Me next!

Marta stands. They play another round of charades. (Actors, make this different every night of the production. You're welcome.)

MINA
I guess this is what we're doing for spring break.

HENRY
I like it.

Milorad stands. Henry looks excited.

HENRY (CONT'D)
Your turn! Yes!

Milorad puts two logs on the fire and the flames jump. He then approaches the pool and grabs the skimmer from its hook on the outer wall of the pool house.

Jane gets up from the sofa and walks toward the kitchen door.

MINA (to Jane)
Where are you going?

Jane holds up her finger and goes into the house. Milorad begins to skim the pool.

<resume>

I return with my red ukulele and Mother's guitar. She takes hers from me and strums it and tunes it. I do the same with my uke. Then I play a chord and she matches it, then she plays a chord and I match it, getting a few notes wrong along the way.

"How about 'Pick the Lock' gets a darker feel?" she says, "Like this?" She plays a chord that's like "Servitude" by Fishbone—daunting. Some birthday wishes come true.

Milorad is over by the pool, working.

"Milorad!" I coo. "Stop working and come sit. You haven't given us a charade yet!"

He waves with his free hand as if I'd just called his name from across a busy street. You can see in his eyes he is somewhere else. Maybe on the Dragon Bridge in Ljubljana. Maybe back on his farm in Serbia, which he has never told us about.

<pause>

EXT. PATIO—NIGHT

Henry and Milorad are over by the pool, where Milorad is skimming the pool water, which is about two feet below the usual waterline. Henry and Milorad see something in the pool. Henry points. Milorad nods and dips the pool skimmer.

JANE

Stop working, you two! This is supposed to be a party!

MINA

I think they found something.

MARTA

Oh God.

GEMMA

I hope it's not snakes. It's the one thing I can't handle.

JANE

Oh man. Remember all the snakes that one year?

GEMMA

That's what I'm talking about.

MARTA

Oh God.

Milorad has something in the net. He and Henry look at it and then look at each other. They seem to be discussing what to do with it. Milorad points toward the firepit. Henry looks over, a thinking frown on his face.

<resume>

Milorad says, "Stand back."

All of us lean forward, though, to see what's in his net.

It's a rat, of course—drowned and dead—not just any rat either.

In one motion, he dumps Brutus onto the fire and rather than fizzle out and pop and crack with added water, the fire roars up and burns enormous.

We all sit back. Mother continues strumming her guitar. I continue strumming my uke. Milorad returns the pool skimmer to its hooks on the side of the pool house. Henry sits by the firepit with the iron poker and pokes the rat, over and over, as if he's making sure it's dead.

The tree frogs in the hothouse match our chords as we strum.

Natural as singing. Natural as dying.

I look at the scene from on top of the pool house—from on top of the town, from space, a bird's eye—and I see us, a family who has freed itself from something both terrible and fascinating.

How easily tricked we can be. How easily influenced. How mean.

How simply honest we can be. How beautifully influenced. How kind.

I will sing songs about it forever.

ACKNOWLEDGMENTS

Books do not write themselves. This one, especially. I owe thanks.

At Dutton—Andrew, we count things in decades now, and I love that for us. Julie, Carmela and Venessa, Anna, Theresa, Kristie, Natalie, Rob, Kaitlin, and every single team at Penguin Random that works so hard to put books into the world, thank you. A toast to Anne, the best damn copyeditor in the galaxy.

Michael Bourret, I tell everyone I have the best agent. I do not lie.

Big thanks and love to David Macinnis Gill for holding my hand through this book. And to Cory McCarthy and Martha Brockenbrough and e. E. Charlton-Trujillo for minding me like good siblings. And to Beth Zimmerman for walking with me through some very serious days, hoo boy. And to Jax for being so damn solid. Friends, family, and every good neighbor, you know who you are—thank you for helping me get this book done with your generosity and kindness. I love you.

Andrea, Jane, Jennifer, and Diane—I am so grateful. (People, thank your therapists.)

Thank you to every teacher, to every librarian, to every bookseller who puts my books in the hands of the readers who need them. Special shout-out to Lauryn Hill for "Forgive Them Father," where I first understood that everyday people lie to God.

Listen. Domestic violence is a common reality. Falling in love with an abuser can happen to anyone and it's far more nuanced and complicated than it looks from the outside. What matters is that you know: You deserve authentic love—the verb. Love that allows you to ask questions, share ideas, and communicate so it stays. Safe love. Love that doesn't lie. Love that doesn't betray. Love that doesn't hurt. You're worth it. I promise.